Finding Home

by

Casey Dawes

Mountain Vines Publishing

Book cover design by GetCovers
Edited by CEO Editor (ceoeditor.com)

Published by Mountain Vines Publishing
Missoula, MT
Contact email: info@ConciergeSelfPublishing.com

To the amazing teachers, paras, and staff at Target Range School
who work daily to educate the next generation.
And to one special little girl who stole my heart one year.

Chapter 1

Once again, Samantha Deveaux regretted she'd given up cursing.

The two-story solid sandstone courthouse anchored the center of the roundabout. Imposing. Following the roundabout past the obviously watered lawn and dark green shrubs, she missed the entrance to the parking lot on her first pass.

"Mommy, why are you driving in circles?" eight-year-old Audie asked from the passenger seat. "You're making me dizzy."

The huge smile on her daughter's face told Samantha her daughter was getting a kick out of her predicament.

"For fun." And she did it one more time simply to keep the smile on Audie's face.

The move to isolated Teton County on the Rocky Mountain Front had been hard on her daughter, pulling her away from lifelong friends and her beloved grandmother who was a better mother to Audie than she'd ever been to Samantha.

"Why are we going here?" Audie asked when Samantha pulled into a parking place.

"Just more stuff we have to do to live in a new place. Hop out," she said as she pushed open the driver's door of her beige secondhand Toyota Camry to walk to the passenger side. The car wasn't her first choice, but the brand-new pale yellow one had been way beyond her reach as a para-teacher in Billings.

Operating on her own time schedule, Audie pushed the door halfway open, then became distracted by a bright red ladybug crawling out from the windshield wiper well. As usual by late morning, her daughter's hair looked like no one had ever run a comb through it, the flyaway brown locks, so like her own, glistening from the hot August sun.

At least here in Choteau, a cool breeze floated in from the mountains now and again, unlike the overheated Yellowstone River valley they'd left a few weeks before.

Patiently, she waited for her daughter to complete her examination. Let the teachers in her new school try to move what could be an immovable object. Samantha had learned long ago to roll with her daughter's timetable whenever possible. Besides, it gave her time to breathe and pretend everything in her life was normal, the total opposite of reality.

"But why, Mommy?" Audie asked when she finally got out of the car. "Why did we have to move?"

To keep you safe.

"I got a new job, remember? Now I can be a real teacher."

"Instead of being a paratrooper," Audie said, tilting her head and trying to hide a little smile.

"Para-teacher, silly."

They walked up the steps to the courthouse, going one level at a time as Audie played her own internal game.

"But aren't para-teachers real teachers, too?" Audie asked.

One would think. Many paras had teaching degrees and wanted a full-time job but didn't want to move to a town of fewer than a hundred people like Two Dot, Montana. So they stayed in the state's five big cities and prayed for an opening.

"Almost, sweetie, almost. C'mon, kiddo, we have to get this done so we can visit the new school."

"Okay." Finding her next gear, Audie walked ahead so quickly, Samantha had to rush to keep up with her.

After checking the directory, she located the motor vehicle office. Good lord, why were all these people here? Didn't they have to work?

With a sigh, she pulled a number from the dispenser and sat, smoothing her floral skirt and crossing her legs at the ankle the way she'd been taught by her old-fashioned mother. Too bad her mom hadn't given her any useful lessons, like how to get a job that paid more than minimum wage or to stand up for herself.

"I want to look at the license plates," Audie said, standing squarely before her, her blue eyes wide behind glasses with frames of the same hue.

God, she loved her daughter. As much of a challenge as a child on the Asperger's scale could be, Audie had no artifice and a heart of gold.

"Sure, just make sure that's the only place you go."

"Okay."

Samantha smiled and glanced at the red numbers on the displays above the clerks' heads—one for registrations and one for driver's licenses. Too bad changing an address wasn't something she could do online.

Pulling out the high school math curriculum from her

oversized bag, she flipped to the spot where she'd left off and began to review her notes. The job was only guaranteed for a year, and she had to make as good an impression as possible to be invited back.

No pressure.

The hum of conversation, its tempo measured by a toddler beating on a chair with a plastic brick, surrounded her as she concentrated.

The freshman curriculum seemed standard enough: quadratic equations, vector analysis, applying mathematics to real life. The sophomore geometry curriculum had its own difficulties. Sometimes kids who grasped basic math never got solid in shapes and their measurements. The trick was to make this come alive for students who were number-challenged. Common Core had helped some, hindered some, and left parents baffled. Her time in Billings as a para-teacher with learning-challenged students had given her an intimate understanding of the problem.

That, and dealing with her own daughter. She glanced up.

Audie stared at the rows of specialty license plates available to Montana drivers, everything from fishing to quilting to schools and the two rival Montana teams: University of Montana Grizzlies and Montana State University Bobcats. They all supported some cause for an extra registration fee. Budget-constrained Samantha was going to use whatever plate the state decided to give her.

A lanky man with raven-black hair trimming the edge of his Choteau Bulldogs cap was squatting next to her daughter.

Samantha dropped the curriculum on the chair and dashed over, her heartbeat ramping up.

"Is she bothering you?" she asked, not wanting him to take offense at being told to back off. No need to start a ruckus in the heart of a small town.

A pair of deep gray eyes turned up toward her, and the man rose to his full height, a good seven inches above her own five foot three. He had on a soft blue Carhartt shirt, jeans, and pointed-toe cowboy boots, like most ranchers in Montana. The difference was an ornate silver buckle adorning his brown leather belt.

He yanked the cap from his head.

"No, ma'am," he said. "We were simply having a difference of opinion about the best license plate. She likes the ones with cats and dogs while I'm kind of partial to the one with the horse." He held out his hand, "Jarod Beck," he said.

She shook his hand. Warm. Strong. Callused.

"Samantha Deveaux. This is my daughter, Audie. We just got to town last week."

"Figured that," he said. "I don't remember seeing you before."

"I'm the new high school math teacher," she blurted out.

He shook his head. "Not my best subject." Then he grinned.

It was a good smile, the kind that made children and animals feel easy. No wonder Audie had been comfortable enough to start a conversation.

"Number seventy-six!" the clerk called out.

Samantha glanced at the paper stub in her hand.

"That's me," she said. "C'mon, Audie."

"But I want to stay here. It's so boring over there."

"I'll keep an eye on her," Jarod said.

Samantha glared at him.

"Or not." He raised his hands in mock surrender.

"Number seventy-six!" the clerk repeated.

She had to get this done. "Okay." She walked to the counter and glanced back at them. He grinned.

"How can I help you?" the clerk asked once Samantha handed over the pink slip with the number. She had once been a redhead, but the color had faded and was flecked with gray.

"I need to update my address on the license and registration. Can you do both so I don't have to get back in line?"

"Seems reasonable. Sure. License and registration, please."

She reached down for her purse. It wasn't there.

H-E-double hockey sticks.

"Looking for this?" Jarod stood next to her, Audie by his side. He held out her purse and curriculum. "I saw them over there all lonesome and figured they were yours."

"Oh, thanks."

"No problem."

Thank goodness for Montana ethics. Sure, there was crime and drugs, just like any other state, but there was also a sense that personal property was just that—personal.

She smiled at him. "Thanks again."

Charged air seemed to surround them for a few moments, then he touched the brim of his cap and walked to the seat she'd vacated.

Audie shook her head and walked back to the license plates.

The sharp tap of heels made Samantha glance over. A put-together blonde strode on her stylish shoes toward Jarod. He stood, and she gave him quick kiss on the cheek.

Disappointment drifted through Samantha. She quickly banished it. Digging through her purse, she came up with the requested documents.

Better be careful or she'd be making up stories from chance encounters and giving people qualities they didn't have, like she'd done with Audie's father, Cody.

"You must be the new math teacher," the lady behind the counter said.

"Yes, I just took the job a few weeks ago."

The woman. "I'm on the school board, and I tell you, it's harder and harder to find teachers willing to come to these small towns, especially if they're single. Not enough of a dating pool."

"Fortunately, I'm not interested in dating. I'm here to focus on the job and my daughter." That was the image she wanted to project: a dedicated teacher who deserved to be kept on long enough to get tenure.

"Is that your little girl over there?" the clerk pointed to Audie.

"Yes, she'll be going into third grade this year."

"She'll love the elementary school. They have a great principal." The clerk handed back her documents. "You'll receive a new registration in the mail in about a week. The license doesn't change until you renew it."

"Thank you." Samantha smiled at the woman.

"Welcome to Choteau," the woman said.

Samantha nodded and turned to get Audie.

The blonde was still with Jarod, smiling, nodding, and touching his wrist. He looked up and gave Samantha a smile and a wave as she took Audie's hand to leave. The woman with him gave her a sharp glance, then spoke to Jarod.

Time to get out of here.

"He's a nice man." Audie waved at Jarod as they left the motor vehicle office.

That earned Samantha another look from the blonde. Who was she?

Samantha would probably find out soon enough. In a place like Choteau, everyone knew everyone.

# # #

Choteau Elementary School was part of a long, low brick complex that also contained the junior high and high school portions of the education system. For a few hundred students, it made sense to keep them together and share resources. The elementary office was reached by a separate door next to the extended wing.

In spite of its size, it was known for the range of special services available to students, no matter their learning or social challenges. It was one of the reasons she'd accepted the position.

"Hello, Ms. Deveaux," said the secretary of the elementary school, an attractive woman with expertly coifed brown hair.

Whoever was the hair stylist in this town was good at her job.

"This must be Audie," the woman continued.

"Yes, it is," Samantha replied as her daughter stared at the secretary, making her own internal assessment.

"Mrs. Wilkins is expecting you." The secretary led Samantha and her daughter to the conference room in the office wing. "I'll let her know you're here." She handed Samantha a stack of papers. "These are for you to fill out and bring back the first day of school."

"I'll probably return them early. That day is my first day teaching at the high school."

"That's right!" The secretary gave her a welcoming smile. "Welcome to the school system. We have a great teacher family here." She paused for a second. "I'm not sure if you heard, but the principal of the high school had to retire—he had a heart attack and needs to avoid stress."

"Being a high school principal can certainly be stressful," Samantha agreed.

"They've scrambled to find a new one to replace him; the vice-principal, Mrs. Helms, wasn't interested. They finally hired Rebecca Johnson. She used to be an elementary teacher and went back for her masters. A female high school principal is going to be a big change in this town."

"Spreading all the education gossip?" A woman with ash-blond hair entered the room. She had the curvy look of someone who'd given birth more than once and the confident handshake of a person in charge. She grinned at the secretary.

"Oops." The secretary didn't look at all chagrinned. "I'll get back to work." With a small wave, she was gone.

"I'm Joyce Wilkins. Won't you and Audie have a seat?"

"You're bossy," Audie announced before sitting down.

"Sorry," Samantha said. "I'm afraid she has no filter."

"Well, at least you know where you stand." Joyce turned her

attention to Audie. "You're right. I am bossy—that's because I'm the boss."

Audie considered this fact. "I guess that's all right."

Joyce grinned. "I think we're going to get along just fine."

Audie gave the principal her "I'm not sure about that" look.

Joyce shook her head with a chuckle. "Well, let's get down to business. You have the forms you need. I'll explain a bit about the curriculum for the grade and give you an overview of the school. I've asked Mrs. Hunt to be here today to meet you both. She's waiting in her classroom."

Even though Joyce tried to include her in the conversation, Audie quickly tuned out. Soon she was out of her chair, inspecting the glass-plated cabinets that held trophies and ribbons.

"I'm sorry," Samantha said.

"No problem," Joyce replied with a grin. "Very few kids can sit through this meeting. They're only doing what most adults wish they could—something more interesting."

Samantha relaxed a little. This was going to be a good place for Audie.

Once they were finished, they walked down to the elementary room.

Mrs. Hunt's third-grade room was full of color, like the woman herself. Her bright top was outdone only by a smile and a welcoming light in her dark eyes.

"You must be Audie," she said.

"I am," her daughter replied. "How did you know?"

"Oh, magic," she said, tossing off the reply.

"There's no magic. You're being silly."

"I'm glad you know that, but are you sure?"

"Pretty sure." Audie's voice held a note of doubt.

"Well, we'll just have to figure that out this year, won't we?"

"Okay."

"Let me show you our classroom."

The dark-haired woman walked Audie around, explaining the different areas to her daughter, including a large tank where a turtle inspected the girl staring at him and the smaller tank where some type of lizard couldn't be bothered to move.

The knot in the pit of Samantha's stomach unraveled just a little. For now, her daughter was safe.

Chapter 2

"How about we take a trip to Great Falls sometime next week?" Cassandra Sanders suggested to Jarod as they walked down the courthouse steps, her expensive-smelling perfume wafting around them. "I could use a good dinner. Fifth and Wine is a great place, and I'm getting to know the owner really well. I can get us some great discounts on some of the more expensive varietals."

"I'm not sure I have time for that," he replied.

"Really, Jarod, you need to get out of this town as much as I do. Winter is going to settle in soon, and then we'll be stuck."

"I *like* Choteau," he said defensively.

"So do I."

"Good, we can do a movie Friday night. I'll take you to dinner before." That should be enough.

"Are you sure I can't entice you into something more exciting? We could do something really scandalous, like rent a hotel room together," she said with a whisper and a suggestive smile.

"You know I'm not ready for that step." If he ever would be. He'd grown up fast, sown a few wild oats on the high school rodeo circuit, but he'd quickly sobered to the realities of casual sex.

And the next step wasn't possible until both the ranch and his training business were solid.

"You know we can have something more than a night, don't you?" The seductive look was gone. "I really like you, Jarod. We could be good together."

He had his doubts about that. He never had figured out what this slick attorney had wanted with a country boy like him. Or why she was even in this small town. She should be at some big city law firm, which was exactly where she had been before moving from Chicago to Choteau.

"Anything more on the mineral rights?" he asked. Time to get away from uncomfortable subjects.

"I thought your sister was handling that," she replied, a frown lessening her charm.

Jarod pulled his cap from his head and slapped it on his thigh before returning it to its perch. Mineral rights had been a thorn in his family's side since the county decided to tax the rights separately from the land property taxes. The deed they had for the ranch wasn't clear on who had the mineral rights, and, much as the entire family had searched, they hadn't found a separate deed for the mineral rights. With the absence of any other documentation, the county had sent them the bill.

The only clue to who might really own the rights was an old Bible with a family tree. Their line had descended from one of the brothers of the original family settlers. The other brother's descendants had disappeared in the 1930s. It was possible that was who had the paper they needed.

His sister, CJ, had hired a private investigator Cassandra had recommended to see if he could find them, but there had been no news in quite a while.

"She is, but since she got the PI's name from you, I thought he might have said something."

"That would be unethical." Cassandra's voice was crisp. "I'm sure he's working at it as diligently as he can. Your family didn't have a lot to go on, if I recall. Tracing families can be a challenge, especially if they don't want to be found." She smiled up at Jarod as they reached her car, a sleek gray Mercedes.

"What do you mean by that?"

"Nothing, really." She looked away from him. "It was just a thought. Now," she said, placing her well-manicured fingers on his faded National Rodeo T-shirt. "Are you *sure* you can't get away for an afternoon in Great Falls?"

"Not interested, thanks." It came out much harsher than he intended. He didn't understand what game she was playing, and it annoyed him that he didn't.

Her hand dropped.

"Sorry," he said. "I didn't mean that the way it sounded. It's that I really can't get away right now. We're getting things ready for winter—"

"It's only August, Jarod."

"Yeah, but you know this state. One day it's summer and two days later there is frost in the morning. Plus I've got Prince ready to sell. As soon as I find him the right owner, I need to execute the next step for my business."

"I could help with that," she said, her smile back to full wattage.

How could he respond without being cruel? He barely knew what he was doing. He certainly didn't want anyone watching him stumble through. She was the type that would be able to figure things out instantly, leaving him feeling like a fool.

"Thanks, but it's something I have to sit with for a while."

"Okay. The offer still stands, though."

"Got it."

"There's a new movie coming in Friday," he said. "We could pick up pizza at John Henry's before."

Her mouth wobbled for a moment, as if she were fighting to control its expression.

"Sounds good." She leaned over and kissed him on the cheek, not hard to do since she was only a few inches shorter than his five foot ten. Then she gracefully stepped into her car and waved as she drove from the parking lot.

He pulled off his cap again but this time threw it on the passenger seat of the truck when he got in. Somehow, it seemed he was dating the lady attorney, but he wasn't quite sure how that had happened.

Was it something he could get out of without causing a ruckus? Townspeople could take sides over a couple's breakup for no good reason. It would be nice to have some choice in who he took out.

The new math teacher had seemed nice and a lot less threatening. Pretty, too.

But he didn't have time for either one.

He put the truck into gear and headed back to the ranch. As soon as he passed the grain elevators leading out of town, he put business behind him and let the beauty of the country seep over him. While there was haze from distant wildfires, the Rocky Mountains still stood sentinel against the sky. To the east, the golden prairie grass led past Freezeout Lake and the city of Great Falls, to become the wheat fields and ranches of mountainless eastern Montana.

He pulled onto the long drive that snaked to the family ranch on the far size of a hill. The ranch house, added to and remodeled over the decades, was situated to have a view of the mountains. Nothing better than sitting on the porch during the long summer's evening and watching the sun set over Beck land—land that was his duty to keep for the next generation, if any of his siblings ever got around to having kids.

"Where's Dylan?" Jarod asked Birdie, the family's longtime

housekeeper, when he walked into the kitchen from the mudroom.

As usual, the tiny woman was sitting at the table, chopping something or other for dinner and watching her favorite talk shows on the flat-screen television on the wall above her.

"Hello to you, too," she said putting down her knife and wiping her hands on the apron strewn with apples. "What's got your nose out of joint?"

"Sorry." He filled a mug with the ever-present coffee. "Cassandra saw me at the courthouse. She wants more than I can give her."

"Why are you two dating anyway?" she asked.

"Beats me." He examined the dark brew.

Same as always. Deep brown with an acidic film on top that was going to rot out his stomach one of these years. Unlike tea leaves though, it didn't give him the answer as to what the attorney really wanted. And he was sure in his bones that she wanted something from him that had nothing to do with relations between a man and a woman.

"Dylan and CJ are out in the south pasture somewhere. That drone they ordered came in, and they're trying to figure out how far they can control it. Seems they think it would save time checking fences."

"If Dylan would spend more time helping me out and less time on his gadgets and paints, I'd be able to move on with my life."

"That's not fair, Jarod." Birdie's reproof was mild, but it stung just the same. She'd been the only mother he'd known since his teens when his parents died within a year of each other. "First you said you couldn't move on until CJ was settled. Well, she's seeing Nick and she's thriving in that new photo job with the magazine. So now you've come up with another excuse." She picked up the knife and went back to work. "You know that old expression: it's time to do your business or get off the pot."

He chuckled. The housekeeper was as chary with foul language as he was. Swearing was easy to use—coming up with the right word or phrase took more skill. She had a point though. He needed to move on with his life or it'd be over before it had ever begun.

He downed the coffee and headed back out of the kitchen and down to the barn. He leaned against the corral rail for a few moments and watched his rescue horse, Prince, prance through the corral, kicking up dust and checking to make sure Jarod was watching.

"Time to go to work, boy," he said and strode to the barn for the tack.

After saddling Prince, he snared one of the calves from a nearby pen and half dragged, half pushed the stubborn animal to the corral as it howled in protest. He needed to get a few of them halter-broken so his training horses would have something to work on.

Mounting Prince, he clicked a stopwatch and put the horse through the same routine he'd have to face in a rodeo. The animal responded to the slightest movement of roper and calf with precision, shaving a few seconds off his previous best.

If only Jarod were a decade younger, he'd head off to the rodeo circuit with Prince in a heartbeat. Thirty-five wasn't old for a rider, just too old to start out again. As it was, it was time to sell Prince. Getting the right price was going to be crucial if he hoped to expand the operation at a steady pace.

Was his dream of creating a world-class roping horse and rider training center crazy? He didn't know business, but he knew horses, and his riding techniques had shown promise in high school. After his parents died, he'd tried running the ranch and doing some of the rodeo events, gaining several purses and buckles before the reality of ranching life got to him.

"I'm not going to sell you to just anybody," he told Prince as they herded the calf back to its mother, who gave them a good piece of her mind. "No, I'll find a good rider, someone to challenge you but who'll treat you kindly." People who mistreated animals of any kind deserved a slow death in hot oil.

"Dylan helped me place ads for you. CJ's pictures made you look like a handsome devil." He'd put them on a few selected websites that sold rodeo stock. The few responses he'd received so far had either wanted a bargain on the price or something about their personalities had made him hesitate.

The sky was the faded blue of late summer, when the dry earth turned to dust no matter how much ranchers and farmers irrigated in the arid west. Rain dried up before it hit the ground, and thunderstorms were as likely to spark wildfires as bring torrents of water.

Prince nickered and stirred beneath him, as restless as his rider.

"C'mon, boy," he said as he leaned down to unlatch the corral gate. "Let's get some kinks out." Carefully, he secured the gate behind him and they headed toward the south pasture. May as well see what his sister and kid brother were up to.

Snugging his cap on his head, he urged Prince to his top speed until the animal was lathered with sweat and his breath was coming hard, then pulled back to an easy lope. There was nothing better than a bright summer day, a horse beneath him, and his land around him.

Except maybe someone to share it with.

# # #

Jarod spotted CJ and Dylan in the middle of the pasture, huddled over a strange cluster of metal in the back of one of the ATVs they'd used to get out there. The cattle inspected the ground around them, as if trying to figure out why there wasn't an expanse of hay around the motorized vehicles.

"What is it you expect that thing to do for us, anyway?" Jarod asked as he slid from the saddle.

"Ah, the grump has arrived," Dylan said.

"Give him a break," CJ gently punched Dylan in the arm. "He had to deal with the government, and you know how he hates that."

"But it's not really government, you know," Dylan said. "It's just a teeny office with two middle-aged women with the power over whether or not you drive."

CJ gave a mock shudder. "Women terrify him."

"I'm standing right here," Jarod said.

"So he is," Dylan mocked.

CJ ran a hand down Prince's sweaty neck. "You've done a great job with him, Jarod. Any nibbles?"

Jarod shook his head. "Not that I'm comfortable accepting."

"It'll come," Dylan said.

"I hope. I need to get a new one—or two if I can swing it—to train."

"What about training the riders themselves?" CJ asked. "I thought that was part of the plan."

"I really need to have an arena for that. I can't train only in the few warm months we have. I need a structure I can use year round."

"I can—"

"No thanks." He cut CJ off, knowing she was about to offer

some of her deceased husband's money. She'd put some of it into the ranch—he'd been outvoted on that one—but he didn't want to touch what he thought of as blood money. CJ and Ben had never really loved each other, that had been evident the more she talked about him, but she'd accepted a fairly large insurance payout anyway after he'd been shot by a sniper in the Middle East, claiming there was nowhere else it could go.

He'd rather stay single than get involved in something like that.

"Suit yourself," she said without rancor.

"We've just run a test with Hawk," Dylan said, pointing to the drone.

"You named your drone?" Jarod asked.

"You name your horses, don't you?"

Jarod shook his head.

"Anyway, Hawk scoped the fence from end to end in about an hour. Just looking at a few pieces of the feed, we can see where posts are starting to rot and fencing isn't quite as tight as it should be. It would take me half a day to ride the fence, if not more."

"Yeah, but that's because you're fixing the fence as you go."

"Good point." Dylan nodded and gave the expensive-looking ... and large ... gadget another look. "But I think there's a way to target the areas that need fixing and preventive maintenance, declare a fence repair day, and accomplish a lot more in a short time."

"Could be," Jarod said. Anything to give all of them more time for the rest of their lives. The historic family ranch, dating back to the 1800s, bound them together, but they had separate interests and lives: CJ with her photojournalism, he with his rodeo-training business, and Dylan with his paints. Only CJ had found time to add a relationship with her old high-school flame, Nick Sturgis.

"I'm going head this boy home, rub him down, and get the rest of the livestock set for the night." He turned toward Prince but remembered what he'd wanted to ask CJ.

"I ran into Cassandra while I was at the motor vehicle office," he said. "I asked her if she knew anything about the search, the PI being her referral and all. She hasn't heard anything. Have you?"

"Not recently. He did send me an email, along with a healthy invoice, saying he'd located baby Alice's marriage license in Indiana."

"Now, who was Alice, exactly?" Dylan was a technical genius

as far as Jarod was concerned, but asking him to remember something important, like which horse sired which colt, was hopeless.

CJ gave a long sigh. "Remember, great-whatever had two sons. Jacob, our relation, got the ranch, and Seth, the other one, left Montana. Whether or not he got the mineral rights is what we have to figure out."

"Before someone comes in here and starts drilling for natural gas," Jarod said.

"According to Kaiden, it's more likely there will be silver, copper, or some other precious metal," Dylan said.

"Whichever, we want control," CJ said. "According to the family Bible, Alice was Seth's descendent—but we don't know what happened to her."

"Except that she got married in Indiana," Dylan said.

"Yep. Sometime in the 1950s."

"Sure is a slow process," Jarod said.

"Right up there with watching grass grow," Dylan said.

"Exactly." Jarod smiled at his siblings. They'd figure it out. After decades apart, they were finally coming together as a team.

Chapter 3

With a smile, Samantha looked around the classroom the day before school started. A big improvement over the plain, pale yellow concrete walls. She'd hung inspirational posters, difficult equations, and humorous sayings like "Five out of four people hate math."

A few plants lined the windowsills, and when she and Audie had traveled to the city for school clothes, she'd picked up a tiny tank and a gold fish.

She'd also set up a cozy area in one corner with a small rug, a couple of beanbag chairs, and some clipboards she'd scrounged from another classroom. While she didn't know if it would work for teens, an unstructured place to figure out thorny math problems had always helped some of her elementary students.

The windows were open most days, airing out any lingering smells. The previous teacher must have had a fondness for scented purifiers; the room had a lingering scent of rose petals. It was a little overpowering.

"Getting settled?" Rebecca Johnson, the principal of Choteau High School, stepped into the classroom.

"I think I'm ready."

"Your first full-time teaching job can be a bit nerve-wracking," the principal said. "But I know you'll do fine. The references from the Billings school were all high praise."

Samantha's cheeks heated. She'd been happy with the job she'd had, but there was Audie's future to consider. Para-teachers barely made above minimum wage and received no benefits. It wasn't a sustainable way to live.

"Thank you for the opportunity," she said.

"Like I said, I'm sure you'll do fine. If you have any questions at all, feel free to ask me or Ginny Helms. If you want to know anything important, though, ask the secretaries. They really run the school."

Samantha smiled. "True in most schools, I believe."

"You got that right. I'll see you at the staff meeting in a half hour."

"I'll be there."

"Is she your boss, Mommy?" Audie asked once the principal had left.

"Yes, honey. I've got to make sure everything is perfect for her." Everything. Failure was not an option.

"Nothing's perfect," Audie pronounced. "You told me it's okay for me to make mistakes. If I can make mistakes, so can you."

If only her mistakes were the kind that resulted in a skinned knee or a broken plate. No, Samantha Deveaux made world-class mistakes, like becoming pregnant by the biggest druggie in Billings. He'd told her it wasn't the right time for him, as if there were ever a right or wrong time for a child, and taken off for Nashville, hoping to make his mark in the country songwriting field.

He'd been talented, but he'd also been irresponsible.

She wouldn't trade Audie for anything. Hopefully, Cody had the good sense to stay out of their lives. She was a grown-up; no need for any more drama.

Tomorrow she'd walk into her classroom, take control of the class, and keep it that way. With life, everything was about keeping things the way they needed to be. Only then could she keep her daughter safe.

Samantha reviewed her lesson plans for the next few days one more time. The files she needed were set on her computer, and after much explaining from the high school's technical support woman, she was confident she could get them up on the smartboard. Copies of pre-assessments were made, and she had plenty of pencils and erasers. She'd thrown out the scented whiteboard markers she'd found in a drawer and had stacks of four different colors.

Over the last two weeks, the house she'd rented had begun to look more like a home. This Sunday they'd visit another church and see if she could find the right fit.

Everything was coming together.

"C'mon, Audie, it's time for me to head to the staff meeting," she said. "You're going to go to the library with some of the other teachers' kids. They've got some high school kids to help you do crafts."

"I'd rather be with you, Mommy." Audie's smaller hand grasped hers and hung on tightly. She'd done remarkably well with all the changes so far, but they were reaching the end of her comfort zone.

"It'll be okay. That way, I can concentrate and we can get the meeting over as quickly as possible."

"O-kay." Her daughter put as much world-weariness in that one word as she possibly could. With any luck, the kid wouldn't become a con artist like her father.

Audie settled, Samantha walked to the multipurpose cafeteria for the meeting. Several others greeted her, including her fellow math teacher, an older, fussy-looking man named Bruce Weber.

"I see you've made some changes in the classroom," he said. "Definitely an improvement."

"Thank you."

"You'd better rethink that corner spot, though. It's obvious you've never taught teenagers. They'll be up to all types of mischief."

"I'll keep my eye on them," she replied. "I think it might help some of them relax about math."

"Mathematics is a serious discipline—it needs structure."

And Bruce Weber needs to retire.

"Thank you for your input," she said, and walked to where the language arts teachers, a friendlier pair, sat. Anger and fear sparked along her entire nervous system. Her fellow math teacher had been in the school for more than twenty years. He had tenure. Was staying on his good side without giving up her teaching principles going to be possible?

# # #

The lanky teen who wanted to buy Prince seemed like a nice-enough kid, and he certainly had ambition. What he didn't have was cash.

"I can work it off," he told Jarod earnestly. "I've helped my dad out all my life. I'm a hard worker. You'll see."

"I believe you," Jarod said, shifting from one foot to the other.

On the other side of the corral, Prince pranced, showing off his prowess, as if this were a test for who got the mares.

"He sure is pretty," the kid said.

"Yeah, but he's also a skilled roping horse. I'm asking seven grand for him. It'll take forever to work that off. I'm sorry, I just can't do it."

"I get it. But he sure is a nice horse." The kid gave a last look at the animal before turning toward the beat-up Toyota pickup in which he'd come to the ranch. "See ya." With a wave, he got in the truck and drove out, respectfully driving slowly to keep the dust down.

"Tough call," Dylan said, leading one of the work horses behind him. "Seemed like a nice kid."

"Yeah. It's something I have to think about."

"What?"

"How to give kids who are just starting out a chance without going bankrupt."

"Hear you."

"Where are you off to?" Jarod asked.

"Checking fences. Not everyone has the time to laze around like you and CJ."

Jarod laughed. "And what do you call it when you disappear for days at a time with your painting gear?"

"I'm preparing for my future. You know, when you get married and have a passel of kids and you don't need me anymore."

"That's not happening."

"I hope it does," Dylan said, his expression becoming serious. He turned the stirrup toward him, stuck the toe of his dusty boot into it, and gracefully swung into the saddle. "This ranch is in your blood more than anyone else's. You're going to need to make some people to inherit it." He nudged the mare and trotted toward the eastern edge of Beck land.

Jarod stared after him a few moments before a rumble and the clank of metal behind him made him turn.

A late model Ram pickup followed by a horse trailer came down the drive.

Buyer number two.

An hour later, he drove out the drive without Prince. He had the cash, but when he rode Prince, he was hard on the horse, sawing at the mouth. This was a man who blamed his failures on his horses, and Jarod wouldn't sell, even though the man threatened to smear his name as a trainer and horse seller.

Jarod had shrugged. He'd been through worse.

Well, that was it. They were the only two buyers. Business progress was going to need to wait a little longer. Besides, Dylan was right: fences needed to be checked in the valleys before they drove the cattle down for the winter.

He took a deep breath and headed toward the back where the working horses were corralled. He'd saddled up a gelding and was leading him outside when a worn but sturdy pickup came up to the barn. A stout man climbed from the driver's side, his cowboy hat dusty and stained, and his boots in pretty much the same condition. The same kid Jarod had seen earlier stepped from the passenger side.

"Hello," the man said, holding out a beefy hand. "Jake Brown."

"How can I help you?" Jarod shook hands and nodded at the teen.

"This here's my nephew. We're up from Dupuyer way. His dad's a cheap SOB, won't even get the kid a horse. What kid in Montana doesn't have a horse?"

"He's not just any horse, Uncle Jake," the teen said. "He's a really good rodeo horse."

Jake waved his hand. "How much is this horse?" he asked Jarod.

"I'm asking seven grand."

"Pretty stiff."

"He'll bring home the prizes, as long as the rider handles him right."

"Well, all my nephew's ever talked about is riding the rodeo circuit, so let's see this animal."

Jake approved of Prince, and before the kid got on the horse's back, he took time to talk to Prince and stroke his nose. His riding was gentle but sure. With time, he'd have the chance Jarod had wanted so long ago—to be a champion rider at the National Finals Rodeo.

"They look good," Jake said. "Still, seven grand."

Jarod hid his grin. The haggling was about to begin.

A few hours later, the check was in his hand and Prince was on his way to his new home.

# # #

"Mommy." Audie stood in front of Samantha, blue eyes vivid with adult seriousness. They'd arrived home from school a short while before, and Samantha was correcting a few papers before she started dinner.

She took a deep breath and braced herself for the attorney-like logic of Audie's request, whatever it was. "What do you need?"

"A horse. I definitely need a horse."

"We have no room for a horse." *Besides, I'm scared to death of them.*

"We can leave it at someone else's house. That's what Jaiden said. She has a horse, and it lives at a big barn somewhere over there." Audie waved her hand to the north of town.

"And who is Jaiden?"

"My new friend."

"I'm glad you're making new friends, sweetie, but we can't buy a horse. They are very expensive."

"Not this one." Audie held out a crinkled piece of orange paper. "This was on the bulletin board at school. Mrs. Hunt said I could have it."

Samantha flattened out the piece of paper. Beneath the picture of a pretty paint with a star on her forehead, the price read $4,500.

It may as well have been ten times that amount.

The text below gave details about the horse and where it was located. For a mere $250 a month, she could keep the animal at the current location.

"You don't have to give me an allowance," Audie continued to produce her arguments. "And I'll take care of it. I'll feed it and pet it and tell it stories."

Samantha's heart wanted to break in two. Much as the beasts terrified her, most little girls loved horses. Anything that made her particular little girl more normal, anything that got her involved outside, would be wonderful.

And it was totally beyond her ability to make happen.

Her daughter stood in front of her, eyes wide and lips parted.

"Honey, I can't afford a horse."

Everything on Audie's body slumped. "That's okay, Mommy. I understand."

Dear Lord, give me an idea of what to do.

Maybe they could afford riding lessons. She could skimp on her clothes a little more. Teenagers wouldn't notice if she wore the same thing twice in a week.

She looked at the flyer again.

Triple Bar Riding and Boarding.

"How about we go look at him ... her?"

"Really, Mommy?" Audie examined her as if trying to determine the trap in the words.

"I can't afford to buy her."

"Oh."

"But we can look at the horses and see if there is anything else you can do there." She grinned at Audie. "Maybe they'll let you feed them. We could bring some apples. I hear horses like apples."

And they eat them with big, yellow teeth.

"Okay. I'm going to go read now. Mrs. Hunt gave me a book to read. It's a horse named Misty. She lives on an island back east somewhere."

A memory stirred.

"Misty of Chincoteague?"

"I think that's it." Audie ran to her backpack and dug through it, finally holding a well-worn paperback in the air. "Yes! I'm going to read now."

Small footsteps thudded down the hall as she ran to her bedroom.

A horse. Good Lord, her daughter wanted a horse. It was probably natural; she was getting to an age most girls liked the animals, a stage Samantha had definitely *not* gone through.

With a sigh, she clicked her cell phone and called the number on the flyer.

A man with a kind voice answered.

"My daughter saw your advertisement for the horse," she said.

"Yes, it's a really fine mare, but my son's decided he wants to do dressage, and Misty is a roping and cutting horse, not suitable for all that fussy riding. I have the money to indulge my son—they're damned expensive horses—so I do. Hate to let Misty go, though."

Samantha had no idea what dressage meant, but if the sport was as fancy as the word, it probably was expensive.

"Well, I can't really afford a horse or its upkeep."

"Sorry to hear that."

"But my daughter is ... um ... different." This was always the hard part. Much of the time Audie looked and acted normally, but the way her mind worked wasn't consistent. She was also easily frustrated.

"How so?" The man's voice was kind.

"Let's just say she needs a little extra TLC. Actually, no, that's not right. She needs ways to give out the abundance of love she's got wrapped inside of her."

Maybe a kitten. Could she satisfy Audie with a kitten?

"Anyway," she continued. "I was wondering if I could bring her out to meet Misty. She'll love that name by the way."

"My wife named her. Some kid's book or something. Sure.

Bring her out. I'll show her the whole thing. She must be about ten—that's when girls get all horse crazy."

"Eight." Samantha frowned. "Is that too young?"

"Not in this state," the man said. "My boy was on a horse by the time he was five. A small horse, but he was still up there. They bounce well at that age."

"Bounce?"

"Just an expression. We give 'em helmets to protect their heads, but they're young enough they don't sustain the injuries old folks do when they fall."

Images of an old woman lying on the floor weakly saying she couldn't get up flooded her memory.

She shook them off.

"Well, come on by whenever you want. We're just north of town; turn west on Stenson Lane and go about a half mile. Triple Bar Riding and Boarding. You can't miss it."

"Thank you, Mister ...?"

"Jenkins. But just call me Bob."

"Okay, Bob. Thanks."

She ended the call and leaned back in the kitchen chair. One step at a time, her mother said frequently. That might work for her. Her mother lived a small life. She'd grown up in Billings, still lived in the same house she'd purchased with Samantha's father, and still worked two to three minimum wage jobs to keep it together. It was the kind of life Samantha was determined not to have in her fifties.

Sometimes things had to be done at the same time, but it sure took a lot of ball juggling to keep it together, especially when there was a special needs child to handle. But at twenty-eight, she was ready to launch. She was finally in control of her own life, or as much in control as any single mother could be.

She'd been a mess in high school, and Audie's teenage years weren't too far away. They needed to be settled in a place with a strong high school for her daughter and a well-paying job for her. Admittedly, it would have to be out of Montana somewhere, since state wages in practically any job were low and public schools penalized those teachers who moved later in their careers with the "Montana rule," only acknowledging five years of previous experience no matter how much the teacher really had.

But Samantha had to keep her daughter away from the drugs, loser kids, and bad decisions she'd made as a teen. And far away from Cody.

She thought she'd seen the last of him when he ran off to Nashville. Her life had seemed even more secure when he was sentenced to prison in Tennessee for ten years for selling drugs. But he must have been a model prisoner, because now he was up for parole.

Maybe God would have the answer.

Chapter 4

There were several churches in Choteau—seven if Samantha counted correctly. A few she discounted immediately; their theology had never appealed to her. The rest, except for maybe the Blackfeet and Buffalo church, she was open to trying. Her mother had never been a churchgoer; retail jobs had interfered too much. But once Audie was born, Samantha had found a small community church that fit her need to have a weekly conversation with her higher power.

"Do we have to go?" Audie whined.

"Yes. I'll set the timer, and when it goes off, you have to get up." Something she'd read had suggested giving kids on the Asperger's scale deadlines and setting timers. Most of the time it worked, but there was the odd occasion when Audie had a hissy fit and didn't want it.

Fortunately, now wasn't one of them.

"I'll ask God for a horse," she said confidently and got out of bed.

Well, that was easy.

At least it started that way. By the time they got to Choteau Community Church, the service had already started. She grabbed a bulletin and found seats at the back. A few people glanced over and gave her a friendly smile. She nodded back but returned her gaze to the service bulletin, with glances at the congregation and people around her.

The inside of the frame building was light and airy, a theme continued by the light wood of the pews. People seemed attentive. The bulletin told her there were programs for children during and outside the services.

Like most small towns, churches were the hub of community.

Next to her, Audie colored intently. Hopefully, her attention would last until the end of service.

"Please pray," the pastor intoned.

Audie immediately clasped her hands and bowed her head.

"Please, God, find me a horse. I'll be really, really good for Mommy. I promise. Amen."

Mission accomplished, she immediately got back up, colored for a few more moments, then looked at Samantha. "Can we go now?" she whispered.

"A few more moments," she whispered back. She also wanted to leave before the rest of the congregation. No need to establish connections until she'd chosen exactly the right place for her and Audie.

"Can we go look for a horse now?" Audie pestered as they made their escape to the car.

"Sweetie, I told you we can't have a horse."

"To ride. You said I could ride."

"I said I'd see about it." She used her mommy-warning voice. "Before anything though, we need to have lunch."

"But then, Mommy? Please, you promised."

"We'll see."

Once home, she made a peanut butter and jelly sandwich for Audie, cutting off the crusts so her daughter would eat it. Ham and cheese did it for her. A big glass of milk and a glass of fresh lemonade completed the meal.

Audie sat down and dutifully chewed through the sandwich and slugged down the glass of milk. She stared at Samantha's half-eaten sandwich.

"We're going when *I'm* done, so you may as well be patient."

Audie rolled her eyes, a reaction she was becoming distressingly good at.

"Remember, we're just going to ask about lessons. And we're definitely not buying horse."

"Even if that horse is Misty?"

"Even if."

A half hour later they were driving north.

The trip didn't take long, but Samantha enjoyed the crisp autumn air and sharper angle of the sun reflecting off the granite of the Rocky Mountain Front. Dark shadows showed sharp crevices etched in the craggy peaks. Yet all around them, waving stalks of brown grass softened the harshness of what natives referred to as the backbone of the world.

Triple Bar turned out to be a good-sized spread with fences of neat white wooden slats she'd have expected more in Kentucky than Montana. Several horses grazed in the fenced-in place closest to the barn. There was also a large structure that probably contained an arena for indoor practice. It would be the perfect place for Audie to have riding lessons. Maybe she could swing it.

When she stopped, the car door slammed as her daughter raced toward the nearest horse. He … or she … was safely behind a rail, but he could still get that massive head containing those large teeth too close to a little girl.

"Audie! Wait!" Samantha ran. She had to keep her from doing anything stupid like petting that horse!

Two men came from the barn, leading a paint horse that looked similar to the one on the flyer.

Audie stopped. "Look, Mommy! It's Misty!"

Samantha raced to close the distance between them. "Don't get too close. He may bite you!"

"My horses don't bite, ma'am," the older of the two gentlemen said. "They're trained to be gentle, particularly with young children."

The pair reached the railing, the younger of the men leading the horse to the rail. He looked familiar.

"Good afternoon, Miss Deveaux," he said, touching the brim of the cowboy hat perched on his dark black hair.

She sorted through her memories since she'd been in Choteau. Not any of the parents or teachers she'd met. No shopkeeper or government official.

Government. She had it.

"Same to you, Mr. Beck." She smiled at the older man. "And you must be Mr. Jenkins."

"Bob," he said. "I told you to call me Bob."

Jarod waved a hand at Audie. "Remember me? We met at the courthouse."

"Of course I do," her daughter said in a tone that indicated he was being ridiculous to think otherwise. "Are you here to see the horses?"

"I'm here to buy a horse." Jarod pointed to Misty, and Samantha's heart sank. "Isn't she a beauty?"

"No! You can't buy Misty! She's *my* horse." The pitch of her voice began to skyrocket and her eyes scrunched. "You can't! I said you can't!" The oncoming tantrum was going to look more like something a kindergartner would pull, not someone in third grade. But it was part of the problem.

"You can't! You can't! You can't! She's mine!" The words became wails as Audie lost her grip on language and became frustrated.

Samantha wrapped her arms around her daughter as the tantrum escalated, holding her tightly to calm her fears and keep her safe from spinning out into something unforgiving like a rock or a fence post.

Jarod slipped through the rails and walked toward them, and she shook her head. He stopped but crouched down so he was eye level with Audie.

"Hey, kiddo," he said. "I didn't know anyone wanted this horse as much as I do."

"I do," she said. Her voice, though still raspy with tears was more level. "She's mine," Audie whispered again.

"Maybe there is a way we could share her," Jarod said.

"I don't think that's possible." Samantha needed to put a stop to his good intentions. "I don't have the funds to buy and board a horse." She loosened her grip on Audie and crouched beside her. "Remember, honey, we talked about this."

"I know. But I was hoping." She looked over at Misty. "She's so pretty."

"Yep," Jarod stood and held out his hand. "Would you like to meet her?" He glanced up at Samantha. "If that's okay with you."

"She's really gentle," Bob said.

"Okay."

Audie took Jarod's hand without any hesitation, and they walked to the large animal.

"Horses make you nervous?" Bob asked.

"Yes. They seem so, well, big."

He chuckled. "They are that. Kind of like overly large puppy dogs, though. They love to play. They're herd animals. Once they learn that humans are okay, they can't do enough for us."

Puppy dogs with hooves.

"But I don't know anything about *him*." She gestured to the man with Audie.

"Jarod Beck?" Bob continued. "He's one of the best men in the county. When his father died the way he did, Jarod stepped up, gave up his dream of being a rodeo star, and ran the family ranch. Now that his sister, CJ, is back, though, it looks like he's going to take some time for himself. He's starting a business to train roping horses for the rodeo."

"Is he married?" she blurted out before thinking.

"No, ma'am." Bob said. "I always thought Jarod would have a dozen kids by now, but he never stuck long with anyone. Dozens of young ladies have shown him they're interested, but nothing lasted."

Jarod sliced an apple into pieces with a pocketknife, handed a few to Audie, and had her hold out her palm to the horse. Audie giggled as the animal, with those teeth exposed, sniffed her hand before using her tongue to delicately lap up the slices and crunch them.

"Jarod's as good with horses as he is with kids," Bob said. He glanced at Samantha. "Let's walk over there. It would be better for your daughter to see you overcome your fear than stay scared."

That might be true, but her feet still dragged as she followed him closer to the horse.

"Mind if I put her through her paces?" Jarod asked Bob. "I want to make sure she can be trained the way I want her."

"I have no doubt she'll be exactly what you want, but go ahead."

Jarod went back into the corral, untied the mare, and swung himself on her back.

He made it look so easy.

When her mother had taken Samantha for her first riding lesson, telling her that she'd get past her fear of horses if she learned to ride, she'd struggled to pull herself onto the saddle. The horse had fidgeted and started trotting around the arena before she was fully seated.

It was a long way down to the ground where her ten-year-old body hit and knocked the wind out of her. She never went back.

This man looked strong and sure on the back of the mare, first circling the corral, the hooves making muted thuds in the soft dirt. He turned her one way then the other, then backed her up. However he got the animal to do it, the mare never protested anything he asked of her. He turned back to them and trotted over, the gear gently clinking as he rode.

Audie gave him enthusiastic applause.

"Why, thank you, ma'am," he said with an exaggerated bow.

"Sold," he said to Bob as he slid back off the horse. "Do you want to do the paperwork now or when I head back with the horse trailer?"

"But ..." Audie's voice was soft. Thankfully, she didn't sound like she was going to go into tantrum mode again.

"Ah, yes. My new partner." He walked to her and crouched again. "Do you know how to ride?" he asked the little girl.

"No. Mommy's scared of horses."

The kid had some form of ESP. Samantha had never told her that.

"She is? Well, we'll have to fix that." He stood. "I would like

33

to give your daughter riding lessons on Misty."

She opened her mouth to protest.

"No charge. All you have to do is get her to the ranch once a week." He smiled. "Maybe we can get you a little closer to a horse, too."

"Yes, Mommy! You can get on and ride with me."

"Why would you do that?" she asked.

"Because every Montana kid should know how to ride a horse, even if they've outgrown being a kid." He smiled at her, an expression that lit up the depths of his gray eyes.

Careful.

"But I also want Misty to be used to all kinds of riders."

"I thought you were training rodeo horses."

He glanced at Bob, who shrugged.

"I am."

"So, you're really doing this just for Audie."

"Guilty. But for you, too. It's tough being a new teacher at the high school. Kids can be a real pain. I know because I went there." A fly buzzed around his ear and he flicked it away. "C'mon," he added. "Take a risk."

She did not take risks. Everything was planned out well in advance and executed precisely, like mathematical formulas.

"How about we try it for a month?" Maybe Audie would get bored. "And she has to learn how to take care of the animal. You know, brush it, that kind of thing. No excuses." Her daughter loved the fun part of any activity, but cleanup could often be a struggle.

Whatever it took, she'd learn to tolerate a horse. If Audie wanted to ride, she'd make it happen.

No way was she going to be less than a perfect mother.

"Good," Jarod said. "I'll see you next Saturday at this time. The ranch is about five miles south of town on the right. If you give me your number, I'll text the address."

They made the arrangements, then somehow she convinced Audie to leave. All the way home the girl sang, "I'm going to ride Misty; I'm going to ride Misty." It drove her nuts, but it was far better than the alternative.

# # #

"She sure is pretty," CJ said as Jarod unloaded the mare from the horse trailer, Misty's hooves rattling against the metal ramp.

"Did you spend a lot?"

"Not really. And I got a good price for Prince, so I have some money socked away for another one." He led the horse to the corral, unhooked her lead, and let her loose.

The mare looked at him as if to say, "Aren't you coming?"

They both chuckled.

CJ helped him raise the trailer ramp and secure it to the body. When it was latched, he gave Misty another look. "She was almost too cheap," he added, "for her skill level."

"Maybe they didn't know what they had."

"Could be. Or maybe they know something they aren't telling." He shook the thought from his head. He'd known Bob Jenkins all his life. "Probably not. Bob said their son didn't want to do rodeo but some fancy thing called dressage. Good thing he's got money to burn after developing that gizmo for vineyard owners to measure the stats of their grapes." He pulled his Bulldogs cap from his head and thumped it on his knee before waving away a few flies with it and slapping it back on his head. "Californians have gone crazy for wine. Not sure why. Give me a cold beer any day."

"You are hopelessly stuck in the past," she said.

"No, I'm not." He grinned at her. "Think of all the microbreweries starting up all over Montana. I'm on the front end of the curve."

"A once-in-a-lifetime occurrence."

"Quit busting me."

"Oh, little brother, I've got years to make up for."

"Don't you have to go see Nick or something?" he asked to get her out of his hair. He wanted to see what Misty could do and make sure she was going to be safe for that little girl.

And her mother.

"What's that smile about?" CJ asked.

"Nothing," he said, climbing into the truck cab and bringing it to life with a roar. "Mind your own business," he yelled from the window. "Go see your boyfriend."

He pulled the trailer to the side of the barn and unhitched it from the back of the truck. If he was lucky, CJ wouldn't tease him about that smile.

His luck had never been that good.

But he couldn't have stopped it if he'd tried. There was something about Samantha and Audie that made him want to assure them everything would be okay. In one small way, he could make their lives better. And it felt really satisfying.

For much of the rest of Saturday, Jarod tested Misty on all the aspects she'd need to be a good calf-roping horse for rodeo. His scribbles about how best to go about training her took up three pages of yellow legal paper. It wasn't that the horse didn't know what to do—it was getting her to do it more quickly and sharply.

Thankfully, CJ spent the night with Nick, and Dylan had gone to Helena for the weekend. Even Birdie had gone to Great Falls for what she termed a girls' night out.

Blissfully alone, a situation he loved and hated all rolled into one.

He pulled leftovers out from the fridge, put them in the microwave, snapped open a local beer, and settled at the kitchen table. Pulling out the latest James Lee Burke book, he settled in for a harrowing tale from the popular Missoula author. It surprised Jarod as much as anyone else that he loved reading books filled with a high body count and horrible deeds.

Ironically, it kept him from looking at the dark side of real life. How did CJ stand it? She'd been in war zones for years, documenting horrors he couldn't even imagine and didn't want to. Now she was staying closer to home, but there was still enough tragedy locally: abused kids, trafficked women, kids who died too soon from a bad decision on prom night.

He said a quick prayer of thanks for his dinner and to keep people he knew and loved safe before he picked up his fork. Even reheated, meatloaf and mashed potatoes were close to the top of the list of his favorite foods.

A half hour later, the dishes were done and he was settled in front of the television watching rookie league baseball using an internet connection Dylan set up one spring when Jarod was bemoaning his lack of opportunities to watch Montana baseball. Tonight the Great Falls Voyagers beat the Missoula Osprey in a lackluster game.

Halfway through, Jarod's mind wandered back to the scene at Bob's place. Teaching kids to ride was not part of his business plan; Samantha had been right about that. But when Audie had looked at him with those wide, blue eyes, she'd obliterated any excuse he might have made.

But the girl wasn't the only one who'd taken a nick from his heart. He would have done anything to erase the stricken look on her mother's face when she realized he was there to buy the horse.

There were a few single mothers he knew in town, even though he wasn't involved with any of them. They looked permanently stressed out.

A total contrast to the put-together Cassandra.

Which brought him back full circle to the question that had been haunting him since they'd met for dinner and a movie a week ago.

What was he doing with her? And why couldn't he shake the nagging feeling she wanted something from him—something he wasn't going to like?

He should break it off, except in his mind there wasn't anything to really break off. They'd drifted together after a few coffees when he'd gone to her office on business. If he was lucky, he could drift right back out without causing a fuss.

Coward.

All right, maybe he would have to be more upfront about it. He'd worry about it while he was riding fence next week. Despite Dylan's hopes with the drone, he'd had difficulties with sight lines over the rugged terrain.

Jarod clicked off the television and headed to bed.

Chapter 5

"You're doing what?" Dylan asked the following Saturday as Jarod sorted through saddles to find the right one for his pint-sized student. The air was cloudy with dust. Even though a lot of the saddles were no longer used, Jarod made it a practice to oil the leather and check the straps and hardware at least once a year, but dust accumulated rapidly in a space filled with hay and animals.

"Teaching a little kid to ride," he replied, trying to make it sound like the most natural thing in the world.

"*What* little kid?" Dylan asked.

"One I met the other day. When I was buying the horse."

"Whatever possessed you to do that? Don't you have enough to do?" His brother cocked his head and eyed him. "Or are you trying on the whole kid and family thing to see if it fits?"

"You're nuts." Jarod shook his head, but his lungs cramped slightly with panic. Was *that* what this was all about? An unconscious wish to have a pretend family?

Like the rest of his siblings, he'd had his whole life planned out when he was a teen. Get to the professional rodeo circuit by the time he was twenty, accumulate some cash, come home, and marry his high school sweetheart. They'd have five kids, several dogs, and horses.

The fact that she might not wait for him never occurred to him, and that he would have to abandon both dreams when his father died had been incomprehensible to his fourteen-year-old mind.

But he'd done what had to be done.

"Oh, look," Dylan said. "Here's CJ's old saddle from when she was a kid. That should do." He hauled the tooled leather piece from its holder. "Sure is a pretty thing. Remember when Dad gave it to her that Christmas?"

"Yeah. She wanted to go out and use it right then, even though we were in the middle of a two-day blizzard."

They chuckled, and ease draped back over Jarod's shoulders.

"That'll be perfect. Thanks, man."

"Have you heard anything from Cameron?" Dylan asked as they walked into the bright sunlight.

"Nothing. It's been a long while since he went out on patrol. A month before Easter, wasn't it?"

"Yeah, coming on six months."

"I hope he's okay." It figured. Their younger brother had committed to one last mission before coming home from the Middle East for good, but it might the one to get him killed. Jarod would have to send up some extra earnest prayers tomorrow and get the prayer circle to add Cameron to their list.

"Me, too," Dylan said. "I keep trying the communications center, but they've stonewalled me—told me they'll let me know when they know but that everything is working as it's supposed to."

"Bureaucracy at its best." Jarod leaned against the corral fence. Rolling hills led to the sudden wall of granite that was the start of the Bob Marshall Wilderness in the Rockies. Some days he wanted to simply run away from all his problems—past and present. The Bob, as everyone in Montana called it, would be the perfect place. He turned toward Dylan. "I feel like everything's hanging like a deep, dark thunderstorm over the mountains. A strong gust of wind and the storm of life is to come down on us again."

"Old Mr. Doom and Gloom," Dylan kidded. "Life includes more than bad luck and tragedy. Someday, I hope you get that. For me, I'm going to ignore that you even thought that, slap an easel and paints on my horse, and head up toward the aspen grove to see what I can find. You need me for anything else?"

"I got it."

"Don't be mean to the little girl now."

"I won't." Jarod opened the gate to the corral, snared Misty's halter, and snapped on a lead. After tying her to the railing and cleaning her hooves, he curried her to loosen the dust and dirt and brushed her down, running his hand over her to make sure she had no injuries he didn't know about. "Rolling in the dust again, were you?" he murmured. "That's no way to get ready for a pretty little girl."

Misty arched her neck around and gave him a look indicating she didn't care what he thought, she was going to do what she pleased.

Just when he'd finished saddling her up, an older-model Camry inched down the dirt drive.

"Showtime," Jarod said to the horse. He let himself out of the corral and tried to lean nonchalantly against the railings, hoping that his smile didn't look as ridiculous as it felt. Was it because of the girl or her mother?

As soon as the car stopped, before the engine turned off, the passenger door opened and Audie shot in a straight line to Misty, causing the horse to take a step back.

"Audie!" Samantha shouted, leaping out of the car. She must not have put it in park because it started to roll forward on the slight slope.

# # #

Samantha looked around when she saw a look of horror pass over Jarod's face. Behind him, Misty danced in the corral, the whites of her eyes visible even from this distance. He grabbed Audie by the waist, picked her up, and started running to Samantha.

"The car is rolling!" he yelled.

She jumped back in and stopped the car. Idiot! She could have killed her own daughter.

Forcing back tears, she walked toward them.

Jarod put Audie down and crouched beside her. "There are rules about horses," he said. "If you want to come here and learn to ride, you need to obey them. Never, ever run to a horse that way, especially if she doesn't know you."

"But we already met. Last week."

"Not good enough," Jarod said. "It's a rule. Are you willing to obey it?"

"I suppose."

Jarod shook his head. "Promise."

"I promise." She pointed to Misty's hooves digging up dust. "Why is she doing that?"

"Because you made her scared," he said.

"Don't be silly. I can't make a horse scared." She scrunched up her nose. "Can I?"

"Yes, you can."

"Oh."

"That's why we have rules." He looked up at Samantha, who nodded. "Your mom is right about one thing. Horses are big animals. If you startle or scare them, they might do something to hurt you. Not on purpose. Because they are moving back and forth

40

and don't see you."

"Okay. Now can I go see her?"

He shook his head and rose. "Nope. First you're going to practice getting out of a car and approaching her with respect."

Wow. For having no children, the man was good.

"Do I have to? Can't I just get on her?"

"Back to the car, Audie," Samantha said.

"I don't want to."

"I can't let you ride until you practice," he said, his voice brooking no argument.

"Okay." With slumped shoulders and a shuffling walk, Audie returned to the car and threw herself onto the passenger seat.

"Now walk over to Misty slowly and calmly."

Audie pulled herself from the car and walked slowly by him and Samantha, eyes on the ground beneath her. Occasionally, she stopped to kick a clod of dirt out of her way with her tennis shoes.

"She doesn't have any boots?" he asked Samantha.

"Only snow boots, and it's a struggle to get her into those."

"She's going to need boots."

She frowned. "I'll see what I can do."

"What did you do before you came to Choteau?" he asked, now walking behind Audie as she carefully made her way to the corral.

Did he expect her to follow him?

She took a deep breath and caught up to him.

"It, uh, took me a while to finish my degree. My mom helped out with childcare, but it was still tough because I had to work odd jobs, too. Then I had to do practicums and student teaching. But, even once I had all that, the only job I could find was being a para-teacher—minimum wage."

"Really? That's all?"

"Yeah."

"What does a para-teacher do, exactly?"

"I worked with kids with special needs—learning disabilities, emotional difficulties, stuff like that. Kids who need some extra help that classroom teachers don't have time to give."

"Sounds tough."

"It can be. But it's rewarding, too." Her eyes widened. "Audie, don't!"

Audie jerked her hand away from Misty's nose and gave her a look that crossed between a glare and tears.

"Shh. It's okay," he said, putting his hand on Samantha's

upper arm.

It took everything she had not to pull away.

He dropped his hand.

"She's moving nice and slowly, just like I taught her."

He was right. Audie was calmly moving her body around the horse—not her normal mode when she was excited. This could be good for her. Then Samantha made the mistake of looking at the size of Misty's hooves ... too close to her daughter's tiny feet in tennis shoes.

She pushed down her panic.

"Alright, let's get you on the saddle," Jarod said and led Audie through the gate to Misty's left side. "You're going to need to be careful because you have on tennis shoes. You should be wearing leather boots."

"Mommy will get them for me," Audie said confidently. "Won't you, Mommy?"

"We'll see," Samantha said. One more thing to add to her already stretched-thin budget.

"That means 'no,'" Audie whispered to Jarod. "She thinks I don't know what it means, but I do."

"We'll figure it out," he said, with a glance toward Samantha.

She kept her face expressionless. He'd better not mean he was going to get the boots for Audie. He'd gone far enough in the generosity department. She didn't want to owe anybody anything.

He must have gotten the picture because he turned back to Audie. "Now, I'm going to give you a leg up. Put your left foot in my hands, grab on to the horn right here." He pointed to the part of the saddle he meant. "Then swing your leg over. Got it?"

Audie studied her feet for a few moments and nodded.

Samantha had moved a few steps closer to the horse, her heart thumping in her chest.

"Just a sec, kiddo," he said to Audie. "Let's get your mom to see it isn't really that scary." He slipped through the corral railings. "Come with me," he said, holding out his hand as he would to Audie. "I'll keep you safe."

"Promise?" She attempted a smile.

"Yes." He took a step and she followed. He smiled at her, but she barely saw him. Her gaze was pinned on Misty.

Slowly, he opened the gate and led her through before latching it.

Misty nickered.

She froze.

"It's okay," he said. "It means she likes you. Let's go over here by Audie." He got Samantha about two feet from the animal before she balked.

"This is as far as I can go." Her voice was so thin it almost blew off in the currents of air drifting down from the mountain.

"Okay," he said, letting go of her hand and turning to Audie. "Let's show your mom how it's done."

"I'll be careful, Mommy," she promised. "Misty's a really nice horse."

Jarod made a cradle with his hands and crouched down.

With one more check of her shoes, Audie stepped her left foot into his hands.

Slowly, he lifted her daughter so she could reach the horn and waited until she was straddling the saddle. He glanced at Samantha. "She's heavier than she looks."

"Don't I know it," she said, her face relaxing a bit more.

He adjusted the stirrups to fit Audie's legs. Then he handed her the reins and showed her how to hold them. "Misty has a real sensitive mouth," he said, "so don't yank hard on the reins. First, your mom and I are going to walk you around the corral so you get the feel of the horse under you. Then I'll teach you how to start and stop her."

Audie's grin was wide but had just a little wobble. The view from the top of a moving thousand-pound animal was very different from the ground. She must be mustering every ounce of bravery she had to handle it.

Jarod took the lead in one hand and reached for Samantha's hand with the other. "It'll be okay," he said. "Just a little walk around the corral." He looked at her feet. "Don't suppose you have boots, either," he said as they started off slowly.

"I don't ride," she said firmly. "I have no intention of ever doing so."

"Uh-huh. Just be careful where you put your feet then. You don't want those pretty shoes covered in horse poop."

Audie giggled, and even Samantha chuckled.

As he slowly led them around the space, the sounds of the ranch washed over them: chickens squawking over whatever was perturbing them, far-off lows from the cattle, a conversation drifting from the ranch house windows, all overlaid by the steady clop of the horse behind him. The sun beat down, strengthening the aroma of horse all around them.

Her shoulders relaxed an inch, and she allowed herself to

take a quick look at the man walking beside her, only to encounter his gaze.

She switched her view to the mountains in the distance.

"You must really love it here," she said, turning back to him once again.

"I do. If there's any way possible, I'm going to live here until they cart me out in a pine box."

"Do they even do that anymore?" she asked.

"Probably not. Maybe a gigantic Ziploc bag."

This time she laughed, her body's tenseness easing at the same time.

When they reached the gate, he opened it to let her slip out. Then he turned to Audie and began to instruct her on the particulars of guiding a horse.

Samantha forced herself to lean against the railing as she watched Jarod patiently go through the methods used to steer the big animal around. He was sure and competent, and the horse the model of patience.

She let her gaze drift from the scene in front of her to the rolling hills and mountains beyond, trying not to think about the text message she'd received the week before from her mother. After a week of stewing, she still didn't know what to do about Cody's release.

So she looked at the scenery instead. It was very different from where she'd lived in the shadow of Billings' Rimrock Canyon, carved by the Yellowstone River centuries before. The city sprawled from the canyon's narrows to the town of Laurel sixteen miles southwest. Sometime in the second half of the 1900s, those with money had started migrating to the top of the canyon walls, crowding out the isolated spaces where for decades teenage boys had taken their dates to show them "how the city lights spelled out Billings."

But Audie hadn't been conceived in those dark reaches. Instead, nineteen-year-old Samantha had joined Cody on his mattress on the floor, convinced that being on the pill made her invulnerable to pregnancy. The theory had worked for the first three years they were together.

Then it had failed her.

"Hello," a female voice said next to her.

Startled, she gripped the top of the railing to avoid falling as she twisted toward the voice.

Chapter 6

"Hello," Samantha replied.

"Sorry, didn't mean to startle you. I'm CJ, Jarod's older, and very much wiser, sister." CJ Beck was a trim woman with well-developed arms below her T-shirt sleeves. Her skin was sun-darkened, and small lines skirted her gray eyes, which, despite their warmth, held a level of wariness.

"I'm Samantha Deveaux, the new math teacher, and that's my daughter, Audie."

"Yes, Jarod said you were coming."

Ah … his sister was here to check her out. She couldn't blame CJ. Although Jarod seemed confident, she'd sensed a vulnerability where Audie was concerned. Was it just her child or all children?

"Jarod mentioned you, too," Samantha said. "He said you'd just returned home, but he didn't say from where."

"The Middle East. I was a photojournalist there for over a decade."

"It must have been tough."

"It was."

Her voice indicated the two words were the end of that piece of the conversation. Samantha waited to see where CJ would go next.

"So what made you pick Choteau?" CJ asked.

"Pretty simple. They offered me a job with a possibility of a tenure if I lasted. It's a small town, but it's close enough to Great Falls and not in a totally depressed area of the state. They also seem to have good options to support Audie. She's on the Asperger's scale." What she didn't add was that as soon as she received tenure, she'd begin looking for a position in a big city away from Montana, someplace Cody could never find them.

"What does that mean?"

"She processes things different from you or me. She's brilliant in some areas and has great difficulty in others. Her social skills aren't always there, either."

"Sounds like a lot of us," CJ said with a grin. "If you ask my

45

brothers, they'll tell you I have no social skills whatsoever—particularly when it comes to them." She relaxed her stance and stuck an elbow on the closest railing.

"How many brothers do you have?" Samantha glanced at the corral, hoping Jarod would finish soon so she could escape.

"Four. Jarod and Dylan—he's the next oldest—live on the ranch and manage it. Cameron's in the army overseas, and Kaiden, the youngest, is supervising operations in the Bakken oil fields. And I work for a Montana magazine as a photojournalist."

"Hard-working family." Samantha gestured around her. "Nice ranch. You must love it here."

"I do in some ways. It's been in our family since the 1880s." A frown appeared on CJ's face, then disappeared. "One of us better have kids soon so we can pass it along."

Would that be CJ? It seemed rude to ask the question.

"Probably Jarod," CJ continued as if sensing the unasked question. "I can't have them."

"Oh, I'm sorry." Averting her gaze from Jarod's sister, she watched Audie for a while. Without him leading her, she managed to walk the horse around the corral, a smile beaming on her face.

"Would you want more children?" CJ's question startled her.

"Uh, I'm not sure." She turned back. "I'm not exactly in the market for a man at the moment—there are too many other things going on."

"Oh." CJ sounded disappointed. Was she matchmaking for Jarod? If so, she was headed in the wrong direction. Samantha's stay in Choteau was temporary, just long enough to prove herself.

"That's it for today," Jarod said. "Now ride Misty back toward your mother. Show her what you can do."

Samantha tried not to think about the horse steadily coming toward her, and focused on her daughter. It would be okay. Audie needed this to boost her confidence and get her outside.

Jarod tied the horse to the railing near Samantha, giving her a nod as he did so.

"Hi, CJ," he said.

"You're pretty patient with her," CJ said.

"Does that surprise you?" he asked—a genuine question.

"You were never that way with me."

"You were impossible," he said with a chuckle.

"Probably true," CJ acknowledged.

Samantha envied them their easy banter. When she was a kid, she thought being the only child was perfect, except for the times the house was too quiet.

Jarod helped Audie off the horse. "Now," he said, "you're a little small to carry that saddle yet, but you can help me get it off of Misty." Patiently, he showed Audie which buckles to undo.

Misty sniffed Samantha's arm, the soft muzzle gentle against her skin.

It took everything inside her not to jump back with a scream.

"Look, Mommy, she likes you."

Great.

"Afraid of horses?" CJ asked quietly.

Samantha nodded, unsure what would happen if she spoke.

"Jarod will cure you of that. He's good with people. Other people, that is. See you around." CJ touched her arm and walked back toward the house, leaving Samantha face-to-face with the horse.

"Pet her, Mommy."

As if she were raising her hand through Jell-O, Samantha touched the long nose.

Misty stayed still.

Emboldened, she gave the horse tiny strokes until Misty nickered and shook her head.

She snatched her hand away, and Audie giggled.

"C'mon, kiddo, your mom'll be fine. Let's get this saddle into the tack room."

They left her alone with the horse.

For a few seconds she stared at it, then the muzzle was back, sniffing the railing as if searching for her scent. Maybe the animal really did like her. She reached her hand up again and stroked the wide cheek. Misty patiently waited.

"Want to give her some apples?" Jarod asked as he and Audie returned. They'd come from the barn and were now on the same side of the corral fence as she was. Jarod held out his hand with slices of the fruit.

"Mommy, it will be okay. Misty is nice."

She had to do it for her daughter, didn't she? And maybe a little for herself. In a state with more cattle than people, it wasn't practical to be afraid of the horses that worked them.

"Okay."

"Hold your palm straight, like this." Jarod demonstrated.

She held out her flat hand, trying to keep it from trembling. Jarod lay two chunks on her hand and guided it to below Misty's mouth.

The horse's muzzle dipped. Soft whiskers and puffs of air tickled her palm before a wet, but not too slobbery, tongue swiped up the apple pieces.

"Good horsey," she said before pulling her hand back to safety.

"Good job, Mommy!"

She smiled at her little girl. Audie had always been her champion, even in the worst of times. Her sunny disposition was another trait she'd inherited from the father who never believed anything could go wrong. Hopefully, her daughter had received a dose of practicality from her mother's genes as well.

"Same time next week?" Jarod asked, handing her a clean rag for her hand.

"Okay." Then she remembered. "I don't know what I can do about the boots though."

"I'll see if I can come up with something. Maybe there's an old pair of CJ's around here."

Her spine stiffened. "I'll figure it out somehow."

"As you wish," he said, the smile fading from his lips.

"Thank you."

"Thanks, Jarod!" Audie threw her arms around his hips and squeezed before running to the car.

Samantha gave a wave and followed her daughter.

# # #

Samantha pulled the Camry into one of the last remaining spots at Choteau Community Church. After the visit last week, she'd run through her options and decided this was the best fit for her and Audie. The modern playground and grouping of picnic tables gave her a positive feeling, as did the neat landscaping and well-kept building.

"Let me see you, honey," she said as Audie got out of the car. She finger-brushed her daughter's hair lightly, trying to make it look like it had been combed that morning instead of the week before. She'd vetoed the extra piece of toast and jam in the car, so the dress was still presentable.

She smoothed her own blue shirtwaist, took her daughter's hand, and walked up the steps to the greeters to introduce herself and Audie to the pair. "The new math teacher," the woman said. "Welcome. My daughter says you are a lot easier to understand than the guy who just retired. So glad you're here." She pumped

Samantha's hand.

"Um, thank you." Her cheeks warmed, and she quickly guided Audie through the church doors and found a pew as far back as she could, putting her against the right side of the gray nave.

"There's childcare if you need it," a woman with a stylish brown hair sitting next to her whispered.

"That's okay, thank you. I'd like to keep her with me today."

"First time?" The woman, who looked to be in her mid-thirties, smiled.

"Second."

"That speaks well for us. I'm glad."

The praise band began right on time and she gave herself over to the music and prayer. Next to her, Audie swayed with the music.

As the service went on, she gazed around at the congregation again. There were plenty of gray hairs but also a significant number of young families, always a good sign. The minister, Pastor Steve, was probably in his forties. She recognized several of the people she'd met around town and a few fellow teachers.

In the front, most of the people were paying more attention to the service than she was, so all that was in view were backs of heads. She forced her attention back to the minister's words as he spoke about repentance.

"When someone truly repents," he said, "he turns back to God and changes how he lives. He no longer continues to sin. Now ..." He leaned forward on the lectern. "Being human, he or she probably stumbles. We all know how difficult habits are to change."

Muffled chuckles filled the congregation.

"But our job, as his neighbors, friends, and community is to support him in his struggle, to help him find the right path. We cannot shun a man or woman who is turning their face to God once more."

Would Cody ever turn away from drugs? For a few months, about the time Audie was conceived, she'd had hope, but he'd quickly fallen back into old ways. Had prison changed him in any way—good or bad? What if he came back to Montana? If he did and he was clean, would she have the courage to let him back into Audie's life? That seemed to be what the minister was proposing.

Not a chance. Audie was too vulnerable. No matter what, she was going to keep her away from her father. Besides, Cody was a smooth talker—the perfect salesman for anything, and he totally believed what he was saying. At the time, at least.

But it never lasted.

When the service ended, the woman next to her held out her hand. "Hi, I'm Trish Small, and this is my husband, Brad."

"Nice to meet you. I'm Samantha Deveaux, the new high school math teacher. And this is my daughter, Audie."

"Welcome," Trish said, and her warm smile said she meant it.

They chatted as they moved down the aisle to greet the minister. Like Trish, the man was welcoming and pleasant, encouraging them to join the congregation at the picnic tables for an after-church coffee hour. She and Audie followed them down a path to where coffee urns steamed on a stand next to the church building and the tables were covered with bright tablecloths and mounds of food. Warmth spread through her bones.

"Look, Mommy! It's Jarod!" Audie let go of her hand and raced toward a small group of people.

Uncertainty replaced the warmth.

Audie tugged Jarod's hand, and he looked over at Samantha, a welcome smile on his face. He said something to the small, bird-like woman next to him, then followed Audie to where Samantha stood.

"I didn't know you came here," he said.

"I just made my decision yesterday."

"So you were church shopping?"

"Something like that." Would he condemn her for the laxness of her commitment to a particular faith?

"Well, you picked the best as far as I'm concerned," he said. "It's not the one my parents used, but I needed a new perspective after they died. The people here reached out when I showed up. They're friendly, so you should be able to find others to do things with once the winter weather settles in."

"I didn't realize both your parents died. I'm so sorry. It must have been hard." Without thinking much about it, she put her hand on his arm in a gesture of sympathy.

He patted it. "Thanks," he said, looking directly into her eyes.

A brief connection touched her. They could be friends, the two of them. Good friends.

She pulled her hand away.

"Jarod, I've been looking for you. I was hoping you didn't have plans for lunch." The blonde from the courthouse wrapped her well-manicured fingers around Jarod's arm.

"Oh, hi, Cassandra. This is Samantha Deveaux and her daughter Audie. I'm teaching them to ride."

Samantha opened her mouth to correct him, but his quick glance in her direction prompted her to stop. There were undercurrents here she didn't understand.

"This is Cassandra. She's a family and estate attorney here in town," Jarod said, finishing the introductions.

"Nice to meet you," Cassandra said.

"Will you excuse us for a moment?" Jarod asked.

"Of course."

The pair walked away from the rest of the congregants, and Samantha led Audie to the beverage table where she got an iced tea for herself and a lemonade for her girl. She turned back to look at the people, not knowing who was best to approach.

"It can be a bit intimidating." Trish Small stepped up next to her and refilled her coffee cup. "Other than college, I've never lived anywhere else but here. And college terrified me. I think you're remarkably brave moving to a new town."

"Thank you."

"Let me introduce you to some of the people. I'm sure you have some of their children in class. You teach freshman and sophomores, right?"

Samantha nodded.

"So you have my daughter, Beth."

"Ah, yes." Beth Small was a chatterbox who looked a lot like her mother.

Trish crouched to Audie's height. "Do you recognize any of your classmates here?" she asked.

The girl nodded, suddenly shy, a characteristic she didn't display very often. She pointed to a few kids her own age who were playing on the slides.

"Why don't we go over there first and then you can play if you want," Trish said, warmth in her voice.

Once Audie was embraced by the other children, Trish began to make her introductions. After a blur of names and faces, they approached the small woman she'd seen Jarod with. She turned out to be Jarod's housekeeper.

"More like his mother," Birdie said. "I keep hoping he'll find a wife, but he seems to like the cows and horses better." She cocked her head like a finch inspecting a seed. "Aren't you the lady with the little girl? The one he's teaching to ride?"

"Yes." For all of her small bones, the woman in front of her intimidated the heck out of Samantha.

"Ah," Birdie said.

What did that mean? She glanced at Trish, who shrugged.

"Sorry," Jarod said as he approached the group. "I had some things I needed to straighten out."

"Oh?" Birdie asked.

That woman could punch more meaning into a syllable than anyone she'd ever met. Unfortunately, she didn't know how to decipher it.

"Like I was saying," Jarod continued, "this is a great little church. I hope you enjoy it."

"Yes," Birdie added.

"Thank you," Samantha said.

"Be sure to ask for help if you need it," Trish added. "Sometimes life can throw more at you than you can handle by yourself."

"Thank you," Samantha repeated.

Her phone buzzed against something in her purse. "Please excuse me," she said.

Her mother had texted.

Mom: Cody called me and asked where you are.
Samantha: What did you tell him?
Mom: That you've moved.
Samantha: You didn't say where, did you?
Mom: Of course not. But he's smart. He may figure it out.
Samantha: Thanks. I'll give you a call later.

She fought down the panic. No matter what, she had to stay calm for Audie.

"Something has come up," she said after returning to the group. "I have to get home."

"See you next Saturday," Jarod said.

"And be sure to bring Audie inside for a piece of pie. Trish has promised me two brimming with huckleberries," Birdie added.

She nodded and retrieved Audie. Just when she was feeling safe, Cody had to reappear. How should she handle it? Truthfully, there was a nowhere in Montana she could really hide for long, not with Audie. The state was often described as a small town with long roads. It certainly fit the bill.

She wished she could stay in Choteau. But if Cody got too

close, how could she?

Chapter 7

"Any idea if CJ kept any of her old boots from when she was a kid?" Jarod asked as he, Dylan, and Birdie sat down for Sunday dinner. The old-fashioned dining room brimmed with heavy furniture and the savory aroma of roast chicken.

"I doubt it," Birdie said. "When she realized that she was staying in Montana for good last winter, she methodically went on a cleaning spree from one end of the house to the other."

"Yeah, I couldn't find my checkbook for days," Jarod grumbled.

"That's 'cause she put it in your desk, where it belongs," Dylan said with a grin.

"Anyway, any of her old clothes and stuff she didn't need any more went to the thrift store. If she had them, they're gone."

"Darn," he mumbled, then helped himself to mashed potatoes and a leg from one of the two chickens Birdie had cooked.

"Green beans," she ordered.

"I was getting there." He didn't need a wife; the housekeeper henpecked him enough. He dug into the potatoes—salt, cream, and butter combined with a hint of garlic. Although the food was basic, Birdie always found some way to twist it so there was enjoyment in every bite.

As he chewed, he contemplated the problem of the boots. He really needed two pairs—one way or another he was going to get Samantha on a horse.

"Kaiden sent me a text," Birdie announced. "He's coming home for Thanksgiving, and he's bringing a girl."

"A girl?" Dylan asked.

"That's what I said."

"Does this mean our little brother is going to get to the altar before we do?" Jarod's fork clattered against his water glass as he used the utensil to gesture his incredulity.

"Could be," Dylan said. "I'm in no rush, and it doesn't appear you are either."

"I'm not sure about that," Birdie said.

"What do you mean?" Dylan asked.

"Yes, what do you mean? I officially broke up with Cassandra today," Jarod protested, stabbing another piece of chicken.

"That was never really serious," Birdie said, waving her hand dismissively.

"Cassandra thought so," Jarod said then regretted it. He tried to keep his personal business out of family gossip and vice versa.

"I wondered why it took you so long to dump her." Birdie efficiently cut her chicken slices into bite-size pieces. She was the most pristine eater he had ever seen. Even chicken legs fell under her sharp knife and accurate fork.

"I didn't dump her," he protested. "I just forced her to come to the mutual understanding that we aren't right for each other. I don't want a woman who's more focused on her career than our relationship. And I don't want to discuss it anymore." He tried to make his voice firm.

"Just one more thing," Dylan said, his teasing expression fading. "Did CJ ever tell you how to find the spot up in the hills? The one that looks like the photo that hangs in Cassandra's office? Or maybe the attorney herself explained it?"

While seeking Cassandra's help on a tax matter, CJ had noticed an old black-and-white photo that looked familiar based on the mountains behind their ranch. Without the attorney's knowledge, she'd snapped a picture of it with her phone. After several trips across the land, she said she'd found the same spot and taken her own picture.

"It's not something I ever brought up with either one of them," Jarod said. The fact that Cassandra had the photo had always bothered him. What was she doing with a photo of their land that looked like it had been taken in the 1920s or '30s?

Odd.

He stabbed a bean. Unanswered questions were starting to pile up, and no one was making any headway in answering them. Who owned the mineral rights to the ranch? Why did Cassandra have that picture? Where was Cameron?

How was he going to get boots for Audie without offending Samantha?

"I think CJ is going to beat you all to the altar," Birdie said, sipping from her glass of white wine.

"She already did," Jarod reminded her.

"Again," Birdie amended.

"You really think she and Nick are that close to making it

permanent?" Dylan asked.

"She's hardly ever here these days," Birdie reminded them. "And when she does come, she's often got Nick's son Trevor in tow. I give them until Christmas."

"That means," Dylan pointed to him, "you're going to need to find someone else to do the books. And it's not me."

"I can handle it," he said.

"We tried that," Dylan replied. "It took CJ months to straighten it out."

He couldn't argue that. With his dyscalculia, it was hard to keep anything involving numbers accurate.

"Isn't Audie's mother a math teacher?" Birdie asked. "I got that impression at church."

Jarod laid his knife and fork across his empty plate and picked up his beer glass. "She is, but that doesn't mean she can do books. Besides, why would she want to do that?"

"For the same reason you are teaching her daughter to ride." Birdie's tone implied he was a tad dense for not getting this himself. "She likes you."

"It's not like that," he protested.

"Whatever you say," Birdie replied. "But it might be a way she could afford a pair of boots."

He *was* dense, but there was no point in letting the housekeeper know she was right.

"I'll think about it."

Once he'd helped clear the dishes, Birdie booted them both out of the kitchen. Dylan headed to his cabin to put the finishing touches on a painting he had hopes of selling.

Jarod tried to settle in front of the television in the family room to watch sports, but he couldn't concentrate. It was just background noise for the thoughts battering his mind. He squirmed in the dark brown leather chair, like a kid too long in school. Finally, he picked up his phone and dialed CJ.

"Remember that picture in Cassandra's office?" he asked when they'd connected. "You said you found where that was. Can you give me an idea?"

"It's up toward the northwest corner of the ranch. The area we graze only if we can't get the cattle fattened enough for market. Why, are you thinking of going up there?"

"I need some time to think. It's as good a place as any."

"I'll send you a copy of the photo I took."

"Thanks."

"I'll get home again soon to help you with the books," she added. "With fall hunting season coming for Nick and some heavy-duty assignments up in the Yaak, it's been tough to find enough time to fit everything in."

"I understand," he said, even though resentment tensed his muscles. CJ had just started to help out after returning from the Middle East, and now she was pretty much gone again. How was he going to get started on his dreams if he couldn't count on anyone to help out? Maybe he simply wasn't supposed to do anything besides take care of the family ranch until the next generation came along, whenever that happened.

His phone dinged, and he brought up the picture.

Yes, now he remembered the place.

After letting Birdie know he was leaving, he headed to the corral. "How about you and me take a ride?" he asked Misty. Without waiting for an answer, he headed to the tack room and picked up a saddle, blanket, and bridle. The leather was newly cleaned. Dylan must have done it.

At least one other member of the family contributed to the ranch they all owned.

He was building a good steam of resentment. That wouldn't do anyone any good, especially him. He took a few deep breaths and concentrated on prepping Misty for riding, losing himself in the rhythmic strokes of the brush on her hide.

As soon as the horse was ready, Jarod led her out of corral and shut the gate behind him. He trotted her down the road, away from the ranch buildings, then let her out in a gallop. Misty stretched out and took the lead while being mindful of his subtle commands.

Soon he found his own rhythm and drifted into the amazing symbiosis between himself and his horse. Thoughts ceased. All that existed was the thunder of the hooves on the hard ground, the wind in his face, and the heat from the animal beneath him.

When the trail began to climb, he pulled back from the gallop to a trot. Not the most comfortable of gaits but effective in working the kinks out. The trail steepened, and he slowed to a walk, adjusting his weight to aid Misty as she worked her way up hills already golden brown from August heat.

The echo of a bull elk bugling startled him. Right time of year, odd time of day. Must be a young buck defeated by a more experienced bull, but it could be an older male, frustrated his time was passing.

Just like him.

Nonsense. He was only in his mid-thirties. There was time.

He needed to implement the next part of his plan. Teaching Audie to ride had taken his attention from his search for a second horse. The man who'd purchased Prince had paid well, and Misty had been purchased for far below what she was worth. Bob Jenkins had given him an additional 5 percent discount because he was helping the little girl.

But was it Audie who was distracting him? Or her mother?

He rounded the top of another hill, and the Crown of the Continent stretched north before him. A new glistening of snow painted the tips of the Rockies. Winter would be here far too soon, and with it the constant feeding of cattle.

Now was when he had to act. When he got home, he'd take a look at the animals for sale. If need be, he could go to Wyoming, Utah, Idaho, or the Dakotas for the right horse.

He took his cell phone from his shirt pocket and thumbed to the picture CJ had provided. The mountains in the picture were the same as the ones before him, but the angle was wrong. He needed to go a little more south and west.

Why would his ex-girlfriend have this picture? Just one more question in his ever-lengthening list. The sheer number of them made him want to ignore the entire lot. This may be a wild goose chase, but for some reason he didn't understand, he felt the photo was a link to where the document for the mineral rights of the ranch might be. It made no sense, but his gut was sure just the same.

He headed Misty south, letting her take her head as he let his internal ramblings take theirs. There were times he could almost hear his great-whatever-grandfather Jarod talking about the importance of land and family roots. The Becks had been part of the great migration from the Midwest in the early 1880s, lured by books like *The Beef Bonanza, or How to Get Rich on the Plains* until the winter of 1886 destroyed thousands of cattle and the era of the Open Range ended.

Most of Grandfather Jarod's relatives left, but he'd stuck it out by getting a law degree and starting his ranch dynasty with a local school teacher.

At least that's what family lore told them. What happened after that remained a mystery, as if there'd been a decision never to talk about some subjects again.

The flash of an animal a few yards in front of them made

Misty shy and dance for a few moments, kicking the pebbles from the edge of the trail so they bounced down the hillside.

"Okay, girl. Steady." This was a problem. He couldn't have her doing unexpected things, especially with Audie on her back. Something to start working out of the horse. It could be done, but it took patience, trust, and a lot of time.

He glanced to a nearby rise. A full-pelted coyote stared back, a beautiful animal, but one that could be deadly on the ranch if it developed a taste for newborn calves—something he and Dylan would have to look out for come calving season next spring.

The coyote trotted off and he urged Misty a little farther down the trail.

There.

"Whoa," he said and gave a slight tug on the reins.

An instant stop. At least that was well-ingrained in Misty's repertoire.

He slid his phone from the pocket and compared. The trees were higher and bushes weren't where they had been, but the overall layout was correct. Now, what could be so important about this site that Cassandra had a photo of it in her office?

Comparing again, he realized that it wasn't quite right. The picture had been taken a little lower down the hill from his location.

He dismounted and, reins in hand, went to the edge of the trail and looked down. Somewhere below, the landscape almost turned in on itself, folding beneath him. Pulling his binoculars from the saddlebag, he scanned around where he stood but could find no way down to where the picture had to have been taken. Could the way up be from the valley floor below?

He checked the level of the sun. Time to head back. He took another shot with his phone, then plugged in the GPS coordinates.

Before remounting he turned Misty around, not willing to risk her spooking in the narrow spot.

The easy rhythm of the ride back gave him time to look at the one thing he'd forced from his mind: Samantha. She was an attractive woman and probably more than capable of doing his books, but ...

"What do you think, Misty? If she does my books, won't she get entangled in the ranch, in us? And what happens when things don't work out? Not only does she get hurt, but Audie will be devastated to be taken away from her favorite horse."

He didn't add that it was likely to happen anyway. As soon as

Misty was fully trained, she was going on the market. He couldn't afford to keep her around and, without the indoor arena, he couldn't take on students.

Misty shook her head and snorted.

"That's your opinion? Not very useful, if you ask me."

Maybe the horse was right. It was time to put away all the questions rumbling in his mind until another day and simply enjoy the heat of sun on his face, the lowing of cattle in the distance, and the view of God's good earth. Who knew how long any of it would last?

Chapter 8

Monday morning. Six weeks into school. Routines were being established, and Samantha was more at ease in the classroom. In spite of her fellow math teacher's sniping, students were learning the concepts they needed to acquire. Fall testing, coming in the next week or so, would measure their current status. Then she'd really have to get to work. Improvement in test scores was one of the criteria for being hired back a second year.

"Of course," Ginny Helms had whispered to her in the last teacher's meeting, now that everyone is getting in gear, the disruptive kids will start flexing their muscles."

Ginny had given a few suggestions of who to look out for, but the one Samantha remembered was Jim Van Sutton Jr.—the sheriff's kid.

And now, true to his reputation, Jim sat in the front row, stating football team members didn't have to do homework during the season. They had more important things to do.

He was dressed in the sports-hip uniform of soccer shorts, black T-shirt with a logo from a team she didn't recognize, and Bulldogs cap worn backward. His large feet, encased in sloppy, untied sneakers, protruded from the space taken up by his desk. The kid was four inches taller than she was, made of solid muscle, so she'd need to re-establish her authority quickly.

"Funny," she said, "I didn't read that in the rule book." She looked down at her record sheet. "And take off the hat."

A snigger came from the back row—one of Jim's hangers-on. She'd separated them early. Now she looked at him with what she hoped was a firm teacher glare.

He smirked.

Turning her attention back to Jim, she gave him the same look. Maybe if she did it often enough, she'd perfect it.

He, too, smirked.

She placed a minus next to Jim's name. "As far as I'm concerned, that's another missed homework," she said. "As I said at the beginning, homework is an important part of your grade. It's also an important part of your learning."

Jim shrugged.

She struggled to hold her temper.

"Moving on to the lesson for today. Why is a ≠ 0 important in this equation?"

In the back row, Sarah's hand shot up.

God bless that girl.

"Yes, Sarah?"

She forgot about Jim and his buddy as Sarah and the majority of other students worked through and solved quadratic equations. They were learning! That was all that mattered.

As they clumped together at the end of class to head out the door, Jim and his buddy looked Samantha's way, and Jim whispered something to his friend. The boy laughed and they looked back at her with a smile that made her a tad sick to her stomach.

Hopefully, it was just a stage they were going through. Still, their obvious disrespect was going to have to be dealt with or she'd start losing the whole class.

She stacked her papers neatly, made sure all the pens and pencils were in their assigned spaces, and straightened a few desks before heading to the principal's office.

Rebecca Johnson's office was a bright area, with a few plants and personal lamps providing a warmth most principal's offices didn't have. Clutter covered bookshelves—various miniatures of bulldogs, a few trophies, and art projects obviously made in school to give Mom for Christmas and other days. Samantha had a similar collection.

"My three kids are still in elementary school," Rebecca said as she sat behind her desk. "I never know what to do with it all."

Samantha nodded, tongue-tied in front of her boss. In Billings, the principal had rarely met with her, and his mode had been to spit out what he wanted and dismiss Samantha back to wherever she really belonged. She was thrilled when she finally received her degree and could climb the rung beyond the para-teacher pool.

If only schools knew how much work paras actually did.

"How is Audie settling in?" Rebecca asked.

"Good. She likes her classes and teacher and seems to be thriving, especially since she started taking riding lessons."

"Oh? I didn't know you had a horse." Rebecca smoothed back a stray hair. Even at the end of the day, she somehow held together the polish she displayed in the morning.

"I don't. It's ... well, complicated. I'd hoped to get her lessons at the ranch north of town."

"Triple Bar Riding and Boarding," Rebecca filled in.

"Yes, that's the place. Anyway, Audie fell in love with a horse, but someone named Jarod Beck bought it, and now he's giving her riding lessons." God, she'd been hanging around Audie and her friends too long. With her run-on sentences, she was starting to sound like them.

"Jarod Beck?" Rebecca tapped her pen on the paper calendar that topped her desk. "I went to school with CJ. I think that's her younger brother."

"Yes." When was Rebecca going to get to the point of this meeting? There had to be a middle ground between the slam bam, thank you, ma'am of her last boss and the moments of small talk that could last the entire conversation in Montana.

"First-quarter grades are coming up faster than anyone is ever ready to handle. I wanted to make sure you knew the procedure and ask if you have any concerns."

She had lots of them—Audie's happiness, Cody's imminent arrival in Billings, her job performance—but that wasn't the subject at hand.

"If you give someone a bad grade because they deserve it, how hard will parents push back?"

"It depends on the parent. Who do you have in mind?" Rebecca leaned forward.

"Jim Van Sutton."

"We'll have to tread carefully on that one. His father is a good sheriff but has a blind eye when it comes to his son. Document everything, and if the sheriff gives you any problems, I'll back you to the hilt."

Law enforcement. The last time she'd tangled with them, she'd been arrested for possession. Fortunately, it was a juvenile offense that no longer appeared on her record.

"Don't let Junior get away with anything. He's got an attitude, that one—especially for a freshman. I'd hoped one of the older kids would take him down, but they're probably too afraid of his dad. But he wants to be a football star, and the coach isn't going to let him play without good grades and behavior, so that'll straighten out eventually. Anyone else?"

"No. The others who are struggling are having problems with the material. I'm giving them extra time after school or during lunch."

"That's kind of you. Don't stretch yourself too thin, though." Rebecca smiled. "You're doing a good job, especially for your first year teaching."

"Thank you."

"How are you getting along with Bruce?" she asked.

Samantha hesitated for a brief second, and Rebecca's gaze sharpened.

"Fine," she finally replied.

"Don't let him bother you too much. He's a good teacher but set in his ways. Unfortunately, he thinks those ways are the only ways that work. We appreciate the new perspective you're bringing to math. For the first time in a long time, we're seeing kids getting excited about the subject. You have a gift—now all you need is experience."

"Thank you, again."

"No problem." Rebecca rose. "Let me know if you have any difficulties at all."

"I will."

Samantha's step was lighter returning to her classroom than it had been when she came down to the principal's office. Teaching gave her energy—no matter how tired she was when she got to school, she perked up in front of the classroom. When a student finally "got" a concept, especially if they'd been struggling, it gave an extra boost to her day.

And now Rebecca said she was doing well!

Jim Van Sutton, bring it on!

The students had started to trickle in for the next class when her phone buzzed. She glanced at the readout.

"I'll be a minute," she said to the class. "Take out your textbooks and find the page written on the board."

Mom: Cody called and said he's coming back to Billings. He's still looking for you. Says he wants to see his daughter.

Samantha: He had his chance. He wanted nothing to do with her.

Mom: He wants a second chance. Says he'll go to court if he has to.

Samantha: He has to find me first. I have to go. Thanks for letting me know, Mom.

Should she start looking for another job right now? Or find

an attorney to help her keep Cody away? Definitely not Cassandra. Something about the attorney put her teeth on edge. Or maybe it had been her proprietary hand on Jarod's arm at church when they met.

Thumps of books hitting the floor and teenage chatter made her turn around.

She'd think about that later. Right now, she had a job to do.

# # #

"Mommy. We *have* to go see Misty this week," Audie said as she stared at cartoons and shoveled Cheerios in her mouth the second Saturday in October.

Samantha had missed one of the scheduled riding lessons, and Jarod had needed to help his sister and her boyfriend out with something during the other. He'd offered to reschedule, but she'd begged off, concerned that she still hadn't figured out how to get Audie a pair of leather boots. She'd tried the thrift store in town, but there hadn't been anything that fit her daughter comfortably. Getting blisters would defeat the purpose of protecting Audie's feet. Getting them online was a risk, and that left a trip to Great Falls.

And there was precious little left of her first paycheck as it was. There'd been a lot of expenses setting up a new household and getting ready for school, including teaching supplies she'd purchased with her own money. Boots were simply not in the equation.

But Audie was right. She needed to get out in the fresh air before warm temperatures disappeared entirely. Already there was a chill at the edges when the sun dipped below the horizon.

"We'll go today," she promised.

"Yea!" Audie leapt up, the milk from her cereal bowl sloshing onto her jeans. She looked down at the white drops on her pants, brushed at it, and looked up at Samantha. "Oops," she said, shrugged, and giggled.

"Oh well," Samantha said, trying to keep a straight face. "It will wash out. How about you go change?"

"Misty won't care," Audie declared.

"I will."

Audie eyed her as if gauging her seriousness. With a dramatic sigh, she handed Samantha the cereal bowl and flounced into her room.

Samantha let her smile loose. It was good for Audie to have something to care about, otherwise she could construct an entire world without interacting with a soul. Samantha would just have to pull up her big girl panties and confess to Jarod she hadn't been able to get boots yet. Maybe next paycheck.

She glanced at the calendar when she entered the kitchen with Audie's cereal bowl. The pages lived on the refrigerator at Audie height, along with a collection of her latest drawings and other things her daughter deemed important, including the flyer about Misty.

Second week in October already. Soon the flurry of holidays would begin, including Halloween, which meant a costume for Audie. She hoped it would be something easy this year. In the past, with her mother's assistance, Samantha had created a fairy, a clown, a cat, and a pumpkin. Without access to fabric stores and patterns, it was going to be a whole lot harder.

She would have to take that trip to Great Falls after all.

"Mommy, I'm ready," Audie announced. She'd changed into a second pair of blue jeans, a plaid shirt that, for once, was buttoned correctly, and a red bandana she'd found at the thrift store the last time they'd gone.

"It's not time."

"That's okay. I just wanted to show you. I'm going to learn to be a real cowgirl, just like on television." Audie turned on her heel and went back to the living room.

Samantha chuckled and tidied up the kitchen.

# # #

A sense of relief passed over Jarod when he watched the Camry slowly navigate the dusty drive. For the first time he noticed the tread on the tires. It was barely there. Come winter, Samantha was going to be in a lot of danger.

He needed to find a way to help her out and keep her pride intact. Because they'd missed the last two planned riding lessons, he hadn't had a chance to ask about the bookkeeping.

"Oof!" he mocked as Audie ran to him, threw her arms around him, and squeezed. He hugged the warm little body close to him, a wave of tenderness flowing through his veins as he gazed at the top of her head, covered in flyaway brown hair. She really had a sweet heart, this kid.

He glanced up at her mother and smiled.

"Sorry," Samantha said. "We're still working on boundaries."

"No problem."

Audie released him. Facing the corral, she took slow, steady steps toward Misty.

Good for her.

He walked slowly behind her. Samantha hesitated for a moment but followed.

Someday soon he was going to help her get past her fear of horses. There were programs all over the country that connected troubled youth and horses. So far, it looked like bonding with one of the herd animals made things a whole lot better in the rest of a person's life. Could it do the same for Samantha? There were times she seemed skittish as a mistreated colt.

Although maybe her life was just fine and he was reading it all wrong.

"Nice job," he told Audie when he reached the fence.

She looked up at him expectantly. "I brought an apple. Mommy cut it up for me." She pulled a well-used plastic bag from her pocket. The apple slices had obviously been checked several times between town and the ranch.

He chuckled. "Go ahead and feed Misty."

There was a sharp intake of breath beside him.

"It's okay," he whispered.

He kept one eye on the girl's actions and the other on a black storm cloud hovering over the mountain peaks. According to Birdie, their in-house weather monitor, it was supposed to snow as far down as four thousand feet this evening and tonight. They were a little below that, which meant at least flurries.

And dropping temperatures.

Early this year again. He understood the overall earth's temperature was rising at a rapid rate, but it sure wasn't acting that way in his little corner of Montana. Would the grass manage to survive the first few storms, or would a hard freeze require breaking out feed in a few weeks?

"I'm done," Audie said.

"Then let's get her saddled up," he said. "First we have to check her feet, curry her, and brush her." He glanced at Samantha, who had her arms crossed, her white fingers clutching her upper arms.

"You look cold," he said. "Why don't you go on up to the house?"

"I couldn't do that. I don't know your family. I'll just wait in the car."

"Audie, keep petting Misty. Your mom and I need to talk."

"'kay."

He caught up to Samantha, who was already stalking over to her car, and took her elbow gently. "Come with me."

She shook him off. "I'm fine."

He raised his hands in a sign of surrender. "Sorry. I shouldn't have grabbed your arm like that. But I beg to differ. You are decidedly not fine. It's cold and you're not dressed for it. Your car is not going to be any warmer, not with the gusts of wind we get around here. Birdie's in the kitchen and you know her from church. So get your things and come on up with me."

"But Audie ..."

"Is fine. She knows to stay outside the corral unless I'm there."

Samantha considered this, her eyes wide with what looked like lurking fear. Who had done this to her?

A powerful wave of anger washed over him. If he ever found out, he'd like to give them a taste of their own medicine.

His expression must have changed, because she took a step back.

He took a deep breath and deliberately softened his stance. "C'mon. Birdie will enjoy the company."

"Okay." Her voice was small.

He walked her up the slight slope to the front porch, up the steps, and through the front door. Once they left the small entryway, the living room spread before them, dark wood and leather furniture brightened by colorful throw pillows and vibrant native blankets.

"Wow," she said, "this is amazing. So solid yet comfortable at the same time."

"They built them that way in the 1800s."

"Is that how old this is?"

"Mostly. Like many old places, it's been added onto over the years. Kitchen's this way." He led her back to Birdie's domain, a large open space that had been remodeled close to two decades ago and sadly needed a do-over.

"Samantha!" Birdie exclaimed, standing and throwing out her arms. "So good to see you. Sit down, sit down. What do you take with your coffee?"

He chuckled as Samantha obeyed as rapidly as everyone else did.

"Enjoy," he said, as he started from the kitchen. Then a thought struck him. There was an easier way.

"Birdie?"

"Uh-huh?"

"Remember your idea on how Samantha could help us out?"

Samantha looked at him, her brow furrowed.

"Yeah." Birdie turned her steely gaze toward him, as if already anticipating what he had in mind.

"Could you talk to her about it?"

"Coward," she said.

"Yes, ma'am," he replied and left before she could add anything else.

Chapter 9

"What did he mean?" Samantha asked Birdie as the woman placed the cup of coffee before her.

"Are you sure you don't want anything with it?" Birdie asked as she pulled down two plates and opened a box on the counter.

"I take my coffee black, thanks."

"Just like Jarod," Birdie said. "I hope you like pie. This is one of Trish's—you know her from church. Peach."

"Just a tiny slice, please." She wanted to refuse, but her mother had taught her a long time ago to accept food offered in another woman's kitchen. Anything else was a slight to her.

Mom may have had a rough life and kowtowed way too much to men, but she had never shirked the responsibilities of civility. As a result, everyone liked her.

"You catch more flies with honey than with vinegar" was one of her favorite sayings.

Birdie slid a plate in front of her. Brightly hued peaches oozed from between two pieces of flaky crust. A sweet, fruity aroma drifted up on the air currents.

Samantha took a bite. "Oh my," she said.

"Exactly. Trish swears she doesn't use lard, but I don't know how else she pulls this off."

Samantha forced herself to slow down and thoroughly taste the next piece before swallowing. As she did, she let the warmth of the kitchen flow over her. It was a comforting space, where good, solid ranch food was created and wisdom dispensed over a cup of tea or coffee. The vibrations of large celebrations lingered, family gatherings over decades.

Nothing like she'd grown up with. Thanksgiving was dominated by Black Friday sales that had relentlessly crept into the actual Thanksgiving Day, so she was usually farmed out to some other family for the holiday. Christmases were celebrated with two or three packages, often donated by well-meaning strangers, under a used artificial tree. Occasionally, her mother found something Samantha had wanted for years on special, but it was usually ill-timed, like the Barbie she'd gotten the year she'd declared all dolls lame.

Her mother had been a clueless parent. She was determined to do better by Audie.

"Well, that scowl certainly doesn't belong with Trish's pie," Birdie commented softly. "Something wrong?"

"No. Sorry. I was thinking about something else."

"Anything I can help with?"

"No. Thanks. The past can't really be changed, can it?"

"Not really." Birdie swirled her coffee with her spoon. "But you can adjust your viewpoint about it, put it in perspective."

"Uh-huh."

Birdie chuckled. "You're young yet."

"I'm twenty-eight."

"Like I said—young."

Samantha took another bite of pie. Time to change the subject.

"So what is it Jarod wanted you to ask me?"

"That boy. He really needs to ask you himself, but since we need someone's help so desperately, I'll do it." She stirred the coffee again. "Do you know what dyscalculia is?"

"It's when people mix up numbers. They're fine with letters, unlike dyslexics, but have the same type of problem with digits."

"Jarod has it."

Where was this going? She didn't have the skills to provide real help for people with the problem. "I don't understand."

"He's figured out his own methods to handle what he needs to run the ranch, but bookkeeping is beyond him. CJ straightened it out when she came back from the Middle East, but he's starting to struggle again."

"She can't help?"

"She and her boyfriend, Nick, are spending more and more time together. It's kind of sweet, really. They were high school sweethearts, but life intervened and they went their separate ways. The good Lord brought them back together, although neither of them would ever admit that."

Samantha dragged her fork over the last bit of peach filling on her plate, stabbed the last piece of crust, and savored it. She'd let Birdie ask whatever it was she wanted, then refuse. She didn't need to get any more tangled up with Jarod, or this family, than necessary.

"Did you have a high school sweetheart?" Birdie asked.

Samantha snapped her head up.

"I understand the assumption, but no."

"Sorry, I didn't mean anything by it." Birdie shook her head. "My mouth gets away from my brain sometimes. It's none of my business."

"No problem." She let the silence hang. It was nobody's affair how Audie had arrived on this earth. The fact that she was here was enough of a blessing.

An outside door opened and heavy boots stomped into the room beyond the kitchen—probably a mudroom. Murmured voices preceded Audie's appearance.

"Mommy! Mommy! Jarod says there's pie!!!" She turned toward the housekeeper. "Is that true, Birdie?"

Birdie gave her a great big smile and said, "Absolutely, there's pie for you! How about a nice, big glass of milk, too?"

"Yes, please."

Samantha smiled.

"Does that apply to me, too?" Jarod asked, his large presence taking up space in the kitchen.

"I'll cut the pie," Birdie said, "Otherwise half of it will appear on your plate. I know you boys. You can get your own coffee."

"Yes, ma'am." Jarod tipped an imaginary hat. He no longer wore the Bulldogs cap that was his customary headgear.

Nice to see. Call her old-fashioned, but it bothered her to see men with caps and cowboy hats on their heads inside, particularly in a restaurant. It was a trend she could live without.

"Go wash your hands," Birdie told Jarod. "And make sure Audie does the same."

Jarod took Audie to the kitchen sink where he studied the girl's height and the distance to the faucet.

At home, she had a stool in the kitchen for her daughter. She was about to get up and help, but Jarod boosted Audie up and squirted soap in her hands. She gurgled a happy giggle and said, "Silly! You put too much soap on my hands. Now they have to take a bubble bath. I love bubble baths. Do you?"

"Uh ... I can't say I've ever had one."

"Didn't your mommy ever give you one? My mommy does."

A shadow passed over his face.

Samantha rose. Too much she didn't know about this family. "Let's dry your hands, sweetie." She plucked Audie from Jarod's arms and steered her toward the dry towel Birdie held out to her. "Thanks."

Once everyone was seated, she tried to come up with

something to say. What had she and Birdie been talking about? Nope, that wouldn't do.

"How was your riding lesson?" she asked Audie.

"Great! Jarod said I'm going to be a real cowgirl someday." She took a bite of the pie. "This is really good, Birdie. Can you teach my mom to make it?"

"I wish I could, but I bought that pie from Trish. She goes to church with us. Maybe she can teach your mom."

"Mommy, please! I l-o-o-ve this pie!" She took another bite.

"We'll see."

"That means probably no," she translated to Birdie.

"But it could mean yes," Birdie replied.

"I don't think so." Audie used her serious, grown-up voice. The one she used when she was trying to impress someone about how well she knew something.

Jarod chuckled. "She sounds just like CJ, doesn't she?"

"Uh-huh," Birdie replied.

"I want to be a cowboy for Halloween," Audie announced.

"Not a cowgirl?" Samantha asked.

"I don't want to wear a skirt." Her daughter sounded like she'd tasted something incredibly yucky.

Samantha loved the femininity of soft skirts and dresses. Her daughter was a total opposite. That should make the issue of what was needed to be a cowboy minimal. She could pull it together from stuff around the house.

"So what does a cowboy need?"

"A horse?" Audie asked hopefully.

"I don't think they're going to let you bring a horse to school."

"For trick-or-treating at night." Audie cocked her head in a way that indicated she thought her mother was being totally foolish.

"Sometimes cowboys don't have horses," Jarod said. "I do a lot of walking. I think you'll be okay without a horse. Besides"—he leaned forward and dropped his voice to a whisper—"if your horse does her business, you're going to be the one to clean up after her."

"Oooohhh." Audie wrinkled her nose. "Okay. No horse. I need jeans, a shirt, and a bandana."

"We've got all those," Samantha said.

"A rope," she added.

"We can lend you that," Jarod said.

"And boots."

Ugh. She looked at Jarod. He looked at Birdie, who shook her head.

He sighed.

What the heck was going on?

"Audie, I need to talk to your mommy for a minute, okay?"

"Okay." Her daughter picked up her fork and went back to attacking the slice of pie.

Samantha followed Jarod into the living room. He gestured to a door at the far end.

The door opened into a beautiful corner office with a rustic but beautiful desk and classic red leather chairs. A bookshelf lined with solid volumes covered half of an outside wall, while dark brown drapes framed the windows. What looked like a Charles Russell iron statue had center stage on a small table.

A man's office.

"This was my dad's, and now I pretend I run the ranch from here."

"It looks like you do a bit more than pretend," she said.

He shook his head. "I'm good with the physical part, but the numbers have me beat. Just when I think I've got it figured out, CJ or Dylan tells me I'm wrong. And I don't understand bookkeeping at all."

"That makes two of us."

The edges of Jarod's mouth turned down, giving him a sad hound expression.

"I was hoping you could help. Not for free; we'd pay you. You have a math degree. You've got to be better at it than I am."

"I couldn't do it for money. I'm not a bookkeeper." She shouldn't do it at all, but truth was, she was lonely. Most of the teachers at school were married and involved with their families. Trish, the pie maker, had invited her over for coffee any time she wanted, but she had yet to take her up on it. Having coffee with a friend was one thing, but what was she supposed to do with Audie in the meantime?

"Is that a yes or a no?" Jarod asked.

"That's a 'we'll see.'"

"Audie says that means no."

"But, as Birdie pointed out, it could mean yes, too." She smiled at him. He'd done so much for Audie that she really needed to give him something in return. Otherwise, she'd owe him, and that was never a good balance, especially with a man. Living with Cody had taught her that well. "I tell you what. I'll take a look at it and let you know if I can help at all."

"Thank you, on one condition."

"What's that?" She studied him warily.

"Let me get Audie some boots. I'm really afraid her feet are going to get hurt in those tennis shoes. I can get a decent pair online for about thirty bucks."

She chewed on her lower lip as she thought it over. It would probably take about an hour to figure out the mess, and a decent bookkeeper could cost way more than that. It seemed fair, and she didn't see any hidden traps.

"Okay. Thank you. When do you want me to start?"

"Yesterday," he said with a smile.

"That much of a mess?"

"Oh yeah." He stood there, looking like what he was—a good man way over his head. "But let's order those boots for Audie. Halloween's only two weeks away. You can look at the books next week while Audie's here for her lesson. They can wait that long. CJ threw some money at the feds for federal taxes. It's probably more than we owe, but something's better than nothing."

That was the longest set of words she'd ever heard him string together.

She walked to the living room. "Audie, can you come here for a moment? Jarod has something to show you."

Her daughter pounded toward them, peach smeared around her lips, her hands sticky with syrup, no doubt.

"Whoa," Jarod said. "How about wash your hands and face first? Bathroom's that way."

Audie's shoulders slumped. "I suppose," she said and walked off in the indicated direction.

She grinned at Jarod. "Thanks."

"No problem."

Maybe it would be exactly that—no problem. As long as Cody didn't find them.

# # #

Life had settled into a settled, if frenetic, routine. The boots arrived, perfectly Audie, with blue swirls decorating the top. The kid positively strutted her importance as a cowboy, explaining to Samantha that the West wouldn't be what it was without cowboys.

"Yes, sweetie," she said while correcting papers about a week before Halloween. A few more minutes and then it would be time to get Audie into the shower and ready for bed. If she was lucky, she'd have a chance to look through a few pages of a homemaking magazine she'd picked up with the weekly groceries before she fell into her own deep sleep.

Her phone buzzed.

"Hi, Samantha," the text began. "This is Trish. I hope you don't mind that Jarod gave me your number. I didn't want to wake you with a call. I know how hard teachers work, and with a young one it's even more difficult. Anyway, some of the church women are getting together to plan our holiday events. I thought you might like to join us. There will be childcare."

The meeting was that Thursday night at seven. It would be good to get out of the house, and it was one of the reasons she joined a church, to get involved and support a community.

"Sure," she texted back. "I'll be there. Anything I should bring?"

"Just your creativity. There will be things for the kids to do."

She wouldn't go empty-handed. Audie had asked for bananas last week and, as usual, had eaten only one before she'd been bored with them. Samantha had the perfect recipe for banana bread.

The next night after supper, she and Audie drove the short distance to the church. The air at night was chilling, and the colorful leaves were more off than on the trees at this point. In another two weeks, Daylight Savings Time would end, thankfully after Halloween this year.

Audie was bundled in a coat Samantha had managed to find in the thrift store after realizing last winter's wouldn't fit. How did these kids grow so fast?

The warm lights of the church hall welcomed them.

"Will they have games?" Audie asked. "I'm not sure I want to play games. I might want to read my book."

"I'm sure they will let you read if you want." Carefully, Samantha pulled the foil-wrapped banana bread from the back seat.

"Why are you bringing that?" Audie asked.

"Because it's the right thing to do. It's always good to go someplace with something in your hand for the person you are visiting."

"But we're not visiting anyone," Audie said, walking the path to the hall's entrance.

Her daughter's irrefutable logic sometimes stumped her.

"Not really, but it's still nice."

"Oh."

Apparently the answer was good enough because Audie didn't ask any other questions. As soon as they were inside, she dashed to the Sunday School wing where Trish's daughter, Bella, was waiting.

Trish and the other women in the group were seated around a rectangle table, magazines and folders scattered across the top. Nearby, a coffee urn steamed on a table already dotted with a few plates of cookies as well as one of Trish's pies. Plates, cups, and saucers were aligned on one side.

"What did you bring?" Sally, a lean woman whom she imagined was a runner, asked. The woman could pack away snacks during Sunday coffee hour like no one she'd ever seen.

"Banana bread."

"Ooh, I love banana bread. Let me help." Seconds later Sally provided a plate and knife from the church kitchen and took the bread from Samantha's hands.

She glanced over at the rest of the women. Trish's mouth was twitching like she was trying to swallow a laugh, and a few of the others were shaking their heads.

"Get yourself a cup of coffee and come sit by me," Trish said when she'd gotten control of herself. "Do you know everyone?"

"Yes, thanks. What are we here to plan?"

"We always have a Thanksgiving dinner in the afternoon of the holiday for those who can't afford a feast or new people in town who don't have a big family."

She nodded. Trish meant people like her, but her plans were to go back to Billings for Thanksgiving with her mother, who blissfully did not have to work Thanksgiving night or Black Friday, if the weather was good enough for the five-hour drive. If it didn't, it was nice to know there was an alternative other than microwaved turkey dinner.

"Sounds like a great idea," she said.

The women got down to business. It was amazing how organized they were.

"We've done this for years," one of the older women announced. "Along with the Christmas bazaar. That's coming up sooner than we're ready for."

"We'll be fine," Sally said. "You ladies always have it nailed."

"It's time some of you young ones took more part," a tall, rawboned older woman said. Samantha had heard that she'd been a one-room schoolhouse teacher in Eastern Montana a long time ago.

Sally rolled her eyes.

"I saw that," the woman said.

"Okay," Trish said, clanking her coffee cup against the plate that held the remnants of a few cookies. "We have the tasks outlined." She pointed to the list on a movable whiteboard. "How about everyone go up and take a few?"

Samantha signed up to bake pies with Trish. Purchasing anything was beyond her means, and she wouldn't be in Choteau on the day of the feast. In a way, it was sad. She would like to get to know more of her neighbors.

But duty called. Her mother had called the Sunday before, making sure she was coming back home for the holiday. She'd said she had something to tell Samantha but didn't want to do it over the phone.

Worry niggled the back of her brain.

Around nine, the meeting wrapped up. In addition to the pie baking with Trish, she'd signed up to help run the bazaar a few Saturdays before Christmas. Snow would probably arrive by then, and Audie's riding lessons would be over. Jarod had told her that he'd started saving for an arena, but the process was a slow one. He was still on the lookout for another horse to train.

As she drove a sleepy Audie home, she thought over some of the expenses she'd seen in the ranch's accounts that didn't make sense. Why would a ranch need a private investigator? And how was she to account for the money CJ was pumping into taxes? She needed to find an accountant who would be willing to answer questions without charging her—or the ranch—a fortune.

Chapter 10

Halloween passed in its usual scary and over-sugared way. Audie strutted her way through, objecting to the heavy coat Samantha insisted she wear while trick-or-treating but enjoying the attention she got from neighbors as she showed them her rope and tipped the pink cowboy hat Jarod had gotten her along with the boots.

In the midst of all the festivities, Samantha had somehow gotten her grades turned in on time at the beginning of November. Now she was facing the event she'd dreaded most: parent-teacher conferences.

"I don't understand how my son got a C- in math." Jim Van Sutton Sr., a tall but heavily built man, squeezed into a student desk in front of her, his Stetson posing on the one beside him.

Because I was feeling generous.

"His grades are based on test scores, homework completed, and participation in class. I gave them the rubric I would use for scoring at the beginning of school."

"What the hell's a rubric?" he asked.

"It's a scoring sheet. I've made up a few for parents who ask about it." She handed him one. "As you can see, I'm marking not only correct answers but neatness and completion as well."

"You said participation, too. I'm sure my boy participates. He's not afraid to speak out."

"That's true." How best to say this? "But talking out of turn and goofing around isn't the kind of participation I'm looking for." She tried to look stern, but from the expression on his face, she wasn't pulling it off.

"You've dragged down his entire grade point average. He did fine with Bruce Weber last year. *He* understands how the system works. My boy needs the discipline of football." He leaned forward, his heavy leather belt, mercifully without a gun, groaning as he did. "He's on probation now, thanks to you. I know it's your first year, but if—"

"Can I come in?" The principal stood in the doorway. "I heard you were here, Jim. Good to see you again." Rebecca held out her hand.

The sheriff pried himself out the chair and shook it.

Samantha slowly exhaled.

"Ms. Deveaux has gone over Jim's grades with me," Rebecca said, "as she did with all her students. As a first-year teacher, I wanted to make sure she was following school guidelines."

"And ..." Jim shifted his weight and almost glared at the principal, as if daring her to uphold his son's poor results.

"Mr. Van Sutton." Rebecca placed the knuckles of her two fists on Samantha's desk. "Our faculty will not be bullied in any way. If you have a problem with anything—anything—that one of our teachers does, you will come see me. You will not threaten them." She straightened. "Now, as I was saying, Ms. Deveaux's grades checked out. She aced it. Every one of them can be backed up by her rubric. She told her students what she was expecting. It was up to them to carry it out. Some didn't do it."

Jim's expression hardened. It must have worked on criminals, but it didn't budge the principal one inch.

"We'll see about that," he said, picking up his hat. "Don't forget I'm a member of the school board and you are on probation as much as Ms. Deveaux or my son."

"Duly noted."

He strode out of the classroom.

"Well, that was interesting," Rebecca said. "I hope there aren't too many more like him today. That took every ounce of control I had."

"Thank you," Samantha said. "I can't believe you stood up for me like that."

"Oh? Do administrators have a habit of throwing their teachers under the bus? Bad policy, especially with someone who has the potential you do to be a phenomenal teacher. We don't get many of them in rural Montana."

"Is this a bad time?" Trish Small stuck her head into the classroom. "We have our parent-teacher appointment now, but I can wait a bit if it's inconvenient."

"No," Rebecca said. "Everything's handled, thanks." She left the room as Trish came in, a hint of floral scent arriving with her.

Samantha sank back in her chair.

"Bad parent?" Trish asked with a smile.

"Unwilling to see the truth parent," Samantha said.

"Let me guess—the sheriff's kid."

"How'd you know?"

"Beth is pretty chatty," Trish said, her grin expanding. "Takes after her mother. Plus, the sheriff attended our church for a while. When he found out he couldn't run things, he departed for a more amenable congregation. He's a good sheriff, though. I'll give him that."

Small towns. Everyone knew everything.

But she had to be careful. The days of requiring a squeaky-clean schoolmarm were gone, thankfully, but communities still expected their teachers to act better than most. A sheriff could be a bad enemy.

"Beth is doing really great in class," she said. "She's my top student."

"Doesn't surprise me. She's got the same math brain as her dad. She says she wants to be a math teacher like you."

"Aw, that's sweet."

"Yes, but—and don't get me wrong—Brad and I are encouraging her to set her sights higher. She's got some of the top math scores on the state tests."

"I understand. It's great when kids have parents to encourage them to be their best."

"I take it that wasn't true in your case?"

Samantha hesitated. Trish was too easy to talk to.

"It's okay. I overstepped my bounds," Trish said. "I just wanted to stop in briefly to encourage you. I don't have a problem with Beth's grade in math. Is there anything else she could be doing? I don't want her to get bored. Maybe some extra-challenging work?"

"That's probably a good idea. Maybe I can locate some more difficult homework for Beth and some of the others who are getting these concepts so easily." She smiled at Trish. "Thank you. That's a great idea."

"I'm glad. It was nice chatting with you, but my daughter's real problems are in English, so I'd best head over that way," Trish said, her voice formal as she slid from the student desk with more ease than Jim Van Sutton had done.

"No, stay for a bit, please," Samantha said, waving her back down. It would be a relief to share it with someone, and she trusted Trish. It was a big step since the last person she'd shared the information with had held it over her head like a big club.

"My dad ... he got into meth right after I was born. He had problems keeping a job. He was always annoying someone, usually a boss, by saying the wrong thing and getting fired. Drugs helped him cope, he said. Then he realized that there was money to be made." She paused, the heartache of watching her beloved father become a stranger so fresh it could be happening again right now. "The more he sold, the more he used. He was barely holding it together."

"I'm sorry." Trish put her hand on top of hers. The warmth seeped through her skin. She hadn't realized how cold they were.

Samantha looked at a corner of the room where she'd hung posters of math symbols and their meanings. There was comfort and order in math, unlike the chaos of her life.

She swallowed hard.

"He was selling everywhere he could, including Wyoming. Crossing the state line got the feds involved. There was a car chase, and he veered to the wrong side of the road, slamming head first into a passenger car." She spoke rapidly, the words coming out before she could stuff them back. "A salesman coming to Billings was in the car. He didn't make it." She drew a long breath, the intake of air cool on her quivering lips.

Trish let the silence linger for a few seconds before she asked, "What happened to your dad?"

"Prison. It wasn't the first time he'd come in contact with the law, so it was a long sentence. He's in a place in Rawlins." She shook her head. "Then I had to go and repeat the experiment."

"Audie's dad?"

"Yeah."

"I'm so sorry." Trish looked around the classroom. "This really isn't the place to talk about this—too many potential ears. How about you come over on Sunday afternoon? Beth will be home—Brad and my son, Sam, are going hunting—so she can entertain Audie while we have some girl time over a glass of wine. Sound good?"

It sounded incredibly adult and wonderful.

"I'd like that," Samantha said with a relieved smile.

"Good. About one sound good?"

That would give her time to get home, change from their church-going outfits, and have a sandwich.

"Perfect."

"Now, let me go see what I can do about my daughter's English grade." Trish stood. "Let me rephrase that—let me see what I can get *her* to do about the English grade."

Samantha chuckled. Trish was one of the parents every teacher wanted.

The rest of the afternoon ran smoothly. A few parents who had scheduled appointments didn't show, but the rest were concerned about their child, although few indicated they weren't going to do much about it.

Sometimes it felt like parents expected teachers to do all the heavy lifting in their child's life.

She closed her notebook, packed up her things, and headed to the elementary side of the building. Keeping in mind her own perspective on parents who'd shown up, she was going to listen constructively to what Audie's teacher had to say about her.

"Mommy!" Audie ran to her from her perch in the chair outside the office door. "I've been waiting and waiting." She pointed to a big clock that decorated one wall. "You're late. You can't be late for Mrs. Hunt. She's going to shake her head at you." Audie tugged on Samantha's hand. "Hurry!"

Samantha walked a bit faster down the hall, arriving at the third grade teacher's door a bit flustered. "You need to wait here," she said, pointing to a chair next to a table lined with crayons and pictures to color. "I need to talk to Mrs. Hunt by myself."

"Okay." Audie grabbed a sheet of paper. "I'm going to make one just for you, Mommy." Her tousled head bent over the paper.

God, she loved her daughter. She watched for a moment, savoring the memory. Several of the older women at church had told her that the time went too fast and to pay attention while childhood was happening rather than deal with regrets later.

It was probably wise advice.

"Ah, Samantha," Mrs. Hunt's greeting was warm and welcoming.

"I'm sorry I'm late."

"Nonsense. You had your own set of parents to deal with this afternoon. How did it go? It's your first time, isn't it?" She gestured toward one of the adult chairs placed in front of the desk.

"For the most part it was okay. There was only one challenging parent."

"There always is." Audie's teacher laughed, a good, hearty, belly laugh. "My problem parent was someone who thinks toughening up his eight-year-old to the point of being a bully is a good strategy." She shook her head. "But let's talk about your delightful little girl."

"I hope she's being good."

"In her own unique way, yes, she is."

Mrs. Hunt went through the results of Audie's standardized

tests, schoolwork, and strengths and weaknesses. Samantha was impressed with her thoroughness. Hopefully, she'd be that good someday.

"One of the concerns we have with Audie is in regard to personal space."

"What do you mean?"

Mrs. Hunt seemed to search for the right words. "I'm not sure when the world became so politically correct that a child's hug isn't seen for what it is, but here we are. Audie's growing up, and things that were acceptable in first and second grade will no longer be common next year. She's not the only one in this category."

"I'd never thought about it. She's such a loving kid, it kind of spills out of her."

"That's true." Mrs. Hunt smiled. "What we're trying to do is get her to ask first. 'Would you like a hug?' That sort of thing."

"Makes sense." But it was sad all the same. A little more loss of childhood innocence. "I'll work on it with her."

"Thank you. Other than that, she seems to be settling in well. More of a loner than other kids, bossy at times, but she does play with the other kids during recess."

"Sounds like you've gotten to know her pretty well," Samantha said. "Anything else she needs help with?"

"She's doing well in all her subjects. The biggest problem is getting her to finish her work in a timely manner. She's easily distracted, but she's trying."

"I'll work on it."

"Nothing to worry about," Mrs. Hunt said, rising. "You're a good mother. She'll be okay."

"Thank you." Mrs. Hunt smiled. "Can I give you a hug?"

"Yes."

The teacher enveloped her in an embrace that made Samantha feel as safe as she'd ever been.

# # #

"There's a lot I don't understand about Jarod's logic with his finances," Samantha confessed to CJ the following Saturday. Jarod's sister had agreed to spend time going over how she'd managed the mess she'd inherited from her brother.

"It's sort of an ignorance is bliss system," CJ said with a smile. "If he can't understand something, he moves on, makes a guess, or marks it 'see accountant,' which would be me, by the way. Also, he's terrible at receipts, so if he pays with cash or even a credit card, it may not be entered in the system because he's used the paper to start a fire or something." She shook her head. "And you know about his problem with numbers—switching them around and all."

"So, Ms. Accountant," Samantha said in mock seriousness, "what's this payment to a Peter Carlson? There's an equal deposit that's not categorized."

"Ah, that." CJ was silent for a while. "I guess if Jarod trusts you to handle the books, I can trust you with more of the family business."

The ins and outs of the Becks' life became stranger daily. Much as she liked Jarod and his siblings, should she get tangled up in it all? But curiosity won out.

"I'm used to knowing things and not blabbing them all over the place," she said with a small smile. Teachers knew way too much about children and their families to gossip about them. At least most of them did.

"I'm sure, just like I'm sure rumors circulate all the time in this damn town. Why, I heard just the other day that you and Jarod are getting married in the spring. Something you aren't telling me?"

Samantha stared at CJ, who was looking at her with a stern expression. "What? That's totally not true. How can people even think that?" She'd have to correct that rumor really fast. What if Audie heard it?

Then she noticed CJ's lips. They were fighting hard to hide a smile. Finally, with a burst of air, she laughed for a good long minute. All Samantha could do was stare. The woman seemed to be milking every last bit of humor from the situation.

"Sorry," CJ said, wiping at her eyes. "Nick's been training me to laugh again. I haven't quite got the hang of it. A work in progress."

"You didn't find much to be humorous about in the Middle East, I suppose."

This time CJ's lips didn't move. "No," she said, in a tone that said the discussion was closed.

"So, anyway, who is Carlson?"

"He's a PI we hired."

That was an answer she hadn't expected.

She wasn't going to ask what for.

"So, professional fees. Where did the deposit come from?"

"Me."

"Well, that does complicate things a bit, but I'm not a tax accountant. I'll mark it as part of your contribution and let him or her deal with it next spring."

"Don't you want to know why we hired a PI?"

"I don't need to know, and it's really none of my business." Samantha leaned back in the soft leather chair. This half-answer stuff was getting tiring. She just wanted to finish up for the day, grab her daughter, and go back to the quiet, if lonely, space of her home.

"Sorry. I went about this all wrong." CJ picked up a glass piece in a teardrop shape from the desk, stared at it a moment, then put it back down with a thud. "My dad's Rotary award. Wonder why Jarod kept it?"

"Why wouldn't he?"

CJ shook her head. "When I talk with someone like you, someone who didn't grow up in Choteau, I realize how fucked up our family is—sorry for the language." She glanced at the crystal again. "My dad was complex. I'll just leave it at that. Jarod can tell you the whole story if he wants."

More secrets. She'd had enough of that growing up. She let her gaze wander back to the screen and placed her hand on the mouse.

"Before you start, let me tell you about the PI," CJ said. "There may be more expenses coming, so you should understand it." She got up, walked to the bookcase, and returned with a worn Bible. Flipping it open to one of the early pages, she pointed to what looked like a family record.

"When Great-whatever Grandpa Jarod settled here, he and his wife had two sons: Jacob and Seth. Jacob stayed and inherited the ranch. What we aren't sure of is whether or not Jarod bequeathed the mineral rights to Seth." She pointed to the bottom of one of the tree lines. "The other problem is that this ends with a baby named Alice, born in the 1930s. If that was the end of Seth's line and they had the mineral rights, what happened to them? If neither of those things are true, where is the documentation for the rights?"

"So that's why you hired a private detective."

"Yep."

Curiosity overcame her. "And that's all you know," she stated.

"Well, I got an email from Peter yesterday. He's learned that

Alice lived through childhood and graduated from high school in 1952 in Jasper, Indiana. Then she disappeared again."

"It certainly takes a long time to find someone."

"He said she probably got married—that's what most women did right after high school in the 1950s. Once he finds those records, and maybe the next generation, the pace should go more quickly. More records are accessible online."

She could see why the family was concerned. Mineral rights had been a big deal in Montana since the original gold and silver claims in the 1800s. They became more vital as the Treasure State's riches were raped from the ground by eastern conglomerates. Wall Street bankers got rich while Montanans spent their lives in the tunnels of the copper mines.

"Meantime, we're paying the mineral property taxes, or rather I'm paying them." CJ's gaze shifted away from her.

"That contribution should probably be run through the books as well," Samantha said.

CJ seemed to consider that.

"Makes sense," she finally said. "Any other questions?" she added.

"Not at the moment." At least none that she was willing to ask.

Chapter 11

Jarod stood in the driveway watching Samantha's car climb the slight rise. Audie waved frantically out the window. With a smile, he gave a wave back. That kid was becoming permanently attached to his heart.

And that was a problem. From what Samantha had let drop, her idea was to stay in Choteau long enough to get tenure, then move to a large city, maybe even out of the state, to a place that would have more teen services and a college for Audie when the time came.

She'd stay long enough for him to care and leave just in time to give his heart its final break. If he ever were to find someone to build a life with, it would have to be someone for whom a small town was a forever choice.

"She's getting under your skin," Dylan said as he walked up, tablet in his hand.

"The kid? Yeah, Audie's an interesting challenge."

"I meant the mother."

"I don't think so."

"You keep telling yourself that, big brother," Dylan said.

"What's up?" Jarod asked.

"The drone took some interesting pictures up in the northwest corner of the range." Dylan turned so his shadow covered the tablet screen and clicked an arrow.

Everything looked normal until the drone reached a portion of the fence not too far from where he'd found the site of the picture. Then a whole section of fence went missing. Not just a few strands or a fence post that had rotted, but a good two hundred yards of barbed wire had been cut and pulled aside.

"Looks more like humans than cattle," he said.

"That's what I was thinking."

"Rustlers?" Jarod asked. With more and more cowhands, especially older ones, hooked on one kind of drug or another, modern day rustlers were as much of a concern as they were in the 1800s.

"I can't think of another explanation," Dylan said. "But it

seems like an out-of-the-way place for an easy in and out operation. The southwest corner is just as remote, but the forest service roads run near there."

"Sounds like we need to take a ride." He measured the distance between the sun and the horizon. Daylight savings had just ended, which meant there'd be less light in the afternoon. "Let's head out in the morning."

Dylan nodded. "I'll get Birdie to put together some sandwiches and coffee so we can grab and go first thing."

"Sounds good."

While his brother headed up to the ranch house, Jarod turned back toward the barn. May as well make sure the horse gear they'd need was easily accessible.

# # #

The chill of approaching winter frosted the grass of the higher elevations as Jarod and Dylan road their horses up the foothills early Sunday morning. They'd left at sunrise, and by eight thirty were about at the place where the drone had identified the broken fence.

"You're missing church," Dylan observed.

"God will understand," Jarod replied. He was the only one in the family who still went, although they'd all been raised with regular Sunday school and church attendance. Birdie had tried, but each one of them had fought her every week as soon as they felt they were old enough to do so. It didn't take much before she gave up the battle.

Except for Jarod.

He couldn't explain why it was important to him, only that it gave him the anchor he had so desperately needed when his father had died in an epically stupid manner coming home on icy roads from visiting a mistress in Lincoln.

The only change he'd made as an adult was to switch to his current church with Birdie. They'd made an unspoken agreement that family memories were best left in the graveyard with his parents.

"So, has Cassandra left you alone?" Dylan asked a little farther up the trail.

His younger brother could be darn nosy.

"Appears that way."

"Just as well. There's something about her."

"You just don't like Easterners," Jarod said with a grin.

"Montana born and bred can be trusted. Anyone else can stay at arm's length."

"That's going to bite you someday."

"And how's that?" Dylan asked with a grin.

"Don't know. I just have a feeling that someone is going to come along and make you eat those words."

"That'll be the day." Dylan laughed.

Two grouse exploded from the sagebrush near the trail. Wings beating furiously, they teetered into the air like a squawking chicken knowing its fate was to become a dinner entree.

Jarod grinned at his brother.

"Looks like we missed a meal," Dylan said.

"Yeah. And we're going to miss hunting season if we don't get out soon. It'd be nice to have some elk or deer in the freezer. A change from beef."

"Still have most of that big trout I caught in the summer. I'll have to grill it some night before it gets too cold."

"We should see if Nick wants to go out before the season ends," Jarod said.

"He's an outfitter. I'd think he'd be a little tired of it."

"CJ says he's not doing fall hunting trips anymore. Tired of too many out-of-state men using the fall hunting trip to prove their manliness."

"See. I'm not the only one who thinks Montana should be for Montanans."

"Yeah. Next thing I know, you're going to have one of those bumper stickers that says the state's full."

Dylan laughed.

"Seriously though, we should check with Nick. If he's going to be part of the family ..."

"Really think he and CJ are going to tie the knot?"

"Birdie thinks so," Jarod said. "And that's all it takes to convince me."

The trail emerged from the sagebrush and rock environment to a small dip in the rolling hills. In the spring and early summer, a small stream ran through the middle, but now it was a dry gulley. To the right, where the fence should have been, was a bunch of barbed wire curled up on itself and a downed fence post.

He and Dylan headed toward the destruction. They slid off their horses and untangled the wire enough to find the ends.

"Looks cut," Jarod said.

"Yep." Dylan walked over to the fencepost. "Looks like the cattle pushed this over, however. It's snapped."

"How many head do you think we've lost?" Jarod asked. "Think they were rustled? Or something else?"

"Let's take a look on both sides of the fence. Maybe that'll help. If it's rustlers, there should be truck tire tracks." Dylan shrugged. "Still seems like a dumb place to make a killing stealing cattle. It's coming on winter, not many are going to be up here, and the terrain is rough."

"Didn't this land just get bought by a Californian?" Jarod asked as they climbed into their saddles and headed onto the neighbor's property.

"Yeah. Don't know his name. I'll look it up tomorrow."

"Okay."

They followed the tracks of the cattle farther down the little valley until it became little more than a gulley. There they found three of the cows in a nearby grove of trees, seemingly befuddled by the lack of grass.

"Looks like a bunch more went up those hills." Dylan pointed at a place where the ground was churned up. "Definitely not rustlers. No way to get a rig up here."

"Then what?"

Dylan shrugged. "Beats me." He looked at the cattle. "How about you get these three back and I'll ride up there a bit to see if I can't get the rest? I don't figure there's more than ten. There's just not that many of 'em up here."

"Okay. There should be some branches in here I can use for temporary posts. I'll get that dug in and start stringing the wire back."

"Sounds good."

"Dylan, be careful. We don't know what or who is responsible for this or how dangerous they really are."

"You've been reading too many spy novels," Dylan said as he clicked his horse to get him moving up the hill.

Jarod found some solid branches, collected the cows, and herded them back to Beck land, all the while puzzling over the mystery of the cut fence. Who would do such an inane thing?

He'd finished pounding the branches into the ground as far as he could when Dylan arrived back with another eight cows.

"It's not perfect," he said to Dylan, "but it'll do until someone can get back up here with real posts. Help me string the rest of the wire."

Using extra wire they'd brought with them, they made a solid barrier to wandering cattle.

"Think we got them all?" Dylan asked as he held the wire for Jarod to secure.

"Won't really know until we count them all in the spring."

When they were finished, they loaded their tools back into their saddlebags and mounted the horses.

"Let's ride up that ways a bit to see if there's any reason for the damage on this side of the fence," Dylan suggested.

Jarod nodded, and they headed upstream from the property line. About five hundred yards from the fence, they found some of the grass trampled, but it wasn't clear whether it was from a horse or a cow. Their luck improved with a single shod hoofprint in the dry drainage. Definitely a horse. A few more isolated prints led them to where the drainage went into a narrow canyon, too close for a horse and rider. They dismounted and looked for traces of the rider leading the animal.

"Find anything?" Jarod asked.

"Nope," Dylan replied. "It's like he just up and vanished." He pointed down the canyon. "If you could just follow that through, where do you think it would lead?"

"Hard to tell from down here."

"Then let's go back to where we could climb the hill."

"Sounds good."

Dylan held the horses while Jarod scrambled up the steep slope to a space where he could see more than the narrow canyon walls. The lowering sun gave a pink outline to the granite mountains while highlighting the golden brown of the grasslands on the hills closer to him.

The view was familiar. He pulled out his phone and found the picture CJ had sent him, the one was on Cassandra's wall.

A different angle, but the same section of mountains. Everything was centered on this small section of property.

But why?

He half walked, half slid to where Dylan waited.

"There's something about this area. It's in a similar area as Cassandra's picture."

"Interesting."

"We'd need a whole lot more time and manpower to be able to do a thorough search."

"Kaiden would be the right one," Dylan said. "That boy has

always had more knowledge in his little pinkie about land and what's under it than the rest of us combined." He swung himself into the saddle.

"Remember all those rocks he used to tote back to the house?"

Dylan laughed. "Think he'll ever come home?"

"Not permanently. Despite his desire to bring everything underneath the topsoil to the top of it, he feels the way the rest of us do about our land. It needs to stay as close to what it's always been as possible."

"NIMBY," Dylan said.

"Huh?"

"Not in my back yard. We all want stuff that some of the most destructive practices get us, like copper from Butte, but we don't want to look at what we have to do to get it."

"Got it." Jarod chewed that over in his mind as they headed home. Energy and mineral extraction in pretty much all its forms was pretty ugly. Even the rows of solar panels he'd seen on his annual trips to Las Vegas couldn't match the hardscrabble beauty of the high desert.

"Think we'll hear from Cameron soon?" he asked.

"I hope so," Dylan said. "I'd hate to think he's lying somewhere injured."

"Or worse."

Jarod didn't want to think about the "or worse" part. Their family had already been through too much unnecessary loss. He gazed out at the grassland rolling toward the prairie. His family's land. But if someone didn't hop to it soon, ultimately, it would belong to a stranger.

To lose the ranch would tear him up.

"I'll meet you back at the ranch," he said to Dylan, then urged his horse into a hard gallop. Heading toward home, and the oat bucket, made the animal comply immediately. The pounding hooves were louder than the fear in his soul.

Chapter 12

Samantha and Audie arrived at Trish's home about twenty minutes after one on Sunday. "Sorry," she said as she entered the homey living room. Overstuffed furniture was littered with bright pillows, magazines, and remotes. Half-full glasses of water dotted a few of the tables, competing with more magazines and books as well as a tablet.

It was a lived-in space that didn't bespeak the grinding poverty she'd known as a child.

"Nothing to be sorry about," Trish said. "I had kids. For the first ten years of their lives, I never made it anywhere on time. Now I'm always late to pick them up from one place or another. Makes me glad Sam is getting his driver's license. One less thing to do."

Audie walked up to her. "May I hug you?" she asked gravely.

"Of course." Trish gave the girl a big smile and held out her arms.

"Mrs. Hunt is teaching her about boundaries."

"What a fraud!" Trish laughed. "That woman is the biggest hugger I know, and I don't ever remember being asked about it."

Samantha smiled, a little of the tension she normally carried in the upper regions of her back unknotting itself.

"Beth!" Trish called out. "Audie's here."

Beth's daughter, who had her mother's brown hair and sunny disposition, came into the living room, crouched, and held out her arms.

This time there was no hesitation and Audie crashed into her and squeezed, almost knocking her over.

"Audie! Be careful!" Samantha said, more loudly than she intended.

"It's okay, Mrs. Deveaux," Beth said. "I do gymnastics. I've fallen off the balance beam more times than I can count. Makes this kind of stuff easy." She unwrapped Audie's arms from her neck. "How about we go in my room? I've got some games we can play or coloring if you'd like that."

"Okay." Audie held out her hand and the pair walked down

the hallway.

"Now for our playtime," Trish said with a smile. "Kitchen's over here, and there's a great little nook we can use.

She followed her host into an industrial-sized kitchen. Serious ovens lined one wall with what appeared to be a walk-in freezer on another. The island in the middle held an industrial mixer, food processer, and several rolling pins. A tray with nuts and small crackers was placed next to a bottle of red wine and two glasses.

"We added this on when the pie business began to take off," Trish said, noticing her glance. "It comes in handy for lots of other things, too, especially as my son and his friends have developed hollow stomachs that constantly need feeding." She picked up the tray. "This way."

She led the way to a spacious nook with a small, round table and comfortable chairs. Three windows arranged in a semicircle gave a view of the foothills to the west. "Brad and I have our coffee here practically every day," she said. "In the spring, we'll sometimes get a herd of deer or elk, pheasants, a flock of turkeys. It's quite a show." She placed the tray on the table and indicated a chair.

Samantha sat while Trish opened the bottle of wine, then brought it and the glasses to the table, smoothly filling them before she took her own seat.

"Cheers," she said, lifting the glass. "To new beginnings. I hope you are ready to make Choteau your home for a long, long time."

Samantha hesitated.

"I can't believe I put my foot in it with a simple toast." Trish shook her head and set her glass on the table. "What did I say?"

"I'm not staying," Samantha blurted out.

"Why not?" Trish asked. "The kids say you're a good teacher, and Audie seems happy. Unless you're worried about the lack of dating material. That is a problem in this town."

"No, that's not it. I'm not interested in dating."

"Not even Jarod?"

"It's not like that. He's just been giving Audie riding lessons."

Trish considered her wine for a moment, then took a sip before speaking. "I can understand why you think that," she said. "Especially since Jarod wouldn't know he was interested unless someone hit him over the head with it. I'm counting on Birdie for that one. But you can't be that blind, can you?"

Where was all of this coming from? Had she missed something from Jarod? Yes, they were friends of a sort, but she didn't think of him that way.

"Or maybe not." Trish answered her own question. "You don't know the history."

"I know they've got plenty of secrets. You know I'm helping out with the bookkeeping?"

Trish nodded. "Brad is CJ's accountant."

Samantha picked up her own glass but didn't drink. "It just seems there are lots of things that don't make sense to me. I'm not asking you to explain, but it makes me uneasy."

"Because of your own past."

Could that be true? Probably. She nodded.

"What makes you think he's interested in more than riding lessons and bookkeeping?" she asked.

"Because he talks about you."

"I'm sure he's talked about other women before. I mean, he's in his mid-thirties. He's had to have girlfriends."

"He did in high school. Everyone figured he and the girl would get married, take over the family ranch because none of the others were really interested, and raise a passel of kids. But then the parents died, and he had too much responsibility, especially after CJ bailed. He kept putting his high school girlfriend off and eventually she found someone else."

"That's hard. But if he's still stuck on her ..." She didn't need anyone's leftovers. Heck, what was she thinking? She didn't need anyone, especially someone who was tied to Choteau forever. Her little girl needed more opportunities.

"No. He's dated a few times but nothing stuck. He goes to Vegas for the National Rodeo every year, but what happens in Vegas ..." Trish shrugged.

"Well, it doesn't matter too much anyway," Samantha said. "My plan is to stay until I get a few years of experience, then begin to look in one of the bigger population areas to give Audie more choices."

Trish studied the contents of her glass, placed it back on the table. "I'm disappointed to hear your plans. You've got Beth engaged in math in a way I've never seen. She's usually bored to tears. Not with you."

Samantha's breath shortened. High praise indeed. Teaching was often aimed at the middle abilities of a class. There wasn't much time to do anything else. If she was reaching the ones who were naturally talented at math, it was great. She'd have to check in with some who were struggling. She didn't want to leave them behind.

No teacher did.

"I don't see any other way to make sure Audie gets what she needs."

"And what is that?" Trish asked. "What can a big city give her that a loving community can't? She's already made lots of friends from what I see at church."

"She needs to have her brain challenged. She doesn't always think like everyone else."

"And yet she's going to need to learn to live in a world with everyone else."

Trish's words stopped her short. Was she only looking at this thing one way? Would it be possible to stay in Choteau and still get Audie the help she needed?

But staying in Montana meant Cody was bound to find her.

"I can't." She forced out the words.

"Something to do with your ex?"

Samantha couldn't answer. Sobs of frustration threatened to break out.

Trish pushed the snacks toward her. "Have some of these. I got them at Costco in Great Falls the last time I was there. I'm halfway addicted to them."

Numbly, Samantha picked up a few and put them in her mouth. Hot and sweet.

"Do you want to talk about it?" Trish asked softly.

"Yes. No. I don't know." Shame welled up from deep inside her. "I was so stupid."

"Not a one of us escapes that curse," Trish said. "The character-defining moment occurs after you realize you've made a mistake."

"I've tried to be a good mother to Audie," Samantha mumbled.

"You're an excellent mother to Audie, and she isn't the easiest child to handle. Changing homes and towns is difficult for most children, and yet Audie seems to be adjusting well."

"Jarod has a lot to do with that. She adores him." Even as she said it, she realized Trish had been right. Audie wasn't the only one with feelings for Jarod. All that was going to do was make it harder to leave.

"And your ex?"

97

"Just got out of jail in Nashville. He's a musician, singer-songwriter—more songwriter than singer. He was doing okay in Billings. He sold some club drugs on the side—Ecstasy mostly. He said it was just until he got his big break." She shook her head. "I believed him. I felt if I supported him, he'd get his breakthrough. Then he got the offer to go to Nashville and he left ... alone. He never did hit it big. I guess in his own way, he was as naïve as I was."

She swallowed hard. She'd never strung it all together like this before. Her mother had lived through it, but Samantha had never discussed it with anyone else.

"I take it things didn't quite work out that way."

"Not in any way at all. He got his break—at least he thought he did. One of the big Nashville names wanted to record one of his songs with a 'few changes.' They wanted him in Tennessee. That's when I turned up pregnant."

"Ugh. Timing sucks."

"Yep. He said I could only come if I got rid of it.'"

"Harsh."

"Yes." She looked out the window at the clouds rushing by, pushed by the strong westerly winds. Life could be like that—speeding along so fast there was never time to think through what was best.

"I made the right decision for me and kept her."

"So what's the problem now? If he didn't want Audie then, he's not going to want to be bothered by her now."

"That's what I thought. But my mom has heard from him. Apparently, he wrote her before he got out, saying he understood the mistakes he'd made and wanted to make amends and get a chance to meet his little girl."

"Maybe he has changed. Doesn't Audie have a right to know him?"

"He had his chance. No do-overs."

"Now who's being harsh? Forgiveness isn't only for the person you're forgiving," Trish said. "You're carrying a lot of bitterness."

"I'm fine." She didn't want to talk about it anymore.

Trish raised her hands in surrender. "Got it."

Tension circled the small table.

"I'm sorry," Samantha said. "There's just so much going on. Too many decisions to be made and I've not really recovered from the move or the new job or leaving home ..." The sobs began before she could catch them.

When Trish took her arms and urged her up, she went along, a puppet under her friend's direction. She was led into the living room and helped to the soft couch. Trish wrapped her arms around her. "Just let it out. There's no point in holding on to all of it—it'll only send you to an early grave."

She tried to pull herself together, but it just spilled out as if she were an overfull reservoir. There was nothing else important to her. Except Audie.

Oh my God. What if her daughter heard her? She stifled her cries and began to get herself under control. She wasn't even sure she knew what she was crying about.

"Better?" Trish asked, handing her a box of Kleenex.

"I'm not sure. It certainly doesn't solve anything."

"No, but it can leave you with a clearer head, letting all those noisy emotions free."

"I should be getting home." She stood.

Trish did the same.

"If you want," she said, then put her hand on Samantha's arm. "Promise me one thing."

"What's that?" she asked leerily.

"To think more about forgiving your ex and maybe yourself as well. Talk to someone—me, the pastor, Birdie, Jarod—just someone."

"That's more than one thing," Samantha said.

Trish laughed. "True."

# # #

Samantha tried not to think about Trish's suggestion or the whole darn mess over the next two weeks. She had enough trouble keeping her students focused on the task at hand. Even the poor grades some of them had received didn't seem to daunt their enthusiasm for the upcoming four-day weekend. The end of hunting season took its toll as well, as students—male and female—skipped school to get the family's deer or elk. For some it was tradition, for some sheer necessity.

As the students in her class became more excited about the holiday and the time to go visit her grandmother neared, Audie became a complete mess. One day she was calm and collected, the next she refused to do anything her mother or teachers asked of her. Samantha was ready to tear her hair out.

Maybe having a second parent around wouldn't be such a bad idea.

Never.

The only person Audie was at ease with was Jarod, at least until he told her they may have to suspend their lessons when the snow fell. When it was time to put the gear away, she did it but made a great show of banging things around and tossing the brush into the bin harder than it needed to be.

"I didn't realize how much she relied on these lessons to stabilize her," she'd confessed to Jarod after Audie stomped to the car, arms crossed, cowboy hat crushed on top of her head.

"Me either."

"Thanks for everything."

"Maybe there's something we can do during the winter months that will help," he'd offered.

"I'll think about it."

Great. One more thing to ponder as she took the four-and-a-half hour drive southeast to Billings. At least she'd gotten their books straightened out. He'd asked her to come once a month to keep it that way, and she'd agreed. He'd been so helpful with Audie, it was impossible not to do so.

On the Wednesday before Thanksgiving, school got out at noon. Quickly, she gathered Audie and started the long trek. One of Trish's pies was safely nestled in the trunk, along with her daughter's favorite green-bean casserole, prebaked yams stuffed into empty orange skins, and a bottle of her mother's favorite wine.

The sky was dark and cloudy as they left. Hopefully, they'd leave the storm in the shadow of the Rockies and the plains would be more forgiving. Their luck held until they turned down the road through Judith Gap. The road wove between the Big Snowy Mountains and Little Belt Mountains, providing a straight shot for massive winds. In fact, one of the largest wind power projects was located in the broad canyon.

"Have you learned about Lewis and Clark yet?" she asked Audie. Montana elementary school history was heavy on the expedition and the fate of the Native Americans after the territory was declared part of the United States.

"Only in some of my books. They walked a lot. I wouldn't want to walk with them."

"Me either!"

The car rocked with a gust of wind, and dots of white

appeared on her windshield before melting quickly. Hopefully this would be the worst of it. She continued her conversation with her daughter, trying to distract herself.

"Did you know this place was named after a friend of Lewis and Clark?"

"Must have been a girlfriend," Audie said matter-of-factly. "I did not know that."

Samantha grinned. Sometimes her daughter's turn of phrase struck her funny bone, especially when such an adult structure came out of a kid with mussy hair and oversized glasses.

The wind was steadier now, and the snowflakes larger as they slapped the windshield. She slowed the car, feeling for the road under her tires. So far it was still warm enough not to ice, but it would only be a matter of time. Making Billings by nightfall would be difficult if she had to stay at this speed.

"Is your seat belt on good and tight?" she asked Audie.

"Yep." Audie buried her nose back in the book she was reading. Thankfully, she had a strong stomach. Samantha had never been able to read in the car.

She gripped the steering wheel. Just stay steady on the road. Follow the taillights in front of her but not too closely. The highway people had installed reflectors on both sides of the treacherous road in an effort to keep drivers from sliding into the side ditches.

All she had to do was keep control.

She risked taking one hand off the wheel to turn up the playlist she'd created before leaving on the trip. Suddenly, the mellow music became like fingernails on a blackboard. It was too calm. Life wasn't calm. This trip wasn't calm.

It took all she could do to restrain herself from ripping the cord out and throwing it on the back seat. She took a deep breath instead and slapped her hand back on the wheel.

They'd make it. She'd make sure they would. And once they got to Billings, everything would be fine.

Chapter 13

Except it wasn't.

It had started out well enough, Audie bouncing up and down as she greeted her grandmother and launched into several hours of non-stop, out-of-sequence stories. Samantha's mother avidly listened.

She'd never had that much time for Samantha.

"Whew, that girl can talk," Mom said when they'd finally gotten Audie to bed and were sitting with glasses of wine on two ends of the living room couch. "I'm just glad you're here safe. The drive must have been terrible. Maybe you should have stayed in Choteau."

"Being here was important," she said. "Besides, you said you have something to tell me."

"I'd hoped for a little more time before we got to that, but knowing you, it'll only eat away at your insides until you know. Actually, there's two things."

"Well, start with the worst." Samantha tried to smile encouragingly. Her mother, always too bony for her, her face aged by sun, wind, and the cigarettes she'd smoked up until Audie was born, looked even more worn than usual.

"I'm not sure it's the worst from your perspective, but it's not good. There's no way to sugarcoat it." She picked up a nearby spoon and twirled it, a habit she'd picked up after she quit smoking. "I've got the cancer." She gestured toward her chest. "From smoking."

"Oh, Mom." Tears welled in her eyes. She gathered the frail figure in her arms and held her, like she'd hold Audie in her arms when she was confused or frightened, as tears spilled down her own cheeks.

They sat like that for a few moments before they separated almost by instinctive agreement.

"What do the doctors say?" Samantha asked.

"It's early stages, so it's only in the lungs."

"Well, that's good."

"It still means surgery and all the other goodies that go with it, radiation and chemo." Her mother's wry sense of humor reasserted itself. "A brand-new adventure."

Samantha forced a smile.

"I'll be here for you. Just tell me when it's scheduled, and I'll take time off from school."

"You don't need to do that. I do have friends, you know." Her mother's smile was a shadow of its usual self.

"Nonsense."

"The surgery isn't until February. We'll discuss you coming back when the time comes. Now, who is this Jarod Audie kept babbling about?" Her mother took a long sip of wine and settled back onto the couch as if she were about to read a good romance novel.

"He's teaching Audie to ride." She told her mother about Misty, and Audie's total melt-down in front of the cowboy.

"He must be a nice man to take such a step," Mom said.

"He is." She gave her mother a stare. "And that's all he is. A nice, friendly man. I've got plans, remember?"

"Yes. And I also remember that life has already happened while you were making other plans. Why don't you go with the flow?"

Because I don't want to end up like you, living not much beyond the poverty level most of your life, even though you worked so hard I never saw you.

But she didn't say a word of it.

Instead she grinned. "Because a man is not a plan, remember, Mom? You taught me that."

Did her mother's gaze shift for a second?

"True. But that doesn't mean you have to spend your life alone."

"I'm happy. Audie's happy. I have a good job with benefits. It will be enough."

Her mother considered this for a moment, then smiled, but it wasn't one that went all the way to her eyes.

"But I'll be here for you, Mom. I promise."

"I know. Thanks." She looked at her empty glass. "And now it's time for me to go to bed. We have lots to do tomorrow before dinner."

Samantha stood. "It's going to be great having Thanksgiving dinner with you."

"I know," her mother said, also rising. "I'm sorry we didn't have them very often while you were growing up. But it couldn't be helped."

"It's okay." She gave her mother a hug, treasuring the warmth of their contact. Her mom had done what she thought was right, staying married to her dad and never going back to get an education to advance herself.

It was a path Samantha would never follow.

When she woke the next morning, it took a moment to realize where she was. That awakening was quickly followed by another. Her mother had told her only one of the things that were on her mind. After the cancer news, anything else had to be easy, right?

Audie dashed into the room. "Grandma's making pancakes! Get up, Mommy!" She turned and pounded back to the kitchen.

The Macy's Thanksgiving Day Parade blared from the television, but it was the aroma of coffee and sizzling butter that drew her into the kitchen.

"Morning," she said working her way to the coffee machine where the fixings were already laid out. "This is nice of you. I haven't had pancakes in so long."

"Mommy never cooks breakfast," Audie said. "She's too busy getting ready for school."

"Getting you ready for school, you mean," Samantha replied with a grin.

"Well, okay. Getting both of us ready for school."

She laughed and shook her head. "Anything I can do to help, Mom?"

"No, sit down and enjoy your coffee." Her mother flipped three pancakes onto the plate, added some butter to the top of the stack, and put it at Audie's designated space. Huckleberry and maple syrup jars were already on the table. "Do you need me to cut them?" she asked Audie.

"I'm a big girl now," Audie said. "I can cut them myself." She sawed away at the stack.

Her mother looked at her and shrugged. "She gets more like you every day. You're going to have some interesting times when she gets to be a teenager."

"I'm trying not to think about it."

"Probably the best idea." Her mother went back to the griddle.

It was difficult to come off the roller coaster of teaching every day and relax. Samantha's mind still raced with lesson plans and papers she needed to grade this weekend—before they took the long trek back to Choteau.

"Have you heard a weather forecast?" she asked.

"Not since yesterday some time." Mom turned toward her, one hand on her hip and the other gesturing with the spatula. "I know the trip yesterday was bad, but there's no sense in thinking about going home until Saturday. The way the wind blows here, the weather people are wrong as often as they're right."

"Yes, but if bad weather is predicted, it might be safer to leave Saturday."

"Worry about it then. Today is Thanksgiving. Let's be happy that we're safe, sound, and here."

A cancer diagnosis probably gave someone a different perspective on things.

"Sure."

A plate of steaming pancakes appeared in front of her.

"Yum."

"They're really good," Audie said. "Can Grandma come home with us? She cooks better breakfasts than you."

Her mother laughed. "You are so nice!"

"No, I'm not. I just want better breakfasts." Audie gave her grandmother a lopsided smile.

This time Samantha laughed. Her daughter would probably never develop a good filter, but sometimes her sheer honesty was refreshing. It beat the games adults played.

"So what do we have to prepare today?" she asked when her mother sat at the table with her own stack of pancakes.

"Turkey, stuffing, salad ... you've got the green-bean casserole and yams; I've got canned cranberries, au gratin potatoes ... I think that's it. Thanks for the pie you brought. It looks yummy. Huckleberry."

"That's what you asked me to bring."

"And I picked up vanilla ice cream. That should do it."

"That's more than enough for three people."

There was that shift thing with her gaze again. Samantha didn't imagine it this time.

"That means there will be lots of leftovers for you and my girl here." Mom squeezed Audie's shoulders. "Are you all done?"

"Uh-huh," Audie said, keeping her lips as close together as possible so she wouldn't spew out the last bit she had in her mouth.

"Chew and swallow," Samantha said with a warning tone. "Before you get up from the table." One of the things she was grateful for as a high school teacher was not having to supervise kids eating. What they could do with their food was sometimes beyond horrific.

She finished up her own breakfast and got Audie cleaned and dressed before taking her shower. On her way back to the kitchen, she paused at the living room window.

Leafless trees allowed a view of the sky and the steep cliff that led to the airport's perch and more clusters of ranches and houses. The Rimrocks, as they were called, were as familiar to any Billings native as the Yellowstone River that carved through the town. The bad weather had moved on, at least temporarily, and the cloud-dotted sky was a crisp blue.

It had been her home as long as she could remember, and it was odd that now it wasn't. But that was life. It kept rolling on, regardless of what anyone tried to do to stop it or change its direction.

Audie's squeal broke into her thoughts.

"Mommy, look! It's Big Bird!" She clapped her hands. "Do little kids still watch *Sesame Street*?"

Samantha smiled. "Sure do! I'm going to help Grandma with the turkey."

"Okay." Audie turned to become sucked into the television just as the latest have-to-have toy advertisement appeared.

And so it began.

The sweet smell of onions and celery rose from the stove where her mother already had started the stuffing process. Next to the stove, she was whacking away at cremini mushrooms on a wooden cutting board that she'd used ever since Samantha remembered.

"What do you need?" she asked.

"Can you chop the pecans? Apron's over there." Her mother had always insisted on wearing an old-fashioned checkered apron she'd probably sewn herself when cooking.

Samantha donned the garment and went to work. The mound of nuts was more than she remembered there being in the past. Her mother must be planning mega-leftovers. When she was done with the nuts, she put them in a bowl next to her mother.

She may as well get the turkey out.

Not in the refrigerator.

"It's in the cold storage out back," her mother said. "If you're looking for the turkey, that is."

"Yep."

"I put it in an ice bath last night to thaw overnight."

The cold storage room, little more than a hallway that held her mother's canned vegetables and fruits, lived up to its name, at least during the winter months. Still, it was an awfully long time for a turkey for three people to be sitting.

Except it wasn't a meal for three. The thing was huge—well over twenty pounds.

Shaking her head, Samantha hauled the turkey from its water bath.

"Are you feeding an army?" she asked when she slid the bird into the sink and began to prep it.

"Not really." Her mother's back was still to her.

There was something going on. "Mom, Cody isn't back, is he? You didn't invite him?" The ends of her fingers tingled.

"Of course not. He's your business. You handle that the way you see fit." She doused the flame under the pot and added the bread crumbs to the savory mixture. "I asked a friend to come," she said quietly. "I'm not sure if he'll show up, but I want to be prepared."

"Wait a minute! You're dating?"

Her mother's response was a loud laugh.

"Oh, no. First of all, I'm still married. Second, not every man is a romantic interest, especially at my age. We can be friends, you know."

"*Why* are you still married?" At least once a year Samantha felt compelled to ask her mother this question. Now seemed as good as time as any.

"Never felt the need. I loved your father before he took a wrong turn. I'd always hoped he'd get it together, but then ..." She shrugged. "All my time was eaten up by raising you and working." She smiled at Samantha. "And I don't regret a minute of it." She dried her hands on her apron. "Now, let's get that bird stuffed and in the oven. It's going to take a while."

An hour later the turkey was roasting, the smells already filling the house with remembrances of holidays past, as infrequent as they had been. They'd made short work of the pots and pans they needed and prepped for the next round of cooking.

"How are you going to fit everything in with that turkey?" she asked.

"I have it all figured out. You didn't get that mathematical brain out of nowhere, you know." Mom grinned.

A wave of affection washed over her. Her mother had made a lot of sacrifices so Samantha could get the education she wanted, in spite of having a child. And it had still been difficult. How hard it must have been for her mother in the same situation.

Maybe she should grow up and cut her mother a break.

"Shall we go see what the youngster is doing?" her mother asked.

"Sounds like a plan."

Although the television was still on, Audie's attention had wandered to her tablet she was avidly reading. She barely looked up when they entered the living room.

"What are you reading?" Mom asked.

"*The Black Stallion,*" she said. "Mommy got it for me before we left home. It's so good, except it's about a boy and horse. It should be about a *girl.*"

"She's horse mad," Samantha said.

"Can we see Jarod when we get home?" Audie asked. "I don't have to ride—I just want to see Misty."

"I'll call him next week. I think he'd be okay with that."

"We should call *now*. He needs to know we're thinking about him on Thanksgiving."

"Next week," Samantha reiterated more firmly.

"Now." Audie dropped her tablet on the rug, stood, and put her fists on her hips. She glared at her mother.

Samantha's own mother had to turn away to hide her laughter.

"You know his number," Audie said.

"Can't you wait? He has his own family. He should spend time with them."

"But he *needs* us."

Need was a strong word for her little girl to use. What could an established rancher need from a single parent and her little girl?

Maybe he was lonely and she couldn't see it through her own need to be in charge of everything and everyone around her.

"Now, Mommy."

The whine in her voice told Samantha her daughter was about to lose it. Should she hold her ground or give in? She glanced at her mother.

"Call him," Mom mouthed.

It was Thanksgiving, and she was grateful he'd given so much of himself to Audie.

"Okay."

"Yes, Mommy! I'll get your phone." Audie pounded to her

bedroom and returned with the phone Samantha had left on the bedside table.

She flipped through the contacts and found Jarod's number. After dialing it, she started to panic. Calling on a holiday was too intimate—it implied a relationship they didn't have. As soon as it started ringing, she thrust the phone at Audie.

"You talk to him."

Her mother arched an eyebrow.

She ignored it.

"Hi, Jarod!" Audie said. There was a pause, then she asked, "How did you know it was me?"

Another pause.

Then a giggle.

"Silly horse." She turned to Samantha. "Jarod says Misty chewed on her stall. He thinks she misses me." Into the phone she said, "Happy Thanksgiving! Tell everybody else. Mommy says so too." A pause. "She's right here. Do you want to talk to her?"

Not in the plan, but how could she ignore him without being impolite?

She took the phone Audie thrust at her.

"Hello? Sorry about that. I couldn't get her focus off of calling you."

"It's sweet," he said. "I really like that about her. She must have gotten it from her mother."

Her mind scrambled for a reply.

"Sorry. Was that a little too much?" he asked.

"A bit. No problem." She swallowed. "Do you think Audie could come see Misty next week? Not to ride. She knows she can't do that. Just to pet her."

"That would be fine. Dylan, Nick, and I are going hunting for the next three days, but we'll be back after that."

Dylan said something in the background.

"I'm not going this year," Jarod said to his brother.

Another comment from Dylan.

"Shut up," he said. "No, not you. I'm sorry. My brother is being a jerk, as usual. Normally, I go to National Finals Rodeo—it starts this week. But this year, I've got too much to do and I don't want to spend the extra money. So come Saturday."

"Okay. Sounds good."

"How was the trip? I'm glad you called. I was concerned when Birdie told me it was snowing from Judith Gap east."

"I held it together," she said.

"White-knuckled?"

"Absolutely."

He chuckled. "I'm glad you're safe. Is everything else going well?"

"So far so good." What would it have been like to be snowed in for the holiday? Maybe Jarod would have driven into town and brought them to the family dinner. A wave of sadness passed over her.

"I'll see you a week Saturday," she said, trying to put a positive spin on things.

"Saturday it is. Happy Thanksgiving."

"You, too."

She clicked the call ended button and slumped into the closest chair.

"Just a friend?" her mother asked, shaking her head.

"Really," Samantha said. "Just a friend."

Audie cocked her head and stared at her mother for a few moments, then went back to her tablet.

"I'm taking a walk," Samantha said.

"Bundle up. It's cold outside."

"Uh-huh." Samantha grabbed her jacket from the hallway hook and stepped outside. If it was cold, it didn't penetrate the warm jacket, gloves, and hat she'd donned.

Jarod thought she was sweet.

Where had that come from? And why did it make her so uncomfortable?

Because there was no space in her life for him. She was going to have to reinforce the distance between them somehow. Staying in Choteau the rest of her life would mean ...

What, exactly?

Jarod was kind to Audie, and she liked her job. If he was developing feelings toward her, would that be the worst thing in the world?

Darn. She needed an instruction book or maybe a crystal ball so she could see where the future led.

One day at a time. That's all she could live. If she were lucky, Cody would come back, figure out he needed all his energy to get his life on the straight and narrow, and leave them alone. As she turned the corner, she sent the wish flying to heaven and concentrated on the familiar neighborhood.

A pink tricycle lay on its side in the front yard of a pale brown house with faded red trim. Several cars were crammed in the driveway. Who had lived there when she was younger?

Ah! She snapped her fingers. Dorothea—an old-fashioned name for a feisty kid with brown, kinky hair. What had ever happened to her? Or any of Samantha's old classmates? Once she got involved with Cody and his crowd, she'd dropped them all. They weren't cool enough.

They probably had steady jobs and happy, intact families.

Water under the bridge. She was making up for lost time now. Kicking at some leaves on the sidewalk, she continued to circumnavigate the block, something she'd rarely had the time to do while Audie was growing up.

When she got back, it was time to help her mother create the rest of the feast. It all seemed like too much food. Soon, however, the sweet smell of yams joined the sharp aroma of turkey nearing its completion.

"Audie, come help me set the table," Mom asked.

Plates clinked and clunked as Audie tried her best.

"Why are we setting four plates?" her daughter asked. "You, Mommy, me. That's only three."

Why indeed? Who was this man who was coming to dinner?

"We might have a special guest. He may come or not. But if he does, it would be nice if he knew we were expecting him."

The Becks had too many secrets for her taste, and now her mother was holding out on her.

They had just hauled out the turkey when the doorbell rang.

Her mother looked around like it was a foreign sound.

"I'll handle the vegetables. You can get the door."

"Okay."

But Audie had gotten there first.

"Who are you?" she asked. "Grandma said someone special was coming. I thought it was Santa Claus. You don't look like Santa Claus."

A familiar laugh swept through the house.

It couldn't be. Her mother wouldn't.

She put down the pot she was holding and went to the front of the house.

Her mother had.

Chapter 14

The laugh Samantha had remembered, but she recognized the face only from photos. Her body went rigid.

Was it really her father? If so, he'd aged greatly, and his skin held a pallor that looked like it would never completely disappear.

"You must be Audie," the man said, holding out his hand to the little girl.

"How do you know my name?" she asked suspiciously.

Her mother crouched. "He's your grandpa."

"How come I never met him before?"

"Can I let him in before we answer that?"

Audie eyed him up and down.

"I suppose so." She stepped around the two and walked to where Samantha stood. There was no space between her shoulder and Samantha's hip.

"Come in, Jake," her mother said. "Before the open door sucks all the heat from the house."

"Thanks, Maddy."

"Why don't we all go sit down?" Mom said, gesturing to the living room couch and chairs. "I'm sure there are things you want to know."

Dear God, why had her mother thought it was okay to invite her father to Thanksgiving dinner? Or anywhere where she and Audie were? The kid's father had been in prison, and now she'd find out that her grandfather had been in prison, too.

If it had been up to Samantha …

A look from her mother stopped her thoughts mid-sentence. It was the same look she'd gotten when, as a kid, she'd even been thinking about doing something wrong. It had stopped her then, too.

Her father had taken the recliner, the one her mother had always used, and her mother perched on the end of the couch closest to him. Samantha sat at the other end, as far away as possible, with a squirming Audie pulled next to her.

The room was still, an awkward silence creeping in on cat's paws.

Her father cleared his throat. "It's good to be back home."

This isn't your home.

"I'm glad you decided to come back when the time came, Jake," Mom said.

Nice little euphemism for "getting out of prison." Samantha's lips settled in a thin line.

Mom looked at her and Audie. "We are glad you're here. *All* of us."

This wasn't the Waltons. Why was she trying to pretend they were one happy family?

"Costco said I could come in for an interview next week," he said.

"That's wonderful," Mom said and gave Samantha another pointed glance.

"Yes," she forced out. "It is." She'd heard people leaving prison had a tough time finding work, forcing a great many of them back into the familiar life behind bars.

Audie slipped from her arms and edged closer to her grandmother, her gaze steady on Jake.

He smiled at her.

"Are you Mommy's daddy?" she finally asked.

"Yes, I am."

"Then how come I've never met you before? Why don't you live with Grandma?"

He was quiet for a moment.

"Because I did a very bad thing when I was younger. Actually, I did a lot of stupid things, and *then* I did the bad thing."

"Was it a really bad thing?"

"Uh-huh."

"What was it?"

Jake looked at Samantha, but she shook her head.

"I'll tell you when you're older. Anyway, they sent me to jail for a really long time."

"You were in jail? Were they mean to you? What did they make you do?"

How could she stop this? She didn't need her daughter's insatiable need to find things out to continue the conversation.

"Sweetie, Jake has just come to visit for Thanksgiving. You don't need to ask him all those questions."

"But I want to."

"Audie ..."

"He's my grandpa! I want to know things." Audie's voice took

113

on the tenseness that meant a full-blown tantrum was coming if she didn't get her way.

There had been too much going on already for her daughter. The long drive yesterday through the snow, the craziness of making dinner and the parade, and now a never-before-seen grandfather. Way too much stimulus.

"It's okay," Jake said. "She deserves to know."

"Be careful," she warned.

"I will."

"Yes, Audie, I was in jail. And there were some people who were mean, but most of us were okay with each other. We did our jobs, like you do in school. If we didn't behave, we were punished."

"Were you sent to the principal's office?"

"Something like that." Her father had a sad smile on his face. "I was pretty good though, so they let me out early."

Audie nodded solemnly. "Do you love my grandma? And Mommy?"

His gaze lifted to Samantha's face. "Very much."

She hardened her heart against that look. It was too much. He'd killed a man. Nothing would ever be enough.

He nodded as if he understood how she felt and then turned back to Audie. "I will love you, too. I'm sure of it."

Her daughter considered all this information for a moment. It was too much. She was too young.

What was she going to think if Cody ever came around again? That all men went to jail?

"Okay," Audie announced. "You can stay."

"Thank you," he said simply before looking at Samantha.

She kept her face neutral.

"There are things to do in the kitchen," her mom said. "I remembered the kind of beer you like. Would you like one?"

"That was kind of you. Thank you."

"Audie, why don't you find a movie on TV? *Miracle on 34th Street* should be on. Then you and Grandpa can watch it together. Samantha, can you help me?"

Samantha seethed as she followed her mother, who went straight to the fridge, pulled out a bottle of local beer, and popped the top. "Can you take this to your father?"

She snatched the bottle from her mother's hand, marched to the living room, handed it to her father, and went back to the kitchen. Her mother was trying to act like the man hadn't been gone for twenty-five years.

"Stop it!" her mother hissed. "Right now!"

"How could you have invited him?" she hissed right back.

"He's still my husband."

"Do you love him?"

"Well, I'm no longer in love with him, but I care about him a great deal. You've always known that. I know you have never approved, but you are a guest in my house and you will treat him with respect."

She took a step back. Her mother hadn't talked to her like that since she was a kid. Even then.

"Sorry, Mom. I'll behave." It would cost her every bit of God's good grace to do so, but her mother was right. She'd been rude.

Twenty minutes later they were ready to eat. Even though she wasn't a regular churchgoer, her mother said grace, as she had done before every meal while Samantha was growing up. Even her father's voice didn't sound rusty.

"Now dig in," Mom said, taking a few slices of the turkey and passing it to Jake. He helped Audie get some on her plate, then passed it to Samantha. She forced herself to be gracious accepting it.

Somehow they made it through dinner to the huckleberry pie.

"Ah, my favorite," Jake said.

No wonder her mother had asked her to bring that flavor.

"It's really good. Beautiful crust."

"A friend of mine makes pies in Choteau. She sells them in restaurants and stores."

"This is my favorite, too," Audie announced and went back to eating the sweet, berry by berry.

It could take all night.

"I need to head out soon," her father said. "They must need people desperately at Costco. My interview is tomorrow."

"On Black Friday?" her mother gasped. "That's unusual."

"I thought so, too. I remember you working so hard at retail, especially around the holidays, even after Samantha was born. I didn't feel like a very good provider—a man. I guess that's one of the reasons I did all that crazy stuff, to prove to myself that I was capable of having a wife and child." He shook his head. "People can bring stupid to a whole new level."

But he still killed a man. There was no getting around that.

She stayed quiet, though.

"I can't eat anymore," Audie announced. "But it tastes so good."

"I'll tell you what," her mother said. "Let's take it inside the kitchen and wrap it up. Then you can help me a little bit while Grandpa and Mommy chat."

"I can help," Samantha called out.

"No, you stay there and talk with your father."

She picked up her wineglass. None left.

Her father grabbed the bottle on the table and poured what was left into her glass.

"You're right," he said. "My remorse, even changing myself to be a better person, doesn't make up for what I did that night or the tough life you and your mother had. But it's all I have. Fairly quickly after I got into prison, I took a good look around me. There were a lot of men there who thought they were really smart. And they were in some ways. But they couldn't control their impulses, and they didn't think things all the way through. They didn't worry about the consequences to other people.

"And I realized I had a choice. I could continue down the same road I'd been going and end up back in prison again and again, with more damage to others on my hands. Or I could do something different. I didn't know what it was, but I knew I could figure it out, given time. And with the strict sentence the judge handed down, I had plenty of time to think.

"Your mother answered when I finally wrote her, but it was mainly to let me know how you were. She told me about your awards, your strength, and your own fall from grace. We bonded over your struggles and how you overcame them. Somewhere along the way, she forgave me."

His blue eyes, so like the ones that gazed back at her when she looked at the mirror, were steady on her.

"Thank you for telling me all that, but it doesn't change my mind. I know, by rights, since I made my own mistakes, I should be able to forgive you. But I didn't kill a man."

The brightness in his eyes diminished.

"I hope you'll let me see my granddaughter when you come to Billings," he said. "Can I write you?"

"It's Mom's house. If we're here, I can't stop you from seeing her here. But not anywhere else. I have to protect my daughter. She's very vulnerable."

"I suspect she's not as vulnerable as you think, but she's your daughter. That will be fine."

"I'm not giving you my address in Choteau," she said. "So you'll need to continue to get your information from Mom." God, she sounded so harsh. "I'm sorry. I didn't intend to sound so mean, it's just ..." Just what? She sipped her wine, trying to come up with the answer.

He waited for her, his expression neutral, probably schooled by prison life not to show any emotion. What a horrible way he'd had to live.

But he needed to pay for his sins.

Another opinion fought to be heard, but she suppressed the idea. What with Cody around—that was it!

"I don't have any emotional space right now to think this all through. A new job, a new place to live, helping Audie adjust, and now Cody is out of prison, too. It's going to be too much for my daughter."

"And you. But to let you feel more secure, I want to remind you that I don't even know who Cody is. Even if I did, I wouldn't tell him a thing."

"Thanks." She looked around at the plates still lingering on the table. "I'd better help clean up."

"Me, too."

Without saying more, they stacked the dishes and brought them into the kitchen, where Audie and Mom were singing old songs she'd heard when she was a kid as they cleaned up the preparation mess.

"Oh, thank you," she said when they brought in the first batch. "Now, Audie, let's refill this sink with fresh water and new suds, and you can help me wash. Mommy can rinse."

"I guess that leaves me to dry," her father said.

With the simple, normal act of cleaning the kitchen under her mother's direction, Samantha began to relax in a way she hadn't since her father had first walked through the front door. Memories of her dad edged back into her memory, other nights when they'd shared this simple ritual as a family.

When the dishes, pots, and pans were done to her mother's stringent satisfaction, her father bid farewell. He didn't attempt to hug Samantha, but Audie threw herself into his arms and told him he was the best grandpa ever.

Tears stung her eyes. Her daughter was so free with her gift of love, like she'd been at that age, before circumstances ripped it away. Could she ever love again? The answer was uncertain.

# # #

The day after Thanksgiving, Jarod and Dylan loaded up the horses, their gear, and some sandwiches Birdie had supplied and headed up to the trailhead where they were to meet Nick. CJ had to spend time in Big Fork, capturing the town's preparations for its annual Christmas celebration, so he'd readily agreed to the hunting trip.

Snow held off, but the air nipped their exposed ears and noses as they unloaded at the other end. The horses stomped their feet and snorted, their breath visible in the mountain cold. Falling leaves had bared the deciduous hardwoods and most of the tamaracks, but the rest of the pines and firs stood vibrant against the blue sky and deep gray granite of the mountain peaks. Jarod took a breath and filled his lungs with the vibrant wilderness air.

Nick arrived, and they helped get out the horse and mules he'd brought and followed his directions to pack the three mules. Each man's clothes, sleeping bag, and rifle were already on the horse he was riding.

"Where's the kid?" Dylan asked.

"In Seattle. His mother decided she wanted to start seeing him on a regular basis again, to see if I'd trained the bad out of him."

"Never saw much bad, myself," Jarod said. "Trevor seems like a normal, mixed-up, hormone-driven, teenage boy."

Nick laughed. "That about covers it." When the animals were loaded to his specification, he said, "I figure we'll take the trail up by the Middle Fork. It gets us to some good spots to set up a base camp, close to small meadows well below the snowline where I've found deer and elk before. Jarod can go first, and I'll bring up the rear and lead the mules."

"Stuck in the middle again," Dylan sang.

"Only 'cause it takes two of us to manage you," Jarod said.

"Oh, it's going to be a fun trip," Nick added with a groan.

"You're the one who wants to be part of the family, bro," Dylan said. "If you thought one brother was a pain in the ass, wait until you have four—especially when they're Becks."

"Hup!" Jarod said and squeezed his knees. His horse, Whiskey, began down the trail, his gait smooth and rhythmic, which was why Jarod had chosen him for the trip.

Dylan took off right behind him and in the distance, Nick brought up the rear, their horses' hooves clattering against the rocky trail bed.

Although they saw some elk and deer sign along the trail, they didn't spot the elusive animals. Nick spotted some bear scat near the spot he'd chosen to stop for lunch and water the horses.

"They are getting to be more and more frequent," he said. "We'll have to be extra cautious at night." He pointed to the coolers tied to the mule behind him. "We should have plenty of ice to hold an animal after we get it. We can either handle two deer or one elk. Once we get that, we'll need to head back."

"Got it." Jarod said, content to let his old friend take the lead. Even when they'd gone camping as teens, before their great rift when Nick dumped CJ for another girl, Nick had been the savvier one about the wilderness.

As they continued on, he gave himself over to the rhythm of the horse swaying him in the saddle. Most of the songbirds had gone south, leaving the forest to the year-rounders: woodpeckers hammering away, caws of ravens and crows, and the occasional screech of a hawk. Ground squirrels scurried about storing food for the winter that inevitably bore down on this part of the country.

It was good to be alive.

And it was well past time to let his family's history keep him trapped. All the work on the ranch wouldn't matter one whit if there was no one with whom to leave it. And his training business wouldn't build itself. He needed to do something strategic—maybe take a risk financially and build that arena in the spring. If need be, he could borrow the money.

But what about the other? A family required a woman, and he'd been through most in the county without success. Few modern girls wanted a life of hard work with no fancy reward.

What was Samantha's background? She seemed satisfied with what she had in town—almost grateful for the security. But there was something in her background that made her leery of giving too much of herself to any other person.

His horse snorted, almost as if to say, "You're a fine one to talk."

Yeah. If Jarod wanted to change, the first person he needed to upend from his set-in-concrete ways was himself. But he'd rather face a grizzly than open up his emotions to another person … woman.

Chapter 15

"Up ahead there's a fork in the road," Nick called out to Jarod. "Take the right. About fifteen minutes from there is the meadow I thought we'd use for base camp."

"Sounds good," Jarod called back.

"Sure you've learned your right from your left yet?" Dylan taunted from behind him.

"Shut up," he replied.

"Is that any way to talk to your younger brother? Fine example you're setting."

"Sometimes it's the only way that works."

Jarod nudged his horse to the right trail, trailed by Dylan's laughter and a muffled snort from Nick.

"Glad to see things haven't changed between you two," the outfitter said.

Jarod growled.

Within fifteen minutes, he came upon a good-sized meadow near a mountain stream tumbling over a set of large boulders spaced enough to leave pools of water between the layers. In November's chill air, the stream was low; in spring the roar would make it difficult to sleep anywhere near it.

"This the spot you mean?" he asked Nick as he and his mules pulled up beside him.

"Yep. We can corral the horses over there, set up the tent here. There's a solid branch on that tree over there we can use to hoist food and the ice chests up at night to keep them from the bears."

"Sounds good," Jarod said.

"Well, then, let's get to work," Dylan added.

Under Nick's supervision, they efficiently set up camp. The man knew what he was doing. When it was all up, he handed them each a sturdy trowel. "Pick a direction to go do your business," he said. "Leave no trace."

"Yes, sir." Dylan saluted. "I will leave no poop behind."

Jarod shook his head. "Is there time to see if there are animals nearby?"

Nick checked his watch, almost a relic in this day and age, but a lot of the places he went wouldn't have cell coverage. "I think so. Depends on how starved you are."

"I can wait," Jarod said.

"I've got an apple," Dylan added.

"Then let's go. We can walk there. It's a short way over that rise."

Stretching his legs after all the time he'd spent in the saddle felt good. The way led close to the stream through a wooded area. The trail was easy but steadily uphill. Near the top of the rise, Nick indicated they should be careful where they stepped to avoid snapping twigs or starting a skitter of rocks. When they emerged from the tree line, they could see the meadow was empty. Nick walked out, staring at the ground.

"They were here recently, probably today," he said, pointing at the dark pellets on the ground. Nearby there were several impressions of hooves, too large to be deer. "They probably didn't go too far. They may even come back here tomorrow."

"Our luck wouldn't be that good, would it?" Jarod asked.

Nick shrugged. "You never know."

Back at camp, Nick pulled out what they'd need for their meal, and they set about making dinner, each with a beer in their hand. Steaming food was soon ready, and they sat on logs they'd found and set up around a campfire.

Dinner was full of good-natured teasing and reminiscences from their childhood years. Nothing had turned out the way they'd planned back then, but their lives still held goodness, and they were all making a living after a fashion.

"Nick, when you first started your business, how did you fund it?" Jarod asked. "I mean, it's an expensive start-up. You need horses, gear, and supplies."

"And advertising," Nick said. "Nothing comes without advertising these days. Website, social media, all that. It's a good thing I've got the wintertime to update all that crap. Except now, with me taking over the store for my parents in the winter, that time's going to be even tighter."

"Did CJ tell you I'm trying to create a horse and rider training business?"

"Yeah, she mentioned something like that. How's it going?"

"I've trained and sold one horse and I'm working with another. I still have enough cash to purchase another horse but haven't found the right one yet." He grinned. "And I seemed to have roped myself into giving riding lessons to an eight-year-old girl."

"Only 'cause you like her mother," Dylan said.

He ignored his brother.

"So how did you get funding?" Jarod asked. "To make a real impact, I'm going to need an indoor space to work with the horses and riders during the winter."

Nick nodded. "Makes sense. Truthfully, I tapped my parents to purchase my first two horses. That gave me a base to start taking a couple of people on guided fishing trips. Those are still my favorite kind of outings."

"Oh." Well, that wasn't much help to him. The family money was tied up in the ranch, and he was trying to start a separate business.

"That wasn't my only source. But it gave me enough to get started. I got a business loan with help from the Small Business Administration. I had to jump through a lot of hoops and create a really solid business plan, but it all opened my eyes to the possibilities and risks of outfitting. Like I have mega-insurance. You should, too."

"Darn, I hadn't even thought of things like that."

"I'm sure the pretty teacher would help you with your plan. You got her straightening out the books now."

"Give it a rest, Dylan," he said. "Besides, that was Birdie's idea."

"How much do you need?" Nick asked.

"Last time I checked indoor riding arenas, it was around a hundred grand when all was said and done. I've got about ten thousand to invest. At this rate, it's going to take a long time to get up and running."

"You're going to need a loan then. Can you borrow from the ranch?"

He snorted. "The ranch is barely supporting itself. And with the question of mineral rights still hanging out there, who knows how much money we'll need in the future."

"Then you're going to have to go for a loan. Check in with SBA. They're good folk."

"I will, thanks."

Dylan rose to his feet. "Speaking of horses, I need to see a man." He pointed west. "I pick that direction." He sauntered off into the night, trowel in hand.

Nick and Jarod looked at each other and laughed. "He hasn't

changed a bit, has he?" Nick asked.

"Nope." Jarod stood. "Thanks again, man."

"No problem. I'm just looking for a piece of that elk I know you're going to bring down tomorrow."

"Good to know you have faith."

They gathered the pots and pans they'd used for cooking. Nick filled a large pot with the water that had been heating on the fire, and they set to work cleaning up.

"Why's Dylan ragging you so hard about this teacher?" Nick asked.

"He thinks I like her."

"So I gathered. Well, do you?"

"Of course not."

"Don't feed me BS, Jarod. I know you too well," Nick said.

He'd never put how he felt about Samantha into words. He wasn't sure he understood it himself.

"Well, she is pretty. I can't deny that."

"Always a good start." Nick handed him the plates to dry.

"Yeah, but there's more. She goes to church—same as mine. And the fact she's a teacher ... well, I respect teachers."

"That's a switch. You couldn't wait to get out of school at the end of the day."

"I still couldn't sit still in a classroom."

"I get that. But I know what you mean. With Trevor, I've gotten to know a few of them. Most of them are hardworking and care about the kids. They spend their own money on the things schools should have on hand. Like every group of people, there are some who need to find another profession, but there aren't too many of them."

"And she's just nice. So patient with her daughter, who can be a handful. The kid is so smart and loving, but she can swing into a tantrum if she gets confused or doesn't get her way." He shrugged. "I just like her."

"So why not ask her out?"

"Aw, Nick, that time's over."

"That's what I thought until your sister convinced me otherwise." The flatware came Jarod's way. "You should try. What do you have to lose?"

His heart.

"So what are you gossiping about over here? Anything juicy?" Dylan rubbed his hands together with a gleeful smile.

"Yep," Nick said as he dried his hands in spite of the two dirty pots still beside them. "We've elected you to finish the pots while we tend the horses." He hung the towel on a nearby stand he'd brought with him and pointed to the wash water. "All yours. Do a good job or we'll make sure the bear gets you."

Leaving a grumbling Dylan, they headed over to the corral.

It was good to have friends.

# # #

Returning to school was a jolt. With only three weeks until Christmas vacation, the kids were no more settled than they had been before Thanksgiving. Teaching was a struggle.

To make it worse, Audie had become enamored with the idea of a grandpa and constantly pestered Samantha to let her talk to him on the phone when she called her mother. Audie was having a tough time understanding why her grandparents didn't live in the same house.

"But they are still *married*," she whined.

If she wasn't talking about her grandfather, she wanted to talk about Misty.

Samantha was going to go crazy.

Then one evening Jarod called.

"Hey," he said. "I've got something for you if you eat elk."

"You got one?"

"Yep." He sounded proud enough to burst his buttons off his shirt. "Bull elk. Four pointer. Nick took it to the processor he works with in town. I have to pick it up tomorrow. Would you be interested in a few steaks and ground meat?"

The food would help stretch her budget.

"That would be wonderful," she said before her pride reasserted itself. "I'd like to pay you for it, something—"

"Not necessary," he said. "I'm just being neighborly."

"But you've done so much for us."

"My pleasure. How was your holiday?"

"Good ... and strange."

"Strange?" he asked.

She told him about the unexpected appearance of her father.

"And you haven't seen him since you were a little kid?"

"Nope." She stared out the window at a nearby streetlamp. Bits of snow drifted lazily in its light. "It's snowing."

"Finally got there," he said, sounding like he was grinning. "Been going here for an hour."

"Is getting out of there hard in the winter?"

"It's more of a pain than anything else. We have a plow and all our vehicles have four-wheel drive. We try to discourage visitors till spring, especially those with not-so-good tires."

He was right, but getting tires was a huge expense. She was trying to put it off as long as possible.

"Audie's going to be disappointed," she said.

"I'm sure we can find a way to get her out here."

"It'll be too much trouble." And, she would be trapped out there without a vehicle of her own, no easy way to escape if she needed to do so.

Although what she needed to escape from she didn't know.

"I'll stop by tomorrow about 4:30 with the meat. That work for you?"

"Of course. Thank you. Are you sure I can't do anything in return?"

"Entirely," he said. "But I'll think on it." His voice developed a teasing note. "How about you agree ahead of time to anything I ask? That will make it easy to get my creative juices flowing."

She laughed. "Now I'm sure *that* is a very bad idea."

"C'mon, take a risk," he wheedled in a tone remarkably similar to her daughter's. "You know me. Would I ask you to do anything against your best interest?"

"Not that I know of."

"Well, then?"

"How about a 90 percent guarantee?" she asked.

"Nope. All or nothing."

"Why do I think I'm gambling with my future?"

He laughed. "Nothing that horrible is going to happen." He waited and the phone hummed anticipation.

"Okay. I guess. But ..."

"See you tomorrow." He hung up.

She stared at her phone. What had just happened? Unease roiled her stomach.

"Mommy, why do you look so funny? Who was that? Was it Grandpa?"

"No, it was Jarod," she said without thinking.

"Jarod! How come you didn't let me talk to him? How is Misty?"

"He's coming over tomorrow so you can ask him yourself." She smiled at Audie.

"Oh, goody, goody, goody!" Audie spun herself in a circle, a big grin on her face.

Was her daughter getting too close to the rancher? What would happen when she had enough time into her job that they could move to a bigger city? And what if Cody found them?

Somehow she needed to put some distance between her small family and the Becks. No good could come of entangling her life with theirs.

She should never have made that promise.

# # #

On her break at school the next day, she received a phone call from the school secretary.

"Rebecca needs to see you. It seems Mr. Van Sutton wants to set up an appointment with you and the principal to go over his son's math grades."

"Again?"

"He's concerned his son won't be able to play football next week if there isn't improvement."

Maybe if his son was concerned, he'd put a little more effort into the class.

"Any idea when?"

"Rebecca will discuss that."

"Okay. I'll be down."

Samantha glanced at the papers spread across her desk. Shutting down her computer so nosy students couldn't investigate, she made her way to the principal's office.

"Sit down," Rebecca said, her tone more formal than in the past.

Was she in trouble? A frown wrinkled her forehead. Hopefully, Van Sutton wouldn't want to see her tonight. She hadn't made any arrangements for Audie, and there was Jarod.

Her expression must have deepened.

"It's not that bad," Rebecca said. "I'm just annoyed that Jim's wasting our time like this. The problem isn't with you. It's with his son."

Samantha was unsure of what her reaction should be.

"Sorry. Bad day. Every time I turned around there was another kid thinking he or she knew more than any adult. I know it comes with the territory, but sometimes it's exhausting. Will tomorrow after school work for you? I know you have to pick up Audie, but she can stay with the office staff. They like her a lot."

"Sure." At least it wasn't tonight.

"We'll come up with some kind of plan. But first I have to see what the man wants." A ping drew Rebecca's attention back to her monitor. "Tomorrow after school, then. Just bring some samples of the kid's work with you, okay?"

"Sure." That was the problem, though. There wasn't much.

She stood and left to get back to her room in time for the next class.

# # #

After providing Audie with a snack when she got home that night, Samantha spread out the few papers that Jim Van Sutton had turned in and brought up her grade chart online. Out of the twenty homework assignments she'd given out in the first quarter, he'd completed five, along with five written excuses from his parents as to why he couldn't complete another five.

Sheesh. Talk about enabling a kid.

His classroom work was lackluster—he often skipped problems he deemed too hard and never went back to work them. The test scores corresponded to his lack of study. They were the lowest in his particular class, and was fifth from the bottom overall.

It was a pretty bleak picture, but she wasn't sure what his parents expected her to do about it.

The doorbell rang.

Sweeping the papers into a pile and shutting her laptop, she went to the foyer only to find it opened by an overeager Audie.

"I missed you, Jarod!" She held out her arms and he crouched and hugged her.

"You know what?" he asked.

"What?"

"I missed you, too, but Misty missed you even more."

"I want to see her!"

"You can come out on Saturday. Your mom and I already talked about it."

"You did?"

"Yep. Mom agreed it was a good idea."

"Thank you, Mommy!" Audie flung her arms around her.

She smiled at the top of the tousled head, then looked up. A jolt went through her.

It was if he were a totally different person standing in front of her. Instead of a stranger or a kind man who helped her daughter to ride, she saw his soul. Years of pain and hiding were visible in his eyes in a ways she'd never seen before. All pretense was stripped away.

"What?" he asked. "You look like you've seen a ghost."

Well, that was one way of putting it.

"Nothing, really. Just something I remembered."

"Okay."

His eyes shuttered again, leaving the friendly rancher behind.

"I've got two elk steaks, a roast, and two packages of ground meat for you." He held up the plastic bag in his hand.

"That's a lot of food."

"Audie needs strong muscles to ride. Protein gives her that. Can we stick the meat in your freezer?"

"Oh, sure." She unrooted herself from the floor and led the way back to the cozy kitchen.

"Pretty place," he said, handing her the packages as she tried to find space for them in the relatively tiny freezer compartment.

"Thanks. I like it. Convenient to school. We could walk if we had to. But then we'd actually have to get up and get going on time, something Audie and I both have trouble managing some mornings."

"I understand that," he said, ruffling Audie's hair as the girl shadowed him around the kitchen. "These dark mornings around the winter solstice can sap any normal human being's will to climb out from under the covers."

"Coffee?" she asked, holding up a cup.

"That'd be nice." He twisted the cap he held in his hand.

"There's a coat rack by the back door," she said.

He shrugged off his coat and hung it with the hat on the rack, Audie dogging his every step.

Her attachment to the man was so not good.

"Can I have some hot cocoa?" her daughter asked.

"Not before dinner. You just had a snack, and that's enough sweets for now."

"Not fair," she said.

She shook her head at the familiar childhood complaint.

After pouring the two cups of coffee, she sat down across from Jarod. "How are things going at the ranch? Any slower this time of year?"

"Somewhat. That's how Dylan and I were finally able to go hunting. We just made it before the season ended."

"So, were you the only lucky one?"

"Nick got a nice whitetail buck. That'll keep him and Trevor going over the winter."

"Oh, Trevor is Nick's son. I never put two and two together, but then, I've never met CJ's boyfriend."

"We think it's getting to be more than a boyfriend."

Apparently bored with this line of conversation, Audie announced she was going back to her room to read her book.

"Wedding bells?" she asked with a smile.

"I'd like to think so, but they each might be too skittish for that."

She tilted her head.

"CJ's husband died while they were in the Middle East—right after they'd had a major blowout."

She gasped and shuddered. "That's horrible. I can't imagine how you recover from that, much less move on. And Nick?"

"Bad breakup with Trevor's mom and then a lot of wrangling over the kid." Jarod shook his head. "I hate when that happens. It's tough on the kids."

"Yeah." What did he think of her single motherhood? It hadn't appeared to bother him up to now.

"Sometimes divorce is inevitable, but unless one of the spouses is a child abuser," he said, "I believe every effort should be made to let the kid know he or she has two parents."

"Got some strong opinions for someone who's never been married or had a kid." Her voice was sharp.

He glanced toward the living room, then peered into the coffee cup before setting it back down. "That didn't come out the way I wanted it to. That is how I feel, but I do know that I'll never really understand until I'm in someone else's shoes. I imagine you had good reason to not stay with Audie's father."

"The best," she said, trying to keep the bitterness from her tone. "He's the one who left. He didn't want her—wanted me to get an abortion, and I just couldn't do that."

"I'm glad you didn't," he said. "She's an amazing little girl."

They gazed at each other for a moment, the tension dissipating into the air.

"Well, then ..." she said.

"Would you go out with me Friday night? For dinner. Nothing fancy. They don't have that in this town."

"I don't think I could. Audie ..."

"I'm sure there's a teen who'd be interested in earning a bit of cash. I'll even split the babysitting cost."

She laughed. "You must really want a date."

He grinned. "I do. I didn't think I would want to go on a date with a woman ever again, but I want to have dinner with you."

"Did things end that badly with you and Cassandra?" she asked. She'd seen the blonde only that one day at church.

He shrugged. "We kinda drifted into that. I'm not sure I ever asked her out. She just assumed things. But I ended that a lot more cleanly than it began." He leaned forward. "So will you go out with me this Friday?"

There were a gazillion reasons why she shouldn't, but it had been so long since she'd gone out—not since high school, really. Cody had come into her life as a teenager and then gone back out without a lot of notice. Just when she'd gotten her feet back under her and was ready to date, he reappeared and she was hooked on his bad boy persona one more time.

Having Audie had forced her to take a good look at herself and focus on what she really wanted to do with her life.

He sighed. "That's a heck of a lot of thinking for dinner. I guess I'd best be going." He stood. "Thanks for the coffee."

Standing as well, she put her hand on his arm. "I'd be happy to go out with you."

Chapter 16

With a stack of notes in her hand, Samantha walked down the hallway to the principal's office. It was an ordinary high school corridor, lined with steel gray lockers. Streamers, papers, and odd coat sleeves tried to escape from their confines, and stickers—not sanctioned by the school—were defiant decorations.

Her low-slung heels clattered on the neutral shaded flooring, chosen no doubt for the lack of ability to discern dirt from color. Samantha had dressed conservatively this morning—a navy-blue dress with pearls.

This was nothing less than a fight for her livelihood. It didn't matter if Jim Van Sutton was the sheriff or not—she was right about his son. Rebecca had said so. But would the principal back her up when confronted? The man in charge in the school in Billings had been notorious for taking a parent's side in any dispute with a teacher.

Even though she was ten minutes early for the meeting, the sheriff was already there and in an animated discussion with Rebecca.

Samantha walked in, and Van Sutton rose slightly from his chair, enough to be polite but not enough to be anything but habit. Still, it was more than she'd ever gotten from his kid.

"Good afternoon, Miss Deveaux," he said. "It's good to see you again."

"You, too, Mr. Van Sutton," she said, taking her seat.

"I was just telling Mrs. Johnson here, I've been thinking a lot about our last meeting when we discussed my son's grades. I was just explaining that Mr. Weber might be a better fit for my son. Jim can be a little headstrong, I'll give you that, and an experienced male teacher may be able to make him work harder. No offense meant, ma'am."

Right. She glanced at Rebecca to take her clue.

"And, I've been explaining to Mr. Van Sutton," the principal said. "Can I call you Jim? Let's dispense with the formality. It's a small town, and we've known each other for years."

"Of course," he said.

"As I was saying, Samantha, I was just explaining to Jim that it's not possible to meet his request. Bruce Weber teaches the upper grades while Samantha handles freshmen and sophomores."

"It's really too bad you had to put an inexperienced teacher on the payroll." He glanced at Samantha. "No offense."

"Actually, Samantha is experienced and came highly recommended."

"Oh? I thought she'd never had a classroom before."

"I taught in Billings, Mr. Van ... Jim," Samantha corrected her instinct to be more formal with the sheriff.

"Teaching is teaching, Jim." Rebecca added. "Samantha has worked in a classroom, and that's what counts. Everyone needs to start somewhere. Even you were a first-time sheriff at some point."

Score one for our side.

Jim pursed his mouth, his moustache bouncing with the movement. "Well, then, what can we do? My wife wants to buy a planner for him."

"That would be a good start," Samantha said. *Where was his wife?*

"She couldn't make it today," he said, as if reading her mind. "She had something to do in Great Falls."

How could something be more important to a mother than her son's education? And why had the sheriff scheduled the meeting when his wife couldn't make it?

"I see," said Rebecca, giving Samantha a look she interpreted as a command not to explore the matter any further.

"I'm glad we agree about the planner," the sheriff said, turning to Samantha. "Now if you could just fill out his planner every day with the in-school and homework assignments, that would be great." He smiled as if not even anticipating an argument.

She fought back the urge to sputter.

"Now, Jim, it's not her job to do that," Rebecca said. "It's your son's job. Same as you have to do your own police reports."

"I dictate them to my secretary."

A bit of power with a dash of sexism. Samantha's favorite combination. Ugh.

"The point is," Rebecca said, her words staccato, "*we* believe it is your *son's* job to write down his own assignments. He's fourteen. He needs to learn to grow up. Take care of his own ...

stuff. What we *can* do"—she looked over at Samantha and she nodded, even though she had no idea what she was agreeing to do—"is have Samantha check at the end of class every day to see if he does it."

"And then she'll make him sit down and do it," the sheriff said with a nod. "That would work."

"Noooo," Rebecca said, drawing the word out and shaking her head. "She'll keep track. At home, *you* will ask to see it. No excuses. If he's not doing it, it's up to *you* to discipline him."

"That seems like a lot of extra work for me," Jim complained.

Rebecca started to shrug, but must have thought better of it. "I agree, but I can't see any other way for you to keep track of what your son is doing so you can make sure he stays eligible for sports."

"I'll make sure he has plenty of time to do it in class," Samantha added.

"We'll see how this works," the sheriff said. He gave Samantha another glance. "Are you *sure* he can't be transferred to Mr. Weber's class?"

"Quite." Rebecca rose. "Thank you for coming in today, Jim. It's nice to see a parent so concerned about his son's education."

Samantha fought to keep her expression neutral. She extended her hand. "Nice to see you again, Mr. ... Jim."

"Um, yes." He pumped her hand, then left the office, slapping his hat on his head as he went.

"Sheesh," Rebecca said when he was beyond hearing. "I've had worse demands—you'd be surprised what parents expect us to do—but how can he be a leader of the community when he can't even lead his own child?"

The more Samantha learned about parents, the more she understood their kids. It was the way it was. Private schools had the luxury of turning away the kids who simply couldn't succeed. Public schools took everyone.

"Thank you," Samantha said. "I appreciated the backup."

"You are doing a stand-up job," Rebecca said. "I would expect nothing less of myself."

Samantha smiled. "See you tomorrow."

Within minutes, Samantha gathered her things, her child, and drove to the local fast food place to give Audie the treat she'd promised. Cleared of her concern about the Van Suttons, her mind scrambled to the next topic on her worry list: the date with Jarod.

# # #

Jarod stared at his image in the mirror. A date. What had possessed him to ask Samantha out? He didn't even know how to dress for anything like a date. When he'd gone out with Cassandra, not only did she arrange the time and venue, she'd told him how she wanted him to dress.

Sometimes he did the opposite to annoy her.

But he wanted to get it right for Samantha.

At least his favorite button-down shirt was ironed. God bless Birdie. He tried to help out around the house, but he was hopeless at it. The space to do anything was always too small, and he'd broken more dishes than he'd washed. She usually shooed him away within ten minutes.

"Rocking it, big brother," Dylan said.

He glared at his younger brother. "Wait'll next time you go out on a date."

"I don't date."

"Not around here, but you do make those trips to Helena every month or so."

"It's business," Dylan said with a smirk. "What goes on in Helena, stays in Helena." He patted the doorframe. "Have fun. She's a nice person." Then he walked back down the hall.

Nice to have permission. Now if Jarod could only make it past Birdie before walking out the door.

The housekeeper had remarkably little to say other than the admonition to treat Samantha well. He threw on his coat, trotted to the truck, and put it in gear to head north to town.

The last snowfall had quit after a few hours and was mostly gone except for a few patches of white in shady spots, so driving was easy, giving him far too much time to think.

What was he going to talk to her about all night? She wouldn't be interested in his ranch problems. Why had she agreed to go out with him at all? He was a bunch of years older than she, more weathered, and more emotionally broken.

He pulled up in front of her house, a pretty little cottage with blue paint and white trim. It looked like the woman herself, organized with a feminine flair. Most women he knew had given up skirts and dresses years before, even in church. She took care with her appearance. It was old-fashioned, but he liked it.

It made him want to keep her and Audie safe from any harm

that might head their way.

Hopelessly out of date, but he was stuck with it. Hopefully, she wouldn't consider it a strike against him in this modern age where women could do everything.

Before he could open the door, Audie yanked it open. "I was waiting for you, Jarod!" She flung her arms around him.

He gave her a quick hug and smiled at Beth waiting at the living room entrance. "Ms. Deveaux said she'd be right out. She just needed to finish something."

"Let me show you something," Audie said, tugging him into the living room. "I made it in school."

He admired the handmade pinched pot gaily decorated in primary colors.

"Mrs. Hunt got them put in the fire," she told him. "We made them as Christmas presents for special people. This one's for my mom."

"Shouldn't it be wrapped or something?" he asked.

"I'll wrap it before Christmas and put it under the tree," the girl said matter-of-factly. "But it's too pretty to hide before then."

"I see," he said, and looked up at a rustle in the entrance to the hallway.

Samantha could have been a teen on a first date, vulnerable and unsure. Her light brown hair was held back by ribbons threaded through the top, allowing a clear view of her eyes, eyes as blue as the Montana sky. Her dress, a subdued blue of a similar hue, gracefully flared at the hips and draped below her knees.

He rose to his feet. "You look lovely."

"Thanks." She came into the room and assumed her parent-teacher authority. "Audie, behave for Beth."

"We'll be fine, Mrs. Deveaux. You have my cell phone number, right?"

"Yes, thanks." She bent and gave Audie a hug. "See you later, sweetie."

Her daughter had already moved on to some other idea and was tugging at Beth's hand.

"Enjoy yourselves," Beth said.

"Yes, thanks." Samantha's eyes darted back and forth, as if she were looking for an escape route.

He took her hand and led her to the coat hanging on a hook in the entrance way. Lifting in from its place, he helped her into it, picking up the ends of her hair from underneath the collar. His fingers brushed the back of her neck, heightening his awareness of her closeness.

"There's a new restaurant that opened a little north of here, closer to Dupuyer," he said. "I hope you don't mind a little drive. I'll need to stop and get gas, but after that it should only take about fifteen minutes."

"Sure," she said. "Sounds great."

"Good." He guided her down the front walk to his truck and helped her up into the passenger side. Pickup trucks were great for all kinds of things but not for dates once a man reached a certain age. However, a fancy BMW or Jaguar was never going to be part of his fleet, so may as well set the right expectations.

She was quiet as he drove the few blocks to the Exxon station.

"How is school going?" he asked.

"Fine."

"Ready for Christmas break?"

"Yep."

He went for broke. "How's Audie doing?"

"Well. Really well."

Maybe pumping gas would give him inspiration. He pulled up to the station's island and hopped out. "Just be a moment," he said.

He'd begun pumping when a too-familiar car, a gray Mercedes, pulled into the station.

Fantastic. His first time out with Samantha and they had to run into Cassandra. But when the driver's door opened, a man got out and walked to the pump. Seconds later, the passenger door of the car swung open.

Cassandra, her blond hair as neat as always, was bundled in a thick coat. She walked toward him with a big smile. "Jarod!" she said, planting a kiss on his cheek before he could react.

He glanced at the truck cab. Samantha was focused on them, a slight frown on her lips.

"Hello, Cassandra," he said. "Nice to see you." He let his gaze drift to the man pumping gas.

"Oh!" she said, following his gaze. "I thought you knew each other since you're neighbors. That's Dave Brockman, an old acquaintance of mine."

The man gave Cassandra a sharp glance, as if he begged to differ with her analysis, then shifted to a brief smile and a nod to Jarod. He had the overly fleshy look of someone whose enjoyment of good food and wine was beginning to catch up with him. The dark brown hair, almost as expertly kept as Cassandra's, reminded him of a style he'd seen on some British actor somewhere.

Something Cassandra had said snagged his mind.

"Neighbors? Did he buy the outfit on the highway just north of our ranch?"

"Exactly. He's building quite a place there. I'll make sure he invites you—and your family—to the housewarming."

"That'd be neighborly." The pump clicked off. He'd also be sure to contact Dave Brockman about the broken fence. He and Dylan had been too flat out getting cattle down from the higher elevations and double-checking the fencing to do any further investigations.

Cassandra smiled and waved at Samantha, who gave a half wave in return.

"I'm glad to see you going out, Jarod. Anyone I know?"

"And you, too." He ignored her question. "Glad to see you've moved on."

"Oh, it's just business."

Dave stiffened. Looked like the man may be searching for more than friendship.

"See you around," he said, placing the nozzle back into its holder and pushing the gas door shut. "I gotta get going or we'll be late." He touched the brim of the Stetson he'd worn. "See you around."

She put her hand on his arm. "Don't be a stranger."

He escaped before she could do anything more, gave a quick nod to Dave, and climbed into the truck. In a few seconds they were back on the town's main road.

"It seems like she can be a bit much," Samantha said.

"That's for sure." He smiled. "Thanks for understanding. That is long over, and like I've said, never really got started in the first place."

"Who was he?" she asked.

"Dave Brockman. He's apparently my new neighbor."

"Looks like he's from California."

"Why do you say that?"

She shrugged. "We got a lot of them in Billings. Their skin is almost always a little too tan, and they look like they've stepped directly from a TV commercial."

"But which came first?" he asked. "Do they look like commercials, or do commercials look like them? Most of them are filmed in southern California, you know."

"Oh, so you're an expert on commercials as well as a rancher?" she teased.

"Only the ones that come with sporting events, particularly rodeo. Do you like rodeo?"

"I'm not sure," she said. "I mean, I've been to one or two events at the state fair but nothing more than that."

"I wanted to be a calf roper," he blurted.

"Were you good?"

"I won some buckles." He'd been proud of his wins, envisioning a career that ran all the way to the finals.

"What happened?"

"Life." He shrugged. It would be a long time before he spoke at length to anyone about the horror of identifying his father after the crash and his mother's slow descent into death that followed.

If ever.

"I'm sorry." She was gentle. "I don't know the details, but I can hear the pain in your voice."

"My father died in a car crash when I was fourteen. My mom died of cancer about a year after that." He forced the words out, leaving his throat raw. "But this is supposed to be a nice night out. Those events are something I'd rather not talk about tonight."

"No problem. Tell me more about the rodeo. Are those bulls really as big and mean as they look?"

"Yep. They breed them that way." He pulled into the parking lot of the new restaurant, a rustic one-story building that had been created out of an early 1900s hunting lodge. The weathered wood was lightened by red trim. Flowerboxes, covered with pine branches, red berries, and silver bows, added to the welcome.

He pulled the iron handle to open the door. "After you," he said, his hand automatically touching her back as she went before him.

Were men supposed to do that anymore, or was the best policy no physical contact? Too late now. It felt natural to him. If she objected, she'd have to let him know.

The memory of the warmth on the back of her neck returned. Though it was accidental, it definitely crossed some kind of line. He'd have to be more careful.

But as he followed her to the table, the desire to touch her in places other than the back of her neck grew within him. She was gentle and sweet, but her life appeared to have left some scars. He'd have to take things slowly.

The hostess, an older woman in a loose black dress, handed

them each a menu with her well-manicured, ring-encrusted hand and described the specials. Her hair and makeup had the polished look of someone from a big city, but her smile held the genuine warmth of a lifelong Montanan.

Interesting combination.

"What's her story?" Samantha asked, echoing his thoughts.

"I'm not sure." He flipped the menu. The back contained a few paragraphs entitled "Our Story." He indicated the page to Samantha.

"Our story begins in Lewistown, Montana, where we both grew up," she read aloud. "Our mothers were close friends who enjoyed putting together small dinner parties. We learned to enjoy food beyond the burgers, steaks, chicken, and trout that filled the plates of most town residents. It also led to dating and falling in love.

"We both attended the Missoula College culinary program and began to work in the industry, Katherine drawn to the management aspects and Kurt developing proficiency in the kitchen. Big cities called and we migrated to Chicago, eventually developing our own restaurant.

"After twenty years in the restaurant business, the pressure cooker of a city high-end restaurant got to us. We'd never had time for children or to ourselves. The sins of a chef—too much stress and a short temper—affected our lives, and we yearned for the simple life with which we'd grown up.

"We chose Choteau because of its proximity to Glacier National Park and the Bob Marshall Wilderness and named our new restaurant LeGorille in honor of the French cooking we both enjoy. We are planning to keep the restaurant small, with the menu changing based on availability of ingredients and the chef's mood.

"Bon appetit!"

She put the menu. "How nice! They follow their hearts, and we get fine dining."

He nodded. Some people's dreams really did come true. All it took was hard work and perseverance. He could do it too.

"If you could follow your heart," he asked her, "what would you do with your life?"

Samantha looked blank, like she had no answer for the question. "I haven't ever thought about that," she said. "It's just been one foot in front of the other for the past eight years. First cleaning up my act, then getting my degree, getting some experience, and finding a job so I could take care of my daughter. I suppose if I have any plan for the future, it's seeing Audie successfully launched."

He knew exactly what she meant. "That's the way it was for me after my parents died. Doing what had to be done to keep the family together, even if that meant giving up everything I'd planned for my own life." He leaned forward a little. "But didn't you have dreams as a little girl?"

"Are you ready to order?" the waitress asked, placing small plates with tiny sauce-covered mushrooms—one each—on the table. "Or do you need more time?"

He stared at the mushroom. Gesturing at the plate, he asked, "And what is this?"

"That is the amuse-bouche," she replied. "A small sample to whet your appetite."

"Okay." He looked at it dubiously. If this was what fine dining entailed, he'd have to learn a whole new language. "I think we need a little more time, but can we have a wine list?" That seemed like a sophisticated thing to ask for, show he was a man-about-town, even though he had no idea what to glean from it.

The waitress shook her head. "Chef Kurt chooses the wine depending on the dish ordered," she replied. "He believes wine to be food as much as everything else. It has to blend. However, I can bring you a small glass of Beaujolais to start you off this evening."

"That will be fine," he said.

He glanced over at Samantha after the waitress left.

"Ooh la la!" she said with a grin and picked up her fork. Somehow she managed to slice the mushroom in half and placed the piece gingerly in her mouth. Then her expression changed, as if she'd just tasted heaven.

If he tried to slice it, he had no doubt it would fly across the restaurant. Instead, he stabbed it and stuck it in his mouth.

Instantly, he understood her rapture.

The both slowly chewed, swallowed, and picked up their menus. It was going to be a meal to remember.

Once they'd ordered, he went back to the question he'd asked earlier. "What dreams did you have as a girl?"

She looked up at the ceiling for a moment, then brought her gaze back to his. "A lot of the usual girl ones: ballerina, actress, doctor saving the world from some horrible disease." She flipped the ends of her hair, then shook her head. "Not the last one. I wish

I were that noble, but doctoring has never been my thing." She leaned forward. "This is going to sound weird and hopelessly old-fashioned, but when I was a kid, all I really wanted was a normal home—you know, white picket fence, mother and father, dog with a wagging tail. I wanted to know we weren't going to eat pancakes for dinner five nights in a row and that when school came, I'd have new clothes some kid wouldn't mock."

"You were poor," he said with a new understanding for her need to control everything around her.

"Very. Mom did the best she could, but once Dad went to prison, life got pretty tough. She was determined to hang onto the house, so everything else got the short shrift."

"Is your father the man Audie calls Grandpa?"

She nodded. "He got out. Apparently he and my mother have been keeping in touch and she's gone to see him."

"And you don't approve."

"He killed a man," she said flatly.

"And so he shouldn't be forgiven?" he asked gently.

"God has the power to forgive. I can't."

"But your mother has. And Audie's head over heels with the idea that she has a grandpa."

Samantha looked away. "Audie's a kid," she said softly. "She'll learn."

His heart ached for her. Her upbringing had robbed her of most of her faith in others.

The waitress came by with two steaming plates of coq au vin and placed them on the table. "I'll be right back with the wine," she said.

Amazing aromas rose from the dish in front of him: savory, sweet, and rich. Small stalks of what looked like broccoli huddled next to mashed potatoes. A touch of garlic rose from the fluffy, white mound.

His mouth moistened with anticipation.

"Here is your wine, a cabernet sauvignon from the Napa Valley. The chef picked it particularly for the flintiness of the taste that complements the very rich sauce of the coq au vin."

The language of wine was also a mystery to him. Who needed stones in their beverage?

"Do you need anything else?" she asked.

He shook his head. "This looks amazing."

She nodded and slipped away.

"All this in Choteau," Samantha said, her eyes large as she

stared at her plate. "I'm not sure I've ever had anything this grand." When she looked up, he was surprised to see tears glistening in her eyes. "Thank you."

"Enjoy," he said, his heart filling with wonder that he could affect her with so little effort. Growing up must have been more difficult than he imagined.

"Where is it you aren't going this year?" she asked. "When you were on the phone with me over Thanksgiving, you said you weren't going somewhere."

"Oh, yes. I usually go to Las Vegas for National Rodeo Finals in December," he said. "But this year life got too hectic moving cattle and double-checking fences."

"Why was this year different? Did you have problems?" she asked.

"Apparently. We wouldn't have even realized it, but Dylan splurged on this fancy commercial drone after he sold a painting in Helena. The drone found a stretch of broken fence in the northwest corner of the property. We figured we better check the places we winter the cattle and tighten everything up to make sure they wouldn't stray." He picked up his glass and examined it, although he didn't really see what he was looking at. His mind's eye reviewed the strange cut in the fence. "That corner was the only place we found. It look like someone cut the strands, but we couldn't find any reason why. There were no tire tracks to indicate rustlers."

"There are still rustlers? I thought that went out with the Old West," she said, holding a steaming fork of potato and chicken in the air to let it cool off.

"Oh, they are much more efficient about it now. They back up a semi, cut the fence, and hustle those cows right into the truck. It can take a big bite out of a ranch's income." He frowned. "That's why it didn't make sense to cut the wire where they did. No way to get a truck up there—all ravines and steep slopes."

"But the cattle like it?" she asked.

"The darn things sure do," he said. "Hard to get them out of the trees come fall."

He dug into the meal again. It was too good to leave a shred, except for maybe those green things.

"Any idea what these things are?" he asked, stabbing at them.

"Broccolini rabe," a male voice said above them. Based on the uniform, it was the chef. "It may not be a vegetable you're used to. I've sautéed them with a little bit of garlic and red pepper flakes, then drizzled some balsamic vinegar over them. Try them."

Jarod tentatively cut a small piece and stuck it in his mouth. Like the coq au vin, the flavors burst almost in layers onto his taste buds.

"It's good," he said in amazement after he was done.

"Of course," the chef said. "I hope everything else is to your satisfaction?" His gaze rested on Samantha.

"It delicious," she said, a warm smile gracing her face.

"Good. Tell your friends. We'll be open until mid-January, then my wife and I head south for a few months and re-open in late April. Come back again soon."

He left as abruptly as he'd appeared.

Samantha chuckled. "The man spent too long in the big city."

"Or maybe it just came with his name."

"Huh?"

"Kurt."

"Oh, that's a groaner." But she grinned.

"But it could be the city living. I've never wanted to spend much time in one. Billings is even getting too big for me."

"Yet you go to Las Vegas for the rodeo."

"That's different. I spend a lot of time in an arena—familiar territory. There are people I've known for years there. In spite of all the competition, it's a tight-knit family. Maybe you and Audie could come with me some year."

A mask fell over her face.

Dumb thing to say, especially on a first date.

"I didn't mean together together—but so she ... and you ... could see the rodeo." He sounded like an idiot.

"No, I understand," she said. "It's just that, well, I don't know that this"—she waved her hand between them—"is a long-term thing. I've got plans. Much as I'm not wild about a big city, it will probably be the best place for Audie to get the education she needs, particularly in high school."

"There are no white picket fences in big cities," he said.

"No." Her voice was wistful. "But whatever it takes, I have to do it for my daughter, just like you did for your family." She pushed the chicken around the plate with her fork. "And, truthfully, there's another problem. Audie's dad ... well, he's not someone I want her to be around. And I have to keep her away from him."

While it didn't seem fair to Audie's father, Jarod didn't know enough about the situation to comment. "I understand," he said, leaning back in his chair and taking a sip of the wine. It was as rich as the meal. Putting on a smile, he said, "But we can enjoy ourselves in the meantime."

"True." She smiled back and lifted her glass as well.

They ate quietly for a little while.

"So when you go to the rodeo do you look for something in particular?" she asked.

"A few things. I study the ropers, see what improvements I'd make if they worked with me. Ideally, I would love to be able to hand them a business card and invite them up for a trial lesson, but with winter as long as it is here, that's impossible."

"Unless you have an indoor arena."

He nodded. "Everything hinges on that. I'm hoping to have enough saved so I can get a loan in the spring and start building. I'd also like to get a lead on a second horse. Maybe one that isn't performing up to par in his owner's estimation."

"Oh," she said, a puzzled look on her face.

So he explained the intricacies of calf roping and the small details that made the difference between a loss and a win while they finished their entrees. She was a smart listener, asking questions that made him think through his assumptions and make the explanations clearer.

As they talked, the tension in his back eased and he began to truly enjoy the meal.

Chapter 17

Samantha didn't think she could eat another thing, but when the waitress recommended a *tarte au poire* made with pears and almonds, they agreed to try it. A small glass of amber liqueur came with it.

Once again, the combination of flavors touched different points on her palate: sweet, tart, savory. After the heavy meal, the small sliver of tart and tiny amount of liqueur rounded out the richness of the wine-infused chicken.

As they finished off, both of them gushed with their appreciation of the chef.

"Kurt he may be," she whispered to Jarod, "but the man knows how to cook."

"Glad to hear that." The hostess stood next to them, a smile on her face.

"I'm sorry. I didn't ..." Nothing like putting her foot in her mouth. What was the woman's name? Katherine.

The smile broadened, and Katherine waved her hand. "I've lived with the man for more than twenty years. When he's cooking, conversation is always on his terms. Outside of the restaurant, he's a sweet, loving guy, but here his focus is on ingredients and combinations. People are an afterthought."

"Which is why you manage the front," she said.

"Exactly. We fit together—two pieces of a puzzle. It's nice when it works that way. How about the two of you? Have you been together long?" The hostess looked at Jarod.

"No, ma'am," he said. "I've been giving her daughter riding lessons and asked her out for the first time tonight."

"Ah," she said. "You must be Jarod Beck. They were right about your manners, although I'm not sure about the 'ma'am' part. Makes me feel old."

"How did you ...?" he began.

"Small town," Katherine and Samantha chorused and grinned at each other.

"Which, if the current gossip is correct, makes you the new high school math teacher," Katherine added. "The one that's giving poor Jim Van Sutton Jr. such a hard time with his grades, according to his father."

What exactly were the gossips saying about her?

"Guilty," she said.

"Well, I've interrupted you long enough." Hands on her hips, Katherine inspected them. "I hope it sticks. You two look good together. And come back." With that, the hostess left as quickly as her husband had.

Jarod shook his head and raised an eyebrow at Samantha.

She quietly laughed at his expression and he joined it. Bubbles of pleasure let loose under her skin. What would it be like if she could let go and let God take her where He would?

Who would she be if she had that much faith?

"What a delicious meal," she said when the last crumb of tart had been swept up and the glasses drained. "Thank you. This was very generous of you."

"My pleasure," he said with a smile. "It's been a very long time since I enjoyed a fine meal with a fine lady."

"You are flattering me," she said. "I've never been a 'fine lady' in my life, and likely never will be."

"You are to me," he said, his voice lowered to a half-whisper.

She stared into his eyes. He was serious. She swallowed and desperately tried to think of something to say to end the moment.

He took her hand. "I wish you'd let go of all your preconceived ideas about what is best for Audie. Stick around. Find out if we," he gestured in direction of the kitchen, "fit together."

"I couldn't ... I can't ..." It would mean throwing all her plans out the window. If she weren't in control, bad things could happen—worse than eating pancakes five nights in a row.

"C'mon, Samantha, at least try it out." He withdrew his hand, but his gaze stayed intense. "Then if it doesn't work out, you can move on with a free conscience."

She had a free conscience now.

Or did she? Looking into his face, she knew they'd already moved beyond riding lessons for her daughter. They'd become friends, if not more.

It was still a bad idea.

"What if someone gets hurt?" she asked.

"We're adults. We'll handle it. But if we don't try, we'll never know."

"I'll think about it," she said.

He cocked his head and gave her a wistful smile. "Without

Audie here to interpret, I'll have to accept that you mean exactly what you said."

"I do."

He nodded. "We should go."

All the way home, she debated the pros and cons of going any further with Jarod Beck. He must have sensed her need to be quiet, because he let the radio fill the cab with holiday tunes. When the pulled up to her house, he cut the engine and turned to her.

"Would you mind," he asked softly, "if I kissed you?"

He looked so hopeful she didn't want to turn him down. So she didn't. Instead she leaned closer to him. "It's fine," she whispered, "as long as we don't fog up the windows."

He chuckled, then got closer to her and placed his lips on hers.

It wasn't a passionate kiss but a sweet one full of hope.

Dear God, help me find my way through this.

# # #

Cody Drake stepped off the Greyhound bus and walked quickly into the station. After nearly two days, he was sick of the bus, tired of company, and nauseous from vending machine food. He needed to find a decent place to stay. Fast. Something that wasn't where his old crowd hung out. The counselors at the prison had drilled that into him.

Stupid. His whole damn life had been stupid. But the worst thing he'd ever done was tell Samantha to get rid of the baby. He was glad she'd ignored him.

He had a kid. A little girl. He hadn't been a daddy up until now, but that was going to change. He'd get on his feet and then find out where Samantha was hiding.

After using the restroom, he splashed water on his face, rinsing off the dusty grime of too many people in too small a space. Was it possible to wash off the stench of prison? He doubted it.

He took the crumpled piece of paper from his pocket. A name, address, and telephone number. Scanning the area, he found what he'd expected, not a pay phone in sight. Just the same tired people dragging luggage and small children that he'd seen in every bus stop in his travels.

His cell phone, although returned to him, was pretty useless;

it had been turned off for nonpayment of service months ago. Nothing to it but find a cab or hoof it across town to an older section with small houses and large trees.

He stepped out into the glaring sun. Even in December, the high altitude intensified the sun's warmth. Shrugging the backpack high on his shoulders, he took a step, then realized what was pulling up beside him.

Damn. Another bus. But it would be crosstown and not cross-country, so he'd be able to survive.

He hopped on and found an empty seat, easy because the vehicle was almost empty. As they traveled toward the town center, he idly watched the scenery roll by. It hadn't changed much in the few years he'd been gone. A few trees replanted here and there, fresh paint slapped on houses, but not much else. There wasn't much breathing room, which was why all the new construction was happening up on The Rimrocks.

Construction well beyond what he could afford.

One day at a time. That had been drummed into him in group meeting after group meeting. Keep doing the next right thing and he'd succeed in life, maybe to the point of getting into one of those fancy houses.

But right now, he needed a place to live. And a job.

Then he could find his daughter.

Chapter 18

Samantha drove down the snow-cleared driveway. Her tires slipped a little, but she was able to correct them before the car went into a full-bore skid and she landed in a ditch. By the time she arrived at the ranch house, her hands were shaking.

She'd barely stopped the car when Audie launched herself out of the passenger seat. "Where's Jarod?" Audie asked, followed by, "Isn't Misty cold?"

The horse was walking around in a far corral a good distance away. How had Audie possibly recognized the animal? But she was right about the chill. Winter was setting its grip on the land.

"Up here," Jarod called from the front porch. "Stuck in a family meeting. Birdie has coffee and hot cocoa ready for you." He waved them up.

What was it like to have four siblings, especially as an adult? How did anyone get any alone time?

Samantha grabbed Audie's hand and propelled her to the porch. Jarod let them in the side door, then went back to the dining room.

"So how was your dinner?" Birdie asked once she had them set up with their drinks. Audie had taken her e-reader to Birdie's sitting room at the woman's suggestion.

"You don't let any grass grow under your feet," Samantha said with a smile.

"Never learn anything that way," the housekeeper retorted, settling with her own cup. "It's about time Jarod settled down."

"It was only dinner," Samantha said.

"If you knew how long it has been since Jarod went anywhere with a woman—besides that lawyer lady, she doesn't count—you wouldn't say that."

"Why doesn't Cassandra Sanders count?"

"You know her. What do you think of her? Be honest."

Samantha recalled the times she'd met the attorney, once at church, occasionally in town, and last night before dinner. "She seems okay, just ..." She tried to put her finger on what it was about the woman. "What's that old expression? She keeps her cards close to her vest?"

"I knew you'd get it. She wants something. I just wish I knew what it was. I was real happy when you came along and were able to yank her claws from my boy."

"That wasn't my intention, but really, we're just friends." She sipped her coffee, the comforting smells of a stew heating on the stove providing inner warmth.

"Where did you go?"

"LeGorille."

Birdie shook her head firmly. "Not a friend kind of place." She tapped her finger on her lips. "Not even a first date kind of place. You may think you're friends, but Jarod has something longer term in mind." She pointed a bent index finger at her temple. "I got the second sight. It's the Scot in my bones."

Samantha wanted to laugh, but there was seriousness in Birdie's expression. And she couldn't deny that the woman was correct, not based on what Jarod had said about seeing if they fit together well.

But she wasn't ready to talk about it.

"What do you know about Jim Van Sutton's wife?" she asked. She hated to gossip but knowing more about his background might give her the tools she needed to help the kid.

"Nancy? Why?"

"Her son is in my class, and his father seems to think I should practically do the work for him rather than forcing him to get busy. But I've never seen his wife. I have to think she might be part of the problem."

"Oh, she's a problem, all right." Birdie looked up, as if asking God what to say. She sighed. "In the beginning, they were pretty happy. Then Jim got more involved in law enforcement, ran for office, and won. He's a pretty good sheriff, I have to say. That's when it started, I think. They used to come to our church, and she'd complain a lot about being left alone. When little Jim was born, she complained worse, saying she was getting old, flabby, and unappreciated. Jim did everything he could, but some men, well, they're just not built to be sympathetic."

Samantha nodded. Van Sutton had seemed stuck in some other century, when men were men and women didn't complain.

"She started getting her younger sister to take care of little Jim while she took trips to Great Falls. Then she started staying overnight, and her sister became a live-in housekeeper of sorts. While Jim Sr. isn't one to betray his marriage vows, it must certainly have put a strain on things."

"Poor kid," Samantha said. No wonder the boy was a brat. He was starved for attention from an overworked father and an absent mother.

Birdie nodded. "It doesn't help that people have seen Nancy in the city at restaurants and such with other men. She always seems to have more cash than a sheriff's wife should. People have said some nasty things."

"I'll bet." When Samantha was single and pregnant with Audie, some of that degrading talk had slipped around to her ears.

"Yes," Birdie said, "I imagine you know."

Unexpected tears whelmed up in Samantha's eyes. She nodded.

Birdie moved to the chair next to her and wrapped her arms around her. "It must have been bad, but you're safe now. We're not going to let anything else happen to you. The Becks'll see to that."

"But ... but ... I can't stay. What if ...?" She held back the sobs, but the tears continued to flow. She couldn't put words to the scars left by Cody's instability and her own drug use. What if her past went beyond haunting her? What if Cody really was determined to see his daughter?

She had to leave if he ever came close. She was not going to let him get near Audie and open her up to the crazy world of addiction.

"Whatever it is," Birdie said, "we can handle it. This family is tough. I'd bet my money on these five kids any day. My only complaint is they are all taking far too long to get married and produce a new generation."

Samantha chuckled through her tears. "I suppose I'm part of your grand scheme."

"You certainly are, my dear. I couldn't pick anyone more suited for Jarod if God Almighty placed her right in front of me."

Samantha's laugh broke the remainder of her self-pity.

"Well, I don't know if you are right about that, but to answer your original question, we had a great time at dinner."

Birdie patted her hand. "Keep up the good work."

"Am I interrupting something?" Jarod asked, leaning against the doorjamb.

"No, no, it's okay." Samantha swiped at her eyes as she looked at him.

He took a step toward her, a slight frown on his face.

Audie came barreling out of Birdie's sitting room. "Now, Jarod? Now?"

Samantha smiled at them both, peace erasing the angst that had possessed her moments earlier. Maybe, just maybe, her life would work out for once.

"Sure," Jarod said with a final glance at Samantha. "Let's see what Misty is doing."

Audie pounded to the mud room. Moments later she returned, her coat on but askew, her hat draped carelessly over one side of her head. Her mittens were still stuffed in her pockets. At least one of them was. The other was on the floor a few feet behind her.

Jarod shook his head. Scooping up the errant mitten, he crouched in front of Audie, adjusted her coat and hat, and handed her the mittens. "Put them on."

He was so good for her daughter.

"Coming, Samantha?" he asked, stepping into the mudroom. "Uh-huh."

He brought her coat to her and helped her into it, a momentary flicker of his fingers across her back. So very close. All she had to do was turn around and ...

Birdie cleared her throat.

That woman did have second sight.

The cool, dry air sucked moisture from her skin as she followed Audie and Jarod outside, her daughter animatedly keeping up a stream-of-consciousness, one-sided conversation with him. Samantha pulled her phone from her pocket and snapped a picture of the two of them framed against the red barn, blue sky, and white snow. Even without the photo, it was a memory she'd have forever, the tall man listening intently to the little girl on a beautiful Montana day.

She caught up with them at the corral, where Misty still pranced around, showing off. Jarod and Audie stepped through the railings.

Samantha's throat closed.

What if ...?

As if sensing her fear, Jarod looked over and smiled. "She'll be okay." He handed Audie a baggie of sliced apples, then walked back to the railing.

"But she's so small and the horse is so big," Samantha said.

"Your daughter knows how to handle herself around Misty, and Misty trusts her. They're a good combination. I can't wait to teach her how to rope. She'll be a valuable assistant."

"Rope? Audie's not a cowgirl."

"Why not?"

"Because ... well, we're going to move to a city where she has more opportunity. And I don't even know if they'll offer me a job for another year. I told you that, remember?"

"Jury's still out on that one," he said with a grin.

"I don't think so."

"Okay, then. You and I make a little wager. You get hired on for next year, I get to teach her how to rope."

"And if I don't?"

"Then I guess she won't learn to rope from me." He stuck out his hand.

"You're crazy."

"Like a fox. C'mon." He wiggled his fingers.

What did it matter? It was a cheap way to provide fun for her daughter.

She shook his hand. "Deal."

"Good. Now my next challenge is to get you on a horse."

"That's not happening."

"Uh-huh." He leaned against the railing and watched Audie. "CJ said she told you about the mineral rights and why we hired a PI."

"Yes, why? Is there something wrong with the books? I got them all straight before Thanksgiving, remember?"

"And said you'd come back in December to make sure I hadn't messed them up again." He chuckled and shook his head. "Books are fine. But something weird happened. The PI up and quit on us."

"Any reason?"

"Not really. He said he had a conflict of interest. We just can't figure out how a PI in the Midwest would have a conflict of interest with us."

"Who recommended him?"

"Cassandra."

"Oh, what a tangled web we weave," she said.

"When first we practice to deceive. Shakespeare."

"Sir Walter Scott," she corrected. "I'm amazed you know that."

"I did finish high school, you know." A little bit of irritation undercut his tone. "And I still read. It's numbers I mess up."

"I didn't mean it that way." She allowed her own tone to get huffy.

He looked at her sharply, then gave her a long, slow smile. "Shall we kiss and make up?"

"Good thing you're on the other side of the rail." She grinned back.

"That can be changed." He bent as if to slip right through.

"No, no, that's fine. Stay there." The tension left her shoulders a little more. "So what is it you know about that other branch of the family? CJ said something about Alice, but that's all I remember."

"We know Alice grew up and graduated from high school, but the guy said he couldn't find anything else."

"Or didn't tell you what he'd found," she said.

"He wouldn't do that, would he?"

"I guess it would depend on how conflicted he was," she said.

"You sure do take a dim view of humanity."

"I've been well-schooled," she said, but shrugged to try to lighten the statement. What her convict father had started, she'd finally realized, Cody had put the finishing touches on. "You know Cassandra. You could come right out and ask her if she stopped the PI from going forward."

"I'd rather not stir that hornet's nest. CJ is looking for a new PI. Besides, I need to have a sit-down with this Dave Brockman about our mutual fence."

"The cut wires you told me about last night?"

"Yes." He paused for a few seconds and stared out at the big sky. "There's something about that guy I just don't trust. I can't quite put my finger on it." He shrugged. "Maybe it's because he's with Cassandra. Maybe it's his aftershave."

"His aftershave?"

"Yeah, some heavy, woodsy smell. Reminds me of hippies and tie-dye."

"Sandalwood."

"If you say so."

"I do."

Audie walked over to them, plastic bag dangling from her fingers, Misty following a few feet behind like a faithful dog. "She was hungry." Audie looked accusingly at Jarod. "You aren't feeding her enough."

He laughed. "Misty knows a good thing when she sees it. She eats plenty. But it's not nearly as tasty as anything you feed her."

Misty nudged the little girl with her nose.

"Stop that, silly!" Audie stroked the horse. "I can't wait to ride her again. I wish I could do it in the winter. Do the horses forget?"

"No. Horses are pretty smart. Someday I'll have a place where you can ride in the winter."

"Can I help you build it? I'm strong!" She flexed her bicep like a cartoon character.

"Sure, sweetheart." Jarod's voice softened. "When I'm ready you can help build it." He looked at Samantha. "Your mom can help, too."

She wanted to protest, remind him they were leaving, that they couldn't get that entangled with the life on Choteau Ranch, but she stayed silent. Audie wouldn't understand.

She wasn't sure she understood it herself.

"Say," he said. "Misty's stall could use some cleaning out. It's called mucking. Want to help with that?"

"Sure! Hear that, Misty? I'm going to clean your room!"

"Wish I could get her to clean her own room with that much enthusiasm," Samantha said to Jarod.

"I've got a job for you, too," he said, "if you're willing to help out while you wait."

Physical labor was great for blowing off steam. She may as well. "Okay."

"Good," he said. To her surprise, he took her hand, Audie's too, and they walked to the barn together.

Once they were finished with the chores, they returned to the main house to warm up. Dylan and CJ were still sitting at the dining room table, heads together, photos and paintings scattered all over the table.

"What's this?" Audie asked as she climbed on a chair like she lived in the place.

"Well," CJ said, "I take pictures, and Dylan paints them. See?" She pushed a photo and a painting toward Audie.

"I want to learn to paint," Audie declared. "Can you teach me?"

"Audie!"

Dylan laughed.

"I thought you were learning to ride," he said.

"I am. But we're on vacation. Too much snow."

"C'mon, Dylan." CJ gave him a light punch in his arm. "You can show the kid a few things. It'll prep you for having some of your own."

"I'm not having them any more than you are. That's Jarod's

job, remember?"

"They're still talking about me like I'm not here," Jarod said to Samantha with a shake of his head.

Her phone buzzed. A text message from her mother.

> Mom: This is your father. I borrowed your mother's phone. They've moved up the date of the surgery. Wanted to let you know. She didn't. I won.
> Samantha: Should I go back? When?
> Mom: I'll be here for her. I promise. It will be ok.

Her stomach churned with misgiving. She needed to be with her mother, not this stranger.

> Mom: They've made it for Jan. 7. She wouldn't let them do it until we rang in the new year together, no matter what.

If they moved up the surgery, they must be concerned.

> Samantha: Please keep me posted.
> Mom: I will.

"Bad news?" Jarod asked.

"My mother's surgery date has been moved up," she whispered, nodding toward Audie.

"Too bad. Are you going back?"

"It's not until January seventh. I hate taking time off and dragging Audie out of school right after we've come back. Of course, I could just stay after the holiday. That would make sense."

"Yes, it would."

"But it wouldn't look good on my record."

Jarod took her hand. "Be right back, guys." He led her to the study.

"They're going to understand, but even if they don't," he said, "you need to be with your mother." He released her hand and stared out the window for a few moments. The air in the room almost beat with the intensity of the emotion on his face.

He turned back to her.

"My mother was a sweet person," he said. "A little straitlaced at times, but she loved all of us, and caring for five kids equally can be a challenge. Especially when most of them are boys."

She smiled. From working in school, she couldn't even imagine having sons. Audie was more than enough.

"And I was a rebellious fourteen-year-old. I wanted to do rodeo. I'd escape the ranch whenever possible. I sassed back at my mother, and she loved me all the same. I didn't realize how sick she was."

"You couldn't know. You were just a kid."

He ran his thumb and index finger across his eyelids and pinched the bridge of his nose for a few seconds. "I should have known. I didn't realize until close to the end. After my father died, I was torn. There was the ranch to run; none of us knew how to do it. And all I wanted to do was head to the rodeo. It was my version of running away to the circus."

She touched his hand.

"CJ and Dylan pulled it together for a while, but it wasn't until close to the end of Mom's life I realized what a jerk I'd been." His voice choked. "She needed me here, no matter how much she said I should follow my heart. The rest of the family did, too." He looked down at her hand, reached around her waist, and pulled her close.

For a few moments they stood like that, the heat from his body melding with hers.

Then he released her. "Thanks." He looked directly at her face. "That's why you need to be there."

"But it's just surgery. They may be concerned, but no one is talking life-threatening."

"You don't know. You never know. Go. That way, you'll never have regrets."

She nodded.

A knock at the door, then CJ pushed it open. "I think Dylan's reaching his breaking point with Audie. He isn't used to her energy, poor boy."

"I should be heading back now, too," Samantha said.

"I'll walk you out to the car," Jarod said.

CJ looked back and forth at them. "It's like that, is it?"

"I don't know what you're talking about," Jarod said.

"Uh-huh." She grinned and left.

"Remember what I told you," he said.

"No regrets."

"No regrets."

Chapter 19

Jarod watched the car leave, slipping a little as it navigated the turn to head to the highway. Somehow he was going to have to get that woman tires before she broke her stubborn, prideful neck.

Johnson's place may have some tires; they were a fairly common type. He could definitely install them for her. Anything had to be better than the semi-bald ones she was using. Especially if she was driving to Billings in a few weeks. If anything happened to her or Audie ...

He headed to the house where CJ and Dylan were still sitting at the table, but now they were intently staring at one of Dylan's gizmos, a largish computer tablet.

"She isn't staying for dinner?" CJ asked.

"No, she's got her own life," he replied. "What are you guys doing?"

"Told you he had it bad," Dylan said. "Dinner last night, togetherness today."

"I don't have time. My training business is stalled."

"Well, giving a kid riding lessons on a horse you're planning on training and selling might be problematical," CJ said. "You're going to break the kid's heart."

He slumped back. That *had* been his plan. It would devastate Audie. She thought of Misty as hers. He shook his head. "Yep, I'm a dolt." He leaned forward and propped his elbows on the table. "Okay, you're the brainy ones in the family. What am I supposed to do now?"

"That's good," Dylan said. "You admit you have a problem. That's the first step in the road to recovery."

"You're not helping," CJ said.

The mudroom door thumped open.

"Get your dirty boots off my floor," Birdie said in the other room.

"Sorry," Nick said in reply.

CJ's face softened as she looked toward the kitchen.

Was that what love looked like?

Nick appeared a few minutes later, a plate of crackers, cheese, and sausage slices in his hand. "Birdie thought you needed brain food." He leaned over and kissed CJ. "Hi, honey. Keeping your brothers in line?"

She shook her head. "It's a losing battle."

"So what world problem are we solving today?" Nick asked.

"Jarod's business—and our PI quitting," CJ said.

"What's wrong with the business?" Nick asked Jarod.

"Well, my helpful siblings just pointed out that if I train Misty and sell her, I'm going to break Audie's heart."

"Good point. Sounds like you need another horse. Fortunately, I may be able to help in that department. I was trying to find another trail horse and found a guy over by Kalispell who's closing down his ranch and moving back to where—in his words—there isn't so goddam much snow."

The rest laughed.

"Anyway, he's got some young horses there, not trained for much beyond riding but not set in their ways yet, either."

"When's he selling them?"

"As soon as he can, so the prices are rock bottom. I'll look it up and send you the info."

"Thanks, that's great."

"There," Dylan said, pointing a finger at Jarod. He looked back at Nick. "Next problem. Jarod needs an indoor rink, and he's too chicken to ask for a loan."

"I offered—" CJ began.

Nick shook his head. "Never borrow from family members; you know better than that. What's your bank?"

"First."

"Good. That's my bank, too. Let's go down there Monday morning and talk to a loan officer."

Jarod hesitated. It was a big commitment. If it didn't work, where would he get the money to pay it off?

"Look, Jarod," CJ said, putting her hand on his arm. "We've got your back. You're the one who's been handling everything for a long time, with Dylan's help, but you took on the responsibility of our home. You've done a great job. Now it's time to take care of yourself and your future."

"This ranch is my future."

Dylan nodded. "And we all hope you settle down and have lots of little rug rats to repopulate it. But you gave up your dream once, and none of us want to see you do that again."

"Here! Here!" Birdie said from the entryway.

His heart filled with gratitude. They were right; it was time for him to start taking some of his own advice: stop being so stubborn and accept help.

"Okay, okay. I get it. I'll go with Nick Monday morning, and I'll call the guy about the horses." Maybe he could go the following Saturday and take Samantha and Audie with him. He smiled, caught himself, and said, "Now that everyone is done dissecting me, what are we going to do about the PI?"

"Well, I'm thinking I could do some of the work with CJ's help," Dylan said. "With winter here, there's a bit more time. CJ's going to find someone for boots on the ground in case we need it, but I'm betting we can find out just as much by internet and phone, without paying a hefty fee."

"I'm still bothered by the fact he up and quit for no reason," Jarod said.

"Me, too." CJ gathered up the photos she'd laid out on the table earlier. "Do you suppose Cassandra had a hand in it?"

"Hard to tell," he said. "I know I went out with her—sorta. It was never my intention. She just kind of manipulated me into it. I always wondered what her real purpose was. Now she's hanging around with some Dave guy."

"Brockman," CJ said. "Wears too much sandalwood aftershave?"

"That's him."

"He owns the land where the fence was cut. Dylan, want to see if we can meet with him this week?"

"Sounds good."

His unease had disappeared. He had a way forward. They'd work together for the ranch and each other.

"Now, clear out of here so I can set the table for supper," Birdie commanded.

"Good idea," Nick said. "We need to pick up Trevor from his friend's and get him back to do his chores."

"How's he doing?" Jarod asked. "With school and everything."

"As well as any teenager can do. Grace is finally cooperating more, and we've got a united front where his behavior is concerned. Sending him to the photography program in Missoula was a genius move. He got out on his own, but there was a ton of work to do and some good supervision."

"Good to hear."

There was a flurry as everyone left, Dylan going back to his cabin and paint. He'd make something in his tiny kitchen when he was hungry.

Birdie looked at Jarod. "Mind if we skip the formality tonight?" she asked.

"No problem. I'll grab a sandwich."

"There's meatloaf cooking," she said with a smile. "And there's potatoes in the fridge for reheating."

"That'll do," he said. "Thanks for everything." He gently hugged the housekeeper, the best surrogate mother he could have ever had.

He grabbed a beer, settled into his favorite chair, and turned on the television. In some ways, it was pleasant to have the house almost all to himself. He could quietly get buzzed and ask God for forgiveness when he went to church in the morning.

Where he'd run into Samantha.

Would Audie's father really try to track her down? And what could he do if he did? Choteau protected its own, and she was now one of them. If need be, he'd hire Cassandra to be her advocate in family court. No matter what else she might be, she was a fine family attorney. Rumors were, no one who went up against her won.

"Meatloaf's done." Birdie stood in the doorway. "You look like you have the weight of the world on your shoulders."

"Just thinking."

She waited for a second, nodded, and left the room, apparently deciding he needed the time to himself.

He pulled up a streaming service. *Longmire* would do nicely tonight. He'd seen the series several times, but there was something about the crusty lawman that appealed. If he could have a relationship, so could Jarod. He just needed to find the right woman.

The problem was, he already had—maybe.

Pausing the show, he pulled himself out of the chair and went to fix himself a plate. Nothing beat meat and potatoes, but he added a spoonful of green beans to satisfy the inner critic who wanted him to eat more healthily.

She sounded an awful lot like Birdie.

He propped his feet on the ottoman and settled the plate in his lap. Starting the show, he dug into the food, expecting to get lost in the wilds of Wyoming.

It didn't work.

Maybe if he asked Samantha out again, she'd relax a little more and let go of the need to be frightened. But these were frightening times. He knew what a mother with cancer did to a child, no matter how old that child was. And the reappearance of a father she didn't really know couldn't be helpful. Plus a relatively new job, pushback from the local sheriff, and an unknown threat from her past would stress out anyone.

Was dating her helping or hurting her peace of mind?

He'd call the horse farm in Kalispell tomorrow to set up an appointment. Audie would be excited. A smile came involuntarily to his face. He loved that kid. She fit into his life like a jigsaw piece he didn't know was missing.

And Samantha? Where did she fit? Something a lot more than a jigsaw puzzle piece. If they didn't stay, one thing had become clear to him: he was long past ready for a relationship, and he'd have to pursue it more actively than he had in the past.

He forced his attention back to the show where Longmire was entering the Red Pony, a bar owned by his wise Cheyenne friend, Henry. That's what he needed, a wise friend. Problem was, he didn't really have any. Lots of acquaintances to say hi to and nod to at church, but he'd pretty much become a loner after high school. At first he blamed it on the ranch, but lately he'd realized he'd pulled into himself and never escaped.

There were others now to help. He didn't have to do it all by himself. All he needed to do was let go.

And let God.

Could he? Well, he could try. He may have skipped the finals in Vegas, but there was always another rodeo. Time for him to get back out there and make his training services known. It went against every instinct he had, but it was time to step back out into the world.

# # #

When Samantha stepped into the church, she thought more than a few young women looked in her direction then looked away. Or was she imagining things?

"We saved a seat for you," Jarod said, gently touching her back to guide her to the pew where Birdie was on her knees deep in prayer.

Carefully, she slid in next to the woman, sat, and bowed her head.

Dear God, what am I doing with this man? I don't want to hurt him ... or Audie. Or myself. Please guide me. Amen.

She shot a glance at Jarod from under her eyelashes, but his attention was on a pew closer to the front. His eyes were narrowed and his lips almost in a frown. She followed his gaze.

Cassandra. She'd know that blond hair anywhere. And it looked like the man who'd been with her Friday night. No wonder everyone was looking; it was a situation made for small-town gossip: the exes both sitting with other people. Would there be fireworks or civility? Oversharing or frost?

She had to bite her lip to keep from laughing. There was a movement next to her, and Birdie sat up.

"What's so funny?" Birdie hissed at her.

"Nothing I can explain right now," she whispered back.

"Well, I hope you can after church."

Sonorous chords played on the small organ, and everyone stood.

She went through the motions of the service, but her concentration was disturbed by the presence of the man next to her. Like most churches during December, the small building was getting close to maximum occupancy as people arrived for one of the two major church holidays. Personal space between bodies wasn't to be had.

Having the soft timber of Jarod's voice repeat the same words and sing the same hymns was far too intimate an experience. She needed separation. She'd given herself over to a man before and look how that turned out.

But this is different, a still small voice seemed to say. *He's not trying to manipulate you into his bed. He's just seeing what's between the two of you.*

Was she trying to keep the upper hand because she didn't know how else to behave? Was it the only other decision she could make besides caving to someone else's demands? If she let herself get involved, would she give up who she was to please the other person like she had with Cody?

The Becks may have their painful past and secrets, but they seemed to be there for each other, something she'd never had growing up. Her mother was always working and never stood up for herself, much less Samantha. Cody had taken advantage of her lonely teenage self. No wonder she didn't know how to have a healthy relationship.

But what if she dug down deep? Would she discover a well of

courage she didn't know she had?

Belatedly, she realized everyone was standing up. "Amen," she chorused with everyone else. The service was over, and she hadn't heard a word of it.

Once they shook hands with the minister, Jarod took her hand and they walked with Birdie to the community room. The warmth of his grip comforted her, but she could almost hear the tongues clacking and wagging. Oh, she and Jarod were making gossip fodder this morning!

Audie ran over with a plate full of cookies. "Look, they have Christmas cookies, Jarod! I brought some for you." She glanced at Samantha and Birdie. "You can have some, too."

Samantha laughed at the dismissal of them as bystanders. Jarod had certainly captured her daughter's heart. How could she rip her away from this? Was the best education system in the world better than the love and safety of family?

Jarod released her hand and made a big deal out of selecting a cookie. "Now let Mommy and Birdie pick theirs," he said and straightened, his face set in a neutral expression.

"Hello, Jarod," Cassandra said. "Samantha, Birdie." She nodded at each of them. "I don't think you two have met Dave Brockman. He's bought some land for a summer place and is thinking of making it a permanent move."

"Nice to meet you." The man held out his hand, a faint whiff of sandalwood accompanying it.

She and Birdie took turns shaking it.

Audie checked out the new adults, turned on her heel, and took her plate to join the other children at the kids' table, where Beth was patiently pouring juice into Dixie cups.

That girl was a saint.

"What made you pick Choteau of all places?" Birdie asked.

"I knew Cassandra was here," he said with a smile as he looked over at the lawyer. "We'd met in college and again years later at a conference in Chicago. I was a hedge fund manager. I still have a few clients, but there's no need to stay on the hamster wheel if you don't have to."

"How will you work from here?" Samantha asked.

"My clients are all over the states, from Nashville to Hawaii," he said. "Internet and phone works here as well as anywhere else. It's beautiful country, with wonderful people." He glanced at Cassandra again.

Oh. He had a thing for the blonde. Good luck with that.

"Anyway," Cassandra said, "he's looking to join a church, become part of the community, so I thought I'd bring him here. It's been so long since I've come. I'm a really bad churchgoer." She looked at Jarod as if he had the power to absolve her of such a crime.

He cleared his throat.

"Do you have any previous affiliation?" Birdie asked. "I mean, what were you raised?"

"My parents never had time for church," he said. "I think they were married in a Presbyterian church. I don't really have a faith. I just figure it's a good way to become involved in a community. Most everyone in a town like this goes to church, don't they?" He smiled again, his teeth perfectly white against a lingering tan created in some warmer place.

He was nothing like Cody, yet every sentence he spoke reverberated with some hidden meaning.

"Are you going back to Billings for the holidays?" Cassandra asked her. "That's where you're from, isn't it?"

"Yes. My mother is expecting us."

"I'm sure she'll be happy to see you and your daughter—Audie, isn't it?"

"I'm sure she will."

"I see." She put her hand on Jarod's arm. "What are you doing for the holidays? Maybe we could have coffee, for old times' sake."

Dave Brockman's smile no longer showed those bright teeth.

"I doubt I'll have time," Jarod said, stepping back and forcing her to drop her hand. "However, Dave, my brother Dylan and I would like to get together with you sometime this week if possible. We want to talk about the boundary between our properties."

"Why? Is there something wrong?"

"There might be; we're not sure. We just want to show you what we found and talk it over with you."

"Do I need my lawyer?" Dave said with a glance at Cassandra.

"Not at all. Just a friendly discussion," Jarod said. "This isn't the time or place."

Dave's shoulders relaxed a little. "Sure. Why don't you come out to my place?" He checked his phone. "Say Tuesday afternoon around three? Market'll be closed by then."

"Sounds good," Jarod said.

They shook hands. Dave and Cassandra drifted off to chat with the minister.

"I wouldn't trust that man as far as I could throw him," Birdie said.

"Wouldn't be very far," Jarod said with a faint smile.

"Exactly."

A hubbub erupted at the kids' table, and Audie stood, her chair crashing behind her. Her little fists were clenched by her side as she glared at the girl across from her. Another mother rushed the table along with Samantha.

Jarod must have started after her because Birdie said, "Let her handle this. If a father appears, then you can go to the rescue."

He grumbled but kept a close eye on the situation.

"What happened, sweetie?" Samantha crouched beside her daughter.

"She said I was weird."

"You are," the other girl said. "Nobody likes you."

God, why were little girls so capable of being so mean?

"Hannah!" her mother said, her mouth open in horror. She looked at Samantha. "I'm so sorry."

Samantha wasn't going to tell her it was okay. The sooner this type of thing was stopped, the better for everyone. Bullying only got worse the older someone got.

"Hannah, you apologize. Right now."

"But, Mommy, you said she was different. I'm just telling the truth. Aren't I supposed to tell the truth?"

Samantha drew herself up to her full height, crossed her arms, and glared at the woman.

Hannah's mother turned a satisfying reddish hue. As the old song went, you had to be taught to hate and fear.

"My daughter is unique," Samantha said, attacking every word crisply. "She is smart but looks at things a little differently than most people. And she's a better kid for it."

"She's also got one of the kindest, most generous hearts of any eight-year-old I've ever met." Jarod crouched next to Audie.

Samantha's muscles tightened further.

"You know what you do when people are mean to you?" he asked Audie.

"Hit them?" Audie suggested.

He shook his head and tried to hide the smile on his face.

"You ignore them." He moved in closer and said in a loud whisper, "You see, what they don't understand is, when they say something mean, they're really talking about themselves."

"They don't know it?"

"Nope, they don't."

A slow smile grew on her face, and she looked at the little girl on the other side of the table before turning back at Jarod. "I see what you mean," she said.

"Good. Now, I have a great idea. Why don't you and your mommy come to our house for Sunday dinner? Birdie baked a big chocolate cake last night. Would you like some of that?"

"Oh yes."

Jarod stood and nodded at the woman and her daughter. "Ma'am," he said and tipped his head before taking Audie's hand and reaching for Samantha's.

She kept her arms crossed.

He glanced at her, a frown ridging his eyebrows. "What's wrong?"

"Not here," she said through clenched teeth. She followed them to the coat rack where he helped Audie put on her mittens, then slid on his own coat.

Samantha remained silent as he walked them to her car, but her movements were jerky and stiff. She could stand on her own two feet; she'd proved that long ago.

"What's the matter?" Jarod asked once Audie was safely settled in the car.

"I can fight my own battles," she said.

"I didn't mean ... I was just trying to help."

"Well, don't. Not unless I ask for it. And speaking of asking, I'm not sure giving chocolate cake to comfort a kid is the right approach."

"Sorry," he said, lifting his hands up as if to hold her, then letting them fall. "This is new to me. I've never been a parent. I guess ... I guess I overstepped my bounds."

He had only been trying to do the right thing. "Apology accepted."

"Then you'll come out?" His smile was hopeful.

She'd have a rebellious child on her hands if she said no now. "We'll come."

"I'm glad my stupidity didn't get in the way of chocolate cake," he said, the grin on his face expanding. "Be careful driving to our place," he said. "It's slick in spots."

"Can I bring anything?" She opened the driver's side door.

A blast of wind pushed at her skirt, and she shivered.

"Get in," he said, holding the door against the force of the gale moving down from the north.

She looked at the dark clouds stampeding overhead. "Maybe

we shouldn't come."

"It's not supposed to hit until tonight," he said, "according to Birdie, anyway. She's glued to The Weather Channel. But we'll keep an eye out. Worse comes to worse, I can take you back tonight in the truck. In fact ..." His gaze went to her front tires.

They were going to need to be replaced soon. If only everything weren't so expensive.

"Why don't you head home?" he said. "I'll drop Birdie back at the ranch and come get you. That way, I don't have to worry about you navigating the driveway."

"Won't that be a lot of driving?"

He shrugged. "No big deal. See you in a bit."

Shutting the door, he walked over to his truck where Birdie waited in the passenger seat. She gave a wave as Samantha pulled out.

She should bring something. Her mother had taught her never to visit someone empty-handed. Besides, it evened the scales a bit. But it was Sunday and pretty much everything was closed ... except the ice cream place. They'd advertised they would be open until December 30.

Vanilla ice cream would go perfectly with chocolate cake, and she could definitely get there and back before Jarod made the round trip to the ranch.

"Where are we going?" Audie asked.

"Picking up ice cream to take to Jarod's house."

"Oh, good. It'll be like a birthday party."

"Uh-huh." As long as she didn't expect a present, it would be fine.

The ice cream shop was all spruced up in red and green garlands and sparkling lights. The servers had on elf hats, and Christmas music tumbled from speakers in the corner. It was a fairyland of joy.

Samantha placed her order, and while the server went to get it from the main freezer, an older woman peered over the counter at Audie. "I need a taster," she said.

"Oh, I'm a good taster," she replied.

"I knew you would be. I can tell by looking. Here. Let me know what you think." She handed Audie a spoon with vanilla ice cream with a red and green swirl.

With a serious expression, her daughter touched it with the tip of her tongue, took a small bite, and moved it around her mouth, like a wine connoisseur. Then she handed the spoon back to the lady.

"Too minty," she declared.

The woman nodded. "Exactly what I was thinking. Thank you so much for your help."

"You're welcome."

The woman smiled at Samantha then disappeared into the back.

"She was nice," Audie said. "I like it here."

"Me, too, sweetie."

"I want to stay here forever and ever."

Me too.

"It depends on the school board," she said. "If they decide I'm a bad teacher, they'll find someone else." The young woman returned with their ice cream, and Samantha paid her.

"But you're a good teacher, Mommy. They'll keep you. You're a good Mommy, too." Audie smiled up at her.

Samantha pulled her tight and kissed the top of her head. All was right with the world.

Chapter 20

"Ready?" Jarod asked when Samantha opened the door.

"Almost. We're looking for a boot."

"Ahh." He grinned.

Audie dashed into the room. "Here it is!" She waved a colorful snow boot around. "It was in the laundry basket. It needs to be washed."

"Logical," Jarod said.

"Designed to drive parents crazy," Samantha said.

"That, too."

They shared a laugh. Good, she must have forgiven him for his earlier gaffe. Birdie had been right. He should have stayed out of it.

Samantha picked up a sack from a nearby table.

"What's that?"

"Vanilla ice cream."

"Perfect with chocolate cake."

"I thought so."

He opened the door and let them walk in front of him to the truck. Once they were all settled with Audie in the back seat, he put the vehicle in gear and slowly moved away from the curb. The side streets were plowed last, if at all, but once they got to the highway, the pavement would be dry.

"What do you think about Dave Brockman?" he asked Samantha.

"He's certainly smooth. I think he's also got a thing for Cassandra that isn't returned."

"That would require her to be aware of people out of her own orbit."

"Mr. Beck, that was nasty," she said with a smile.

"Yeah. But true."

"Are you saying bad things about someone?" Audie asked.

"Gotcha," Samantha said.

"I'm afraid I was."

"You shouldn't do that. It could hurt people's feelings."

He was being lectured by an eight-year-old.

"You're right. I'll try to do better."

"It's okay. Nobody is perfect. I keep telling Mommy that, but I don't think she believes me."

"I do too," Samantha protested.

"Uh-huh."

Time to change the subject. "I need to look at a new horse," he said. "Nick said there are some for sale over in Kalispell. If I can make arrangements to see him next Saturday, would you like to go with me?"

"Oh, yes!" Audie said. "Misty needs a friend. I could help pick her out."

Samantha frowned. "I'm not sure that's a good idea. It's a long way. Over the mountains."

"Only a few hours each way," he said. "The government does a good job keeping the roads cleared. We wouldn't go in a blizzard, of course. We could have a nice lunch in Kalispell."

"Please, Mommy? I'll clean my room before we go."

The way to every mother's heart.

"I'll think about it."

"That doesn't mean no," Audie informed him. "It's maybe."

"Good to know," he said as he turned down the drive to the ranch.

"It means I'll think about it," Samantha restated.

He refrained from speaking as he pulled around the side of the ranch where a path had been cleared to the mudroom door. Once snow arrived, Birdie issued her annual edict: this door only.

"Samantha brought ice cream for the cake," he called out after they entered the house.

"Wonderful!" Birdie said. "Put it in the freezer out there, would you?"

He did as instructed, hung up their coats, and led Samantha and Audie into the kitchen.

"Can I help?" Samantha asked.

"Got it. I'll gladly turn over the cleanup when we're done eating, though."

"Okay."

"I'll help with that," Jarod said.

"The others are in the living room."

"Figured." He looked at Samantha. "Beer? Wine?"

"A beer will be fine."

He grabbed two from the fridge, and they headed out of the kitchen. Audie was already halfway on Dylan's lap, distracting him from the game on television while she begged him for drawing lessons.

"How was church?" CJ asked.

"It had its moments," he said. He described in vague terms what had happened with Audie.

"Some people have no clue," CJ said. "Sorry that happened."

"It's not the first time," Samantha said. "In first grade, there was a horrible little girl who picked on her. It never let up. We had to transfer Audie to a different school."

Dylan shook his head. "Whatever happened to tolerance?"

"Not sure," Nick chimed in. "It does seem to be in short supply these days."

Trevor came in from the dining room, his flushed cheeks indicating he'd come in from the outside. A camera hung from his neck.

"Your horse is cool," he told Jarod. "I got a lot of nice shots of him against the snow."

"Let's see," CJ said. He sat next to her, and the two bent their heads over the back of the camera as she flipped through the shots.

"Who are you?" Audie demanded to know as she stood in front of them.

"Who are you?" Trevor replied with a grin.

"I'm Audie. I belong to Mommy and Jarod."

His insides went wonky, and he blinked back a few tears. Samantha shifted beside him. How would she take that pronouncement?

"I'm Trevor. I belong to my dad and CJ."

"We could be pretend cousins," she announced. "I've never had a cousin."

"Me neither. Let's see if we can get everybody to marry each other and then we can be for real cousins."

Audie nodded solemnly. "Okay." Then she walked to them and sat next to Samantha on the couch. Every eye in the room stared at him, and every set of lips was grinning.

"Come and get it," Birdie sang out.

He let out a breath of air as everyone stirred and got up. The hubbub of getting food on the table, saying grace, and serving each other distracted them from the agreement between Audie and Trevor.

Still, something was making his spine itch. Was it because the more he tried to get close to Samantha, the more he seemed to put his foot in it? Maybe he should find someone without a child to date.

No. Unless he was forced to, he didn't want to give up on them. Navigating these waters was trying, but that wasn't what was bothering him; he was sure of that. More like something was coming, something bad.

"I have some news," CJ said when they'd all been served. "Max, my old boss at the agency, was contacted by someone who'd seen that picture I took of the girl in Great Falls." She looked at Samantha. "I happened to grab a shot of a girl who was a victim of"—she glanced at Audie—"some bad men, if you get my drift."

"I do," Samantha said. "It's a horrible situation."

Fortunately, Trevor was keeping Audie entertained.

"Anyway, a national magazine is doing an article on how the situation plays out across a number of states where it's the heaviest. They want me to take the photos. It's an amazing opportunity."

"Not one I'd like to take part in. Those poor, poor girls. But I guess after being in war, that stuff doesn't affect you as much."

CJ shook her head. "It still gets to me. I've learned how to compartmentalize. My photos make a difference, and that's what matters to me." There was an edge to her voice.

Great. All he needed was a disagreement between the two women.

Samantha smiled. "I know you do. I've seen some of your work. I just meant it's something I wouldn't be brave enough to do." Her words were gentle with the same tone he'd use to calm a horse.

CJ nodded. His sister was still a little miffed but nothing that couldn't be healed with a little time.

"How long will you be gone?" he asked.

"A month. I leave right after the new year."

"And what are you going to do without her?" Dylan asked Nick. With a wicked grin, he added, "We could have some fun times."

"Thanks, but no thanks," Nick said. "I'm going to take over my parents' store for a few months. Give them a chance to go south and get warm."

"Lucky them," Birdie said. "The older I get, the more this chill seems to affect me."

Three heads turned abruptly as he, Dylan, and CJ looked at Birdie.

She waved her hand. "Oh, stop it. Until one of you gets married, moves into this old house, and starts producing the next generation, I'm not going anywhere."

Three sets of shoulder blades dropped an inch.

Samantha gave a low chuckle.

"Is it time for chocolate cake yet?" Audie asked.

And with that, the rest of them joined the laughter.

"Not quite yet, young lady," Birdie admonished. "You need to be part of the clean plate club first."

"The what?"

"Trevor, show her how it's done."

The teenager swept up the last bit of meat and potatoes and pointed to his plate. "That, little cousin, is how it's done."

He and Samantha were in so much trouble. Audie was bonding with the family. What would happen if her mother took her away?

Everyone finished their plates to Birdie's satisfaction. Plates were cleared and ice-cream-topped cake slices delivered. He'd just picked up his fork to dive in when the ranch phone rang.

"Excuse me." He strode to the office.

"Choteau Ranch," he said. "Jarod speaking."

"Is this Jarod Beck?" the voice on the other end asked.

"Yes."

"This is Sargent Chaistain, sir. I have some news about your brother, Cameron Beck. He listed you as next of kin."

Jarod sagged against the desk. Weren't they supposed to come to your door if someone died?

"Your brother's unit was hit by the enemy," Sargent Chaistain continued. "He survived, but he has serious injuries. We are transporting him to our hospital in Germany where he'll undergo surgery."

"Where? One of us will get there."

"Sargent Beck specifically asked that no one from his family come to Germany." The serviceman cleared his throat. "He said he needs to deal with his injuries first before he can handle family. I hope you understand, sir."

That sounded like Cameron.

"What are his injuries?"

"The most severe is in his left arm. The doctors aren't sure they can save it."

Jarod felt like he'd been sucker-punched in the gut. Losing a limb would destroy Cameron. No wonder he didn't want anyone to see him.

"Would you please tell my brother that I don't like it, but I understand. Also ..." He swallowed hard. "Also, that his family is here for him, all of us. Whatever he needs, we'll make it happen."

"Yes, sir. Thank you."

After Jarod hung up the phone, he stared out the window at the ranchland covered in snow. Like CJ, Cameron needed to come home. This was a healing place. He could do no better than to have family around to support him and push him when he needed it.

But what would it do to Jarod's plans?

He needed to keep going. If he gave it all up to help Cameron, not only would he annoy his younger brother, but the rest of the family would kick him where the sun didn't shine. They'd made their point pretty strongly the other night.

He heaved himself off the desk and returned to the dining room. Silence descended as soon as he entered.

"That was the army," he said.

"They've found Cameron," CJ said without hope in her voice. "He's alive."

A little of the tension left the room.

"But he's badly injured," he added. "They're flying him to Germany."

"I've got a current passport. I'll get on the next plane," CJ said, half rising from her seat.

"He doesn't want us."

"Any of us?" Dylan asked.

Jarod shook his head.

"It must be bad," Nick said.

"Yeah." There was a tightness in Jarod's throat. "They're afraid he might lose his arm."

Dismay crossed Birdie's face. "Oh, God."

"I'm sorry," Samantha said, touching his hand gently. "It must be hard for you all to have to sit back and wait."

"Yep."

Dylan pushed back his chair. "I'm going back to my cabin. Thanks for supper, Birdie. I probably won't be back for the night." He picked up his plate and walked quietly to the kitchen. A minute later, the side door thudded.

"We'd better get going, too," Nick said. "I need to check in with my folks about a few things, and Trevor has a big project due for history before the holiday."

"I'm almost done," the teen protested.

"We haven't seen anything," CJ said. "Let's go, kiddo."

"Bye, Audie," Trevor said. "Nice to meet you, Samantha."

His sister and Nick were doing a good job with him. When Trevor had arrived in the spring, he'd been a little rough around the edges. But so had CJ.

Now they had to do the same for Cameron.

"Let me help with the dishes," Samantha said to Birdie.

The housekeeper shook her head. "My soul needs a little healing right now. Making order out of things will soothe me. You and Jarod go on with whatever you're doing."

They all took things into the kitchen.

"If you don't mind taking me home," Samantha said to him once they were done, "I need to get ready for school tomorrow, too."

He nodded. It wasn't the time for anything else.

Chapter 21

Jarod stared at the applications in front of him on the desk. Numbers. Why did bankers always need numbers to make them happy? He'd gotten two forms from the bank yesterday, hoping he could get it right on least one of them. Nick had suggested CJ review them before he turned them in.

On the whole, the banker had been encouraging. Jarod's credit rating was thin but good. He'd offered up a half dozen cows for collateral, and the banker chuckled, saying they didn't need it for a loan this small.

Jarod turned to the spreadsheet he'd put together listing expenses and expected income from his training business and set to work. Maybe Samantha would review it. He'd tried Johnson's salvage yard yesterday on the way home, but he hadn't had the right size tires for her car. Randy Johnson said he'd call around to see what he could find but wasn't making any promises.

If he couldn't find them, Jarod was going to have to haul them to Billings himself. No way was she driving all that way on those tires.

Numbers made him cantankerous.

He finished the first pass in time to grab himself a sandwich before he and Dylan were supposed to head over to Brockman's place. He hadn't seen his brother since Sunday. Dylan had been close to Cameron growing up and had never gotten past the fact that Cameron had enlisted in a war that seemed to have no end.

The sergeant had emailed Jarod saying Cameron had made it to Germany safely and the surgery was scheduled at the end of the week. He gave him a contact at the hospital to get updates and wished Cameron the best.

The doctor in Germany had been non-committal but told him Cameron was sedated and resting well. He would recover; it was only a matter of how well.

Jarod's chest was tight. He couldn't imagine his brother without a limb. Cameron had always been active, a star athlete in high school and almost as horse crazy as Jarod. He'd entered some of the same rodeos, the brothers competing head-to-head in roping events. He even eked out a win once in a while.

Jarod bowed his head.

Dear God, protect and keep my brother safe. Let him return home whole so we can help him heal. Show him a path forward if that isn't possible. Amen.

His spirit lightened a bit. He'd done all he could do. Time to tackle the next problem—a mysteriously cut fence.

# # #

Dylan was quiet as they drove the few miles north to the next turnoff. The road to Brockman's ranch house curved around the foothills, leading them to a secluded valley farther west than their own ranch house was located. The road was smooth and even, well-maintained even in bad conditions.

The house itself was polished logs and glass, the kind of home normally found among the rich and famous in Big Sky south of Bozeman. Two stories, it had an upper deck and three dormer windows that reflected the Rockies to the west.

"Why does a single man need that much house?" Dylan groused.

"Because he can," Jarod replied.

They clomped up on the porch, stamping their boots to get the snow off.

"Welcome, welcome," Dave Brockman said. "You're one of my first guests. This place was only finished right before the snow came."

"Nice house," Dylan said.

"You must be Dylan," Dave said. "Cassandra says you're quite the artist."

"Nice of her."

"C'mon in," Dave said, taking their jackets and gesturing toward the living room. "Anything to drink? Coffee, beer, water?"

"Coffee," Jarod said.

"Same for me," Dylan echoed.

"I'll be right back," Dave said.

The living room matched the outside of the house; polished, artistic wood furniture accompanied brand-new leather armchairs and a sofa. A thin, Navajo red rug stood out against gleaming stone floors. Jarod wandered to a bronze of a cowboy chasing a steer. The gold plate identified it as a Charles Russell.

Of course.

"Have a seat, gentlemen," Dave said as he returned with a tray of mugs, sugar and cream, and spoons.

Once the coffee ritual was complete, he asked, "How can I help you?"

Jarod described once again what they'd found.

"And you don't think it was someone trying to steal cattle?" Brockman asked.

"No sign of a truck, and that's how they do it these days. Plus, we're only missing one cow from up there. The rest are all accounted for."

"Well, if I see a stray animal, I'll be sure to call you," the man said with a grin.

"So you aren't missing any livestock," Jarod said, his neck muscles tight as he controlled his temper. Dave Brockman was treating this as a joke when it was life and death for a ranching family.

"Don't have any," he said. "Nor do I intend to. Half dozen horses when I find the right man to handle them. You interested?"

The man's gaze made him uncomfortable. As with Cassandra, it felt like there was a trick behind the question, one he couldn't see.

"I got enough on my plate right now, but thanks for the confidence," he said with an unnatural smile.

Dave nodded. "I'm not sure how I can help you fellas," he said.

"Did you collect all those rocks?" Dylan asked, pointing to a display Jarod hadn't noticed.

"About half," he said. "I'm an amateur geologist. The rest I purchased so I'd know what to look for."

"Silver, sapphires, copper. You certainly have varied tastes."

"No coal?" Jarod asked only half-seriously. Most of Montana's coal was found in the eastern part of the state.

"Coal's dying," Dave said. "It just doesn't know it yet."

"You going to look around here?" Dylan asked.

Dave looked at him sharply. "The land is for me to use and enjoy. Hiking, rock hunting, whatever. If I find something, I'll deal with it then. I've got the mineral rights."

Jarod could almost hear him say, *and you have no idea where yours are.*

"Well, I wish you luck. If you see any strangers on the land or find that stray cow, we'd appreciate knowing about it. Maybe once you get your horses, you can check the fence now and again, just to be neighborly, you know. It's what we do here." He gazed steadily at Brockman.

The man didn't look away, just nodded. "I'll do that."

Jarod stood. "Thanks for your time. And the coffee." He set the half-full mug back on the tray.

"Sure," Dave's voice was hearty. "Stop by any time, although I'm thinking about going down south for a few months. Haven't got enough antifreeze in my blood yet." His laugh was the kind of fake bonhomie salespeople displayed when they were afraid they'd lost a sale.

He and Dylan shook hands and left. As soon as the door closed behind them, they both rubbed the palms of their hands on their jeans. Dylan smirked at him.

"Get in the truck," Jarod said with a grin.

"He's a piece of work," Dylan said as they drove away. "Wonder what he's up to. Did you see all the books on mining on the shelf way in the back?"

"No, missed them, too," he said. "Could that be what this is about? Are there valuable deposits in the back?"

"Not a clue. That's Kaiden's department. But it sounds like the three of us should take a ride up there when the spring thaw gets here."

Jarod nodded, glad Dylan had the same misgivings he did.

# # #

The week had gone by fast, and Samantha was still debating whether or not going with Jarod to Kalispell was a good idea. It'd be really nice if a blizzard blew in. That would settle the matter without her having to make up an excuse.

He'd called to confirm Wednesday night, and they'd spent a half hour chatting about this and that. She'd given him a tentative yes.

So here she was, on a bright and clear December morning, ready to hop once again into a pickup truck and cross the divide to Kalispell. Audie was beside herself with joy.

"Ready, ladies?" Jarod asked when she answered the door.

"Yes! Yes!" Audie ran to the truck.

"I filled a Thermos with coffee," Samantha said.

"Thank you." He opened the passenger door. "Audie, why don't you sit in the back? There's a seat belt in the middle so you can see through the front window."

"Okay."

Once her daughter was settled, Jarod placed the Thermos on the floor in back, right next to another.

"Oh," Samantha said. "You already packed one."

He shook his head. "Birdie."

"Oh."

"It's okay. There can never be enough coffee."

He grinned and helped her to her seat. As soon as he was belted into the driver's side, they headed north. Once they passed the turnoff to Misty's old home, Samantha was in new territory. The prairies rolled relentlessly toward the mountains in the distance. Just north of Dupuyer, a metal sculpture appeared by the side of the road.

"What's that?" she asked.

"The beginning of the reservation. You've never seen it before?"

"No."

"Funny-looking horses," Audie commented. "Are those real Indians?"

"They were created by real Indians," Jarod said. "They're at all the entrances to the reservation."

"I've never been here before," Samantha said.

"Does that mean you've never been to Glacier, either?" Jarod asked.

"Nope. Nor Yellowstone. Mom always promised she'd take me, but work interfered or there wasn't enough money or something."

"We'll go through part of Glacier on the way to Kalispell, but we'll have to come back in the spring. Rent a cabin and explore. Or maybe trailer the horses up here and ride some of the trails."

"I don't ride," she reminded him.

"You will."

She didn't reply as she watched the miles slip by. Here and there an isolated house or trailer, often brightly painted, perched in the snow. Cattle and horses pawed through the snow or munched on hay that had been distributed for them. It could be anywhere in Montana, but it felt different. They were essentially in another country.

"I'd hate to be in law enforcement here," she said.

"Why's that?"

"Which US and state laws apply and which don't? And exactly how do each of them apply? Can they sell property to non-

Natives? Are there special restrictions? It's got to be confusing."

"Yeah, probably is. I've sold and bought cattle and feed from here, but that's about the only interaction I've had with reservation politics and law."

She turned it over in her mind. The same conundrums existed with the Crow and Cheyenne reservations near Billings, as well as the four other reservations in Montana that held other tribes.

Around a bend and down a hill, they came upon Browning, the largest town on the reservation. Jarod drove slowly through the middle of it, past the snow-drifted gas station, cement teepee, and a variety of stores in various states of boom or bust. A relatively new hotel and casino complex anchored the outskirts of town, where Jarod took a left and the truck climbed out of the valley.

She gasped at the ridge of sharp mountains lining the horizon.

"Neat, aren't they?" Jarod asked. "I love this view. It gets even better the closer we get."

"Audie, look," Samantha said. "Isn't that beautiful?"

"Is that where we're going?"

"We're going to go past them."

"I don't want to go that high." A tinge of fear crept into her voice.

"Oh, we won't go over the high mountains," Jarod said. "A long time ago, human beings figured out a way through the mountains that was pretty easy. Now we have a nice, smooth road to take us there."

"We'll be okay," Samantha added. "Jarod wouldn't take us anywhere dangerous."

The mountains did grow more magnificent the closer they got, looming over them as they crossed the cavern of the Two Medicine River and drove through the sleepy little town of East Glacier.

"About an hour to go," Jarod said. "How's everyone doing?"

"I need to go to the bathroom," Audie announced.

"Ah, yes. A good idea," he said. He turned down a small street that was barely paved, turned left again past a row of tired trailers. One more left, then finally back right to the main road to a spot they'd already passed. "Gas station is the best bet," he said, pulling into the wide lot. "Everybody out."

He was waiting in the store when she and Audie were ready.

"We have our coffee," he said. "Does she need anything?"

"Some juice would be a good idea," she said, moving toward the cold case. Apple. That would be best in case something spilled. As soon as she took it out, he reached for it.

"I'll get it," he said.

She clutched the chilled bottle. "I'd rather. You're doing enough for us already." She needed to hang on to some shred of independence.

He looked at her for a moment then nodded. "I'll get Audie set."

"Okay."

By the time she paid for the drink, her daughter was set and ready to go. There was an uneasy silence as they pulled away from the small town. Had she made a big deal out of nothing? She needed to keep the brakes on this relationship or whatever it was. They'd only known each other four months, and the future was unknown.

Her attention was snagged by the beauty around her. Streams ran through the ice and snow, still warm enough to move rapidly. Stark mountains lined the sky to the north, almost as if they were poking holes in that impossibly blue sky. A thrill entered her when they passed a sign announcing Glacier National Park.

"The goat lick is shut down for the season, but we'll have to take Audie down there," he said.

"What is it?" she asked.

"It's a huge salt deposit on the edge of the Middle Fork of the Flathead," he said. "Mountain goats love to lick at it. Sometimes there are dozens of them there."

"Must be amazing to see."

"It is. Choteau is such a perfect spot to live, not too far from a city, yet Glacier is practically in our back yard."

Was he trying to convince her to stay?

As they drove west, he continued his monologue. The town, such as it was, of West Glacier had some funky buildings that were supposed to be haunted, and the Middle Fork broadened to include most of the valley to their north. Sunlight sparkled from the ripples in the water and the snow lining the banks.

When they finally broke free from the mountains it was getting close to lunch time.

"What'll it be?" Jarod asked. "Hamburger, Italian, Chinese, pizza?"

"Pizza!" Audie called out from the back.

Jarod grinned. "I kinda figured that, but let's see what your mother thinks."

"I think that we can get pizza and hamburgers in town. Let's try something more exotic, like Chinese."

"Have I had Chinese?" Audie asked.

Eating out had not been much of an option in Billings—too expensive. "I think maybe when you were five or so. Grandma got a nice bonus at work and brought some Chinese food home. It came in little white cartons."

"Did I like it?"

"Yes."

"Okay. I don't remember, but okay to Chinese."

"Then Chinese it is."

Jarod drove into town and went north until the road broadened out. Big box stores of every stripe lined the two sides of the highway. He pulled into the parking lot of a chain Chinese place and managed to squeeze the big pickup between a wall and an SUV complete with a sticker family on its rear window.

She pulled on her coat and made sure Audie had hers but didn't worry too much about zipping up. The noonday sun made it feel like spring, and most of the pavement was wet with melting snow.

Once they'd ordered, Audie took off for the bathroom. Jarod paid before Samantha could stop him, and she fumed beside him while they waited for the order to be completed.

"Look," he said when they finally sat down with their food. Audie was slowly walking back, examining every poster as she came. "This isn't a big deal. You don't owe me anything. I invited you along because I enjoy your company and Audie's. When I do the inviting, I do the paying. I'm old-fashioned that way. Right now, we're friends enjoying a sunny day ride to see some horses. Okay?"

Was she making a big deal out of something that wasn't? He wasn't someone who kept a quid pro quo list like Cody had, but still it was time to set some boundaries.

"I appreciate it, but I want to be able to talk about it. You can't assume that I'll go along with every decision you make that concerns me and my daughter." She forced her body to stay calm, her expression neutral.

He considered her statement. "I understand what you mean, although I'm not trying to control you." He rubbed the bridge of his nose. "I'll give it my best shot, but my instinct is to do the right thing for the people I care about, and that includes you and Audie. I guess I'm used to handling things on my own."

"Me, too," she said. "But it's important that I maintain the right to make final decisions for us."

"Even about paying for Chinese?" he said with a slight smile.

"Even that."

"Then, Ms. Deveaux, may I purchase lunch for you and your lovely daughter?" He tilted his head to one side.

She'd made her point. "Yes, you may. And thank you very much." She smiled back at him.

"Good." He gazed at her, as if trying to determine if there were any other minefields he hadn't seen.

"Eggroll!" Audie said as she plopped down in the molded seat. "We get these in school sometimes." She snatched it up and proceeded to chomp down on it.

He laughed, and the tension fractured into shiny pieces.

# # #

The ranch was up a quiet country road to the west of town. Samantha sat back in the seat, the rolling land with its alabaster snow and contrasting pine green trees giving the sensation that all was right with the world. No strife or turmoil allowed. Just human beings creating, building, living, and loving. It was a lovely illusion.

She let herself drift with it. Reality was always ready to pounce.

Jarod put his hand on top of hers. "Do you mind?" he asked quietly.

She shook her head. It felt natural given the day.

Three deer in stood in the middle of a field, grazing on stubble that poked through the white fluff. Christmas-card perfect.

They turned onto a paved drive under a log ranch gate with a fierce-looking eagle atop it. Blue spruce lined one side of the drive, the other providing a few of a well-tended log home and a traditional red barn a short distance away.

Jarod pulled up next to a shiny black pickup with the ranch's logo stenciled on the side. "You want to stay here or come with?" he asked.

"You *said* we could see the horses," Audie reminded him.

"It'd be good to stretch our legs," Samantha added, opening the door to the passenger side.

Jarod quickly walked around and helped her and Audie down.

A back door opened on the house, and a man bundled in a beige Carhartt jacket, wool cap, and work gloves walked over. "Jarod Beck?" he asked.

"Yep."

"Nice of you to bring your wife and child. You looking at a horse for one of them?"

"Oh, no," Samantha said. "We're not married. This is *my* daughter, Audie."

"Really?" The man sounded disapproving.

Oh, dear, she'd given the wrong impression. She looked him in the eye. "Only friends. Nothing more. I'm Samantha. Nice to meet you."

He smiled and nodded. "That's okay then. I'm Tom Chapman." He looked over at Jarod. "The horses are over here. Only got two left, both geldings, both about a couple of years old. My wife, she was the one into horses. I built this ranch for her. I'm a dentist. But she's gone now." He ambled toward the corral attached to the barn. "My son's in Oregon. Still a bit on the cold side over there, but I figured I'd try it out. He's offered me a downstairs living area in their house."

Tom Chapman must be lonely.

Audie reached for Jarod's hand, and they followed Tom, Samantha bringing up the rear.

The horses looked them over as they approached. One was a common brown color, but the other was a rich bay with red highlights. There were no markings, just the high and low notes of his coat rippling in the sun as he swished his tail. Ignoring the other three people, he fixed his gaze on Samantha and confidently walked toward her like a feline instinctively picking the lap of a cat-hater.

She was mesmerized by the warmth in his eyes. They had the same trusting look of a Golden Retriever, but there seemed to be more intelligence behind them. On some level, they were communicating. She took a step toward him and hesitated. He stopped as well, waiting for her to make the next move.

Going any farther was out of the question. He was big.

"That was my wife's favorite horse," Tom said. "She swore he could understand what she was thinking. He was always careful with her when she rode, especially toward the end when her Parkinson's made it almost impossible for her to get on him."

"That must have been hard," Samantha said.

"It was. But she was a fighter. Did whatever it took to have the best life possible and not be a burden to anyone else."

"Can I go in?" Jarod asked.

"Sure."

He stopped at the first horse and ran his hands over him. Holding the bridle, he led the animal around, testing his reflexes and response to commands. Then he approached the bay, who was still staring at Samantha. He repeated the same procedure, while the horse stretched his neck, raised his tail, and pranced.

"He seems to want you to know how pretty he is," Tom said to Samantha. "You going to ride him?"

"I don't ride," she said.

"You're going to disappoint him then. He definitely wants to be your horse."

She shrugged, but she couldn't take her eyes off the animal. "What's his name?"

"Laughin' Jack," Tom replied. "I won him in a poker game with a jack of hearts."

She chuckled.

"Can I saddle and ride him?" Jarod asked.

"Sure thing," Tom replied. "I'll show you where his gear is."

Samantha walked over to Audie where she leaned on the corral rail.

"They're pretty," Audie said, "but not as nice my horse."

"Misty isn't your horse," Samantha said. "She belongs to Jarod. He may sell her someday."

"He won't. He likes us too much."

Too much were the right words.

Once again, the horse performed the maneuvers Jarod asked him to do, but Samantha could see the animal was still performing for her. When he was finished, he rode up next to Samantha, slid off the horse, and leaned against the rail. "So tell me," he asked her, "is this a horse you're going to ride?"

"I thought you were buying a horse for your business. One you could train and sell."

"I am, but I need to get you on a horse, too."

"I don't see why that's necessary."

Jarod leaned closer. "Because you're afraid. And I believe if you can conquer your fear of this animal, you can do it in all the other areas of your life where you feel fear."

"There isn't anything else."

He looked at her, one eyebrow arched. Beside him, Laughin' Jack shook his head and nickered.

"Oh, be quiet," she said to the horse. Jack took a step closer, stuck his head over the railing, and nudged her shoulder before she could move back. It was a simple action, then the animal pulled back and waited, his gaze once more intent on her. She moved closer and slipped her hand through the rails. Tentatively, she touched his neck. He stood still. She stroked the soft hairs.

"Maybe," she told Jarod.

"I'll buy him," Jarod told Tom.

"Good," the man said.

Tom served them coffee while they finalized the deal.

"I've got a friend from my rodeo days who wants to bring a few horses along to our ranch so we can tend to them while he visits his ill father. He said he'd pick up the horse and trailer him as well," Jarod said.

"Sounds good," Tom said. "You heading back to Choteau today?"

"Yep." Jarod stood and they shook hands.

"Anyone need to use the facilities?" he asked Samantha with a nod toward Audie.

"Good idea," she said.

"Down that hall."

Samantha showed her daughter where the bathroom was and waited until she was done before going in herself. She stared at her face in the mirror. It was an ordinary face. The circles under her eyes were deeper than they'd been, and no matter how much moisturizer with sunscreen she used on her face, it still showed signs of the hot and dry Montana air. With her flyaway hair, she looked like a classic prairie woman, somewhat weathered and worn. It was only her blue eyes that saved her.

Her mother had always told her she had a nice smile, so she tried it on.

Maybe.

But when Jarod looked at her, she felt like a model on the cover of *Vogue*.

She washed her hands and ran a brush through her hair and returned to the kitchen.

Chapter 22

Monday morning, things consistently went from bad to worse. First, Audie complained about a stomach ache but didn't want to skip school during the last week of fun before the holiday break. Something about a gingerbread man had her in giggles.

Samantha's car started reluctantly, whining for several seconds before the engine caught. God willing, the car would hold together until she returned from Billings. But as she skidded to school, she realized Jarod was right. Going anywhere on these tires was going to be risky.

Jim Van Sutton Jr. smirked his way through math. She wasn't a violent person, but it was tempting to use a stiff washcloth to wipe it off. As he left, he said, "I'm still on the team, Teacher. You've got no say around here. If my dad has his way, you're going to be gone by the end of the year."

She straightened her spine. "I'm not going anywhere."

He laughed and left the room.

Then she slumped back into her chair and put her head in her hands.

"You know," Bruce Weber said as he walked into her classroom, "you're going to need to be a little more political if you're going to work in a small town. That boy's father is sheriff."

She lifted her head. "I know. It—"

"That means he's got pull in this town. All small towns have someone, and he's it. His son's teachers either toe the line or move on to another town." Weber shrugged. "It stinks, but that's small towns for you."

"It's his son's ..."

Weber had already left.

"Responsibility to pass," she said to the empty room.

Tuesday afternoon, she got a call from the elementary school.

"Audie threw up," the nurse/secretary said. "She's running a little bit of a fever, too. Can you come get her?"

"Only if I can find someone to cover my classes," she said.

"Oh, that's right. You're a teacher."

Why couldn't anyone ever remember that?

She checked in with the high school secretary. "Certainly," the woman said. "Bruce is here. He's got a free period coming up. Maybe he can take over. Then Ginny can fill in at the end of the day. She was a math teacher before becoming vice principal. Just a sec."

"All arranged. Bruce will be down in a few minutes."

Great. The man would sabotage her class. Good thing Van Sutton had already come and gone.

"Do you have your lesson plans for me?" Bruce asked when he walked in.

"I've pulled out some extra worksheets on the lesson we're finishing up. I don't want to start anything new this close to the holiday."

Bruce shook his head. "Bad idea. I always give them a big project before a vacation. Several math problems where they need to put everything they've learned into the work. Keeps their minds sharp." He tapped his temple.

"Well, I believe they need the time off. So here you go." She handed him the stack of papers.

"Your little girl is sick?" he asked.

"Yes, nauseated."

"Hope she gets better soon. Don't worry about the class. We'll be fine."

"Thanks."

So Bruce Weber was a human being after all.

She got Audie home and to bed, collapsing in front of the television with a cup of tea when she was done. A moment to herself ... a time to think. If only there were someone to talk to. There were friendly people in town, but she'd been spending so much time with Jarod and his family that she wasn't reaching out to people like Trish who'd been friendly to her.

Life was imploding around her. When she'd gotten to Choteau, her path forward was clear. Get Audie settled, teach school, save money, and get on her own two feet. Start looking in the spring for new employment, just in case the school didn't keep her for another year. Make friends but stay uninvolved. Keep in touch with Mom but unhook from life in Billings.

And keep Audie hidden from Cody.

Not getting on a horse hadn't made the list, but she would have added it if she'd thought there was a remote possibility it could happen.

God was laughing.

Hysterically.

First things first.

Do the next right thing.

One day at a time.

Sayings from the twelve-step program she'd attended for a while came back to her.

Okay. So what really needed to happen next?

Make sure her daughter got well. Nothing else was more important than keeping Audie safe and well.

Her phone rang. She checked the display.

Jarod.

"Hi, there," he said when she picked up. "How are you?"

"I'm fine, but Audie's sick." She told him the girl's symptoms, which somehow morphed into a litany of her problems over the last few days.

"Poor kid," Jarod said. "You, too. Sounds like you've had a rough time since Saturday."

"Thanks for letting me dump."

"That's what friends are for. Laughin' Jack got here today."

"How's he doing?"

"Looking for you, I think," Jarod said.

"He's got a bit of a wait." Maybe forever.

"When are you leaving?"

"We get out of school at noon on Friday, so I'm hoping to head to Billings after that, depending on the weather."

"I think it's supposed to be clear. We'll get snow on Saturday, so best you head out then. I'll miss you."

Would she miss him?

"Yes," was the largest commitment she could make.

"I've got something for you, kind of an early Christmas present. Something for Audie, too."

"We didn't ... I mean, I hadn't thought about Christmas. I was planning on doing my shopping in Billings."

"Makes sense. But it's not a usual Christmas present, and you need it before you go."

"What?" she asked.

"I'll need to get the keys to your car tomorrow while you're at school."

"If I make it to school. But why?"

"It's a surprise. I just need to borrow your car for a few hours."

"Jarod, it's *my* car," she said firmly. "Remember? We talked about this. I need to know what's going on before I can agree to it."

His blown-out breath seemed to tickle her ear. "How about this?" he asked. "I won't do anything to your car that will damage it or change its appearance in any way. For the rest, I'm asking you to trust me. Can you do that?"

He was making perfect sense. A reasonable person would agree, wouldn't they? It was so hard to figure out when giving in was too much and when stubbornness was plainly foolish.

"Okay," she said.

"I'm glad. When would be a good time in the morning to stop in?" he asked.

"I have a plan period from 9:45 to 10:30," she said.

"I'll come by then. Give Audie a hug for me and tell her to get better. I'll talk to you tomorrow."

He hung up, more abruptly than normal.

What could he be giving her? A true Christmas gift. Her spirit lightened, and she smiled. Whatever it was, it wasn't going to be a bad surprise. Jarod wasn't like that.

All she had to do was find the faith to trust in the goodness of other human beings.

# # #

When Jarod called Samantha the next morning, he was happy to learn Audie's illness had been only the twenty-four hour variety and that they were back in school. He made arrangements to pick up her keys, then drove her car to his friend's garage.

The Camry was a good, basic car, and with 150,000 miles on the speedometer, good for another 100,000 at least as long as it was maintained. He noted the oil sticker in the upper left windshield and figured it'd be a good idea to change the oil in the vehicle while he was at it. Maybe give the car a once-over to see what else it needed.

They needed to stay safe.

He unlocked the door to the one-and-a-half story metal building and rolled it aside. His friend had a fascination with antique cars, tinkering with them most of the year. There was barely enough space to work amid the shrouded relics. Slowly, he pulled in through the vehicles to the garage space.

The chill seeped into his bones. Although the garage was heated enough to keep it above freezing, the thermometer stopped there. He closed the door, snapped on the dust-covered and dinged radio, and went to work to the scratchy voice of Patsy Cline.

Using the two-post hydraulic lift, he leveraged the car high enough to replace the tires with the retreads the salvage yard had found, rubber that actually had tread left. A pneumatic wrench made it easy to undo the old tires. He balanced the new ones and put them back on the car.

The work soothed him. Maintaining a car, especially when it came to the basics—engine, tires, body—felt purposeful. The electronics of the newer vehicles and farm equipment could be left to the geeks, people like his brother Dylan.

For him, the work was an act of caring for someone, a specific someone. He gave himself over to reliving their date. The kiss had been a tease. He wouldn't do much more unless they were in a serious relationship, but how was he going to get her from where they were now to that point if she didn't want, or was too scared, to come along?

She was easy until he got too close to those boundaries—steel walls—she wanted to keep erected. He knew what family trauma could do to a young child; his parents' deaths, especially his father's betrayal, had torn them all apart in one way or another. CJ's wound had been the most visible, but Kaiden didn't have an argument without resorting to his fists, Cameron became stoic and guarded, and Dylan disappeared within himself.

And him? He'd shouldered the responsibility and soldiered on. And now he was tired of doing it alone. He wanted someone in his life. He wanted Samantha. But she was right. He needed to find a balance between protecting her and her daughter from every possible danger and allowing them to live their lives as fully developed human beings.

No one came onto this planet with those skills intact. Some relationships worked out because the people involved talked, adjusted, and grew over time. Some people just made a hash of it and moved on.

He turned his mind back to the work, the scream of the wrench, the satisfying thud of the tire on the axle.

Finishing with the tires, he moved under the front of the car to tackle the oil, wrenching out the old filter, draining the black goo, and replacing the filter with the one he'd bought. The smell of oil and old metal was comforting, reminding him of times he'd spent with his dad before everything had gone south.

What would it be like to have a son of his own? He wasn't that old. There was still time. Would Samantha want more kids? It seemed premature to ask but important to know.

When he was done, he looked at the car with satisfaction just as his stomach rumbled. He checked his phone. Two o'clock. Enough time to get to Bridge's Coffee Shop for a burger before running the car back to Samantha at school. Besides, he needed to give it a test drive.

"Hey, Jarod," Mae sang out when he walked through the door. She'd been a fixture in the coffee shop for as long as he could remember. "You're just in time. Slow day. Jimmy was about to shut down the grill and run his errands. What'll you have?"

"Burger, fries, Coke."

"Don't you think you should vary your diet a little?" she asked. "You've been having that same meal since you were a teen."

He shrugged. "I'm a man of tradition."

She laughed. "Burn one and frog sticks," she shouted through the window to the back. The coffee shop owner's diner lingo was iconic if incomprehensible.

"Hear you're taking that new teacher out," she said.

Penalty of a small town.

"Trying to. She's not sure if she wants to be taken out."

"Trouble with her ex, I hear."

"Now, how do you know that?" he asked.

"Have you forgotten who bakes my pies?" she asked.

"Trish told you?" He was astounded. His old classmate was usually so circumspect about things people said in confidence.

"Not exactly. It's a combination of what she said, what Jody Hunt said, and something Samantha herself said when she was here one day."

Gossip central.

"You're going to need to find out what's going on there before you get very far," Mae said as she slid the burger plate onto the counter. "Enjoy." She picked up a spray bottle and some rags and walked to the back of the dining space.

Jarod picked up his burger, bit in, and did as he'd been instructed.

Nothing like a meaty burger after a few hours of labor.

Samantha was going away for a few weeks, maybe longer if she decided to stay with her mother during surgery, which she should, in his opinion. When she came back, there'd be a brief thaw, then a return to even more brutal temperatures as winter demanded its last pound of flesh.

Spring was the best time in the Rockies. They could go to the park and poke around its outer edges. The main road through the park, Going-to-the-Sun, never opened until late June at the earliest. Mamas and baby goats would be hanging around the salt lick.

Maybe they could fall in love in the spring.

The idea took his breath away. Was that what he wanted?

Yep.

He pushed away the unfinished meal, threw down a twenty, and headed back out.

Chapter 23

Jarod hadn't brought back her keys.

Samantha stuffed papers needing correcting, her laptop, and a book she was reading into her huge tote, picked up her purse and coat, and headed to the other side of the building to get Audie. They could walk home if they had to, but it would be no fun with all this stuff.

Her irritation built up a head of steam as she walked out the door, Audie already whining about walking home.

"Hey," a male voice called. "Sorry I'm late. I wanted to make sure everything worked okay."

He stood in front of her car, a bunch of delicate white flowers in his hand. "These are for you," he said, holding them out to her.

She looked down at her full hands, then back up to his face.

"Oh. Sorry. I can be clueless sometimes." He handed the flowers to Audie. "Let me help you." He unloaded her bundles and put them in the back seat. Retrieving the bunch from her daughter as Audie settled into the passenger seat, he extended them to her again.

"Thank you," Samantha said. "But what's the occasion?"

"Safe travels. Part of your early Christmas present. New tires and an oil change didn't seem to set the right tone."

"What?"

"I got you new tires. Well, not new, new tires. Retreads. And I changed your oil. Your ... uh, sticker said you needed it." The schoolboy grin faded from his lips. "Merry Christmas?"

"Oh, Jarod." It was too much. She shouldn't accept it, but it would be mean not to. He'd meant well, and her car was certainly safer.

And it meant a great deal that he'd been so thoughtful and caring, but once again she was forced to accept a fait accompli. Being churlish about it wouldn't be the appropriate reaction, however.

"Thank you," she said, touching his hand briefly. It was the schoolyard, and she was a teacher. Certain proprieties must be maintained. "It's wonderful."

"I wanted you and Audie to be safe." His smile was back but a little more tentative. "I've got a few more errands to run, but I was hoping to take you and Audie out for pizza later."

She shook her head. "Audie's stomach is still shaky. I'm planning a quiche tonight. How about you come for supper?"

"Thank you. Can I bring anything?"

"Just yourself," she said.

He nodded, touched the tip of his cap, and walked over to his parked truck.

As she watched him, a warm glow enveloped her. Would it be so bad to stay? To see how things could turn out between them? To see if he could talk to her before he did things and if she could be less sensitive when he stumbled over her boundaries? Was she finally ready to try an adult, non-addiction-fueled relationship?

She got into the car and drove home. When she walked in the front door and looked around, she panicked. There was so much to do. He'd be here in less than two hours.

"I'm going to throw up," Audie said and ran to the bathroom.

Apparently the stomach flu had decided to make a repeat visit. Samantha dropped her things, went into the bathroom, and held her daughter until she finished. Then she wiped her face and took her temperature.

"Pajamas and bed for you, honey. You need to rest."

"But, school ... the gingerbread man is tomorrow. I have to help the first graders."

"We'll see in the morning. That's why going to bed now is good for you. It'll help you get better quicker."

Once Audie was in bed, Samantha found her daughter's favorite stuffed bear and tucked it in with her. "Jarod is coming for dinner later. I'll see if you're ready to eat when he gets here."

"Okay." Her little girl's eyes were already starting to close. "Can you ask him to say good night if I don't?"

"Yes, sweetie." Samantha kissed her daughter's forehead. Before she'd even turned off the light, Audie was asleep.

# # #

Somehow, she managed to pull together a quiche, straighten up the house, and refresh her clothes and makeup before Jarod arrived. He brought a bottle of wine and dessert, a pint of Chunky Monkey. The scent of winter surrounded him as he invaded the small kitchen.

"Can I do anything?" he asked.

"Open the wine and have a seat. There's no formal dining room like the ranch, so this is—"

"Perfect," he finished.

Perfect only if he didn't look into any of the cupboards into which she'd shoved toys, papers, and other items that had developed feet and moved from their accustomed places. Perfect only if he looked past the deepening circles under her eyes, the ones makeup could never quite cover. She just hoped she got all the vomit cleaned up in the bathroom.

"Stop," he said. "I can see you evaluating, comparing yourself against everyone else. Audie is right. You haven't quite learned that no one is perfect." He stood. "Now, have a seat. You're as worn out as anyone else. I think I can manage to get this on the table."

She hesitated.

"Sit."

It took every ounce of willpower she had to let herself sit. He placed a glass of wine in front of her, then found plates and flatware to place on the table—the one without a tablecloth or placemats. His vase of flowers was the only decoration.

They were so pretty. Thoughtful. He was a nice man. Totally opposite the bad boy she thought she'd loved so desperately when Audie was conceived. Maybe she had changed.

The timer went off and she rose.

He'd found the oven mitts and pointed one at her. "I can handle this. It's not a horse, but I got it."

Soon steaming slices of quiche lay on plates in front of them.

"To safe travels," he said, raising his glass.

"To your business," she responded.

They clinked, set down their glasses, and began to eat. She told him about the threat Jim Jr. had uttered.

"Birdie told me things were rough in the household, but pampering someone like that kid doesn't help anyone, especially not the kid," she added.

"Yet some parents have always done it," he replied. "I think they feel guilty if they don't, or they're trying to help the child out." He shrugged. "Or they feel entitled themselves. In this case, I think it's the first. The problem is, you're the one stuck dealing with it."

"Do you think the threat is real? Could he really get me fired?" That was her real concern. One thing if she made the decision to leave, but she didn't want to be forced out. That wouldn't look good on her record.

"Ultimately, no. But it could be a rough ride. Did you talk to your principal about the threat?"

"No, I put it out of my mind."

"Maybe you should."

"I'll think about it." It was nice to have someone to talk with, something she'd never really had. Her high school friends, if she could call them that, were druggies who cared only about themselves and their next high. Her mother tended to defer to her "do whatever you think is best, Samantha." And her busy college, work, and baby-raising schedule had left no time for true friendships to develop.

"What about your mom's surgery?" he asked. "Did you ask for extra time off?"

She shook her head. Another thing she didn't really want to think about. What if something went wrong?

"You need to be there," he said. "You'll never forgive yourself if you aren't."

"I know that. But what if they count that as a mark against me?"

"You really don't trust people, do you?"

"I trust you," she said with a smile to hide the churning inside her. This conversation was too intimate. He was getting to know her too well.

He chuckled. "You trust me as much as you trust anyone, I'll give you that." He sliced off a piece of quiche with his fork. "Maybe it's different in a big city, but here we look after each other. Life happens to every one of us. We help each other out." He looked down at his plate for a moment, then leaned forward to gaze directly into her eyes.

"I learned that lesson first-hand when I was fourteen. That's when my father died. My mother ... well, she was a good mother, but I always had the sense that bearing children was something she felt she had to do. She'd wanted to be a painter, like Dylan, but she could never get it off the ground."

His expression saddened. "Galleries told her that her work was too pedantic—she colored inside the lines a little too well. I wouldn't call her bitter from that, but she was formal, not exactly the fun-loving parent she'd been when we were little. I know her relationship with my dad changed, too. Not that it excuses him from what he did, but ..."

She got it. Events made people change. She'd hardened her heart when Cody left her alone with her pregnancy.

"Anyway," he added. "Think about it. I figure you can always err on the side of forgiveness and be okay. Your mom raised you as best she could. It's all any of us can do."

"I'll consider it," she said.

The gazed at each other for a minute, something shifting between them as she opened up a little more. Finally, she picked up her fork to eat, looked down, and realized she'd already finished her slice of quiche.

"Want more?" Jarod asked. "What about Audie? Should we feed her?"

Samantha shook her head. "I think it's best if I let her sleep." She took a risk. "She did want you to say goodnight, though."

"Sweet. I'll do it without waking her, promise."

"Thanks."

He glanced outside at the streetlight. Fat flakes of snow were starting down. "I think, however, I'm going to forego the Chunky Monkey. You and Audie enjoy it. Let me say good night, and then I need to head out."

While he headed to Audie's room, she cleared the table. Soft murmurs came from the hallway but didn't last long.

"She is one sleepy kid," he said, returning. "Thanks for dinner. It was nice."

"Thank you for everything you did for me. It's the least I could do."

He moved close to her. "Drive safe. Come home in one piece. That's all I ask in return." Placing his hands on her shoulders, he continued, "And maybe a chance at something more than being friends when you get back."

"I'll think about it."

"According to Audie, that means 'maybe.' I'll take it," he said with a grin. Then he kissed her. "Think real hard," he whispered. "I care a great deal, and I'm willing to do the work necessary to make you feel safe around me."

He released her, put on his coat, and walked out the front door with a wave and a smile.

# # #

The drive to Billings went a lot more quickly than it had at Thanksgiving, thanks to beautiful weather and her new tires.

She'd been worried about a blowout a lot more than she'd realized. Smiling at the sky, she sent a silent *thank you* to Jarod and the spirit who sent him. Then she added a prayer for Jarod's brother Cameron. The only news the family had was that he was recovering from his injuries.

And he still didn't want to talk with anyone in the family.

Twilight was ending when they drove past the airport on the top of The Rimrocks. Another fifteen minutes and they were at her mother's.

"Wake up, sleepyhead," she said, gently nudging Audie, who had her head propped on a pillow and a quilt draped over her. Somewhere near Eddy's Corner, she'd drifted off to sleep and stayed that way. Poor kid wasn't really past the stomach bug that had gotten her.

Pushing open the front door her mother rarely locked, Samantha lugged in the roller bag she'd packed for herself. Audie slowly came in after her, letting cold air through the front door. Samantha propelled her past the doorway and shut it.

"Mom?" she called out.

"Living room." The voice was weak, barely discernable over the news program her mother was watching.

Her mother's body matched the tone of the voice. How could anyone shrink that much in a few short weeks?

"Hi, Grandma." Audie placed her arms gently around her grandmother, as if sensing her frailty. "Are you sick? Do you have a stomach bug? I do."

Her mother smiled. "I'm feeling like someone knocked the stuffin' out of me, for sure," she said. "But I don't think it's a stomach bug. Are you getting better?"

"Uh-huh." Audie gave a big yawn.

"Not time for you to go to sleep yet. We still need to have supper, remember?"

Her mother put her hands on the arms of her chair and scooted forward. Each movement was a struggle.

"Stop, Mom." Samantha crouched so she could see eye to eye with her mother. "I can take care of it. I'll check out the kitchen, and if there isn't anything to make, I'll order in. I'll do a shopping run tomorrow. When's the last time you ate?"

"I had some toast for breakfast. Just haven't felt like moving much today. Don't worry about the shopping. You're father's doing it tomorrow. He's working today. He figured he'd let you get settled tonight before coming over." A vague look passed over her mother's face, like she'd checked out of reality for a second. "Oh. He said he put something in the fridge for dinner."

Well, at least there was that. Much as she didn't want him around, her father was finally helping out the family.

"I'll check as soon as I get Audie's suitcase and my other bag of school stuff from the car."

"Okay." Her mother shifted back, then turned her attention to the television screen.

"Audie, go hang up your coat," she told her daughter on the way to the door.

Samantha yanked the door open and stopped cold.

With his hand raised, as if he were about to use the knocker, stood her ex.

Chapter 24

"What do you want?" Samantha asked, hastily stepping out and pulling the door behind her.

Cody took a step back. "I want to see my daughter."

"You gave up that right before she was born."

"I'm not that person anymore."

"Too little, too late."

"Jesus, Samantha, you're still the same hard-ass you ever were."

"And that, right there, is why you're never coming near my daughter."

"Our daughter." He clenched his fists, then released them. "Because I swear I won't say any curse words around her. I can handle myself now. I've faced the beast, and I know I don't want it inside me anymore. I'm going to meetings. I've got a job." He shook his head. "And I want to see my daughter."

"No." Samantha was rigid with anger and righteousness. Where had he been all those nights she was up with Audie and all those long days when she worked? Partying and chasing wild schemes, just like her father.

"You can't keep her from me."

"Yes, I can," she said with more bravado than she was feeling.

"Even your mother agrees I should be allowed to see her. I'll do it with your supervision if you want. Any terms you want. I just want to see her."

"You talked to my *mother*?"

"Yeah. She's a lot more understanding than you are. She even pointed me to some places that had jobs that might work for me." He stared at her as if trying to fathom what made her tick.

She pulled her jacket around her. Her mother had betrayed her twice now—first with her father, now with Cody. "Excuse me. I have things to do." She pushed past him off the porch and walked toward the car.

He followed.

"This isn't the end of this," he said. "I'll find a way to see her." He stalked down the drive and turned onto the sidewalk.

With her gloved hand on the door handle, she watched him go. How could she trust that he'd changed? He was always a smooth talker. Couldn't Mom see that he was the same old con man he'd always been?

Maybe her mother's cancer was eating more than her lungs. It seemed to be affecting her judgment as well. She looked terrible. Would she survive the operation?

Samantha yanked the door open and pulled out the two bags before slamming it shut. What a mess.

What would she do without her mother?

Dropping the bags, she leaned against the car. It was all she could do not to scream and swear at the sky. Instead, she buried her face in her hands and sobbed.

After a few moments, she wiped her eyes, picked up the bags, and went back inside.

# # #

"Grandpa's here!" Audie shouted, shaking Samantha to wake her up.

What time was it?

Darn, she'd overslept.

"I'll be right out. Is Grandma awake?"

"She's sleeping in the chair in the living room."

"Well, then, don't make too much noise so you wake her up."

"Okay." Audie's face turned serious. "She's really sick, isn't she?"

"I'm afraid so, sweetie."

"Is she going to die, like my goldfish?"

"Someday, sweetie, but not too soon, I hope." Samantha's throat seized on her. After swallowing, she added, "Go back to the kitchen. I'll be right there."

Her mother's wan face haunted her as she walked past her in the living room. There were fresh flowers in a vase on the coffee table, and a blanket was tucked around the sleeping form.

Her father was a strange sight in the kitchen, bringing back a vague memory of him cooking Sunday brunch when she and her mother returned from church. They'd always picked up fresh rolls from the bakery, and he'd prepare bacon and eggs to go with them.

Just like he was doing now.

"Still like your eggs scrambled?" he asked as she came in.

"Um. Yes." She grabbed a mug and poured some coffee. "You've certainly made yourself at home here."

"Your mom needs help." He cracked eggs into a bowl, added a little salt, pepper, and basil flakes, and whisked them together. "She went downhill pretty fast after Thanksgiving. I think she was holding it together until the holiday was over." He looked over at her, his dark eyes shadowed by craggy eyebrows. "Until she could have her entire family together."

She took her coffee to the table where Audie was eating her own scrambled eggs. Her mother was a pushover. She was not.

"I'm going to stay for the surgery," she said. She'd gone to Rebecca at the last minute, and the principal assured her they would handle the absence. "It's important you be there," she'd said.

"That's good," he said. "Your mother will tell you to go back, but she needs you here." Deftly, he scooped the eggs from the fry pan, added a few strips of bacon and a roll, and slid it on the table in front of her. "I got in groceries for the week, although I'm not sure what you and Audie especially need."

"That's okay. I need to go out. I need to ..." Darn. She had to Christmas shop for Audie. The little girl couldn't tag along while she did that. And she couldn't leave her here with her mother. What if Cody came back?

"What's the matter?" her father asked.

"It's just that Choteau's a small town and it's Christmas." She looked pointedly at Audie.

"Got it," her father said. "And your mother's not up to watching her."

"Yes. And ... well, that's not the only thing."

"Are you talking about me?" Audie asked, looking at each of them in turn.

How to answer that?

"I was about to tell your mother what a smart girl you are," Audie's grandfather said. "And how I'd love to spend the day with you. In fact," he said with a conspiratorial whisper, "I think Santa left an early game for us all to play."

"Oh, yes!" Audie said. "Let's go!" She got up and tugged at his hand.

"Not quite yet," he said. "I need to clean up my mess." He gestured at the kitchen.

"Okay. I'm going to go watch TV." She picked up her empty plate and fork and handed it to him.

"Not too loud," Samantha said. "Grandma's sleeping."

"Uh-huh." Audie tiptoed out of the room.

"She's a pistol," her father said.

"You can say that again."

"So, what else is bothering you?" he asked as he took the plate to the sink and began to put things back in the refrigerator.

"Cody, Audie's father, showed up last night."

"Your mother said he'd come back."

"And now he wants to see Audie."

"Seems reasonable."

"Reasonable?" She dropped her fork on the plate with a clatter. "He wanted me to get an abortion. He left while I was still pregnant. What gives him any right to see her?"

"He's her father." Her own father's voice was reasonable. Patient.

And utterly wrong.

"He's made mistakes, just like I did," her father continued. "He's paid for them, and now he's trying to turn his life around." He poured more coffee in his mug and sat down across from her. "He deserves a second chance. We all do. Addiction is a horrible thing. You know that."

"I got myself clean. I didn't have to go to jail to do it—or kill anyone in the process."

He let out a breath. "I wondered when you were going to throw that at me. It took me a long time to forgive myself for being an instrument of that man's death. His family has forgiven me. Do you think you can?"

Never happening. She stayed silent.

Her father shook his head. "You're a hard one, Samantha. I feel for Cody. And I hope that someday you learn to forgive all of us—me, your mom, Cody—for our struggles as human beings doing the best we can." He stood. "In the meantime, go do your shopping. I've got a granddaughter to play with."

She stared at her eggs after he left. No longer hungry, she dumped them in the garbage and placed her plate and utensils in the sink. With a sponge, she wiped off the table and made sure the chairs were pushed in.

After waving good-bye to Audie, engrossed in a game with her grandfather, and giving her now-awake mother a quick hug, she got into her car and headed downtown.

The Christmas decorations mocked her. This was the season of anticipation, joy, and hope, an advent of better things to come.

Instead, her life was being turned upside down. The only thing she could anticipate was struggle and pain.

Why couldn't Cody have decided to stay in Nashville? Why on earth did he want his daughter now?

She shouldn't be as bitter as she was, but she'd watched her mother give in and sacrifice all her life, and Samantha had done the same thing when Audie was born. Where were these men when she and her mother were continually on the brink of losing everything?

Even if she were to do something so foolish as to forgive them, there were no guarantees that the snakes wouldn't turn around and bite her again when she wasn't ready. She needed to keep them all at arm's length, including Jarod.

What a mess.

She parked and began to walk the shops in the revitalized downtown, all glass and steel. She admired the furnishings and artwork in the upscale shops, knowing it would never grace anyplace she lived.

God, she was sounding like a brat to her own ears.

She needed to take care of the things she could control and let go of the rest.

A bookstore snagged her attention. The perfect place to begin.

After locating the children's bookseller, she selected four books for Audie, three of them about horses, including one nonfiction. She found a not-too-heavy picture book of English gardens her mother would love. Her mother's affection for these kind of books baffled her. As far as Samantha knew, her mother had never picked up a trowel in her life.

A new book by David McCullough caught her eye. Would it be something her father liked? She should get him something. Audie, with her large heart, would be devastated if there was nothing under the tree for her grandpa.

Lugging her purchases, she headed back to the car. Her stomach rumbled as she walked past a café, and on impulse, she went in. It had been a while since she'd treated herself to a lunch out by herself. As soon as she looked at the prices on the menu, she remembered why. Still, she stayed. Going home, even if it were by way of the big box stores, seemed too difficult at the moment.

How sick was her mother? How would life be conceivable without her? Even though she'd never been the take-charge woman Samantha had hoped she'd become, her mother was the one constant in her life. Even in the depth of Samantha's addiction, Mom had never turned her back on her.

Just as she hadn't on her father.

Once she ordered her soup and half sandwich, she checked her phone. One message, from Jarod.

JB: Glad you made it there safely. Laughin' Jack misses you. Missy is sad. Tell Audie.
SD: Will do. How is the weather?

He must have had his phone nearby because the answer was immediate.

JB: Snow came in today. Everyone's staying close to home. Miss you.

She should type *Miss you too*, but she didn't.

She stared out at the busy street, contrasting it with the near-empty sidewalks of Choteau. There seemed to be more time to simply be, there—more time to breathe.

And Jarod? Strong, consistent, overbearing Jarod?

He was solid and dependable, and someone she could talk to, even about Cody.

SD: Miss you, too.
JB: How's your mom?
SD: Sick. Very sick. My father is helping out.
JB: Is that hard?
SD: Yes. But last night Cody showed up.
JB: Cody?
SD: Audie's father.
JB: Oh. How does he seem?
SD: We didn't really have a conversation.
JB: Don't you think you should?
SD: Nope.

Silence.
The waitress slid her meal in front of her.

SD: Got to go. Talk with you later.
JB: Okay. Take care.

Well, that was awkward. Sliding the phone away, she picked up one of the magazines she'd purchased at the bookstore and began to leaf though it.

Once her lunch was finished, she took a long walk around the block to the car. Somehow, she needed to find something to take to Jarod as a present from her and Audie. Nothing too personal. Or meaningful. But perfect enough to show her gratitude for all he'd done since they'd moved to Choteau.

The Billings First United Methodist Church caught her eye. She'd gone to meetings there once, only for a short time before deciding she didn't need it anymore. It wasn't her church, but maybe if she got on her knees, she'd feel some relief from this ever-present stress. They said God never gave a person more than they could bear, but perhaps He was being overly optimistic in her case.

Sliding her packages into the pew next to her, she stared at the altar for a long time, searching for that still, small place within herself. It seemed harder and harder to find. Her mind latched on to the very things she didn't want to think about: Cody's threats, her mother's illness, her father's reappearance, what to do about Jarod, what was best for Audie, and how she was going to keep her own addictions at bay.

The last thought brought her to her knees. A hit would be so nice. Just a little oblivion for a while.

Except that wasn't how it was. Once you let it in, the demon took over. He'd chained her to his side for years, invading every crevice of her mind and stealing her free will. The things she'd done to get her fix came back to her, like watching a fuzzy film reel made a hundred years ago. She'd been lucky most of her actions had been stupid, not criminal or fatal. So lucky.

She could never let that monster anywhere near her again. And she could never tell anyone about it.

No, she had to keep control. Not allow anyone or anything to get to her—good or bad.

Her knees ached.

God, she was exhausted from the effort. She wanted to let go, fall into someone's arms, and let them handle it, just like she used to do with her mother. But her mother was fading. Roles were reversed.

Jarod would be safe, a voice whispered.

But could she give him enough in return and still retain who she was?

What if he simply wanted her, warts and all? If he was willing to accept her and work within her boundaries?

Impossible. Nobody was that good. If he ever found out what she'd done ...

Forgiveness was possible.

It was what her father wanted from her.

It was what her mother deserved.

Maybe if she practiced it a little on others, she could find it for herself.

Some of the tension left her shoulders, and peace enveloped her. She slid back onto the pew and let it wash over her. Just for now.

Her face was wet with tears, and she wiped them away.

With a deep breath, she picked up her bags and walked from the church.

Chapter 25

"A little to the left," Birdie said.

Jarod shifted the Christmas tree in its stand.

"You went too far. Back to the right."

He did as he was told. It had been the same for a bunch of years. He pushed the tree right and left, forward and back until the housekeeper found her internal point of uprightness.

It was all part of the holiday. Thankfully, he'd conned Dylan into doing the lights about five years ago, explaining it needed his artistic temperament. Somehow, his brother had persuaded Birdie that his way was best and she left him alone.

"Forward."

Mindlessly, he moved the tree.

Christmas needed kids. How was Samantha doing? God was certainly hurling a lot of things her way. And knowing her, she was going to try to handle it all herself, except that every single one of those things was out of her control. He'd never met anyone who had such a tight grip on life.

"Back."

He put the tree back to where it had been.

What was going to get her to let go? He had faith in a horse's ability to reach even the most stubborn of people, but only if they'd give the animal a chance. There'd been something between her and Laughin' Jack. If only the weather would thaw enough to make it safe to get her on his back. Maybe Jarod should start slowly, just having her groom the horse?

He needed that arena, but the bank hadn't contacted him about the loan yet.

"Jarod! Are you listening to me?"

"Sorry."

"Just move the trunk an inch toward where I'm standing and I think we have it."

He looked over and tapped the tree a couple of times.

"Perfect!" Birdie clapped her hands and, for a second, looked like a schoolgirl. "Dylan!" she yelled, her features fading back into her sixty-year-plus wrinkles.

"I'm right here." Dylan emerged from the office where he'd been doing some software updates.

"Tighten the tree and then you can do the lights."

"Yes, ma'am," he said with a grin before he dropped to the floor and did as commanded. Once the tree was tight, he righted himself. "Now, the two of you can leave while I do the lights," he said with a grin.

"You just want me to do your chores with the cattle," Jarod said.

"Something like that."

Jarod shook his head and went to the mudroom and got his gear. Holidays didn't matter to cows. They wanted to be fed, no matter what.

As Jarod drove out to the pasture, he let the solitude of the landscape wash over him. Snow blanketed the rolling hills, with bunchgrass stalks punching through where the layers were thin. The blue sky, true to its name, went on forever. He never wanted to leave this place until they carried him out, boots first. But more than that, he wanted to raise a family here.

Time was running out for that. Most of the kids he'd gone to high school with had kids entering their teens. Some had gotten divorces, and a few ex-girlfriends had indicated they'd love a second chance. If Samantha was bent on leaving town, especially now that her ex had shown up, maybe it was time to give up on her and take the easy road.

Problem was, he'd never been good at the easy road. Even as a kid he'd stood up for the underdog, cheered his team on even when they were headed for certain defeat. Heck, even picking up the ranch duties after his father died had been the tough choice.

And he'd do it again in a heartbeat.

He let himself through the gate, closed it behind him, and set the wheels in the path made previously. A long line of cows headed his way. Every hundred feet or so, he stopped the rig, got on the back platform, and distributed hay to the pleasure of the raucous cattle.

At the far end of the field, he went through another gate and drove up a hill. From here, he could see the upper level of Brockman's house.

What was this guy's deal? And what was his relationship with Cassandra? There was nothing Jarod could put his finger on, but somehow Dave Brockman was a threat to his family. Could he have been the one to cut the fence and go onto their land, not caring about the straying cattle? If so, what was he looking for?

They hadn't gotten a chance to get back up there before snow fell, and now it was socked in until spring. Would he know what it was if he stumbled across it? Maybe Kaiden, who was due in sometime today, had some ideas. Not that he'd understand what his younger brother was telling him. His geology major seemed to give Kaiden permission to talk in words of only four or five syllables ending in *ist* or *ith*. He smiled. It would be good to have four of them back together for the holiday season.

Better if Cameron could be here. There'd been no word since the original news that he'd made it to a hospital in Germany. At some point he'd return stateside to go through rehabilitation, but when depended on how fast he recovered from the trauma.

Why didn't he want to talk to them? And how would they be able to help him without damaging his spirit? Cameron had always been a proud man, confident and strong.

Losing a limb could destroy him if they weren't careful.

Did war, especially those that never ended, serve any purpose at all? Once he would have answered with an unequivocal yes, but now? It was different when it hit so close to home. Probably why Americans were so detached from the ongoing conflicts in the Middle East. They no longer had any skin in the game.

He needed to shake this off. There was nothing he could do to save the world today. His phone had a signal. Maybe he could make at least one person's life better.

"Hey there," he said when Samantha answered.

"Hey yourself," she replied. "How's it going?"

"Same as usual. I'm feeding cattle, Dylan is being artistic, and Birdie is fussing in the kitchen. How about you?"

"I wish it were that normal. Audie's wound up because it's Christmas, my mom sleeps most of the time, and my father, I'm still getting used to him. By the way, I found the gifts you tucked in the trunk. You didn't have to do that. You've already done too much."

"They're little things. I wanted something under the tree from me." He flushed with warmth. Would she think he was being too possessive again, trying to stake a claim?

He supposed he was in a way. He needed to learn to temper it.

"Nothing from Cody?" he asked.

"He's called Mom a couple of times, and my father spoke to him once. I'm not dealing with him, and Audie certainly isn't going to talk to him."

Much as he didn't like what her ex had done, her approach wasn't going to work in the long run, and it wasn't really fair to Audie's father. What if he was trying to get a new start in life? Didn't he deserve the chance?

Best to tread lightly.

"Do you think he has changed?"

"Not you, too. I knew him too well. Nothing would have made him change his ways. It's only a matter of time and he'll be back down the hole."

"I'm sure you'll figure it out," he said, trying to soothe her feelings.

"I'm her mother," Samantha said, a hard edge to her voice he'd never heard before. "I'll decide what's right for her."

Maybe he didn't know her as well as he thought he did. Or maybe the stress was getting to her.

"Do you have your tree up yet? I've left Dylan to do the lights."

"We've been working on it all week. It's slow going." She took a little breath. "It used to be Mom's favorite thing, making sure the lights were just so. She liked to bury them deep in the tree so it glowed from within. All the ornaments had special memories. She'd spend all day decorating. So far this year, all we have is the tree. Everything else is still in boxes." Another silence. "She says she doesn't have the energy."

"I'm sorry. It must be tough."

A sharp breath of air.

"It is. I'm not sure ..." Another hesitation. "Can you hang on a moment? I want to go outside."

He gazed over the land, Beck land, as he waited for her to get back on the line. These were the hard parts of a relationship, when one person fundamentally disagreed with the other. Acquaintances had problems navigating differences of opinion. Add the emotional component and it increased the opportunity for things to go wonky.

"Hi," she said. "I'm back. Sorry. I didn't know how much my mother or Audie could hear."

"I get it."

"It's just ... I don't know, Jarod. Some days I don't know if I can handle it. Audie knows something bad is happening, and she's starting to act out. And it's the worst way. I could handle it if she were defiant, but she gets all passive-aggressive on me. You know, she doesn't 'hear' me. Or she mishears me deliberately. It's totally aggravating."

He chuckled. "I can imagine. You've got a smart little girl there."

"Too smart."

"Are you staying for the surgery?"

"Yes, Rebecca told me to take as much time as I need. They'd figure it out."

"That's good." He wished he could hold her, comfort her, make sure she knew she wasn't alone. "Do you have any friends around?"

"Not really. I kinda burned my bridges in high school when I got involved with Cody. Then when I finally got my act together, I was heads down for years."

"Too bad. It's hard to go through alone."

"Yeah." She sounded so tired.

"Have you got Audie's presents?"

"Yes, but they aren't wrapped. If she ever gets to bed tonight, that will be the chore. My father has taken charge of cooking meals tonight and tomorrow, so that's a relief. Then it will just be waiting out the rest of the year and getting ready for the surgery."

"You'll make it. Don't forget to take time for yourself."

"I will. Thanks for calling, but I have to go. Cold out here."

"Get inside then. And take care of yourself and Audie."

"Will do."

He slid the phone back in his shirt pocket, re-buttoned his jacket, and headed the truck back down to the ranch as a light snow began to fall.

# # #

With Kaiden's help, they managed to finish decorating the tree and the fireplace—stockings all hung in a row—to Birdie's satisfaction. She'd get up early tomorrow morning and fill them with nuts, fruit, and chocolate, just like she always had. There were even two for Nick and Trevor.

Cameron's was hung but would remain empty, a reminder of the missing soldier.

It was bittersweet.

Jarod poured himself a whiskey after dinner, slumped into his favorite chair, and stared at the gas fire in the fireplace. He'd converted it a few years ago, after Birdie convinced him natural gas was a whole lot cheaper and neater than wood, as romantic as manly men chopping in the cold might be.

Christmas music filtered from the speakers.

The holiday was out of whack; there were missing pieces. Not only Cameron, but he felt the lack of Samantha and Audie.

"You could go to Billings, you know," Dylan said as he slid onto the couch nearby.

"What?"

"You can go to Billings. I know you want to be with her."

"That would be imposing. Besides, I need to be here for the ranch."

"I can handle the ranch. Kaiden is here for another week."

"Uh-oh. I heard my name mentioned." Kaiden perched on another armchair.

Jarod wasn't ready to discuss a trip to Billings.

"Kaiden, when you were doing all your rockhounding, did you go up to the northwest end of the ranch?"

"Once in a while. Why?"

Jarod told him about the fence being cut and the reaction of their new neighbor. "I've been wondering if there is another reason we can't find the mineral rights."

"You mean if there's actually something worthwhile up there we don't know about? And whoever cut the fence was looking for it?"

"Uh-huh."

"Interesting," Dylan said. "Unfortunately, we won't be able to get back up there until spring."

"I can do some research, though," Kaiden added. "Dig back through old records and see if I can find anything, as well as look up geological reports."

"Thanks," Jarod said.

"Now about Billings," Dylan said.

"I'd be intruding."

"Don't you think Audie could use a friendly face and Samantha could use someone in her corner?"

"Well, of course."

"Am I missing something?" Kaiden asked.

"That kid Jarod has been giving riding lessons to—Jarod's got the hots for her mother."

"You're disgusting," Jarod said, glaring at Dylan.

"Have you kissed her?"

"No comment."

"He's kissed her," Kaiden said.

"No doubt," Dylan added.

"If I tell you I'll think about going to Billings, will you two leave me alone?"

Dylan and Kaiden looked at each other with matching grins and clinked their glasses.

It had all been a plot between them.

Jarod harrumphed and picked up a nearby magazine.

They could be right. He'd just have to find a horse near Billings to take a look at so she didn't feel he was trying to run her life.

# # #

Christmas morning passed easily enough. Samantha's parents were happy with their gifts, and there were plenty of things under the tree for her and Audie, including Jarod's gifts. He'd gotten Audie a glass replica of Misty of Chincoteague. For her, it was a picture of her and Laughin' Jack in an intricately carved wooden frame. CJ must have Photoshopped it because she'd never been that close to the animal.

"What's that?" her mother asked.

She handed it to her mother, who turned it so her father could see. "I didn't know you ride horses," her father said.

"I don't. Jarod, the guy who took that picture, is trying to convince me that it's something I must absolutely do."

"That his horse?"

"It is now. He bought it because he thinks Laughin' Jack—the horse—will convince me to get on his back. Of course, he's pretending he bought it for his rodeo horse training business, but he's not fooling me." Even thinking about Jarod relaxed her shoulders. It would be nice to have him here, someone who could protect her from all the demons she knew were lurking, waiting to get her alone.

But she couldn't have it both ways. If she went to him for protection, she'd have to let him take the actions he thought were best at times.

"He must like you a lot," her mother said.

"I think he's in love with her," Audie announced. "And Mommy loves him, too, but she's afraid they aren't perfect together." She shook her head in a very adult fashion. "And Mommy thinks everything has to be perfect."

"And you are perfect just the way you are," Samantha said.

"But that's not why I'm not in a relationship with Jarod."

"Why on earth not?" her mother asked.

"I'm not ready. Audie's not ready."

"Am too," her daughter said.

"There's just stuff," Samantha said. "Stuff I don't want to talk about right now."

"She doesn't want me to hear," Audie added.

Sometimes her daughter was too precocious to stand.

Her father chuckled, releasing some of the tension. "Anyone ready for breakfast?" he asked.

"Me!" Audie jumped up and grabbed her grandfather's hand. "I'll help!"

"That's my good girl," he said. "We'll eat out here so Grandma can stay in her chair. That's why I brought the wooden tray tables."

"Okay," Audie said as the pair left the living room.

"So, this Jarod," her mother began. "Is he good to you?"

"Yes," Samantha said. "Almost too good. Do you know what he did before we left? He put better tires on the car and changed the oil. How am I supposed to repay him for that?"

Her mother shook her head. "Life isn't about even-steven. He did it to take care of you. Audie's right. It sounds like he does love you. Maybe you should give the guy a chance."

"I can't. I don't have tenure. What if they fire me? What am I supposed to do for a job? What if Jarod tries to run my life? And worse, what if Cody shows up like he did the other night?"

"You're going to have to learn to deal with both of them like an adult," her mother said. "From what your father told me, Cody is trying to turn his life around." She looked at Samantha thoughtfully. "You're not much on giving people a chance or even having a conversation about a problem before leaping to conclusions. Did I raise you to be that hard on everyone? I hope not."

"I'm not hard. Just realistic. Better to be prepared than to think everything's fine and give someone an opening to hurt me."

"You're pretty young to be that cynical," her mother said. "The problem with always protecting yourself is, you don't let the good things in either." She leaned back in her chair and took a few breaths.

Her mother was fading before her eyes. Was she going to be strong enough to go through surgery?

What would she do without her mother? Mom had always

stood by her, even when she'd messed up. She'd been there for her every step of the way with Audie. Without her support, she wouldn't have been able to get her degree.

Following in her footsteps, being kind and nice to everyone and forgiving everything wasn't in Samantha's makeup, but maybe it was time to accept that her mother was who she was and she'd done her best—more than her best—to help her out.

"I love you, Mom," she whispered.

"I love you, too, baby," her mother said, her eyes still shut. "Don't ever forget that. No matter what."

Samantha's throat closed up, and she put her hand over her mouth to cover the sobs that threatened to escape. This couldn't be happening. Her mother was too young. She'd only be turning fifty in a month, having had Samantha at eighteen.

She had to get better. People did all the time these days. Cancer survivors lived well into their eighties. Somehow, Mom had to live ... she just had to.

Her father brought out the wooden tray tables and set one up for her mother. "Maddy, are you going to want anything?" he asked gently.

"Just some orange juice," her mother said. "I need it to take my pills." Her hand swayed toward the pillbox on the side table.

"I'll take care of it," he said. "You just rest."

"Do you need help?" Samantha asked.

"No, thanks. Audie's a good little helper. You keep your mom company." He set up the remaining tables, then went back to the kitchen. A moment later, Audie came out, carefully placing each step, an orange juice glass in each hand.

Samantha pressed her lips together to avoid saying anything until the glasses were safely on the tables. "Thank you," she said, letting go of the breath she was holding.

"Grandpa says I'm a big help."

"That, she is." Her father placed two plates heaping with eggs, bacon, and biscuits on her tray table and Audie's. He and Audie high-fived each other, then returned to the kitchen.

A few minutes later, the entire breakfast was out, grace was said, and they were digging in while Christmas music drifted from the same stereo system her mother had had since Samantha was small.

The rest of the day passed in the way that Christmases always did, with the exception of her father's presence and her mother's lack of energy. Phone calls, reading, a classic movie on television, a half-hearted attempt to straighten up. Sometime around three, the blue sky and fresh air beckoned Samantha, and she went out for a walk.

She'd just turned the block when a shout made her hesitate.

"Samantha! Wait!"

Cody.

Tempted to keep walking, she turned around instead.

"I want to see Audie. It's Christmas. I have something for her."

"And who do I explain you are?"

"The truth. I'm her father."

She shook her head. "I told you. I'm not letting you or your friends anywhere near her. It was bad enough what happened to me. I won't let you do that to my child."

"*Our* child. And I told you. I'm clean. I don't hang out with those people anymore."

"And what happens if you slip? What then?"

He fisted his hands but pushed them into his jacket pockets. "I'm doing everything I can to keep straight, Samantha. I can't guarantee anything, but if I do, you can toss me to the curb."

"That's not going to be good for Audie."

"It's the best I've got."

She couldn't risk it.

"That's not going to work. Why don't you find someone else and leave us alone like you did when I was pregnant? We're doing okay. I'm finally on my feet, and it took a heck of a lot of work and time to get here. I don't—we don't need to go backward."

"I can take you to court."

"Please don't, Cody. Please just leave us alone. There's enough stress for us with my father's reappearance. And now Mom, she's so ill." Her voice broke.

"I'm sorry, but you have to let me in. I can help. Take Audie off your hands to give you time to help your mother."

She straightened her back and took a step forward. "Do you really expect to come waltzing back into our lives like nothing ever happened? Think again." She jabbed his chest with her index finger. "Go away. If you bother me again, I'll be the one going to court for a restraining order."

He glared at her, his shoulders rising and falling rapidly as the pace of his breath increased.

Would he hurt her?

She took a step back and shifted her weight, prepared to turn and run.

He shook his head. "I won't do anything to you." He closed the difference. "There's right and wrong here, Samantha, and you're on the wrong side. This isn't the end of this. You've just made it clear what course I have to take. She's my daughter, and I *will* see her. Merry Christmas." He turned and walked away.

She was shaking. Wrapping her arms around herself, she jogged back to the house, not seeing Cody along the way. The sooner they got out of Billings, the better.

Chapter 26

"There's someone at the door for you," Samantha's father said. It was late afternoon, two days after Christmas.

It had better not be Cody. She couldn't be responsible for what happened, not with everything else.

Her mother had been even more listless the day after Christmas. It looked as if she'd made it through the holiday and that was all the energy she had left. Unfortunately, the soonest they could get her into her doctor was tomorrow, and she refused to see anyone else.

The growing stone in the pit of Samantha's stomach weighed her down and sucked the joy from the holiday. It was a toss-up between sobbing uncontrollably and screaming at the next person who crossed her.

"Yes?" she said as she got to the small entryway where her father had left the visitor. As soon as she saw Jarod, the last shred of control she had deserted her. "Oh, Jarod," she said, swaying as her strength left her.

He pulled her close, and the cool mountain air still laced in his jacket cracked her open and she cried again for how sick her mother truly was.

"Let it go," he said, holding her close. "It's okay."

She couldn't hang on any longer. Nine years of struggle to get a degree, raise her daughter, and stay clean poured onto his shoulder. How good it was to finally let go. He was solid. Safe.

The world was not.

Tears finally ran out, but she stayed there, putting off facing the world, including the man she'd just soaked with her tears, a little longer. Finally, she lifted her face to his.

"I must look a mess," she said.

"You look beautiful." He thumbed away a remaining tear and kissed her gently on her lips.

"My manners," she said, pulling away. It was too intimate to be standing like this in her mother's house. "Let me take your jacket. Do you want anything? Coffee? Water? I think we have some wine left, but no beer, I'm afraid."

"Coffee'd be just fine," he said.

"Come to the living room," she said after hanging up his coat on a nearby hook. "I can't imagine where Audie is." She led the way.

As soon as he stepped into the room, Audie leapt from her place on the floor in front of the television and launched herself at him. "Jarod! I missed you! Thank you for Misty! She's beautiful!"

"I'm glad you liked her." Jarod gave her daughter a big hug.

"I convinced her to give you two a minute," her father said, rising and holding out his hand. "Jake Deveaux, Samantha's father."

"How do you do."

Her mother had her eyes open for the first time in hours, steadily watching the scene unfold in front of her.

"And this is my mother, Maddy."

Jarod unpeeled Audie from him and crouched in front of her mother. "Nice to meet you, Mrs. Deveaux," he said. "I'm sorry to hear you are so sick."

"Me, too, young man. But I am happy to meet you. Very happy." She slumped back into the chair, her energy apparently spent.

Jarod rose.

"C'mon back to the kitchen," Samantha said. "I'll get you that cup of coffee." Audie followed them like a shadow.

"How long did it take you to get here?" she asked as he settled into a chair, her daughter still glued to his side.

"About five hours. Roads were clear."

She set a cup in front of him and sat in the chair opposite. Why was he here? Her gaze flicked to Audie. Her daughter must have needed this solid rock of a man as much as she had.

Her gaze connected with his. There was so much to say, but she didn't want to say it in front of her daughter.

"Hey," Jarod said to Audie. "Misty said to tell you hello. And next year you won't have to wait all winter to ride her."

"How come?"

"Because I'm going to build an arena over the summer. And you're going to help me." He touched the end of her nose with his index finger.

"You have enough money?" Samantha asked, afraid of the promises he was making to Audie. Promises she wasn't sure they could keep.

"Nick helped me apply for a loan, and they gave it to me." He shook his head in wonder. "It means I have to ramp up the business a whole lot to pay for it. That's why I'm here. There's a horse for sale in Laurel I need to look at."

"Oh," she said. He hadn't come solely for her. Just as well. "Where are you staying?"

"Holiday Inn on the west side of town."

Her father came into the kitchen. "I figure it's about time to get something going for supper," he said. "I'm planning a macaroni and cheese casserole with ham—lots of ham. We have leftovers from Christmas. You're welcome to stay, young man."

"I'd like that. Thank you."

"Why don't you two go take a walk or something? Audie can help me with dinner, and your mom's sleeping again."

"That sounds good," Jarod said. "Okay by you? It'd be good to stretch my legs after all that time in the truck."

"I'll get my coat," she said. Getting out of the confines of this stuffy house suddenly seemed like a fantastic idea.

And with Jarod, she wouldn't have to worry about being approached by Cody.

The sun was already beyond the horizon when they emerged from the house.

"Days are getting longer," Jarod said.

"Uh-huh. I looked it up once. They get longer by about thirty seconds a day. With less than nine hours of sun a day, it's no wonder I've always felt like I was living in a cave in the wintertime."

He chuckled. "Not into winter sports?"

"No time." They moved down the sidewalk. "And, to be truthful, no inclination either."

"I always figured I spent enough time outdoors already," he said.

"I bet. All that feeding and moving the cows around."

"Not to mention calving in February. Always takes a ton of time to find and tag all those newborns."

"But ranchers decide when calves are born, don't they? Why don't you do it so they come out in the warmer months?"

"It's all economics. Getting cattle to market. The bigger the better, and the more time they have to grow, the bigger they are."

"I'm glad it's your job," she said, slipping her hands into her pockets. Even with gloves, the cold still air was getting to them.

"But there's nothing like the sky in winter," he said. "Even here, although there's too much other light for my taste. Look up."

The stars pinpricked the dark blanket above them. A mass of twinkling lights indicated the Milky Way. What if she could go aloft, like a character in a fanciful children's book, and swim through the bright lights, find the perfect one, and bring it home to hang over her daughter's bed to keep her safe at night?

She stopped as she considered the possibility.

Or maybe they could both sail away in the night sky, away from all the problems that surrounded them.

"It's amazing, isn't it?" Jarod said as he stepped behind her and slipped his arms around her. "Here we are, two small people looking at all that expanse. We're part of it yet separate. But when I want to be reminded about how insignificant our difficulties may be, I take a moment to lift my eyes to something grander."

"And that's comforting? I think it would overwhelm me."

"It's a matter of perspective, I guess. I know it's up to me to do the next right thing but also that there is a lot I can't control and I have to let go of. For example, if we don't get enough rain and the grass doesn't grow, I can feed the cattle or sell some off. But I can't make it rain or make the grass grow. The same is true with life, even though I wish mightily at times it weren't."

"Like when?" she asked.

Jarod was quiet for a bit.

Maybe she'd overstepped.

"Cameron," he finally said. "It's so difficult to accept that he doesn't want the family, at least one of us, by his side. I mean, I don't understand what he's been through, but CJ would. And they were always close growing up." He shrugged. "I think I was too much of a thorn in her side. Anyway, I have to let it be. Pushing wouldn't solve anything." He released Samantha and walked around to face her.

"So much we can't control," she said, thinking about her mother.

"Yes." He took her hand and continued the walk. "And accept that people are doing the best they can with the tools they have."

"I'm not sure I can believe that about everyone," she said, shaking her head.

"I know what you mean, but it's not that you have to agree with what they're doing or let them harm you because they can't help themselves. It means, I guess, believing in their better angels and hoping they will win the fight someday."

"I'm not sure Cody has any," she said.

"Has he been back?"

"Christmas." She told him about her ex's threats to go to court.

"You might not be able to keep Audie from him forever," Jarod said.

"I will die trying."

He laughed. "Let's not do anything so drastic."

How dare he poke fun at this serious situation? She tried to yank her hand away.

"Whoa there," he said, hanging on. "The stars, remember the stars."

He stopped, and she forced herself to look up again. A nanosecond of time, that's all human beings were. She took a deep breath. "Okay. I won't die trying. But I'm going to do my best to keep that from happening."

"Why?" Jarod asked as they turned the last corner before home.

"What do you mean why?" What kind of a dumb question was that? "He's a drug addict."

"But what if he is clean and sober?"

"A tiger doesn't change its stripes."

"We're talking about human beings here."

"Whose side are you on?" This time she was successful in yanking her hand free, and she stomped up the stairs.

He stood at the bottom with a grin on his face.

"What?" she said.

"Well, at least I know where Audie gets her stomping ability."

"You're impossible."

"I try my best. CJ would agree with you."

She opened the door, then glanced back at him. "Are you coming in?"

"I hope so," he said and took the stairs two at a time.

She held the door for him. Once they'd shed their outerwear, they went to the living room. Her mother was still sound asleep. Audie must still be helping. Samantha was about to head into the kitchen when her father came down the hallway.

"Time to get your mom up. She needs some nutrition to keep up her strength. Mac and cheese should be easy."

"Maddy?" he asked as he shook her mother's arm gently. "Time to wake up."

Her mother didn't stir.

Samantha crouched beside the armchair. "Mom?" The slow

rise and fall of her chest told her Mom must still be with them. She shook her a little harder. "Dinner. One of your favorites."

Audie stood in the doorway. "What's wrong?"

"Nothing," Samantha said automatically. "Grandma's really tired, that's all."

"Can I see?" Jarod asked. "I take an emergency medicine class every year. Too many accidents can happen on a ranch."

Samantha gave him her place.

He checked her mother's pulse and her breath as well as gently lifted one eyelid to check her eyes. There was no response to anything he did. Standing, he looked across at her father. "I think it's time to call an ambulance," he said.

# # #

The hospital was finally quiet.

Samantha had taken turns with her father to be at her mother's bedside while Jarod took care of Audie. When the doctors had completed their examinations, one had come to them with a bowed head. They didn't need his words to know.

It was only a matter of time.

Tubes snaked around her mother, the beep of machines the only indication she was still on the planet.

She didn't know if her mother could hear her, but there were things she needed to say.

"I'm sorry, Mom," she began, holding her mother's hand, barely skin, bones, and tendons stretched by unrelenting hard work. "I didn't thank you nearly enough. And I never really tried to understand why you did what you did. It just seemed like life treated you unfairly."

Her heart was cracking apart. The person who had been beside forever was leaving. It wasn't possible. God wouldn't let it happen.

Yet He did every day. Along with a thousand other cruelties human beings seemed to be determined to perpetuate. The curse of free will.

Do the next right thing.

"But you were a real hero, Mom. You did what had to be done, every day, without fail. And, even though you weren't a churchgoer, you had more faith in me and my father than any other mother I knew, no matter how messed up we were. I love you, Mom. More than I ever told you. And now ... now it's too

227

late." It felt like her chest were ripping apart. Samantha laid her head next to her mother and let her tears fall.

She must have fallen asleep like that, because a gentle touch on her shoulder startled her.

"I'm sorry," her father said. "She's gone." His voice choked.

"Noooo." She squeezed her mother's hand frantically. There was no response. Her mother's face was slack. "But I still feel her. Oh, Mama, please come back. I need you."

"Hush, baby girl." Her father pulled her close, and she let him. "It'll be okay. Not now, but it will be as we adjust to the hole in our lives. Remember, Audie needs you now. It's going to be hard for her to understand."

Oh, God, how was she going to tell her little girl her beloved grandmother was gone?

"I'm glad Jarod is here. He seems like a good man. Let him help you. Not all men are as messed up as me and Cody."

She didn't say anything. The world was foreign now. It wasn't the same.

"Mama."

"Your mother has always been right here." Her father tapped his chest. "She's still there. Just like she is in your heart and will always be." They stood like that for a few more seconds, then she backed away.

"Be strong, Samantha. I know you can be. You're stronger than all of us put together. We'll get through tonight, and then tomorrow ... tomorrow ..." He took in a slow breath, quivering with his grief. "Tomorrow, we'll begin again. But for now, let's go home. We can't do anything else for her."

With a last look at her mother, they walked out the door and into the night.

# # #

She got through the next few days, but it was like living in a deep haze. Nothing was ever quite clear. Audie had been far too practical about her grandmother's death, which meant she would lose it over something entirely unrelated someday soon. Jarod was always there, helping however he could, providing a support she was only barely aware of.

Her father was also more of a steadfast rock than she could have imagined.

How was she going to move forward?

One step at a time. There was no other choice. Almost every human being went through this. They survived. So would she.

But, God, it was going to hurt. When she got back home, she'd need to spend some quality time seeping up the comfort of her church family. She'd missed them while she was in Billings.

Home. She was really thinking of Choteau as home.

She and Jarod were returning from a walk around the block after her mother's memorial service when Cody showed up.

"Hello," he said, his tone not as aggressive as it had been in previous encounters. "Your dad told me. How are you doing? How is Audie?"

"We're okay. It's hard, but ..." She shrugged. No words came easily for the pain she felt.

"Can I see her? I'd really like to give her a hug."

Beside her, Jarod shifted his weight. It was subtle, but Cody must have sensed it, too.

"Are you going to introduce me to your friend?" he asked.

"Jarod Beck. I'm a friend of Samantha and Audie's."

"Where did you meet her?" Cody asked.

Samantha held her breath. She'd never specifically told Jarod about the secrecy of her location.

"I don't see how that's any of your business," Jarod said.

"Audie is my daughter. That makes it my business."

"Seems to me, a father is there for his daughter, helps provide for her. I haven't seen you in the picture before."

"You don't get to decide that," Cody answered, widening his stance.

The situation was becoming too charged, like two bulls standing off with each other.

"Enough," she said. "My mother just died. That's all I can deal with right now. The answer is still no, Cody. I'm not exposing Audie to you. Go away. Just go away." Then the tears she'd held back for the last few hours burst through. She turned away from the two of them and went inside.

Her father was in his usual spot in the kitchen. He was always cooking, cleaning, or examining the contents of cupboards, frequently muttering something like, "I didn't know she kept that." Now, however, he was sitting at the table, staring at a newspaper, and, she suspected, not really reading it. A cup of coffee stood nearby.

She retrieved one of her own, wiping her eyes as she poured the brew.

"How you doing?" her father asked when she sat down.

"Not well."

"Me either."

She sipped her coffee and her father stared some more at the newspaper.

"Audie's watching television," he said. "Hope you don't mind. I didn't have the energy to entertain, her and it was the only thing she wanted to do. I found a nature show for her."

"Good. She likes those. It's like brain candy to her. More facts she can stuff into her mind to bring out at inappropriate times."

He smiled. "Yes. She is quite good at that."

"I think she does it to torment me," Samantha said with a smile.

"Could be. Jarod coming back in or heading back to the hotel for the night?"

"He's out there arguing with Cody, unless it turned into a fist fight or something."

"Sorry. I thought if I let him know what was going on, Cody would stay away."

She shook her head. "Cody wouldn't know how to do the right thing if it bit him."

Her father sipped his coffee. "Someday, you're going to have to let go of your anger against him, you know. He's paid his dues and he's trying. He wants to see his daughter. I understand that."

"Well, understand all you want. He's not coming near Audie. She'd only be confused."

"I think your daughter sees things quite clearly," he said. "She'd ask uncomfortable questions, that's for sure, but she'd accept things as they are, something you seem to be having trouble doing."

A head of steam built within her. Why didn't anyone understand?

The front door squealed open.

"Mind if I come in?" Jarod called out.

"Jarod!" Audie shouted. "Come watch TV with me! There's a bug in the desert, and he's climbing a really big sand dune."

"Just a sec. Let me talk to your mommy first."

"Tell her it's almost time to eat. Ask her if we can have pizza."

"I think pizza is a fine idea," her father told Samantha as Jarod walked into the kitchen. "I'll order some and get some fresh air while I do." He headed for the back porch.

"So?" Samantha asked Jarod. "What happened?"

"We just talked," he said. "He calmed down a bit. He knows he messed up, but he's hoping for a second chance—not with you; he knows that's not possible—to be on the periphery of his daughter's life."

"But—"

Jarod raised his palm. "Hear me out, please. I'm not taking sides, but we talked for quite a while. I think he's faced, is facing, the beast inside that drove his actions. Just like your dad. I know it's tough to have two significant people in your life who were addicts, but they've worked to become better men than they were. That's more than I can say for my father. I hold out hope that he might have changed his ways if he'd lived, but he did a lot of damage while he was alive." He gestured toward the coffeepot. "Mind if I have some?"

"Help yourself."

"What you do is your decision, but I hope you think about it a little more."

She glared at him.

"Yeah, I know. Not my call." He poured a cup. "I think I'll go watch the bug climb the sand dune," he said, "if that's okay with you."

"That'd be good for Audie. Thanks."

She watched him walk out, then put her head in her hands.

"Pizza should be here in about a half hour," her father said, reentering the kitchen. "Are you okay?" He sat beside her and awkwardly put his hand on her arm.

"I'm not sure I know how to be an adult. I was always Mom's daughter, and now, who am I?"

"Welcome to the club," he said. "Your mother was an extraordinary woman, one of a kind. She had such faith in people's ability to overcome their worst selves."

Samantha nodded, tears trickling down her cheeks. She swiped her eyes.

He gentle squeezed her arm. "It's hard to lose a parent," he said. "It doesn't matter how old you are. It's going to take some time, but do yourself a favor."

"What?" she said, her voice barely squeaking out from her swollen throat.

"Don't' push Jarod away in the process."

"But—"

"Hear me out. It's very tempting in moments when a person is hurting a lot to push everyone away and make major changes, like move across the country or find a new job. But one of the things the twelve-step programs have taught me is to resist that impulse. Give a decision six months before doing anything drastic."

"I've heard that too," she said.

"Your mom told me about your struggles. I'm sorry." He released her arm. "There's some belief that addictions are genetic, and I feel guilty about my possible contribution."

"I did it all by myself," she said. "With Cody's help, of course. It was bad, and I did a lot of dumb stuff, but I forced myself to do the right thing the minute I realized I might be pregnant."

"Do you still feel the impulses?" he asked. "I know it's something I have to be aware of. It means a lot of self-care, never getting hungry, angry, lonely, or tired."

"HALT," she said.

"Yes."

She took a deep breath. "Most of the time, it's okay, but this past week has been very difficult. Being back here, Mom so sick, Cody ..."

"A lot of stress."

She nodded.

"Does Jarod know?"

"No, and he's never going to. It's all in the past."

"You're smarter than that, Samantha. It's never totally in the past, especially if it's nipping at you like you say it is. You need to him know." Her father leaned back in his chair. "And when it's time, you have to warn Audie of the danger."

"She's only eight."

"These kids grow up faster than you know. And she's not like other kids. Sometimes that hurts. A lot."

She looked up at the pain in his voice.

"I was a lot like Audie when I was growing up," he said. "I had a tough time understanding why other kids acted the way they did. Often they were mean, and I was lonely. When I first got involved with drugs, all I was trying to do was ease the pain."

"I'm sorry," she said, her heart sad for the little boy he once was. So many things she didn't know or understand about other people. "I'll think about what you said."

"That's good." He stood and got himself a cup of coffee. He gestured toward her, but she shook her head.

"There's one more thing we need to discuss," he said. "Your mother left the house to you. It's free and clear, so all you have to pay are taxes and whatever upkeep is needed. I was hoping you'd let me rent it from you."

She swallowed. It made sense. She didn't really know what to do with it, and she wasn't ready to put it on the market. There were too many things she needed to go through, items she couldn't deal with right now.

"Sounds like a plan," she said.

"Thank you."

The doorbell rang.

"Pizza!" Audie yelled from the living room.

"Remember what I said about Jarod," her father said, stopping her as she headed to the door. "He's a good man. Let him help."

Samantha nodded, but she wasn't sure she agreed at all.

Chapter 27

Jarod pushed through the fatigue as he drove onto the road that connected through Great Falls to the highway. He tried to keep an eye on Samantha's Camry behind him but lost her in the busy traffic. He'd get on the highway and pull off until she showed up.

He was bone-tired. Too many emotions. Too many memories tugging for his attention. At least Samantha's mother's death had been relatively quick. His own mother had lingered at death's door for well over a year.

There were times he doubted God had any sympathy for human beings, and this was one of them. Samantha had so much to deal with, why hit her with this now?

He thought back to his conversation with Cody and then a later one with Samantha's father.

"I know it's not my place," he'd said. "But you seem to be a good man, a man my daughter should wake up and take a long look at. If you ever had the inclination, which I think you do, considering you drove five hours just to see her."

"I had to see about a horse," Jarod began, but her father simply waved it away.

"I know a good excuse when I see one. Anyway, if you have the inclination, you have my blessing, for whatever that means. Sometimes I think I'm hopelessly old-fashioned."

Jarod had grinned at him. "So am I, sir. It means something. Thank you."

All of which meant at some point he was going to have to sort out his feelings for Samantha. Some point soon. His brothers all thought he had more than a passing interest. CJ had indicated as much as well, but she hadn't seemed as enthusiastic as the others. Did she know something, or had her time in the war made her wary?

None of their opinions really mattered. The future depended on what he and Samantha decided was possible.

He reached the highway and took the on-ramp. After he got onto the interstate, he pulled over on the shoulder on a rise, turning the mirror so he could see the cars travel up the two lanes. Sure enough, after a few minutes, he spotted the small sedan, and he breathed out his tension. He signaled and pulled in well ahead of her. Once they made the turn off the highway and got back on the two-lane to Choteau, he finally relaxed again, like a horse anticipating a return to the barn.

Too much big city.

He turned his mind back to Samantha. They both had things to do. He had a business to build, starting with a serious look for another horse. Calving season would start way too soon.

She needed time to get her feet back on the ground.

Everyone at the ranch was about to go into a knuckle-down-and-work time of year. But he wanted to keep a connection with Samantha, if he could stop putting his foot in his mouth.

Maybe Bob Jenkins would let him rent out the arena to keep up Audie's riding lessons and get Samantha on Laughin' Jack, although that was a long shot.

He flipped on his favorite country station and hummed the rest of the way to Choteau. The sky was blue, the roads were clear, and life was good.

Although the sun was already low in the sky when they got to Choteau, his optimistic feelings lingered. He'd support Samantha through this period of mourning and then, with spring, they could begin to move forward again.

He pulled up to the curb and leapt out to help Samantha unload her car. In addition to the suitcases she'd brought with her and the Christmas gifts, there were things she'd wanted that she'd taken from the house. There was more to do, but it could wait, especially with her father living in the house.

He was glad she'd made some kind of peace with Jake Deveaux. Although the man had messed up a lot of lives, he was trying to do something right. The past couldn't be undone, but he was working to make the future a better one.

"I know you need some time," Jarod said to Samantha when they were done. Audie had gone to her room to make sure everything was just as she'd left it. "But I would love it if you'd come to Sunday dinner."

She didn't give him an immediate answer.

"If you want, that is."

"I don't think that's a good idea," she said. "I ... Audie ... We both need some time to adjust to this new reality. I need to get back to teaching so I can show them what I can do. And, even if they offer me the job, I don't know if we can stay. It's only a matter of time before Cody finds us."

"You can't keep running from Cody forever," he said, placing his hand on her arm. "It's not healthy for either of you."

"Having him around is what's not healthy," she said, shaking off his hand.

"It's not either or," he said. "There can be boundaries around his visits with her. You can be there. He can come to the ranch."

"That's not an ideal solution either," she said.

"Everything in life is not perfect."

"I do my best to make it that way. As long as I keep control over who she sees and what she does, Audie will be safe. And that's what's most important."

His optimism faded away.

He shook his head.

"None of us are in control," he said. "Cursing at the rain because it's falling or not falling is a foolish waste of time. Trying to control what another human being does or has happen to them is even more futile. We don't have that power." He wanted to make her see, to understand, but her expression was guarded, the truce they'd reached in Billings all but gone.

"I'm not doing a good job at this, but it's what I know," he continued. "We can't keep another person safe, no matter what the threat. I couldn't save my father from himself, my mother from cancer, and I couldn't save Cameron from his determination to join the service. It just can't be done."

"Those were grown-ups. I'm talking about a child. There is a difference. But you don't have any kids, so you wouldn't know."

God, that hurt.

"I guess you're right." He put his hat back on his head. "I'd best be going. The invitation still stands. And let me know if I can do anything else for you."

He tipped his hat, walked out the door, and headed home.

# # #

Samantha wanted to call out after him, tell him she was sorry, that she hadn't meant it, but she didn't.

Why didn't anyone understand the need to protect Audie from Cody?

Maybe it was because it wasn't true.

She tried to ignore the small voice whispering to her.

Being in control had been the only thing that had gotten her through the anguish of drug withdrawal. Memory of the torture had been what kept her away from them, because the craving was always there, a tiny siren song of lust.

So you think you did it all by yourself.

She ignored the voice and walked to the kitchen. Was there anything for dinner, or would she have to get to the market before it closed?

Eggs. Bacon. Good thing Audie liked breakfast for dinner. She'd whip up a small batch of pancakes and her kid would be happy.

Unlike her.

She'd succeeded in making Jarod leave, but it was a hollow victory. Nonetheless, she straightened her shoulders and dragged the suitcases to the washer. She could do what had to be done. Jarod wouldn't try to run her life anymore and she could continue on the path she'd set for herself when she arrived in Choteau.

As she sorted through their clothes, loneliness washed over her.

# # #

"Mr. Van Sutton!" Samantha leaned on the teen's desk and glared at him. "For the last time, stop distracting your classmates with your antics. The next stop is Mrs. Helms's office. I've had enough of you."

The kid looked startled for a gratifying moment but then leaned back in his chair with a mocking grin. "You must have had a bad Christmas," he said. "Santa leave coal in your stocking?"

"Her mother died, jerkface!" one of the girls hissed from the back.

He had the courtesy to blush and look down at his desk.

"Now, class, let us get back to the lesson at hand. Take out your calculators." Like she did a thousand times a day, Samantha pushed away the pain of her mother's death. They said it got easier, but after only a few weeks' time, she was rushing things if she thought she'd get any relief.

Jim was the last one to leave the classroom.

"I'm sorry," he said. "I didn't know."

Her first instinct was to dismiss him, but then she remembered what Birdie had told her. "Thanks, Jim. It can be tough losing your mother, no matter how or when it happens."

"Yeah." He fumbled his big hands around each other.

"You know," she said, "it wouldn't take much to bring up your grade for this quarter. I'd like to work with you to see if we can make it happen."

He cocked his head and pursed his lips before asking, "Would I have to make up all the homework I've missed?"

"While that would be ideal," she said, "I was thinking of something a little less drastic. I've got a few packets I could put together. Complete them and I'll count it for homework."

He still looked leery but nodded his head. "Thanks for the chance."

"Everyone deserves a second chance."

Except Cody.

Not fair.

That pesky voice could really take a hike.

# # #

Everything slipped back into a normal pattern, with the exception that Jarod wasn't part of their lives anymore. She avoided him at church, even thought about finding a new one, but he seemed to sense her desire and made it easy for her, although his interactions with some of the single women who seemed to sense he was free made her teeth clench.

Birdie was not so easy to dodge. For the first few weeks, she echoed Jarod's Sunday dinner invitation but then gave it up. Instead, she'd look at Samantha and shake her head with a sigh.

Samantha didn't know which was worse.

"Something wrong between you and Jarod?" Trish asked one Sunday toward the end of January. The weather had had a brief break, sliding into warmer temperatures as cold air blasts from the north subsided, lulling them into a false sense of believing spring was imminent.

"There is no me and Jarod."

"You did go on a date."

"One."

"And he was that bad?" Trish asked.

"No. It was fine. He was fine."

"And I heard rumors he went to Billings over Christmas to see someone."

"He went to buy a horse."

"Did he?"

"What?" Samantha asked in confusion.

"Did he buy a horse?"

"Well, no. But that was because my mother died." Trish, along with most of the congregation, had offered her condolences the first Sunday after her return. Big happenings were never kept under wrap for long in small towns.

"And he helped you through that."

"Yes." This conversation was getting uncomfortable.

"So why is there no you and Jarod?" Trish asked.

"Because it isn't the right time. I don't know if I can stay. I don't know if he's the right person. What happens to Audie if I take that risk and it doesn't work out? What happens if my ex shows up and I have to leave?"

"Why should your ex showing up affect your life? Aren't you over him?"

"Long past. But he could damage Audie."

"I've seen your daughter in action. I don't think she needs that much protection. What are you going to do when she becomes a teenager?"

Samantha didn't want to think about that.

"Tell you what, girlfriend," Trish said, putting her arm around Samantha and steering her in the direction of her husband, Brad. "You and I need some girl time. I happen to have several lovely fruit tarts I just made as an experiment and a late harvest Riesling to go with them. Brad will be happy to take the kids for a burger or something."

"I'm going to do what?" he said with a grin.

"Play nursemaid to the kids."

"How about I take them skiing or something?"

"No!" Samantha cried. "Audie's too young to ski."

Trish shook her head. "Beth and Sam were five when they started. I think that's a great idea."

"She doesn't have any gear." First horses. Now skis. Samantha was going to have a heart attack before she was thirty.

"I don't have any gear for what?" Audie asked, walking over to them with Beth.

"Skiing," Trish said.

"We're going skiing?" Beth asked. "That's awesome. Are Ms. Deveaux and Audie coming, too?"

"Ms. Deveaux and I are going to have a girl's afternoon. I'm thinking some pampering is in order for your math teacher."

"But I haven't given permission for Audie to go skiing,"

Samantha protested.

"Please, Mommy. I want to go." Audie tugged at her sleeve. "I'll be good."

Samantha looked down into her daughter's face. How could she deny her? It would be a good change after all the trauma of her grandmother's passing. But what if something happened to her?

Trish took her hand. "She'll be okay. The beginner slope is practically flat. Someone will stay with her, right, Brad?"

"Of course," he said. "We can take turns. That way everyone gets to ski."

"What does it cost?" Samantha said cautiously.

"We'll take care of that," Brad said. "She's our guest."

"I can't ..." People were too generous in this town.

"You can," Trish said. "It's the least we can do."

"Well, Mommy?"

"Okay," Samantha said. She couldn't fight all of them. "You can go."

"Yay! I love you, Mommy!"

"You, too, sweetie," she said, giving her daughter a hug.

She took Audie home for a change of clothes and then drove to Trish's house. By the time she got there, the nerves had come back. What was her friend going to ask her? How could she best respond?

"Now for peace and quiet," Trish said after they'd gotten everyone out of the house. "I have some sandwich fixings before we dive into the tarts. I really want to get your opinion on them. I'm trying to decide whether to add them to the lineup or not."

"Do you have enough customers to expand?" Samantha asked.

"There are several new avenues. Of course, it's better when summer and the swarm of tourists arrive, but with the new restaurant and a rumor of a new bed-and-breakfast in town, I'd say Choteau is on an upswing. It's about time."

"It's tough for small towns everywhere," Samantha said.

"Yes, but we have a couple of things that have helped. The first is David Letterman. He's given the town a name. Like him or hate him, people know about him and his ranch. And," Trish raised a finger, "he has clout. That brings me to the second thing. The internet. Thanks to Letterman's influence, added to a few of the other California types who have moved here, we have internet at a decent speed."

"California types like Dave Brockman?"

"Yes, why do you ask? Do you know him?" Trish finished putting the fixings on the center island counter. "Help yourself."

As she built her sandwich, she told Trish what she knew about Jarod's new neighbor.

"Typical," Trish said when she'd finished. "People come from warmer places during the summer months, and then winter sets in way too soon. Only the ones who develop a relationship with the reality of Montana make it."

"Or they want something," Samantha added.

"That's cynical."

"Yes, but there's something about the man just doesn't sound right. Especially since he's friends with that attorney."

"Cassandra Sanders?"

"Yes, that one."

"I know the Becks aren't crazy about her; in fact, I had a hard time trying to figure out what Jarod was doing with her. But I don't know that there's anything more than she's an aggressive attorney. No one wants to face her in family court. The opposite side rarely gets what they want. Brad doesn't seem to have a problem working for her, though."

A chill went through Samantha. Would Cody go through with his threat to take her to court? And would he hire someone like Cassandra?

"So what's up with you?" Trish asked once they'd cleaned up the lunch dishes. "No, sorry ... let me start again. I know that your mother died and that takes some real adjustment. Mine passed last year, and it was life-changing. Fortunately, I've got lots of aunts and surrogate mothers because I've lived here all my life." She pulled a couple of dessert plates from a cupboard. "But it feels like it's more than that. Like you're at some crossroads."

That pretty much nailed it on the head. She was definitely at a decision point in her life.

"I guess, once I got my life together after Audie was born, that was it. I was all grown up. I charted my course, and all I had to do was execute it."

Trish laughed. "That's one of the greatest lies of all time. It trips up every single one of us." She wagged her finger. "This growing up stuff? It's never finished. Never."

"I'm coming to realize that."

"And the path you were on was to get a job, get a few years' experience, and aim for a job somewhere else, right?"

Samantha nodded.

"And then do the same thing all over again?" Trish asked.

"No. The next move is supposed to be the last. I figured I could find something in a big city, probably out of state. Someplace where my ex couldn't find us."

"Tell me something. When you applied for the teaching license, did you have to get your fingerprints checked?"

"Um. Yes." Realization dawned. "I guess I'd be pretty easy to find no matter where I was."

"Yeah. A private investigator could do it in about five minutes. Innocent people are pretty terrible at thinking like a criminal."

Samantha laughed at her foolishness and then sobered. If nowhere was secret, where was the safest place to be?

Chapter 28

Sitting across from Trish in the breakfast nook, Samantha focused her mind on the tart while her friend waited expectantly. Layering a bit of flaky crust, some custard and a blueberry on her fork she put it into her mouth. Tart berry contrasted with smooth sweet cream, finished with the neutral crust.

She opened her mouth to say something, but Trish pointed to the wineglass. "Taste some of that first. I want to know about the entire experience."

Layers of fruity honey coated her tongue, enhancing the lingering flavors of the tart.

"Amazing," she said. "The tart is dynamite, and the wine makes it out of this world. It would be perfect for LeGorille."

"I'm was hoping you'd think that," Trish said. "My biggest problem will be keeping them away from Brad. He thinks they're divine."

"He's a good husband," Samantha said. Would it ever be possible for her to get married again? If she stayed here, it would be awkward to date anyone but Jarod.

As if sensing her thoughts, Trish asked, "What happened with you and Jarod?"

"Truthfully, I pushed him away. It was getting too intense too fast. And he is a bit controlling."

"How so?"

"He'd just leap in and do something without asking. Or pay for things I should be handling."

"Putting new tires on your car?" Trish asked, a slight smile on her face.

"Exactly. That's way too expensive a gift."

"He worried about you. He's that kind of guy—we get a lot of them here in the West—who shows more by actions than by words that he cares. Like you, he's also used to doing things alone. From what CJ says, they've all clashed with him more than once about his tendency to do first and ask later."

"I can't handle that."

"Have you given it a chance?"

"Of course I have." Samantha cringed internally as she said the words. They weren't really true. "Probably not."

"Relationships take work," Trish said. "Especially when two people have been alone for a significant amount of time. Even Brad and I need to talk things out now and then, and we've been at this our whole lives it seems."

Trish had a point, but Samantha had already blown her shot with Jarod by not giving him a chance. "I'll keep that in mind for next time," Samantha said.

Her mother had been right. She was awfully hard on people, probably because she expected them to let her down. On an impulse, though, she'd given Jim Van Sutton a second chance, and so far he was coming through. Not only had he picked up the packet she'd made, but he'd asked for help with something he didn't understand.

Miracles did still occur.

"You could be in a movie with all the expressions that crossed your face in the last minute," Trish remarked, pouring them each a little more wine. "I don't think the jury is in on you and Jarod. Do you *want* another chance with him? If you decided to stay, that is."

"I'm not sure. The Becks seem like a lot to handle. Lots of secrets and a big responsibility in the family ranch, responsibility Jarod has taken on. And there is still a lot of pain there."

"That's true," Trish said. "When CJ first came back, she was a wreck. Nick helped smooth her out and give her hope again. Every day she becomes more of the CJ I knew growing up, before her world turned upside down."

What would happen if Samantha stayed? Would she blow it because she didn't know what to do with a man if he wasn't rotten to her? What if he turned out like her father? Or his father? What if her own internal demon reared its head again?

"Look," Trish said. "I don't know what's running through your mind. Brad and I were sweethearts in high school. We've known each other all our lives, so I didn't have too many questions about what I was getting into. But if you're worried about Jarod's character, don't. He's as solid as they come."

Someone else had said that. Bob Jenkins.

"My whole plan was to keep running, but you're right, that doesn't make sense. I'm going to have to take a stand somewhere."

"May as well be here," Trish said.

"May as well."

# # #

By the time Samantha reached the house with Audie, her daughter was half asleep. She tucked her into bed, made herself a cup of tea, and sat in her favorite chair in the living room, not bothering to put on any lights. Although twilight had long since disappeared, the streetlight had come on. There was enough brightness to could do what she had to do.

Think.

Maybe converse with God a little.

The mistakes she'd made growing up had colored her viewpoint. Everything was suspicious, everyone out to get her. Even if she hadn't been conscious of the attitude, it had affected every choice she made.

And what about the demon that apparently still lurked, the one that had raised its head in Billings? The one that could destroy her life and everyone around her if she weren't careful and in control?

Despite what she'd said to Trish, did it make sense for her to stay in Choteau? Or should they move one more time and get a fresh start? Maybe that would keep the demon satisfied.

But it would devastate Audie. Her daughter had just begun to fit in. If Audie's safety and happiness were priorities, Samantha's choice leaned toward Choteau. Would Jarod's steadying nature finally bring her peace? If she told him about her past, would her fears disappear like fog in strong sunlight? Or would he walk away, not wanting to risk his future with damaged goods?

What if it was already too late and she'd pushed him away too hard? What if he no longer wanted anything to do with her?

There was only one way to find out. She was going to have to make a decision soon.

She sighed and looked at the old clock on a side table, something she'd brought from her mother's house.

Seven. Sunday dinner had been hours ago, and she knew they each took care of themselves for Sunday evening supper. Now would be a good time to call.

She reached deep for every thread of humility and courage she had, wrapped them together in a strong weave, and picked up the phone.

"Hello, Samantha," Jarod said, his voice neutral.

"Hi. Did I catch you at a bad time?"

"No, it's fine. Just staring at numbers."

"Your favorite."

"Yeah. So what can I do for you?" he asked.

This was not going to be easy.

Give it up.

She ignored the demon and pressed on.

"I behaved badly," she said. "You did so much and then I sent you away."

"Don't worry about it. It's all water under the bridge."

"But I was wrong. I like you, Jarod. A lot." Her throat threatened to close.

"I like you, too." His voice had a tinge of wariness now.

"Will you give me ... us ... another chance? There are things you don't know that I need to tell you. I'm hoping if that's in the open, we can work together on the rest."

The long silence doomed her.

The creak of the leather chair in his office prefaced his words. "I've spent a lot of time thinking about this," he said. "I don't think you were wrong. You're just getting your feet under you. I'm ready to settle into something more permanent. I live on a ranch that can sometimes require hard physical work and long hours. My favorite thing in the world is to saddle up my horse and ride the land where I can almost touch the clouds above me. You're afraid of horses."

She didn't have any response. Every one of his points was correct.

"I thought we could make it work," he continued. "I wanted to. But you kept handing me my hat and asking what my hurry was. I'm getting a little bruised, and the push and pull is not good for Audie."

"I'm sorry," she finally got out. "Are you sure there's nothing I can do to change your mind?"

Silence surrounded her.

"Quite sure," he finally said. "I hope you'll understand. See you around."

The line disconnected.

She set it on the end table and stared into the night.

Now what?

# # #

Cody walked into Choteau Elementary School like he

belonged there. That was the secret he'd learned a long time ago: walk in like you owned the place and no one asked any questions. A quick glance at the directory showed him where the third grade classrooms were.

It had been pitifully easy to find out where Samantha had gone. She may have tried to cover her tracks, but Jarod Beck was hanging up his shingle as a horse trainer, and his website led Cody right to Choteau. The town wasn't big enough to get lost in, and the school was easy to find.

It was almost time for classes to end, so he could present himself to the teacher and say that Samantha had asked him to pick up their daughter early and bring her to her classroom in the high school. Which is exactly what he'd do once he introduced himself.

He trudged between the kid-sized cubbies, overflowing with coats, boots, and other assorted kid gear. He barely remembered his elementary years, and what he did consisted of teams who picked him last, nasty little girls, and continual notes that indicated he wasn't performing up to his potential.

He was going to turn it all around now that he was a parent. Reclaiming the lost years wasn't possible, but he wanted to be part of her life.

"Hello," he said to the dark-haired woman sitting at the desk, fiddling with something on her computer while pictures flashed on a screen at one end of the room.

As soon as he spoke, she rose from her chair and strode to where he stood at the doorway.

"How can I help you?" she asked, using her body as a block against him entering the room any farther.

"Hi," he said, putting on his most engaging smile. "Samantha asked me to pick up Audie a little early and bring her to the high school. She needs to do a few things that will make it hard for her to get here in time."

"And you are?"

"Audie's father. I'm Cody Drake. Samantha and I never married."

"I see. And do you have permission to pick up Audie?"

"I do, I do." He relaxed his shoulders and leaned an arm against the doorstop. There were no kids in the classroom. Were they on the playground? Damn cold to be outside.

"Let me check that." The woman picked up the handset of the old-fashioned landline that hung next to the door. "Hey, Tami, this is Jody Hunt. Has Samantha Deveaux given anyone else permission to pick up Audie?"

Cody dropped his relaxed pose. If they were at recess, that would work for him just as well, maybe better. He stepped back.

"Wait a second," the woman said, following him. "You can't just go wandering around the school and picking up stray children. There are laws against that."

"I really am her father," he said, stopping and pulling himself up straight. "There are also laws that say a father has a right to see his child. A right her mother is denying me. How is that fair?"

"I've got no say in what Samantha does or doesn't do, and neither do you unless you follow the rules like everyone else."

"What does that mean?"

"It means if you feel you have a legal issue, get yourself a lawyer."

"A lawyer."

"Yep. For now, I'm escorting you to the office."

He could probably outrun her, but that would be the worst kind of stupid. They'd call the cops, which in this town wouldn't take long. All a cop would have to do is pull his records and he'd be back where he started.

"Okay, okay. I'm going."

She softened a little. "I'm not saying you're wrong," she added as she took another step his way, herding him back down the hallway toward the front entrance. "Just that you need to do this the right way. Like an adult."

A lawyer. It would be worth it. Maybe they would take payments. He'd seen a sign on his way through town: Cassandra Sanders, Attorney-at-Law, in big gold letters.

# # #

"You look like someone rode you hard and put you up wet," CJ remarked as she walked into the barn. "You said you needed help with the books again, so here I am. What happened to the schoolteacher?"

"Didn't work out." He gave the lug nut on the tractor wheel another hefty turn, and the bolt broke. "For the love of all that's holy!" he shouted.

"Wouldn't it be just as easy to swear?" she asked, sweetly. "You wouldn't have to start big, but a little *damn* or *crap* won't hurt. It's so much more satisfying."

He glared at her.

"Or you could stick with what you've got." She shrugged. "So why didn't it work out?"

"Hand me a drift pin, would you?"

"A what?"

"Never mind." Jarod got up from his crouch position and found what he needed. Hopefully, he could mine one of the junk tractors he kept around for a replacement bolt. Better yet, CJ could leave and take her pesky questions with her.

"So why didn't it work out?" his sister repeated.

"We weren't right for each other."

"You're perfect for each other!" CJ stood in front of him, hands on her hips. "She's sweet, and her daughter's a pistol. She went through rough times, like you, and you both are better people because of it. And you both have the church thing going."

Everything CJ said was true if oddly put. That's what made turning Samantha down Sunday night all the more difficult. But he couldn't keep getting close and then being pushed away when she got scared.

"Can you stay out of my business?" he said.

"Oh, like you all stayed out of mine when I came back?"

"That was different. You needed help."

"So do you."

"Yeah, can you find me a bolt?" he asked, a little sarcasm creeping into his voice. Why couldn't people just leave him alone? He needed a little time to get over Samantha so he could move on to his next step, whatever that was.

"I think you're scared."

He let the tools he'd picked up fall back to the workbench with a clatter. "I think you need to take your amateur therapy somewhere else. What's Dylan doing?"

"Yelling at his phone. The legislature up in Helena is close to passing a law he thinks is dead wrong. Since when did he get so fascinated by politics?"

"It's new this year. He's getting frustrated because his paintings aren't selling."

"Yeah, well, I hope one sells soon. He sure can get intense over this stuff," she said.

Jarod picked up the drift pin and hammer again. "If you could make sure last year's books are up to date and correct so I can get them over to Brad for taxes, I'd appreciate it."

"Sure. But that's not the only reason I came over. I found out something new about Alice."

"Really? What's that?"

"She married someone named Greg Stern in 1952. I haven't gotten any further than that, but if she changed her last name, which most women did back then, at least I know to look for Alice Stern."

"That should help. But what if the line dies out or we find someone and he or she doesn't have the deed for the mineral rights?"

"We'll cross that bridge when we come to it. The other thing I wanted to let you know is, Nick and I are heading down to Great Falls sometime this week for supplies. Let me know if you need anything. Calving season is almost here."

"Thanks. Will do." He crouched back down by the tractor wheel.

She started toward the barn door, then turned back. "For the record, I believe you need to rethink this whole Samantha situation. Since you two split up, you've become far more of a grouch than anyone on the ranch would like to live with."

The door thudded behind her.

"We were never together!" he shouted at the closed door.

He held the drift pin against the end of the broken bolt and pounded the heck out of it.

# # #

"Samantha Deveaux?" a young man in a Carhartt jacket and heavy black snow boots asked her as she walked Audie to the car after school.

"Yes?"

He handed her an envelope. "You've been served. Have a nice day."

He walked back down the school sidewalk to the blue car at the edge of the road.

She stared after him as he drove sedately down the road.

"What did he mean?" Audie asked as she settled into the passenger seat. "What is served?"

"It means he gave me this envelope."

"Well, that's a silly thing to say."

"I agree, sweetie." Samantha tossed the envelope in the back, started the car, and headed home, the thrum of imminent danger beating in the back seat like Poe's telltale heart.

Cody must have carried through with his threat.

She knew she should have started looking for a lawyer when Jody Hunt had told her about the incident. As soon as she got home, she'd get on the phone and call Cassandra. She may not like the woman, but, apparently, she was the best in town.

Samantha tried to pretend everything was normal while she got out a snack for Audie and helped her with her homework. Once she'd listened to Audie read to her and checked her math homework, Audie went off to read the latest in the Black Stallion series. The kid was seriously horse obsessed. Fortunately, she'd accepted the excuses Samantha had been feeding her about why they didn't go to the ranch.

February was marching relentlessly along. Soon it would be time to get the obligatory Valentine's cards, with an extra special something for her girl. As usual, Samantha would ignore the holiday for herself.

If only things had worked out with Jarod.

But it was her own fault, so now she needed to do the next things on the list: open the envelope and call Cassandra.

She grabbed a kitchen knife and attacked the offensive paper. With shaky hands, she pulled out the heavy sheets. From the format alone, she could see it was a legal document.

Cody was suing her for visitation rights.

She sank to the nearest chair.

Cassandra Sanders was representing him.

Chapter 29

Dear God, what was she going to do?

There was no one she really wanted to talk with right now except Jarod, and that wasn't possible. Trish had offered help, and since she knew as much about the situation as anyone, Samantha picked up the phone. As soon as Trish got on the line, Samantha told her what had happened.

"Well," Trish said. "You have a couple of options. You can find another attorney and go up against Cassandra in court, and I can pretty much guarantee you're going to lose."

"Or?"

"Or you can contact Cody and work out some arrangement."

"Not happening. And why would I lose?"

"Because Cody does have rights," Trish said. "And Cassandra is really, really good at what she does."

And running was no longer possible. If Samantha left in the middle of a school year, she'd be able to get a job only in some of the worst school districts, where they were truly desperate.

"What would you suggest?" Samantha asked.

"I'd try to get a meeting with Cody and a neutral party— maybe the minister?"

"He wouldn't go for that," Samantha stated.

Trish sighed. "You aren't giving the man a chance," she said. "What if positions were reversed? What if you had done the work to get clean and sober, and, after you gave birth to Audie, they took her away because there was a chance it might not stick?"

"It's not the same," she said, although her stomach got rock hard. What if she hadn't been able to get clean as quickly as she had? Would some government agency have taken Audie away from her?

"Why not?"

"He didn't want her," she whispered. It wouldn't do for Audie to overhear that.

"Yes, there is that. But that was in the past, and much as we would like to, we can't go back for a redo. We can only atone and move forward. It seems to me that's what the man is trying to do.

You can't ignore him. God or bad, right or wrong, he is Audie's father," Trish said. "And she has a right to know him as much as he does her. In your heart, you know that. I'm not sure why you are being so stubborn about this."

What would Audie say if she knew that Samantha had kept her father from her? Her daughter had a strong notion of what was fair and what wasn't.

"All right," she said. "I'll talk to Pastor Steve."

"I'm glad." There was a pause. "I've hesitated to ask, but how are things with you and Jarod? Any improvement?"

"There still isn't any me and Jarod," she said. She told Trish about her call to Jarod and the result.

"Too bad," Trish said. "But don't give up. I know Birdie is rooting for you."

Did nothing escape the notice of this small town?

Once they hung up, she went to the kitchen to get dinner started and mull over her decision. Would Cody listen to reason and work with her? Or would he insist on going to court and getting as much time as he could?

He couldn't have much money of his own, so hopefully he'd work with her. And then what? How was she going to be able to allow him unsupervised time with Audie? Would she have to drive to Billings every week?

The whole idea was impossible. What had she been thinking?

"Mommy?" Audie's voice was tinged with crankiness.

Samantha hoped she could smooth it away. She couldn't deal with any more crises tonight.

"What, sweetie?" she asked in her softest voice.

"I *have* to see Misty on Saturday. I miss her soooo much. And I miss Jarod. Are you guys mad at each other? You shouldn't be."

"We're not mad," Samantha said. "It's complicated. Adult stuff. We're still friends, just not best friends."

"Because he's not perfect," Audie stated.

"That's not true," Samantha countered.

"It is too. But he's nice to me. And I want to see him. And I want to see Misty, and you have to take me."

"Just because you're demanding something does not mean I have to give it to you," Samantha said, tired of trying to work around everyone else's issues. Her daughter was only eight, but she could be exhausting because of how she saw the world. And also because she was eight.

"When spring comes, we'll see if we can find another place for you to ride. Maybe that nice Mr. Jenkins will give you lessons. And because he has an indoor arena, you can ride all winter."

"No!" Audie stomped her foot. "I want Misty!"

"You can't have Misty!" Control was slipping from Samantha's grasp; the demon hovered at the edges of her consciousness.

"I hate you! You're ruining my life!" Audie pounded her fists on Samantha.

For tiny hands, they had an impact. She grabbed them. "Stop it! Stop it this instant!" Even as she yelled, she knew it was wrong. She was only going to wind up Audie more, not calm her down.

The little feet started to kick. Fortunately, there were no shoes.

The demon laughed.

Samantha took a deep breath and sent up a prayer. Then she sank to the floor, bringing Audie down with her. Arms around her daughter's waist, she held her tightly while the girl wore herself out with struggle and tears.

"I know, sweetie," Samantha whispered. "I messed things up. I'm sorry. So, so, sorry."

She hung on for several minutes.

"I love Misty," Audie said amid the sobs. "You have to fix it."

"I'm not sure I can."

"You have to."

Samantha pulled her close and kissed her head. Audie was right. She'd made this mess, and somehow she was going to have to fix it.

Starting with her ex.

# # #

After getting Cody's phone number from her father the next day, Samantha sent him a text.

SD: Can we talk? Without going to court?

A few seconds later, the phone dinged.

CD: That's what I've been trying to do. You wouldn't listen.
SD: I know.
CD: I want to see my daughter.
SD: I understand.

CD: Good. I'm in Billings. At work. Talk tonight? You have my number.
SD: Okay.

Samantha closed her eyes. *Dear God, give me the strength to admit I'm not perfect. Show me the way to the best actions for my daughter.* After a moment, she added, *And please keep the demon away.*

She opened her eyes, took a breath, and went back to prepping for the next class.

Once dinner was done and Audie settled that evening, she poured herself a cup of tea, sat at the kitchen table, and called Cody.

"Hello," she said awkwardly when he picked up.

"Hello. Listen," he said in a rush. "I'm sorry about the whole lawyer thing. I didn't know what else to do. You wouldn't hear me out."

"I know. I ... I was wrong."

"Okay. So now what?"

"What do you want?" she asked, turning her teacup so its flowers aligned perfectly with those on the saucer. "I mean, specifically. I don't think I can leave her alone with you—not quite yet. And you live in Billings."

"We could meet in Helena. It's a longer drive for me, but I don't mind. After being in prison for more than eight years, I enjoy the freedom."

"Are you going to tell her about that?" Samantha asked.

"Not now. I don't want to scare her half to death. But if she ever asks, I'm not going to lie."

"You've changed."

"Mostly. I still do my share of stupid," he said. "But I'm working at it, Samantha. And I'm sorry, really sorry, for all I put you through and for not being there for you when you needed help with Audie. As soon as I get back on my feet, I hope to do something to support her."

"I'm doing fine." Contributions gave people control, like charity groups that tried to change the values of the people they served.

"I see," he said. "I'll start a college fund."

Her irritation persisted, but she kept her peace. She'd promised Audie she'd set everything right, and that was what she was going to do.

They made arrangements to meet at the end of February, when winter should start to loosen its grip.

When she hung up, she put her head in her hands and closed her eyes. It had been exhausting, but the first step was taken. He'd promised to contact Cassandra and withdraw the petition.

How would the attorney take it? Would she advise him to keep going? Or let them work it out themselves?

"Who were you talking to?" Audie said, wandering in from the living room where she'd been watching a nature show.

Tell her now or tell her later?

"Were you talking to Jarod? Can we see Misty?"

"Not yet. There was something else I had to fix first."

"What?" Audie plunked herself down in one of the other kitchen chairs.

"Uh ..." Samantha let out a long breath of air. "Remember when I said you didn't have a daddy?"

"Yeah. I didn't believe you. Everyone has a daddy. I figured mine got lost or something."

Samantha stifled her laugh. If only everyone could have such a practical view of life.

"You are absolutely right," she said. "He did get lost. But he found his way back. He'd like to see you."

Audie frowned. "Does that mean you and he are getting back together? What about Jarod? You love him."

"I ..." Samantha didn't want to deny her feelings anymore, but how to explain feelings that weren't reciprocated to a little girl who expected everything to work out the way she decided? "Your dad and I are not getting together. You don't have to worry about that."

"But what if I don't like him?"

"But you might like him. You have to give it a chance."

"But what if I don't?" The pitch of her voice began to rise.

"Then we'll talk about it."

"And I won't have to see him anymore."

"We'll talk about it," Samantha said, as firmly as she could.

Audie looked at her for a moment, as if deciding whether to continue. Then she asked, "When can I see Misty again?"

"Soon, sweetie." At the very least Samantha could take her up to the ranch on Saturday. Surely Jarod wouldn't deny the little girl a chance to pet her favorite horse.

# # #

"Hi, Jarod." Cassandra took the stool next to him at Bridges Coffee Shop.

"Hello." He really didn't want her, or anyone else for that matter, to bother him right now. He'd spent half the morning signing the loan papers over at the bank—signing his life away was more like it. Glancing up at the old clock in the shape of a coffeepot, he asked, "Buy you a cup of coffee?"

"Sure. I'd like that."

Mae, the owner of the café, came back from the table service, a pot in her hand. She dumped more of the dark brew into his cup. "The usual?" she asked Cassandra.

"Yes. Jarod's buying."

"Oh?" Mae shot him what most people referred to as "the look," the one that told the recipient he was doing something against Mae's personal code. Since no one really understood what that code was, it could be difficult to interpret what they'd done wrong.

In this case though, he had a pretty good idea. Like most everyone else in town, Mae was partial to him dating the schoolteacher, however brief it might have been. And while the town respected Cassandra, even admired her, there wasn't a lot of love lost there.

"So, your friend Samantha is making nice with her ex," Cassandra said once Mae had delivered the coffee and walked off to take an order.

"What do you mean?"

"Oh, you didn't know. Now that Cody Drake has released me as his attorney and it's a matter of public record, I can tell you. He sued for visitation rights."

And Cassandra had represented him. Of course.

He forced a shrug. "It's up to her."

"You don't care anymore?"

"It's none of my business." He refrained from telling her it was none of hers, either. But it was tempting.

"So you aren't seeing her."

Now it was the time to take a stand.

"Whatever's between me and Samantha is exactly that," he said, giving her a long stare. "Between me and her."

"Whoa, cowboy. I didn't mean anything by it."

He looked at the clock again. A minute had passed.

"You had a chance to hook up with Dave Brockman? He's a

really nice guy," she said after enough silence between them had passed for her.

"We did."

"And?"

"Not much." Fatigue settled on his shoulders. He peeled some bills from his wallet, placed them on the counter, and picked up his hat. Placing his finger to the brim, he said, "See you around." Then he strutted out the door, his imagination supplying the sound of the spurs as he left.

A man needed time to think. Maybe Saturday he'd saddle up a horse and try to find a relatively dry path up the foothills. Snow on the ground was still heavy, but the January thaw had diminished it enough in some places to make it passable. And so far February hadn't dumped any new snow. Even the temperature, which normally dropped like a rocket the first few weeks of the month, had stayed temperate. He needed some time to commune with God in the best place there was to find Him— out on the range.

He got in the truck and headed to the market, a list from Birdie in his back pocket. When he walked into the kitchen, bags in his hand, he found Dylan sitting at the kitchen table.

"What's up?" Jarod asked. "Where's Birdie?"

"In her room," Dylan replied. He cleared his throat. "There's news. Cameron's coming home."

Jarod's body tensed. "When?"

"A few weeks. They'll give us particulars. Someone has to pick him up in Great Falls."

"I'll do it." It would be good to have Cameron home. He hoped.

"Maybe CJ would be a better choice," Dylan said. "He was closer to her than to the rest of us."

Jarod started pulling groceries from the bag. It burned him, but Dylan was probably right. No matter how hard he'd tried when they were growing up, he and Cameron were simply cut from different cloth, no matter how much their values appeared the same to the outside eye.

"I'll give CJ a call," Dylan offered. "You're too grumpy to be nice to anyone."

"I've got a lot on my mind."

"So what are you going to do when that little girl wants to get up on that horse again?"

"I'll deal with it then. I thinking Bob Jenkins might be a good teacher for her. I need to train rodeo horses if I'm ever going to get this business off the ground."

"You keep telling yourself that."

Jarod forced himself to keep a steady hand as he put the perishables in the fridge. Wouldn't do to go slamming things around.

"Calving season is coming up soon. I'm going down to the barn to work on prep before I feed the cattle."

"Isn't it my day?" Dylan asked.

"I'll take care of it. The cows don't care about my mood." If he closed the outside door a little harder than needed on his way out, it was fine with him.

Grumpy. Ha.

# # #

Saturday morning was crisp and clear. The bright sun glistened against the icicles that hung from Samantha's eaves, creating a constant drip. The snow around them had been turning slushy for days.

She'd lived in Montana long enough to know that thinking spring was here was a fool's promise in February, but no harm in enjoying the warmth while it lingered.

"Mommy, when can we go?" Audie started badgering her about going to the ranch from the moment she'd gotten up at seven. It was like Christmas morning all over again as far as her daughter was concerned.

"I told you. You're going to have to go at your usual time. And when we go, you wear your snow boots, not your cowboy boots." If it was melting this fast in town, the area around the corrals was going to be muddy. Hopefully, there was enough stone on the driveway and the area where she normally parked to keep her from getting stuck.

Should she call first?

She'd been debating that for days. Politeness dictated a call, but if she were turned away, Audie would be devastated. A meltdown would be inevitable.

Maybe Jarod wouldn't even be there.

That would be better, wouldn't it? But her spirits deflated at the thought.

Somehow, Audie made it through the morning while Samantha attended to her Saturday morning chores of laundry and shopping. While they were at the grocery store, Audie insisted on purchasing two apples, in case Laughin' Jack needed some extra chow.

How was Jarod doing with his new horse? Had he regretted the purchase now that she was no longer in his life?

Why was it people never knew what they had until it was taken away? She'd give anything to have not sent him away when they returned from Billings.

Apples cut and safely in plastic bags, they headed down the road toward the ranch. Everything seemed to have a new lease on life. Several hawks soared overhead, and in the distance a few deer nibbled on stalks of grain that had emerged from the snowy prairie. The sky was blue, but from the high altitude of the land, it seemed close enough to touch.

She carefully drove the road down to the ranch, thankful it wasn't slick. After pulling in and stopping, she and Audie walked toward CJ and Dylan, who were standing by a saddled horse.

Jarod's horse.

"Hi," she said, caution framing her voice. Something was off.

"Oh, hello," CJ said and exchanged glances with Dylan. "Um, Audie ... why don't you hang with Dylan for a bit? I have something I need to discuss with your mom."

"Okay." Audie walked over to Dylan.

"What's up?" Samantha asked as she and CJ moved toward the corral.

"Jarod went out for a ride this morning."

"In the snow?"

"There's cleared paths where the deer and elk have gone through. It's not unusual for him to be gone a good while, but his horse came back without him."

"Oh my God," Samantha said in a hoarse whisper. "He could be hurt."

CJ nodded. "Dylan and I are about to saddle up and go look, so now isn't a good time for Audie to see Misty."

There was no way she could sit around while Jarod could be lying in the snow, cold and injured. "I'm going with you."

Chapter 30

"You don't ride." CJ's voice was flat.

"I did. Once. For a little while." Until she'd fallen off and never gotten back on.

"It's rough terrain."

"I'm going."

Something in her voice must have convinced CJ that she wasn't going to take no for an answer.

"Okay, but don't slow us down."

"I won't."

The walked back to where Audie was animatedly explaining something she'd seen on one of her nature shows to Dylan.

"Hey, Audie," CJ said, crouching to her height. "We need to go out for a little while. Jarod seems to have gotten lost, and we need to find him. Your mommy is going to come with us." She gave Dylan a look and he raised an eyebrow before glancing at Samantha and shrugging.

"Is he hurt? Can I come, too?" Audie asked, her face getting pale.

"He's probably just fine. Sometimes he gets clumsy. But I think you need to stay here," CJ said.

"Hey, why don't we see what Birdie is doing?" Dylan said, holding out a hand to Audie.

"Mommy?" Audie's voice held a crack.

Samantha squatted. "It'll be okay. We need to make sure Jarod is okay. You be brave and help comfort Birdie. She's worried."

"I'm worried, too," Audie said. "What if he's hurt?"

"Then we'll get the doctor to make him right as rain." She'd picked up the old expression her mother had used.

"How can rain be right or wrong? That's silly, Mommy."

"Yes, it is." But it had distracted her daughter. "Now go on to the house with Dylan while I get reacquainted with Laughin' Jack."

"You aren't scared anymore?" Audie asked.

Samantha was petrified. But her worry for Jarod was larger

than her fear of the animal.

"I'm feeling brave today," she said and gave her daughter a kiss.

"I love you, Mommy. Take care of Jarod."

"I will. Love you, too."

She watched Dylan and Audie go up to the house, then turned to CJ. "Show me what to do."

"Follow me," he said.

They went into the dim light of the barn, dust motes dancing in the beams of light that came in from the high windows. CJ led Laughin' Jack from his stall and hitched him to a couple of leads, then handed Samantha a brush.

"Just give him a quick rubdown. We have to get going, but we don't need him getting cranky if there's anything irritating him."

No, no. A cranky horse would not be good.

After CJ left her to retrieve another animal, Samantha stared at Laughin' Jack's eyes. What a dumb name for him. Horses didn't laugh.

As if to prove her wrong, Jack curled back his lip and snorted.

All those teeth.

Well, she didn't have to deal with them. All she had to do was brush him in the back.

Near the hooves. Where he was capable of kicking her.

"Are you going to get a move on?" CJ asked. "Or are we leaving you here with Audie and Birdie?"

"I got it."

Samantha stabbed at the horse with the brush and stroked him a few times with jerky movements. Jack turned to look at her as if to say, "Just get on with it already." Samantha took a deep breath, put her left hand on the top of the horse as CJ was doing, and began to brush in earnest, reminding herself to move around and not just brush the same spot over and over.

"Don't forget the other side," CJ commented.

Samantha gave the coat a few more swipes and walked around Jack's front to get to the other side. As she passed his nose, Jack rubbed her shoulder and blew out a breath that tickled her neck.

"He likes you," CJ said as she grabbed a saddle from the rack and flung it over the back of the horse.

"Uh. Thanks." Samantha attacked the other side with a little more confidence.

Dylan came back in, and he and CJ had all three horses

saddled and bridled in about fifteen minutes. He gave Samantha a leg up, and soon they were following muddy tracks northwesterly from the ranch house. There hadn't been time to get anxious about getting on a horse. Dylan had given her a leg up and here she was.

Most of it came back, but like childbirth, she'd forgotten the discomfort that came from exercising long-disused muscles. Sandwiched between Dylan and CJ, though, she had no choice but to keep up. Bringing up the rear, CJ trailed Jarod's horse behind her.

If it had been any occasion but this, Samantha may have settled into the ride. Out here there was so much peace and quiet, so far from the noise and posturing of other human beings.

They'd been at it more than an hour when Dylan pulled to a stop. "Looks like this might be where he fell," he said, pointing to an area where the snow was packed down by multiple horse prints. "He should be around here somewhere."

"Unless something or someone carried him off," CJ said.

Samantha's heart beat faster.

"Hey! Jarod!" Dylan yelled out. The sound echoed around them. Then silence.

Dylan examined the torn up snow and pointed. "Single track there. It looks man-made." He slid off his horse and followed the path around some trees. "Found him!"

Samantha slid from Laughin' Jack and tore up the path. "Jarod?"

"Here." The voice was weak, but it was Jarod's. He was propped up on a boulder, back against a tree, pain etched in the twist of his eyebrows, which shot up when he spotted her.

"You got on a horse!" His laugh was rusty. "If getting my ankle twisted was the price I had to pay for that, it was worth it."

"You idiot," she said, putting her hand on his solid shoulder. "There's lots of things I can do, and it doesn't take you hurting yourself for me to do it."

"What happened?" CJ asked. "Why can't you ever stay on a horse like you're supposed to?"

"I'm not sure," he said. "There was a loud noise, kind of like an explosion—you know, dynamite."

"Now? In the winter? That doesn't make sense," she said.

"I didn't have time to figure out whether it made sense or not," he said. "I wasn't ready for Whiskey to jump to the side, and off I went. Unfortunately, I landed on my foot wrong. I think the ankle's twisted. And, of course, Whiskey bolted for home before I hit the ground."

"Let me see," CJ said, "although not much I can do until we can get you back home and get that boot off."

"I was waiting for either someone to come or get up the strength to find a branch and hobble home," Jarod continued. "I must have fallen—ouch!" He glared at the top of CJ's head.

She patted his knee. "Yeah, twisted. At least you didn't break it this time." She looked up at Samantha. "Last spring, he got his foot all tangled in a stirrup when he was training Prince. Made the rest of us do his chores for weeks on end."

Maybe getting on a horse hadn't been such a good idea.

"Let's get you home," Samantha said, trying to hide her emotions under the guise of practicality. If they didn't move soon, she was going to break out in sobs of relief. "It's getting cold, and there's a little girl who is very worried about you."

"And you?" Jarod asked. "Were you worried, too?"

She pursed her lips and cocked her head. "I *got* on a *horse*."

He chuckled.

She had to know.

"Jarod?" She shifted her weight on her feet. "Can you forgive me? Please? I'm so sorry I sent you away."

"I forgave you at the time. You'd been through a lot." He gazed steadily at her.

"But when I called ..."

"Forgiveness and repeating the same mistake aren't the same thing," he said, his tone serious.

"Let's go see about some horses," CJ said, pushing Dylan back the way they'd come.

"And there's more," Samantha said.

He nodded.

"I was an addict before I got pregnant with Audie. I got cleaned up, haven't touched anything since, but ..."

"You're afraid something will trigger it. That's why you're always trying to keep everything in control."

She nodded and waited.

He took her hand. "Everyone has dark times and makes bad choices of one kind or another. I'd rather be by your side if you're struggling than watch you crash and burn from far away."

She breathed out. "I've been scared, so scared." She swallowed. "I know I'm not easy, but I'm trying. I'm going to stop running and work things out with Cody. I'm here for the long term." She licked her lips, trying to come up with the right words to convince him.

"And if the school doesn't hire you back?"

She considered that for a moment. "That will depend on where we are. If I have to, I could find another job. There is the internet." She smiled. "I could learn to bookkeep for real and do offsite work."

"Or you could help feed cattle now that you know how to ride and all." The corners of his lips turned up slightly.

"There is that."

They stared at each other for a few moments, all the feelings that defied codification into words humming in the air between them. He slid his arm around her and pulled her closer. "Shall we see if we can make this work?" Jarod whispered into her ear.

"Yes," she said, the final constricting band easing from around her heart.

"Well, then we better get a move on," he said. "My ankle's not getting any better sitting on this rock. Help me up, will you?"

She slid herself under his shoulder, and he leveraged himself up, leaning on her as little as possible. But she still felt his weight.

"One more thing," he said.

"Yes?"

"This." He leaned over and kissed her on the lips. "I've missed that."

"We better haul you back to the house so the two of you can get a room," Dylan said, walking up to them. He took most of the burden from Samantha, and they hobbled down the path.

"Dylan and I were talking," CJ said as they boosted Jarod onto Whiskey and mounted their own horses. "When we get home, we're going to send the drone up here to poke around, see if we can find out what that blast was."

"Good idea," Jarod said, his face paler than usual from the effort.

CJ nodded and steered her horse toward home.

# # #

While CJ wrapped up Jarod's ankle, Audie made him repeat what had happened about five times before Dylan took her to the barn to see Misty. Samantha brewed tea in the kitchen under Birdie's fierce supervision, then sat with Jarod on the couch.

Satisfied that her horse and her friend were okay for now,

Audie pulled out the Walter Farley book she always carried with her and settled down to read. CJ and Dylan took the drone out and sent it off.

"So what did you and Cody decide?" Jarod asked.

Samantha explained the arrangement.

"Want me to come with you, or do you think it will confuse Audie too much?"

"It's probably best if I go alone. I don't want Cody thinking I'm ganging up on him."

Jarod nodded. "Just let me know what I need to do."

"Get better." She nodded at his leg.

"Yes, ma'am." He leaned over and gave her a kiss.

Audie chose that moment to look up. "I'm glad you're friends again," she said. "Told you, Mommy."

"Yes, you did," Samantha said. "I'm glad, too."

"You're staying for supper," Birdie said, settling into one of the armchairs, a cup of tea in her hands. It was a command, not a question.

"Yay!" Audie called from her spot in front of the unlit fireplace.

"Yay, indeed," Jarod said, smiling at Samantha.

She grinned and squeezed his hand. "Thank you very much, Birdie," she said. "I'll be happy to help."

"Thank you."

"You'll never believe what the drone captured," Dylan said as he came back into the living room.

"What?" Jarod asked.

"You know where we found the fence down last fall?"

"By the Brockman property line?"

"Yeah. On our side, about that same place we found the horse prints, only lower down in the canyon. Someone blew out a chunk of the side wall."

"See anyone?"

Dylan shook his head. "Snow was all churned up from an ATV or snowmobile, it looked like. And the damn fence is cut again."

"Ohhh," Audie said with a grin.

"Oops," Dylan said, shaking his head. "I'm going to have to get used to having the kid around again." He tousled Audie's fine hair. "It's a good problem to have."

"When are you going to teach me to paint?" Audie asked.

"Soon, kiddo. Soon."

"CJ staying for supper?" Birdie asked.

"Nope. She hightailed it back to Nick's. When's she going to bite the bullet and move in with the man totally?"

"When she feels good and ready," Birdie said.

As they chatted, Samantha leaned back and let her eyes drift. Forgiveness, whether given or accepted, provided peace. The demon slipped back into the dark recesses, evidently no longer finding anything to feed on.

# # #

Audie studied Cody across the table at the coffee shop in which they agreed to meet, her blue eyes staring acutely into his. Samantha sipped her coffee, striving to let things manifest without her interfering. She and Audie had had many conversations about what Cody was like. By reliving the times she'd been with him over the years, Samantha realized he'd had his own problems growing up, but there had been times when he'd been funny and kind.

"So you're my father," Audie pronounced.

"Appears so," Cody answered.

"What do you do?"

"Well, right now I'm loading trucks for UPS. But I write songs, too."

"Have I heard any?"

"Not yet, but one's being considered by a new country singer."

Samantha's heart lightened a little more. Cody had a talent for music, when he didn't get in his own way. It was good that someone recognized it.

"Oh." Audie considered the hot chocolate in front of her, blew on it for a bit, and tentatively took a sip.

Cody shot Samantha a grin and mouthed, "Thank you."

She nodded.

After another half hour, Audie declared it was time to go home. She gave her father a grown-up handshake, and they parted ways with a promise to figure out how to move forward from there.

"So what did you think?" Samantha asked after they left Helena behind.

"It's weird to have a daddy I can talk to," she said. "I always thought he was dead or something."

Samantha stifled her laugh. Hopefully, Audie would always

say what she thought.

"But did you like him? Are you okay with seeing him again?"

"He's okay. But he doesn't ride horses like Jarod. I'm glad you like Jarod. We're going to be happy with him."

"Yes, we are." Jarod had made her promise to stop by after seeing Cody. He was hobbling around on a set of crutches Dylan had found in the attic, and getting frustrated that he couldn't be as active and mobile as he wanted to be.

Audie picked up her tablet and started playing one of her games. Samantha turned up the music and hummed along as they gained altitude to the high grasslands near Choteau. Winter had come back with a roar, driving temperatures back down close to zero, but the blasting wind that had accompanied the drop in temperatures was mercifully absent today and the roads were clear.

An hour and a half later, they reached the ranch turnoff.

Jarod limped out to greet them.

"Where are the crutches?" she asked after embracing him. She didn't think she'd ever get tired of the touch of his strong body and the gaze of his warm, gray eyes.

"Tired of 'em," he said. "The ankle's getting stronger, and the doc said as long as I'm not overdoing it, I can put weight on it." He looked down at Audie and pointed toward the corral. "I know there's a horse missing you. Shall we go say hi before we go inside where it's warm?"

"Yes!"

Audie rapidly walked to the corral while Samantha and Jarod ambled behind.

"How are things going?" she asked.

"Good. CJ, Nick, and Trevor are helping with the calving, which is a good thing since I'm useless." There was a touch of anger in his voice.

"It'll pass." She patted his arm. "You don't have to be responsible for everything all the time. Let people help you."

"Says the pot to the kettle." He grinned. "I'm trying."

Audie and Misty were engaged in their own form of conversation.

"I had some good news this week," he said. "I've ordered a steel arena and found someone to install it once spring gets here. It all fits within my budget, too." He frowned. "Unless I got my numbers mixed up."

"I'm sure you're fine," she said. "I'm happy to look at it,

though."

"While you're at it," he wheedled, "can you take a look at the books for February?"

She chuckled. "As long as I don't have to tag calves, sounds good to me." She remembered something Dylan had said. "Isn't your other brother, Cameron, coming home, soon?"

"Yeah. He was supposed to be here last week, but there was a delay of some sort. I'm not sure why he's so reluctant to come home, but Dylan says they've told him Cameron will be back by the end of March at the latest."

"You said he lost his arm. I imagine that would be a huge adjustment for anyone. It's going to take time. You are so good with Audie, I know you'll work with your brother, too."

"We were never close, but I'll have to take it one day at a time." He put his arm around her and pulled her close. "You're good for me," he said.

"You're good for me, too." She looked up at him, and he smiled.

"I'm certainly glad you came to Choteau to teach," he said.

"Yes." Letting the invitation show in her eyes, she leaned closer.

"They're going to get married someday, Misty," Audie announced. "So it's okay if they kiss."

"Glad we have her approval," Jarod murmured before lowering his lips to hers.

The End

Will Dylan find success as an artist? Or does fate have something else in mind? Check out your favorite bookstore to keep reading *Leaving Home*.

Have you read the first book in the Rocky Mountain Front series? If not, check your favorite online bookstore to discover *Home Is Where the Heart Is*.

From the Author

My first stop when I moved to Montana in the 1970s was to teach college for a year in Billings. Born and brought up in New Jersey, the city felt like the wild west to me from the moment my dog and I arrived on the railroad platform in a borderline section of town.

There were so many things I learned that year: skiing in Red Lodge, discovering wild mustangs near the Wind River in Wyoming, corn dogs and chili dogs, and yes, how the lights spell Billings when a person is on The Rimrocks.

From there I moved to teach on the Blackfeet Indian Reservation, close to where this story takes place. During the holidays I drove back to Billings, often in the blizzard-like conditions that Samantha experienced. You haven't driven in snow until your only guidance is the taillights of the car in front of you as you creep from reflector to reflector.

During that time I lived in East Glacier and drove from there to Kalispell so often I could do it in my sleep. I felt perfectly comfortable on that drive until a freak May snowstorm made me skid and crash into a bridge not far from the goat lick.

Living in Montana has its challenges, but it is still an amazing and beautiful place to live.

To learn how Maggie, the heroine of *Leaving Home*, adapts to Montana after living all her life in North Carolina, pick up *Leaving Home* at your favorite bookstore.

Thanks for reading my story!

Casey

P.S. Reviews help authors keep writing. Please feel free to leave one!

Leaving Home Excerpt

Dylan Beck checked his phone for about the tenth time that Wednesday as he poured himself a cup of coffee from the ever going pot in the ranch kitchen. He should leave for the airport in about fifteen minutes, giving himself plenty of time to get to Great Falls, park and find the right gate. Not that it would be a big problem in the small airport with a handful of gates.

"When is Cameron coming in?" his brother Jarod asked as he entered the kitchen.

"His text message said he left from Dulles at nine eastern time, which put him into Denver at eleven their time. He had a two-hour layover and thinks he should be in Great Falls by three or four at the latest." He held up his phone. "I'm tracking it and so far it's right on time."

"You and your gadgets," Jarod grumbled as he poured his own cup.

"I was right about the drone," Dylan said.

"I'll give you that."

"Someday you'll need to move beyond the twentieth century."

"I'm content the way I am."

"Now that you finally got the girl." Dylan glanced at his phone, then poured his coffee into a travel mug.

"CJ didn't want to go?" Jarod asked.

Dylan shook his head. "She thought it would be better if only one of us were there so he didn't feel ganged up on. She also said a brother would be easier for Cameron to deal with than an older sister."

Jarod slumped into a chair. "I wish it had turned out differently. Cameron's such an outdoor guy. Losing a limb is going to hamper that big time."

"They've got some amazing technology today," Dylan said, trying to look at the bright side.

"It's not the same." Jarod sipped his coffee. "Where's Birdie?"

"Fixing up the master bedroom for Cameron." Dylan didn't look at his brother.

"He's not going to like that."

"Birdie thinks it will be easier on him. He had a lot of internal injuries from the bomb detonation, too."

"He's going to like being treated like an invalid even less."

Dylan opened the mudroom door. "I'm sure we can figure out something to keep everyone's ego intact. See you."

He zipped up his coat and tugged on his gloves, leaving his longish hair to warm his ears. Cameron's return was putting everyone out of sorts because no one knew what to expect. His younger brother's refusal to allow anyone to visit him while he was in the hospital recovering from his combat-inflicted wounds.

His brother was facing some mental injuries as debilitating as the physical ones.

Dylan put the ranch truck in gear and climbed the drive to the main highway. Turning left, he headed the short distance to Choteau, around the courthouse, and out on the road to Great Falls. Next to the market, a new shop caught his eye.

A combination cheese shop and bakery. Pretty upscale, but the area was changing. New people were moving in, attracted by small-town living and the awesome scenery of the Rocky Mountain Front. If the town could support a niche store like this, maybe someone would finally start a gallery where he could sell his paintings ... if he could sell his paintings.

He'd worn out his welcome at the Great Falls' venues when none of his art sold after a year. The sale of a painting last fall, which allowed him to get a commercial-sized drone for the ranch, had kept him in one gallery in Helena. But as each month passed without a subsequent sale, his spirits sank, in spite of the fact it was winter and most high-end stores were slow.

The road descended into the Freezeout Lake area. Since it was already mid-March, the migratory birds had increased the number of waterfowl massing in the open water. It was the wrong time of day to watch the huge flocks of white geese leave or return from the stubble-strewn farmer's fields, but they should catch it on the way back.

That should bring hope back to Cameron. There was nothing better than the sights of nature to heal a person's soul. It had worked on CJ; it should help Cameron, at least mentally.

Dylan followed the road's gentle curve as it passed the various ponds that made up the refuge. The overhead sky was gray, but not the deep hue that threatened snow, although the wind was picking up, nudging against the pickup with gentle bursts. The solid old truck didn't budge from its path.

Maybe he should give up his dream of being a painter. It was what his mother had done, and the same criticisms she'd heard were repeated to him—solid technique, but nothing distinguished his landscapes from the other dozens produced by plein-air painters rambling around the west.

But if he gave it up, who would he be? With his other four siblings firmly planted in careers, his lack of success stood out more and more. He was unsettled, drifting like an unmoored boat. At the ranch he was second fiddle to Jarod. In the art world he was nobody at all.

The road deposited him at the edge of Vaughn and soon he was on the interstate going to the airport. Time to put away his own internal angst. His brother needed him and that was the most important thing of all.

Acknowledgments

For the last seven years I have been a substitute teacher at a local school, Target Range. I've had the privilege to watch children change as they progressed from kindergarten to middle school. They let me into their world and challenged me daily. Thank you for helping to keep me young.

The teachers and staff have treated me as an equal and allowed little slices of their characters to be used my stories. Thank you Cody for allowing me to visit on you a fate worse than death, and Jodi for being the one to straighten him out, as she does to many of us in real life.

I am blessed with a wonderful editor, Julie Sturgeon, and gifted cover designer, Elaina Lee. Thank you both.

Finally, and forever, to my dear husband who loves me no matter how cranky I get.

About Casey Dawes

Real Life  Real Problems ⟨⟩ Real Love

Casey Dawes writes non-steamy contemporary romance and inspirational women's fiction with romantic elements.

Her stories range from small-town Montana to the Eastern and Western coasts of the United States. Her mostly "seasoned" strong heroines confront their problems and pasts, often to find real love for the first time in their lives.

Currently, she and her husband are traveling the US in a small trailer with the cat who owns them. When not writing or editing, she is exploring national parks, haunting independent bookstores, and lurking in spinning and yarn stores trying not to get caught fondling the fiber!

Follow her on Facebook:
www.facebook.com/CaseyDawesFiction/